BY HOOK & CROOK

S. G. KARAM

CHYMIST PRESS

Art Contributions (with Instagram handles):

Front Cover: @jbott138
Back Cover: @gustu_erik
Back Cover Color: @weswongwithyou
World Map: @shepengul
City Map: @_melnash_

ISBN: 979-8-9915995-0-4 (eBook)
ISBN: 979-8-9915995-1-1 (Paperback)
ISBN: 979-8-9915995-2-8 (Hardback)

LCCN: 2024920487

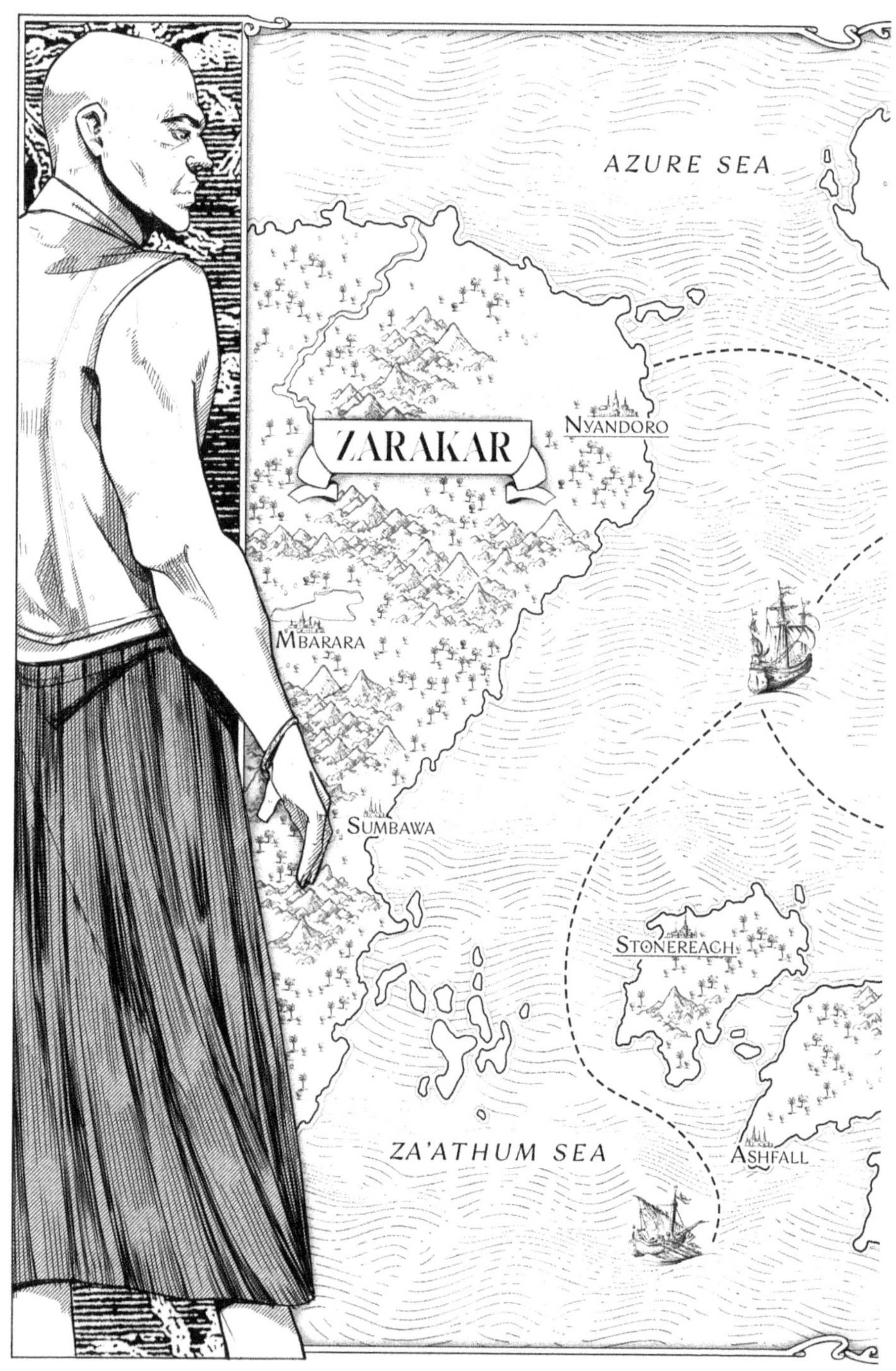

AZURE SEA
ZARAKAR
NYANDORO
MBARARA
SUMBAWA
STONEREACH
ZA'ATHUM SEA
ASHFALL

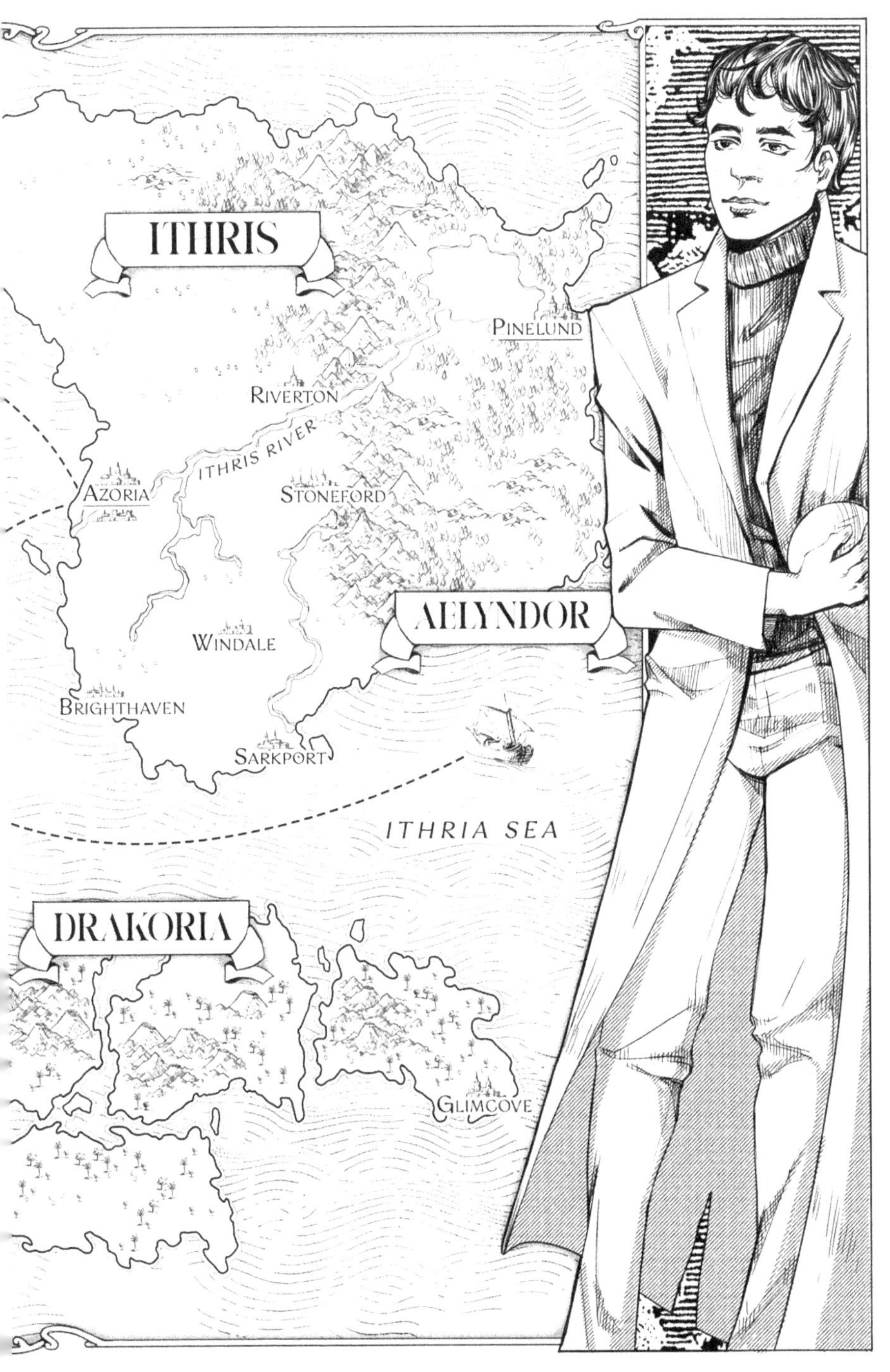

ITHRIS
PINELUND
RIVERTON
ITHRIS RIVER
AZORIA
STONEFORD
AELYNDOR
WINDALE
BRIGHTHAVEN
SARKPORT
ITHRIA SEA
DRAKORIA
GLIMCOVE

N
W E
S
Azure Sea
Foundries
Gaming Commission Headquarters
Ithris River
Shipyard
Market District
Tavern Row
Azoria Research Institute
Estontown
AZORIA

PART 1

AN OPEN WINDOW

1

If there was one thing Lars hated, it was an unlocked window.

It could only mean two things and neither of them was good. Either the owner of the house had no respect for the craft, or someone else had gotten in first. The first option Lars could handle. He barely had respect for his own craft half the time with how *easy* it had become.

The second option was a real pain because it meant he had to deal with the challenge of the score and whatever personalities the competition would bring. And hells, thievery came with some interesting personalities. Some less savory than others.

A tower clock flashed midnight in the distance, snapping Lars out of his musing. Competition or not, he had a job and not many hours in the night to do it. There was only so long he could hang off the ledge of a building, staring at a suspicious unlocked window, without being cast as a total dunce in tomorrow's paper.

He could see the headlines now: LARSON HARROW'S WINDOW PANGS, or perhaps LARS HANGS HIS HAT AND HOPES IN STUNNING UPSET.

"Well," Lars said to a bird that was watching him, head cocked, from a nearby roof. "That just won't do."

Sliding the window open quietly, Lars hoisted himself up onto the ledge and rolled inside. He stood and stashed his lockpicks in one of his many pockets as he scanned the room.

Like most homes of the fabulously wealthy, this one was filled with plush sofas, velvet drapes, and polished wood, every surface cluttered with books and baubles. Dimmed dynamo flambeaus cast a steady, warm light over a thick carpet—perfect for masking his footsteps.

First, he needed to check in. His team might have some ideas about what to expect now that the game was on.

Lars glanced at the flambeaus, each humming with dynamo power, and spotted a small box set into the wall below them. Even the box looked expensive, crafted from oiled walnut that rippled under the light.

Maybe he would be alone tonight after all. No competition, just the usual challenges: traps, guards, finding the right room, transport, and escape. Easy. But he wasn't getting his hopes up. Unlocked windows didn't happen in old estates like this, especially when a four-ton copper statue was in play.

Hells, the things he and Liora could create with four *tons* of pure copper.

Lars made his way over to the small box. He pressed a finger against the wooden cover and watched it slide open on clever little inset hinges. Two small gold terminals jutted out of a small panel, with a tiny pin of copper set into each.

Lars reached into a bag wrapped around his midsection and pulled out a small metallic device dotted with pinholes.

From it stretched a small cloth-wrapped cable tipped with a golden connector. He plugged the connector into one of the terminals in the wall box and waited.

He didn't have to wait long.

A quiet, tinny voice squeaked from the device in his hand. "Lars?" it said. "Glad you made it. We were wondering when you'd get inside. Did you forget your lockpicks again?"

Lars rolled his eyes, grinning despite himself. The only thing better than a skilled crew, he thought, is a crew that kept you on your toes with quick wit. His team was so determined to rib him that he could cheerfully throttle them half the time.

"Nah, it wasn't locked."

"Talk into the squawk please," Liora said.

He looked at the little metal gadget and realized he was talking to the wrong side.

This was only his third job using the new technology. Liora had invented squawks herself after months of brain-numbing shrieks. Her experiments had yielded a small, portable contraption that could plug into any dynamo terminal. It drew power from the city-wide grid while also allowing the thieves to communicate on the job. Her dynamo-wrangling genius was unparalleled.

Lars flipped the squawk over and tried again. "Repeat, the window wasn't locked."

"Ah nuts," came the reply. There was the sound of a quick shuffle on the other end, then a door opening and closing. Liora came back on. "I'm on the way. Jax too. Ya know, just in case. Go get it. Liora, out."

She always sounded so proud when she signed off like that.

The time for daydreams and fiddling around was over. Focusing only on the objective, Lars unplugged the squawk, put it back into its bag, and closed the wooden panel on the wall.

He listened at the hallway door until he was satisfied that no one was stirring nearby. Cracking it open, he cautiously peered through, then slid out of the room. Lars dashed down the hall, inconspicuous as a shadow in the night.

It didn't take long for Lars to reach the room his team identified as the target. Scouting reports had indicated the top-level grand hall was built with reinforced lower floors, using far more beams than would be needed for simple furnishings. No, whatever was kept in that room was heavy. It had to be the statue.

He trusted that Liora would be ready from her position on the roof, and that she brought the right equipment to maneuver and make off with the damn thing.

Despite sneaking past multiple traps—two tripwires, a false floor, and a spring-loaded plate that would drop a net on an unwitting thief—he hadn't yet come across any guards. Any high-profile thief worth their lodes was adept at getting around even the most complex of traps. Humans, mobile and armed to the teeth as they were, posed a far greater challenge.

And yet here he was, about to enter the grand hall itself, and nary a musclebound bruiser was found. Lars inspected the door, found it satisfactory, and entered the dark room slowly. Still no sign of the—

Shit.

A dozen dynamo flambeaus flared to life, bathing the great hall in a harsh, blinding light. He knew, he *knew* that he hadn't triggered any trap, unless his cockiness really did make him that careless.

No, he thought, blinking to clear his eyes, that wasn't it. Someone was waiting—and what's worse, they were waiting for *him*.

As his vision adjusted, his gaze was drawn immediately to the back of the room where the statue stood against a smooth wall.

It stood around four feet tall, a rich orangish-brown color from its small pedestal base up through strong legs, a cunningly wrought torso that appeared draped in flowing, rippling cloth, and finished with heavy armor fashioned from dozens of intricate knives. The hands, too, were knives, cascading out from the wrist in a fierce display of deadly intent. In all the effect was as beautiful and terrifying as the subject itself—Illia, Lady of Knives, a goddess of the old ways, forgotten in the age of dynamo.

Only then did he take in the rest of the room.

The vast hall was adorned with wooden beams covered in gold and copper gilding, and a glossy, waxed teak floor cleaned and polished to perfection. Along the walls were the flambeaus, giving off their bright and unwavering light in a way that oil or wax never could.

Light sparkled around a monstrous crystal chandelier, branching off the ceiling in grand swoops and whorls. Each arm dripped with dozens of flawless crystals that caught the light and set it dancing like brilliant drops of sunshine.

Of course, the beautiful floors, stunning chandelier, and fierce statue meant nothing at the moment. What really mattered were a bound, gagged, and blindfolded collection of guards, a skinny old man with wispy gray hair and silken nightclothes, and a faint older woman also in her nightclothes with hair piled high on her head.

And then there was the tall pile of garishly-dressed pigshit who stood near the statue. He was grinning like a kid who just conned his own mother out of her life savings.

That man was otherwise known as Darius Adalan, master thief and the only guy Lars could imagine bumping into on this heist. No one else had the guts to take on a job like this, particularly when they knew there might be competition.

But where Lars favored stealth and tech, leaving no trace of his passing (except the lack of a few cherished items), Darius liked to put on a show and get the household involved. While the headlines that favored him were far less complimentary than the ones Lars had collected over the years, they were every bit as numerous.

"Darius," said Lars, with a brief nod.

"Lars," said Darius, unable to contain his grin.

Lars stood still for a moment. Then he shook his head, a wry smile creeping onto his face. With a resigned sigh, he crossed the room, grabbed Darius by the shoulders, and pulled him into a tight hug. Darius barked a laugh and pounded Lars on the back.

As he released Darius from the embrace, Lars caught the familiar challenging glint in his old rival's eyes. Their long-standing competition was one of the few constants in his life besides stealing, an unlikely foundation for a friendship between two master thieves. Each encounter was a dance of wits and skill that pushed them both to the top of their game and into the headlines. Standing here amidst opulence and opportunity, Lars felt that exhilarating tug once more—their dynamic about to be tested yet again.

"So glad you could make it," Darius said, "I was starting to think I'd have to take this prize all for myself without a story to show for it."

Lars looked at the group of bound and gagged residents, then back to Darius, raising a questioning eyebrow.

"Well, maybe some kind of story," Darius continued, "but not the kind that stirs up the crowd."

"Speaking of which," Lars said, "if you were waiting on me, I'm going to assume you had some kind of plan in mind. And not one involving the city watch this time."

Darius only sighed. "That was unfortunate. Yes, I had something of a plan, but honestly it all depends on you my friend."

He looked to the statue, with all its powerful femininity and razor sharp knives, then back to Lars. "Eight *thousand* pounds of copper, Lars. How were you planning on carrying it off?"

"How were you? You might have a bit more muscle than me, but that won't help you get her out the door," Lars said.

"Oh, that's easy. You were going to haul it out for me."

Darius paused to gauge Lars's reaction, but if he thought there'd be anything beyond faint disbelief, he was disappointed. "The way I see it, there's enough copper in old Illia here to set us up for years. And our teams at that. Why not go in half on this one?"

Lars shook his head and snorted. "Why in the hells is it always me?" He walked to the statue, then spun to face Darius again. It was time to end the charade.

"So let me get this straight. You snuck in, left the window unlocked, mind—"

"That was just to freak you out," Darius said innocently.

"Sure," Lars continued, "then you somehow rounded up the guards which you could have just avoided, gathered the lord and lady of the house—who I'm sure were sound asleep—dragged them all in here, and waited in the dark for me to show up. All so you could ask me to do all of the actual work for you." He tapped his fingers against his thigh. "Did I get all that right?"

"Lars, buddy," began Darius, feigning offense, "you have no ide—"

"JAX!" Lars interrupted him with a shout, squatting beside the huge copper statue.

Above them on the roof, a roar answered, followed by a dull thud.

The crystal chandelier shook and tinkled, sending tiny beams of light dancing over the walls and floor. Another thud and a crash followed as chunks of plaster and wood rained down. The blindfolded captives started thrashing and making muffled exclamations, unaware they weren't under the collapsing ceiling.

Darius, on the other hand, had been nicked by a falling wooden shingle right above his eye. He winced and raised his fingers to his forehead and pulled them away to find them glistening with a dab of blood.

"Now that was uncalled for, don't you think?" Darius scowled at Lars petulantly just as a huge figure fell through the ceiling and landed in a crouch right in front of him.

Thank the hells for solid floors, Lars thought with a wry smile.

The figure stood up to his full height, all six feet six of him, barrel-chested and thick-legged, with arms like tree trunks and hands that could grasp a man's entire head with room to spare. For whatever reason and despite the balmy weather, he'd decided to cover his entire frame in a voluminous cloak. The hood was pulled far forward to hide his face.

Not that it did any good. There was no one in Azoria—not that Lars had met anyway—as gargantuan and imposing as Jackson Crasher.

"Well now, this is a surprise," said Darius, looking from one man to the other. "Mister Jax Crash himself. Not gonna lie, I thought you were still in prison."

Jax huffed and favored the man with a cocky smirk. "Got out yesterday."

"Right," Darius replied, and truth be told his grin had faded a bit. "So, uh… now what, Lars?"

Lars stood from the base of the statue. He had tried a few times to budge it, putting all his weight against the thicker part of the torso while carefully avoiding the dozens of knives, and it had not moved even a little. He doubted Jax, for all his strength, could do much better. It would be up to his engineer.

"Good question. Jax, knock out Darius and tie him up with the other captives."

Jax stepped forward while Darius took three steps back. He eyed the bruiser, knowing full well he'd do as his boss said. "You wouldn't dare."

A huge crash sounded from somewhere outside, followed by a muffled shout of, "City watch!"

"And that's my cue," Darius said, sprinting for the door. "Pity we couldn't pull this off, Lars old buddy."

Then he was gone. Well, that was one problem down.

✧

Now Lars just had to figure out how to get himself, Jax, and a four-ton statue of razor-sharp delight out of here before the city watch had them all pinned.

If anything else, he'd feel horrible for Jax. The guy just got out of the clink, after all.

"Liora," Lars called, "are you up there?"

A wide-eyed, spectacled face peered over the lip of the hole made in the ceiling, and a long braid of auburn hair fell through it. "Of course," she squeaked, "but I'd recommend we not be here more than a couple more minutes."

At that, the old man started kicking his feet against the ground, a rhythmic thumping that the other captives took up as well. That would make it far too clear to the watch where the thieves could be found.

The captives had been calm this whole time, enjoying their part in the intriguing turn of events. But now that the watch was here and Darius was gone, they were ready to be back on their feet and free of their fetters.

"Boss—" Jax started with a dangerous growl.

Lars made his decision. "Right. Do you have chain up there, Liora?"

"Yes," she said, "about fifty feet of it."

Fifty feet should be enough. "Alright, drop it and get the hell out of here. Leave whatever you have to behind."

"Oh you have to be joking," Liora said, adding something else under her breath that Lars couldn't catch. She saw her well-planned inventory of pulleys, carts, and winches going to waste. "But hey, if you think you can pull it off, I'll see you back at base for the celebration."

She shoved the heavy steel chain through the hole and then disappeared. Soft footfalls on the roof echoed through the room.

"Jax," Lars said, all business with no time for ruminating on what would happen if the guards got to them. "I need you to bust a hole in the wall behind the statue."

"You know we're three floors up, right boss?" Jax countered, but he was already moving to do what Lars said. Every second counted. He slid a heavy club out of his belt and bashed at the wall, tearing open a widening hole.

Through it, Lars could make out the Azure Sea bathed in moonlight. The great Ithris River which slashed through the continent flowed right outside this estate, meeting the sea in a breathtaking estuary that drew the rich and famous—such as their unwitting copper benefactor—like moths to a flame.

Lars's hands moved with frantic precision, his breath coming in short, sharp bursts. Behind him, Jax hacked at the hole in the wall, sweat glistening on his brow, each strike of his club echoing through the room like a drumbeat of desperation. The chain felt heavy and cold in Lars's grasp as he worked to loop it around the statue. His heart pounded with the relentless thump of footfalls on the staircase just outside.

He wrapped the chain around the statue's arm, then threaded it between its powerful legs, the rough steel biting into his palms. A metallic taste filled his mouth; he realized he was clenching his teeth so hard it hurt. Another loop, this time around the shoulders, their edges covered in jagged blades that sliced into his skin like teeth. Blood slicked his fingers, warm and sticky, but he ignored the pain with a focus as razor-sharp as Illia herself.

The chain clinked as he tightened it, pulling it taut. The footfalls grew louder, closer—too close. His blood dripped onto the stone floor, mixing with the dust. One final loop.

One last twist. He slammed the clasp shut, fingers slick with blood. He knew they were out of time.

"Good as it's gonna be, boss," Jax said. His eyes gleamed with excitement as he gulped huge breaths from the exertion. "Now what? Do we push?"

Lars grinned despite the impending danger. "Jax, you couldn't budge it if you tried." He picked up the other end of the chain and put it in Jax's meaty hands.

"Then what—"

Lars cut him off. There was no time. "Jump out the fucking hole, Jax."

Jax quickly looked at the river, three flights down, and gulped. "Oh hells." He braced himself to jump and threw the chain over his shoulder. It trailed behind him as he launched himself through the hole with a great leap.

Well, that went better than expected. Jackson Crasher might be a lot of things, but scared wasn't one of them.

Lars just hoped there wasn't a big embankment between the estate and the river. Most of the place was right on the water's edge with a small foundation below it, as was the fashion amongst the elite.

The long chain continued to exit, uncoiling in loud metal clinks as it raced down to the river with Jax. Suddenly, a huge splash sounded below. Lars whispered a silent thanks to whoever might be listening.

At that moment the door burst open with a sharp crack, and the Azoria city watch filled the entryway with crossbows leveled. Lars counted six of them.

One woman carried a taseshot, a bulky monstrosity of a device capable of shooting a dynamo-infused wire at its target, rendering them immobile, albeit a bit twitchy. A thick, oiled cable connected it to a heavy backpack, crammed with gears and a crank, which another guard spun to build up a charge.

They had come prepared. The guard at the lead, a tall man with more bars and adornments on his crisp blue uniform, took in the whole situation with a glance.

"I knew it had to be you, Larson," the captain sneered at Lars, "there's no way you could resist a prize like this."

Lars made a slight bow, glancing down to ensure the chain continued its descent. "Captain Myrim, it's good to see you. How's the family?"

"Can it," Myrim huffed. Clearly he wasn't interested in banter.

Lars was disappointed. Banter was the best part.

"Now," the captain continued, "step away from the wall, drop to your knees, and explain to me why you saw fit to abuse these poor people." Myrim looked at the collection of people thrashing on the floor and shook his head. "I have to say, it's not your style."

"Ah, that was Darius."

Captain Myrim's eyebrows shot up. "Is he here too?"

"Sorry Captain," Lars said, just as the chain went taut. "You just missed him."

A groan of metal and a screech of wood buckling under weight cut Myrim's reply short. He looked toward the copper statue—a massive behemoth he'd dismissed as impossible to steal with no equipment in sight.

It was moving—slowly, agonizingly, tilting backward toward the gaping hole, the chain groaning as it dragged the Lady of Knives into the outside air.

The floor beneath the statue finally gave with a deafening crack as an abundance of wood and metal tore away. The statue vanished instantly, plummeting through the wall, taking a chunk of the Blackwood estate with her.

Myrim stared at the empty space, mind struggling to catch up, the impossible feat unfolding before him like a scene from a drunken dream.

"It's a real shame, Captain," Lars said, stepping backward as the statue splashed into the river. "Do something for those poor folks, will you?" Before anyone could respond, he turned and dove straight out of the hole and into the night.

Myrim cursed and ran for the wall, followed by one of his guards. The others had the forethought to start untying the captives, pulling off their blindfolds and gags.

Through the gaping hole, a scene of chaotic brilliance unfolded. Lars was swimming toward a smoking steam tugboat that churned through the river, the thick chain trailing behind it.

On the tugboat's deck stood Jax Crash, a massive frame silhouetted against the flickering glow of the engine. He gave Myrim a quick salute before hauling Lars aboard. The winch groaned as it continued to reel in the chain, the statue rising inch by inch from the depths.

Myrim, despite himself, couldn't help but feel a hint of admiration. It was a masterful escape, a perfect blend of audacity and precision.

"Marvelous, absolutely marvelous!" crowed the old man, now freed from his bindings. "I'm Lord Blackwood, Captain. Please write that in your records. In fact, shall we summon the press? I'm ready to give a detailed report."

WELCOME TO AZORIA

2

By day, the capital city of Azoria was transformed. Gone was the breathless silence from the palatial estates of the elite, the raucous gaming, and the less savory activities from the taverns ringing the city's inland edges.

They were replaced by the loud bustle of industry—pounding and escaping steam from forges and foundries, shouts and the occasional crash of cargo at the harbor—and the buzz of excitement as downtown shops, cafes, and street vendors plied their wares to people from all walks of life.

As Lars and Liora made their way through the south end strip, Lars's gaze drifted up, where the towering windmills turned steadily in the coastal breeze. Their blades sliced through the air, silently fueling the city's dynamo grid. The windmills, like the city itself, never seemed to rest.

It had been two days since the statue heist and it was still all the city could talk about. The papers yesterday had flown off the shelves with bold headlines: BLACKWOOD

BURGLED AS RIVALRIES HEAT UP! DARIUS ADALAN CRIES FOUL, LARSON HARROW TAKES IT ALL!

The stories filled thick sheaves of print with sensationalist speculation and more than a few wild details which had Lars rolling his eyes and muttering to himself.

"We need to do something about this," Liora complained. "They called it a 'squawkee' *again*. It's a squawk. Just squawk. I invented it, I name it."

When no reaction was forthcoming, she nudged Lars in the ribs and pushed her big round glasses up. "Right? I name it."

Lars grinned and put a reassuring arm around her slim shoulders as they walked between food stalls and shops of the main Azoria strip. "Right. It's just a squawk." He knew that until he confirmed it, she would never let the question go.

He flipped open the paper he was holding and smacked the middle of the page. "That said, you're still the lucky one. Look what I have to deal with.

"Front page. 'Jackson Crasher, otherwise known as Jax Crash, was the real star of the heist at the Blackwood Estate, reported a rival thief who was present at the scene, on condition of anonymity.'"

Lars almost tore a hole in the paper with how hard he gripped the edges. "No, wait, it gets better. 'The source further expressed that Azoria's own Lars Harrow was, quote, "Not on his game that night."'"

He crumped the paper into a ball and tossed it into a corner bin outside a crowded cafe. Tables and chairs spilled out from the building and into the street. Onlookers gaped at Lars, whispering to each other with glee while clutching their purses and satchels close.

As if he'd ever steal a bag from a common passerby. Lars sniffed.

Liora giggled and reached up to pat him on the cheek. Lars was of medium height and had the lean muscle of an acrobat, but Liora Banz was short and wiry in comparison, with piercing amber eyes and a mass of curly, braided auburn hair.

"Poor Lars," she sang, "letting Darius get under your skin like that."

He laughed and swatted her hand away. He and Liora worked so well together. She knew how to lighten his mood just like she always knew how to pull off a job. People often mistook them for lovers or siblings, the latter proving somewhat true—he couldn't help but think of her as a little sister. A playful little sister who was smart as a whip and twice as noisy.

"Yeah, yeah," he said, eyeing the cafe. Two young men stood up from a cleared table and brushed past, beaming at Lars. He felt one of their hands touch his as a small strip of paper was pressed into his palm.

Giggling, the men left and rushed across the street. Lars flipped open the piece of paper, scanned it, snorted, and tossed it in the trash.

Liora cocked a curious eyebrow at him. "Hot tip or a hot date?"

"Neither," he sighed. "A party invite. It seems we're in demand today."

She snorted and tossed her hair. "You are, maybe. I'm just a burned-out dynamo girl who is overworked and gets none of the credit."

"Yeah," said Lars, "that thousand pounds of copper you pulled is just *so* demeaning."

She smirked but didn't respond. When the job was done and the statue had been pulled into one of their secret dockside storehouses, they had all stared silently at it. Jax,

Lars, Liora, and Keer Basar—he had operated the tugboat—all saw different potential.

Fistfuls of copper coins, jumbles of fresh wire waiting to be tinkered with, fame, glory. Though their fifth team member hadn't participated in this job, they each took an equal cut.

A quarter went, as always, to the local Gaming Commission. The remaining eighth was provided to the city's general welfare fund. There it would be used to maintain roads, fund schools, and ensure the populace had their basic needs met.

The empty table was still open. Lars stepped toward it, eager to take a break. "Cup of coffee?" he asked Liora. "My treat."

"No, I'm going to head back and get the foundry set up. Lots of copper to work with, like you said. But thanks." She reached up and gave him a peck on the cheek.

"Bye—" Lars started, but she was already gone, disappeared into the milling crowds.

Lars took a seat at the table and picked up a menu. He wasn't very hungry, but it was always worth seeing if there was a treat worth trying. Azoria was known for its inventive and delicious foods. Good food, good drink, people-watching, and planning out their next job would make for a perfect day.

Over the rim of the menu he saw a uniformed *someone* making their way to his table, and he smiled, preparing to place his order. The smile died on his lips when he realized it was Captain Aric Myrim taking the seat opposite him.

"Have a nice swim?" Myrim asked.

Lars was surprised—it was about as close to a joke as he'd ever heard from the man. But there was no smile accompanying the words, just a thin-lipped grimace.

Well, this was awkward. They both had their jobs. His was thieving, Captain Myrim's was catching. Without the city watch, burglary wouldn't be as thrilling as it was, and without thieves, Myrim wouldn't get paid.

While the watch had almost caught him—they got far closer this time than the last—it wasn't like Myrim to gloat anymore than it was like him to crack a joke.

"Not particularly," Lars said, "But all in all it was a good night." Myrim just kept staring at him and said nothing.

"I have to say Captain, you're giving me the creeps. Is this a social call or...?"

The captain shook his head as if clearing some vile thoughts. But his face relaxed as he reached up to rub his temple. He sounded tired when he spoke again. Even a little defeated.

"An engineer of one of your rivals was murdered last night. Know anything about it?"

Lars finally understood the man's grim and dour attitude this morning. But he didn't know what to say. It was ridiculous for Myrim to think he would know anything about a murder. In fact, had he known, he would have been the first to report it.

Murder was a heinous crime and something he could not abide by. That said, the thieving community was tight-knit, at least among the professionals. That included the engineers, without whom none of their heists would be possible—or at least, not as entertaining.

"A rival?" Lars said. "Not from Darius's team, was it?"

Myrim shook his head.

"Okay. Then who?"

"He goes by Remus Switcher," the captain said, "based on the east side, right on the border of Estontown."

So, outside the city then. It wouldn't be anyone Lars knew and not someone he'd consider a rival with his standing. He was about to tell the man so, when a deep, powerful voice spoke up behind him and he saw Captain Myrim's eyes widen.

"What's going on here, Captain Myrim?" the voice asked, "Not hassling one of Azoria's brightest stars, are we?"

The captain stood up in a flash.

"Lord Thume! Of course not. Done is done, as the law prescribes." He waved in the direction of Lars. "Though I think you'll read in the papers, I was *this* close to catching him in the act this time."

"But you didn't," the newcomer said.

Myrim looked as if he might say something in return. But Lord Thume slid toward his now empty seat. "Good day, Captain Myrim."

While he was far too proud to appear chastised, Lars thought that Myrim looked nervous. He couldn't blame him. Street corner appearances by Lord Thume were rare, and as one of the wealthiest and most untouchable men in the world, he was a force unmatched.

"Right. Good day, gentlemen," Myrim said, stepping away.

Today was one hell of a day for coming and going, Lars thought.

As Lord Thume took his seat, Lars considered the man. While he wasn't the flamboyant entertainer Lars and his fellow thieves were, he still exuded fame and power. Tall, thick-limbed, with night-dark skin like most of his countrymen, the most striking of his features were his eyes.

The whites were stark white, with large irises like liquid gold ringed in dark bands. Gold eyes were a rarity among Zarakarans, but Thume's made the few there were look like faded brass. He wore a skirt made from dozens of panels of black cloth rimmed in thin leather piping and a black leather vest trimmed with even darker velvet.

Even in his elder years his arms were muscular and imposing, covered from shoulder to wrist in intricate tattoos that blended against the dark tone of his skin, but in his proximity, the complexity of the needlework was intimidatingly clear. He set his hands, covered in gold and copper bangles and rings, on the table and directed his striking gaze at Lars.

He gave off every image of a man with the wealth and vision to change the world. And so he had. Lord Cecil Thume—founder and head of the Ithris Gaming Commission, fierce politician, and global philanthropist— had stemmed the tide of crippling disparity in Ithris following the discovery of dynamo. He had created the very system that made Lars famous and Azoria prosperous.

For that, Lars would be forever grateful.

Lord Thume snapped his fingers, and a serving girl rushed to the table. Setting down two mugs, she poured steaming coffee into each and prepared to take their order. Thume waved her away.

Lars sipped the dark coffee and found it fantastic. "Lord Thume," he began, "It's an honor to share a table with you."

"Please, Larson, call me Cecil. I feel like you've earned that."

"And you can call me Lars." He hated being called Larson.

Thume tested the name. "Lars. I think I prefer Larson. But very well." He took a sip of his own coffee. "I must congratulate you. Your recent exploits netted quite the score."

Lars flashed the man a genuine smile. The statue was a huge boon for him and his team compared to an everyday haul. For Lord Thume, it was a pittance.

"It was a fair amount of copper, my lor—Cecil," he corrected. "We will, of course, be making our tribute to the Gaming Commission."

"And the people, dear Lars, the people!" Thume was insistent on that caveat.

"Yes, of course."

"Of course," Thume echoed. "Though you do realize the combined remainder is a significant amount of money."

Lars wasn't sure he liked where this was going. He tapped his fingers against his thigh under the table, but his face remained impassive.

"If you were to convert that to coinage and spend it over the next several days, it could destabilize the economy quite a bit." Thume paused in his musing and stared pointedly at the thief. "And that wouldn't be good for anybody, would it, Lars?"

Lars laughed, but seeing Thume's penetrating look he snuffed out his mirth. "Sorry. Here I thought you were going to ask for additional taxes."

"Ha! No, no. But please, continue. You were about to answer my question," Thume said.

"Yes, well. I wouldn't worry sir," Lars said in return. "We'll be making some new coinage, of course. But there's also a lot of equipment to replace, new materials to buy—"

Thume waved this off with impatience.

Lars was ready to wrap this up. "Right. We'll be drawing most of it into wire and forging new components. Hells, I doubt my engineer will spend a single copper piece."

Lord Thume drummed his fingertips on the tabletop and drained his coffee. "You have, of course, heard about the engineer murdered in Estontown last night?"

"I have."

"It's a shame," Thume said. "Quite a shame. Good talent should never go to waste."

"Indeed," Lars said. He wasn't really sure what else there was to say.

But nothing else was needed. Thume rapped the table with his fist and stood up, the folds of his elaborate skirt draping around him. "I believe that's that then. Thank you for your assurances, Master Harrow."

"Of course, and if there's anything else I can—" Lars said, standing as well, but Lord Thume had already walked away.

Two strange and unexpected encounters were more than enough for Lars. He gathered his things, drained the last of his coffee, and prepared to head back to his base across the river. The market bridges would soon be clogged with foot traffic, making the return trip a hassle if he didn't leave now. But just as he stood to go, a young woman began making her way toward his table.

"Oh, for hell's sake what now?" he muttered.

"Skipping off without paying your bill, are we, sir?" she said, handing him the tab for his drink and Thume's. "I didn't think the great Lars Harrow would stoop to robbing a humble little corner cafe."

✧

The air at the docks was heady with the smell of saltwater and the sounds of bustling activity. Ships of all sizes, from small fishing boats to large trading vessels, were docked along the piers, their crews unloading cargo and preparing for the next leg of their journeys. The harbor district was a hive of activity, a crucial point in Azoria's trade network, connecting the capital to the rest of the world.

Lord Cecil Thume moved through the chaos with the confident stride of a man accustomed to commanding respect. His presence alone was enough to part the sea of workers, who bowed their heads or stepped aside as he passed. Thume's sharp eyes took in every detail, noting the efficiency—or lack thereof—in the busy harbor.

I built this, Thume thought.

That wasn't entirely true, as the city had stood for hundreds of years and worldwide commerce had existed almost as long. But since the discovery of dynamo thirty years prior, Thume's influence had transformed Azoria's docks from a modest port into a thriving hub of international trade.

The docks now buzzed with activity, ships laden with goods from all corners of the world docking alongside sleek steam-powered vessels. Their cargo holds brimmed with food and fancy, metal and magnets, fueled by the dynamo revolution.

Thume's vision and relentless drive attracted wealth and industry, reshaping the economic landscape and solidifying Azoria's position as the beating heart of commerce and progress in the world. As he watched the organized chaos of unloading and reloading, the disciplined movements of the dockworkers, and the seamless coordination overseen by his harbormaster, a rare smile tugged at the corners of his mouth. This was his legacy—thanks to his power and foresight, a reminder that the city and its people thrived under his guidance.

He approached the harbormaster's office, a sturdy building situated near the main pier, where the largest ships docked. The harbormaster himself was a burly man with a weather-beaten face and a clipboard always in hand. He looked up from his work as Thume entered.

"Lord Thume," the harbormaster said, standing straight to give him a respectful bow. "How may I be of service, sir?"

Thume's golden eyes were piercing, even in the dim light of the office. "I'm here to ensure everything is in order for the next shipment from Zarakar." His deep voice carried a weight of authority, tinged with slight impatience.

The harbormaster nodded, flipping through his clipboard until he found the relevant details. "Of course, sir. The shipment is scheduled to arrive in two nights. We've cleared the largest berth for it, and additional security has been arranged as per your instructions."

Thume's features were a mask of calm, but there was obvious satisfaction etched on his face. "Good. This shipment is of utmost importance. I trust you understand the implications if anything were to go amiss."

The harbormaster swallowed hard. "You can count on me, Lord Thume. We'll ensure everything goes smoothly." Of course he understood the implications. It was his job to ensure safe passage of any cargo passing under his watchful eye, but cargo stamped with the seal of Zarakar—a lightning bolt atop a mountain—required an even higher standard of vigilance.

He had to know that failure was not an option; disappointing Thume could mean the end of his career or worse. The Lord's reputation for perfection and his unwavering demand for excellence left no room for error.

As Thume turned to leave, he paused for a moment as if deciding whether to say more. He turned back to the harbormaster. "You need to understand just how critical this shipment is," he said. "The contents are not just valuable—they are invaluable. Priceless crystals, experimental components, and rare metals that could revolutionize our understanding of dynamo. If anyone got their hands on it, it would be more than a loss; it would be a catastrophe. The very foundation of our economy would be at risk.

"Look at my eyes and say you understand."

The harbormaster nodded vigorously, his face pale. "I understand, Lord Thume. We'll double the guard and keep a close watch."

"See that you do." Thume turned on his heel and strode out of the office, leaving the harbormaster to rally his men and prepare for the arrival of what must be the most important shipment Azoria had seen in years.

As Thume walked back to his carriage, he decided whether or not to be satisfied with the harbormaster's responses. Each step echoed his thoughts, a rhythm of confidence and caution. Testing each and every possible scenario in his head like a lightning bolt branching and arcing its way to the ground, he found no flaw. Everything was, of course, perfect.

Jax Crash, soldier turned enforcer, walked through the busy streets of Azoria. His imposing frame caused many to step aside. Today he was in the market for a new cloak, something stylish yet practical, a blend of form and function that reflected his unique taste. Fashion was very important to Jax, almost as important as food.

The market district was bursting with activity. Vendors called out their wares, their voices punctuating the enticing aromas of exotic spices and fresh baked bread. Stalls overflowed with vibrant displays: saffron from the southern plains, cinnamon sticks bundled from the eastern forests, and fiery chilies all the way from Drakoria. Rich, smoky sausages and cured hams hung from hooks, their savory scents mingling with the sweet allure of candied fruits. Piles of fresh produce—bright red pomegranates, golden sunburst squash, and deep green kale—added a vibrant splash of color to the scene.

Azoria was a dense yet sprawling city, divided by the ever-flowing Ithris River. On the more reputable south end, the polished estates of the elite overlooked the Azure Sea, their opulent homes bathed in sunshine and the coastal winds that powered the city's windmills. Swanky residential and commercial neighborhoods ringed the Azoria Research Institute and other landmarks.

The north end was a raucous madhouse of commerce and industry. With its rowdy inns and gambling halls, Tavern Row hugged the northern banks of the river, a notorious haven for those seeking entertainment—and trouble. To the east, foundries and workshops hummed with the power of fire and steam, feeding the constant churn of the city's dynamo grid.

But it was the market district, teeming with vendors, cafes, and curious onlookers, that truly connected the city's diverse mix of residents, making it a melting pot of culture, petty theft, and opportunity.

That diversity—the melting pot of cultures and culinary delights—made the market district Jax's favorite spot in town.

He paused at a stall displaying an array of fine cloaks, running his fingers over the rich fabrics. The vendor, a thin Zarakaran man with a keen eye for fashion and a keener eye for copper waiting to be spent, approached with a broad smile.

"Master Crasher, a pleasure to see you out of prison. My, aren't you looking positively dashing." He was laying it on thick, but Jax didn't mind. "Looking for something in particular today?"

Jax eyed a striking gray cloak with gold embroidery but dismissed it. Gray was just too drab. "Something sturdy, yet elegant. And it's got to make a statement."

The vendor nodded and pulled various cloaks from the racks, each more elaborate than the last. As Jax tried on a rather fine one, he caught a snippet of conversation from a nearby group.

"...murdered in Estontown, can you believe it? An engineer, of all people."

Jax's ears perked up. He turned, listening more intently without making it obvious.

Another voice chimed in. "His name was Remus Switcher. Poor bloke. They say he was found in the middle of his workshop, stabbed right in the heart with a chunk of crystal if you'd believe it."

Jax frowned, mind racing. He knew Remus Switcher by reputation, though he had never met the man. The news of his murder was unsettling, but Jax couldn't afford to be distracted. He had shopping to do, and getting sidetracked by every piece of gossip wasn't part of the plan.

"Master Crasher, what do you think of this one?" the vendor asked, holding up a deep purple cloak with intricate copper patterns. It was just the kind of look Jax loved—fine enough for a noble and flashy enough to draw attention. Not that the big man ever needed help in that department.

Looking over the fabric with a critical eye, he ran the cloak through his fingers. The material was soft and pliable and would drape nicely over his broad back. "How much?" he said, not in a mood to haggle.

The shopkeeper, unfortunately, was. "Master Crasher, what you hold in your hands is the finest silk and velvet blends from Aelyndor," he said in awed tones. "A treasure, so to speak, of textile genius, that—"

Jax held up a warning hand, cutting the vendor off and looming over him with a deep scowl. "How. Much."

The shopkeeper gulped. "Eight coppers?"

Jax forced a smile and nodded. "I'll take it. Wrap it up for me, would you?"

Nodding and bobbing in a quick, respectful bow, the man packaged the cloak and handed the bundle over. Jax in turn handed him the copper coins, thoughts still on the murdered engineer. As he turned to leave, he overheard another group discussing his own recent heist. Now that was a more interesting topic.

"Did you see the papers? 'Jax Crash Leaps to Glory!'" The young woman's voice was awed and tinged with excited disbelief. "They say he jumped out of a third-story window right into the river. Can you imagine?"

Jax chuckled. He'd always enjoyed the thrill of a successful job, but hearing the public's perception added a layer of satisfaction. The headlines were always a mix of embellishment and fact, but it was nice to be recognized for his part in the escapade.

Standing behind one of the shop's beams, he cupped his hand and called out, "Not a window! Jax bust a hole in the wall with his bare hands!" The gossipers started buzzing anew without so much as questioning where this new exciting detail came from.

With his new cloak draped over his arm, Jax made his way to a nearby food stall. The scent of roasted meat and spices was irresistible. He ordered a hearty meal as his thoughts drifted back to the conversation about the engineer. It wasn't his business, but in Azoria, everything somehow connected back to Lars's crew. Or, more realistically, it came around to bite them.

As he ate, he overheard more conversations about his recent heist, embellished details about the stolen statue ("I heard it was seven feet tall!"), and the ongoing business maneuvers in the city. The capital was abuzz with excitement and tension, as always.

Belly full and his spirits high, Jax decided it was time to head back. There was a lot to discuss—the unsettling news of the murdered engineer, the whispers of his own daring heist that were already making their way through the city streets—and of course, a spectacular new cloak. After months of drab prison garb, he was ready to make a statement.

He navigated the maze of narrow alleyways and hidden passages, the faint sound of waterwheels turning along the Ithris River drifting through the air. Senses alert, his hand never strayed far from the dagger at his side. Trust was a precious commodity in this city, even among thieves.

The dark purple of his new cloak billowed behind him like a thundercloud as he reached the heavy door of the crew's base. Jax paused for a moment, savoring the anticipation, the thrill of the reveal. Then he pushed the door open wide, his entrance a bold declaration of his undeniable style.

Inside, Liora, Lars, and Keer looked up, their faces turning toward him, a mixture of surprise and relief in their eyes. Perfect. The stage was set.

"Got a new cloak," Jax announced, looking downward and grasping the edge of the fabric to hold high for all to admire.

He looked up just in time to see Keer start to clap and Lars's lips twitch into a smile. Liora had a wide grin that reached all the way to her amber eyes, as expected.

"Looks great, Jax," Lars said after sufficient time to let Jax bask. "Come have a seat. We were just talking about murder."

MURDER AND MERCHANDISE

3

Jax raised an eyebrow and took a seat. Their base was a converted inn, and the crew as a whole decided to keep it as it was. It made for a good front as a legitimate business and served as a meeting place, relaxing respite, and drinking spot.

To one side, an old bar stretched across the room—polished wood still gleaming despite the years—and was backed by shelves lined with various liquors and spirits. Cozy seats with worn leather chairs and sturdy stools were arranged around a large fireplace. It was cold this time of year, but always ready to cast a comforting glow. The high ceilings and exposed beams added a rustic charm, while dim lighting created an atmosphere of secrecy and camaraderie.

Lars had bought the old inn for a song, as the saying went. The public believed it to be an incredible show of negotiation. In reality, the clever thief had caught the owner rigging card games and took the tavern off his hands in lieu of exposing him.

"Murder, huh?" Jax said, leaning forward. "Funny, I just heard about something happening in Estontown. Remus Switcher, stabbed with a chunk of crystal. In the heart."

Lars nodded. "That's what we were discussing. It's troubling news."

Murder was not very common in Azoria. The penalties were high, almost always death, and not a pleasant one. Ever since the Gaming Commission had become the most powerful force in Azoria—in truth, for all of Ithris—violent crimes had dropped drastically, with the system adapting to ensure disparities were made tolerable for the common populace.

"That said," Lars continued, "investigating crime isn't our job, is it? I saw Aric Myrim this morning. He's on the job himself."

Liora snorted and pushed her glasses higher. "Lord Commander Captain Commandant High and Mighty Myrim couldn't catch a murderer if they jumped up and down with a bloody knife yelling 'I did it.'"

Keer leaned back in his chair, a thoughtful look on his face. The chair creaked, a relic of bygone days, almost as old as he was.

"Back to it not being our job," he said, "and realize, I'm as cynical as they come." That was an understatement. A Zarakaran by birth, Keer was a brilliant transporter, trapspringer, and naysayer. His sharp wit and even sharper instincts had earned him a reputation on both sides of the Azure Sea. "But something about this is off. Engineers don't just end up dead. And by dead, I mean murdered." He looked at everyone pointedly.

Liora jumped back in. "Right. We've got our priorities, but ignoring this could be a mistake. If someone's targeting engineers, we could be next." She gulped. "*I* could be next."

Jax nodded and patted her fidgeting hand with his own. "Agreed. It's not our usual line of work, but we should at least look into it. See if there's a connection to anything else. Don't want to be blindsided."

Off the cuff, Lars couldn't imagine any reason for someone to murder an engineer. Almost all of the engineers he knew—present company included—were curious, quirky, sometimes a little nosy. But never worrisome enough to kill.

Lars drummed his fingers on the tabletop, deep in thought. "Alright. We'll keep our eyes and ears open. Gather information discreetly. No need to draw attention to ourselves, but let's not be caught unaware."

Keer looked around the table, dark brown eyes meeting each of theirs. "So, what's the plan? Do we have any leads to follow?"

"I'll reach out to a few contacts in the engineering community," Liora ventured. "See if anyone knows more about what Switcher was working on. Jax, you keep doing what you do best: look fabulous, listen, and find out what the streets are saying."

The big man smiled so hard Lars feared his face might split apart.

"And I'll see if I can dig up any information on the crew, the investigation, all of that," Lars said with a nod. "Maybe I can pay our good buddy Darius a visit. If he's not too salty over the Blackwood job."

He looked around the room. "Speaking of, where the hells is our statue?"

Liora flashed him an excited grin. "Don't you worry, Lars. It's at the forge today getting turned into beautiful bars and coins. Tomorrow's payday, guys."

That was the best news any of them heard all day.

"Oh, that reminds me," Lars said. "Lord Thume did say something about our recent score."

Every single smile dropped and the crew turned to look at Lars. Once a score was done, won was won, and the terms were set according to law. What could Cecil Thume want to talk about—other than to congratulate them on a great job not getting caught and thank them for the donation to his illustrious Commission?

Keer broke first and snorted. "Well don't just keep us in suspense, Lars. You might be known for putting on a show, but this isn't fun or entertaining." He ran his hand over his graying hair. "What did Thume say?"

Lars scratched his cheek and grinned sheepishly. "Sorry, I got lost for a second. It wasn't worrisome, but he had some concerns about the effect on the economy if we were to spend all that copper too quick."

"Break it down for me, Lars," Jax said. "Pretend I'm slow."

"I don't think it means anything. Even a big buyer like you couldn't spend a thousand pounds of copper in a few days."

Jax smirked and flourished his cloak. "Wanna bet?"

"Alright, alright," Lars said, "we shall humor the good lord Thume. We all need to contribute some of our cuts to gear and engineering updates anyway. Liora will give you the tally, I'm sure."

"On it."

The conversation turned to more lighthearted matters. At some point Keer made his way behind the old bar and rummaged around until he found a full bottle of Sarkport whiskey. The crew decided as a whole that worrying about murder—and how to avoid spending vast piles of money—could wait.

Drinks were imbibed, and many a good-natured joke made. Jax, bless him, introduced his new cloak at least four more times. Lars had lost count after Keer went behind the bar to bring back a second bottle of whiskey.

After all, they'd pulled off the most lucrative heist Azoria had seen in years, if not in its entire history. That deserved a night of celebration, didn't it?

✧

The sun dipped below the horizon, casting long shadows across the busy docks of Azoria. Bramwell Hargrove, chief harbormaster for the city, finished his rounds with a weary sigh. He surveyed the docks one last time, ensuring everything was in order for the night. The preparations for the upcoming shipment from Zarakar were well underway—the largest berth cleared, and additional security was in place as per Lord Thume's instructions.

Satisfied, the harbormaster tucked his clipboard under his arm and headed home, the sounds of the docks fading behind him. His modest house was a short walk away, just over the river and nestled in a quiet neighborhood where the hustle of the docks seemed a distant memory.

He opened the door, greeted by the warm aroma of a hearty stew simmering on the stove. His wife Yanelle, a rosy-cheeked woman with short black curls, bright eyes, and brighter lips, looked up from her cooking, face lighting up with a smile as he entered.

The harbormaster washed up, and the day's tension melted away as he sat down to dinner with his wife. As they ate, he mentioned the massive shipment that was expected to arrive the night after next. Yanelle listened, eyes widening at the sheer scale of it all.

She asked some curious questions about what could be in the shipment. The harbormaster answered while pounding down spoonfuls of hearty stew. She went on to other topics, but her husband's words echoed in her mind long after they finished their meal and retired for the night.

The next morning, Yanelle left the house for her usual walk, meeting up with her friend Preena at the corner of their street. The two women strolled through the market district, chatting about their lives and the latest gossip. The harbormaster's wife, eager to share the exciting news, recounted her husband's story about the enormous shipment coming in. Preena listened intently as her mind raced with the implications.

After their walk, Yanelle returned home and Preena continued to her morning tea breakfast with a gathering of influential women who prided themselves on knowing the latest news. As they sipped their tea and nibbled on delicate pastries, Preena couldn't resist sharing the tantalizing tidbit. Lord Thume was bringing in a shipment so large, she said, that the harbormaster had to make special preparations. The items included vast amounts of wealth, dynamo components, and who knew what else.

The tea group buzzed with speculation, each woman eager to piece together what this shipment could mean for Azoria. Who was it going to? And who might try to make off with it in a fantastic show of thievery?

Who indeed? One of the women, Shelina Halmuth, a buxom beauty known for her sharp mind and extensive network, left the breakfast early and made her way to the marketplace. She chatted with various vendors, weaving the information about the shipment into casual conversation.

The market was a hub of activity, and the news didn't take long to spread like wildfire. Whispers of the impending arrival of wealth, exotic goods, and potential for entertainment reached the ears of merchants, traders, and customers alike.

By midday, the rumor had traveled from the marketplace to the taverns, where foundry workers, dynamo wranglers, and sailors gathered to share a drink and exchange stories over lunch. In one such tavern, a grizzled sailor huddled close to speak with a young perceptive man with a keen ear and sharp wit. The sailor recounted the story that had been embellished with each retelling. Jewels! Crystal beyond anyone's wildest dreams! No wonder, he said, the harbormaster had ordered extra guards to be posted at the northern end of the docks.

The young man listened very intently, and when the sailor turned to tell his tale anew to another willing listener, he scribbled some notes before he could forget the details.

He left the tavern and headed for the alleyways, where he knew he could find Darius's intelligence broker, Silas Calder. Weaving through the maze of tight back streets, he arrived at a nondescript door and knocked three times. The door creaked open, revealing a figure wreathed in shadows. The young man leaned in, whispering the shipment details with a sense of urgency and pressing a piece of paper into Silas's hands.

The intelligence broker nodded, absorbing the information with ease, and tossed the boy a hefty gold coin on his way out the door. As it closed behind him, he sped toward the fashionable end of town, knowing that this intelligence could tip the scales in Darius's favor. Oh, the boss was going to love this.

Darius Adalan, mastermind at large, lord of larceny, number one thief in Azoria no matter what anyone (including Lars) said, sat at his desk after a hearty lunch. His sharp eyes scanned over plans and blueprints for potential targets. The converted warehouse he called home was filled with the remnants of past jobs: maps with detailed notes, sketches of security systems, and lists of valuable items in at least three different cities and dozens of notable homes. The question wasn't who to rob but when and what.

Just then, the door creaked open, and Silas slipped inside. He wore a satisfied smirk as he approached Darius. Reaching into his coat, Silas retrieved a folded piece of paper, presenting it to his boss with a flourish.

Darius snatched it with light-fingered ease, skilled hands unfolding the paper and smoothing out the creases. His sharp eyes absorbed the details. The scribbled list of items and security measures painted a vivid picture—a shipment beyond any they had encountered before. It was filled with wealth beyond imagination: copper, crystals, dynamo gear, and perhaps even more items worth a fortune on the black market.

As Darius read it, his eyebrows climbed up his head and his expression shifted from curiosity to intense focus. The magnitude of the haul sank in, as did the potential it held for he and his crew. His mind raced with possibilities, already forming a plan. The thrill of a new challenge with potential for massive rewards ignited a fire within him, built off the smolders that lingered since his loss to Lars at the Blackwood Estate.

"This is it," Darius said, eyes narrowing. "The one we've been waiting for."

Silas watched his boss intently. The information he had brought was a potential game-changer for the whole crew. "The shipment is expected tomorrow night," he said. "Lord Thume's made special preparations. Security will be tight, but that's never stopped us before."

Darius nodded, still engrossed in the parchment. He scanned the details again to ensure he missed nothing.

But Silas wasn't finished. "You realize, of course, that no one has ever explicitly stolen from Thume before. Going after his shipment is unprecedented. It could put us in a world of shit, as they say."

Darius looked up at the talented spymaster, considering. "It's a risk, yes. But think about the reward. This shipment isn't just any haul; it's a fortune and a victory we need."

He gave his spymaster a sly grin. "Besides, Thume himself lobbied for the laws that allow it to happen, even against his own assets. The man can't be seen to bend the rules only when it suits him."

Silas nodded, though the concern in his eyes remained.

What Darius said was true—no one was above the law, not any noble nor even the vaunted leader of the Ithris Gaming Commission. Thume's own machinations allowed for this kind of theft, no matter how audacious it may have appeared.

But on the flipside, the man likely didn't give a shit what rules he might be seen bending.

"I can't argue with that. But just remember that if we're caught, the consequences could be more severe than usual."

Darius leaned back, fingers steepled in thought. Not thoughts about whether he should move on the goods, that decision was already made and there wasn't a damn thing anyone could say that would dissuade him at this point.

Now he just had to convince Silas and the rest of the crew. "Every score comes with its risks. We've faced tough odds before and come out on top. This is just another challenge we're more than capable of handling. We play it smart, stick to the plan, and we'll be the first to pull one over on Thume."

The room fell silent, the importance of the decision settling over them. Darius's confidence was infectious, though, and he knew Silas would come around. If they succeeded, the payoff would be immense, and their status in Azoria would be unchallenged.

"We need to move fast," Darius said, looking up from the parchment. "Get everyone together. We have a lot of planning to do, but we have only one night to do it."

Silas smiled, nodded, and slipped out. The door closed with a soft click, and Darius leaned back in his chair, fingers laced behind his head. He knew his crew was capable, and they could pull this off with the right strategy and execution. He could already feel the thrill of the hunt coursing through him, the adrenaline of planning and executing the perfect heist.

The hideout stirred with activity as Silas spread the word. The members of Darius's crew, each with their unique skills and specialties, gathered in the main room. Their faces were etched with curiosity and anticipation.

Darius remained at his desk, sketching out the initial details of the heist on a large piece of parchment. He drew rough outlines of the docks, marking key locations and potential hazards. A few details were known about the number of guards and where they would be posted, but they'd have to play it by ear for the most part.

He grinned. That's how Darius worked best.

The room buzzed with low murmurs as the crew awaited his instructions. Despite any prior concerns, no one in the crew questioned the wisdom of the decision. The potential was just too damn good.

Darius stood, clearing his throat to get the crew's attention. "Listen up," he began. All heads swiveled his way.

"We've got an opportunity here, and a damn good one at that. It's going to take everything we've got. This shipment is our chance to make history—and it's happening tomorrow night."

He eyed each of them in turn, then flashed them all an excited grin. "Let's get to work."

With that, the crew leaned in, ready to begin the meticulous planning that would either lead them to unimaginable wealth or straight into a locked cell.

BALANCING THE SCALES

4

The sun beat down on Tolan's neck as he adjusted his cap, the leather warm against his skin. He squinted, trying to peer past the glare reflecting off the Azure Sea, his gaze sweeping over the docks. This was it. His first day on duty, and he was guarding a Zarakaran galleon. A real, treasure-laden vessel from the legendary land of mines and mountains docked right here in Azoria.

The ship itself was a marvel of craftsmanship and opulence. Its hull was crafted from dark, richly-grained Zarakar hardwood, reinforced with brushed copper and iron bands. Despite weeks at sea, the wood gleamed, a black glossy shine without barnacle or blemish. Its sails were woven from the finest fabrics and lay crumpled at the bottom of the masts. The wide folds of fabric and rope were dwarfed by the height of the massive wood columns, each holding a large, powerful wind turbine.

A gruff man chuckled beside him. "You look like you're about to burst, Tolan," he said. "Never seen a ship before?"

Tolan turned to face his fellow guard, a seasoned veteran named Garin, whose weathered face and cynical grin had seen more than its share of Azorian nights on watch.

"This isn't just any ship, Garin," Tolan said. "It's a Zarakaran cargo galleon. They say it's filled with enough copper to buy a small kingdom!"

Garin snorted, spitting a stream of tobacco juice onto the cobblestones. "Copper, crystals, who knows what else those mountain folk are hauling these days." He rolled his eyes. "But don't get your hopes up, lad. It's just another boring shift. No one's stupid enough to try and steal from Thume."

A figure in a wide-brimmed floppy hat, brown coveralls, and heavy boots trudged by, heading toward the far end of the docks.

"Keep moving," Garin snapped. The dockworker paid him no mind and idled a bit at the corner of the pier. Garin was about to say something else but shrugged and ignored them.

Tolan's youthful enthusiasm might have wavered a bit, but there was no squashing his curiosity and excitement. "But what if someone does try? There has to be some thief out there crazy enough. Hells, we might even catch them! We'd be legends!"

Garin laughed, a deep, rumbling sound that echoed across the docks. "Legends? You'd be lucky to keep your head attached to your shoulders if anyone dared to mess with Thume's cargo. He's got eyes everywhere, lad. And his punishments are creative, to say the least."

Tolan wouldn't be dissuaded. "But that's what makes it so exciting. The risk! The challenge!"

"You're a green one, Tolan," Garin said, chuckling as he shook his head. "Still got that starry-eyed look. You'll learn soon enough. This city is full of dreamers and schemers, but most end up broken or forgotten. Best to keep your head down, follow the rules, and collect your paycheck. Leave the heroics to the fools."

He clapped Tolan on the shoulder, a friendly and condescending gesture. "Now, keep your eyes peeled, lad. Try not to fall asleep on duty. Wouldn't want to miss the excitement."

Garin walked off to harass the lounging dockworker, but they were nowhere in sight.

Tolan straightened with a wistful sigh. His youthful enthusiasm may have been dampened for a moment by Garin's cynicism, but the flicker of hope refused to die. He adjusted his cap and surveyed the docks—the cranes, ropes, and endless rows of stacked crates forming a chaotic, intricate maze. It was a mess of shadows, angles, and perfect hiding spots.

He knew the chances of seeing a heist tonight, especially one bold enough to target a Zarakaran galleon, were slim to none. But the sun beat down on his back, the salty air filled his lungs, and a thrill of anticipation ran through him.

He muttered under his breath, a grin tugging at his lips. "Sure would be a great setup for a heist."

Maybe tonight, he thought, just maybe, the impossible would happen. He tore his eyes from the docks and started to walk, but his gaze kept drifting back, still hoping for something—anything—to stir.

The forgotten dockworker slipped out from behind a stack of crates, broad-brimmed hat pulled low over their eyes. She had watched the ship for hours, noting the guards' positions, the dockworkers' routines, and the flow of cargo moving on and off the vessel. It brought together a meticulous tapestry of observation and analysis, which she added to her mental balance sheet of risks and rewards.

She lifted her head, the brim of her hat tilting upwards, revealing the hardy features of her face, framed by pulled-back chestnut hair. Her round eyes were a clear, piercing gray and took in the positions of everything—guards, light posts, latrines, crates, ropes. It would be a challenge. But every lock has a key. Every system, a flaw.

Lowing her head once more, she shoved her hands into her pockets and left the docks. She puckered her thin lips and whistled the tune to Dynamo Daydream, a new hit that musicians were playing at every tavern and market corner. It was time to report back to the boss.

Darius Adalan stood on the rooftop of the shipyard complex and scanned the docks below. The night was clear, and the moon cast a silvery glow over the city. That was a shame, a bright moon made it far more difficult for him to be discreet. But if he was to be seen, at least he'd be well dressed. He wore a sleek, dark outfit combining style with functionality—leather pants and a tunic with straps that held various pouches and pockets.

He had learned earlier that Lars and his crew were out of the running for this job. A night of heavy celebration following their recent score had left them too hungover to plan anything. They were also flush with copper, reducing their immediate need for another high-stakes heist. The juice wasn't worth the squeeze. While the reminder of Lars's success irked him, it also made Darius more confident in the night ahead.

His eyes locked onto the centerpiece of the night's operation. It was a magnificent ship. Like the nation it came from, the vessel exuded wealth and grandeur. Darius had no doubt the contents on board would be every bit as rich.

From his vantage point, Darius could see guards stationed around the ship, their watchful eyes scanning the surroundings. But he knew every nook, cranny, and weak point, thanks to the intel Inora brought him. She had spent the day dressed as a dockworker taking in all of the pinpointed locations, and formulating her well-crafted plan.

Taking a deep breath, Darius felt the familiar rush of adrenaline coursing through his veins. This was his moment. It would be far different tonight than it was at the Blackwood Estate. He didn't have his team with him that night and had gone on a lark just to liven up the game with Lars.

But tonight, he was ready. With a final glance at the intricate layout of the docks, he leaped from the rooftop, his silhouette slicing through the night air. He landed on a squat building, rolling to absorb the impact before continuing his descent.

As he approached the edge of the docks he signaled to his crew, who were in position and waiting for his command. Silas and Inora, Rurik and Maren, each in turn acknowledged his presence with subtle nods.

Maren moved first. With deft hands, the engineer manipulated a small device connected to a harbor control terminal that would send a pulse through the dynamo-powered lights, plunging the docks into controlled darkness. He glanced at Rurik, who stood ready, the short, stocky bruiser's imposing frame tensed for action.

As the lights flickered out, Rurik sprang into motion. He moved swiftly, hands covering the mouths of two guards before they could react. With precise, practiced movements, he knocked them unconscious and lowered their bodies to the ground. But there was no time to silence all the guards. One of them managed to shout a warning.

Maren swore under his breath but there was nothing he could do. The die was cast.

A cry went up among the remaining guards as they stumbled in the darkness, lighting oil lanterns to make sense of the sudden confusion. They rushed to the main dock, knowing only that some number of thieves were attempting to make off with the ship's haul. Inora took advantage of the chaos, slipping through the shadows to signal Darius. Her hand gestures were clear and urgent: Move forward, *now*.

Darius didn't hesitate.

He ran toward the edge of the dock, bounding up a stack of crates and leaping over the head of a young man in a leather cap still trying to figure out what was happening. Darius spun and delivered a great kick to the shocked guard's midsection. The poor fool splashed straight into the water.

Darius spotted a thick rope dangling from a nearby crane. Seizing it, he swung over the gap and landed on the deck, offering a quick salute to the guards still on the docks. He crouched behind a tall barrel stamped with the jagged peak and lightning bolt emblem of Zarakar.

Silas, watching from his concealed vantage point, nodded in approval. He glanced at their engineer, who was already moving to the next phase of their operation. Maren reached into his satchel and pulled out a dynamo scrambler designed to interfere with the ship's power systems.

Meanwhile, Rurik took position near the ship's entryway. He flexed his muscles, ready to remedy his previous error. It must have rankled him that he'd exposed the crew by allowing a guard to cry out. More than one pursuer shrank back—or even turned away completely—in the face of the eager bruiser.

Darius moved across the galleon's deck, eyes scanning for any remaining threats. He saw a guard hurrying by and ducked behind another barrel.

Timing was everything. As the guard passed, Darius sprang up, delivering a precise blow to the back of the man's head. The sentry fell to the deck with a thud. Darius dragged the body into the shadows to be sure it was hidden from view.

There was no more time for subtlety. Inora took in the situation and shouted, "NOW," indicating that the path was clear.

Darius urged the whole team forward. Silas, Maren, and Inora made their way onto the ship, each taking up their designated spots according to the plan. Silas made his way to the stern, ready to relay any changes in guard positions. Inora moved to secure the guards Darius had encountered along the way. Their engineer went straight to the ship's command center, dynamo scrambler in hand.

Darius knew they had limited time. The guards were rallying, and enough noise had been made that the city watch would be along soon. He raced toward the captain's quarters, where the manifest was kept.

If all went well, he wouldn't need it. If they had to fall back to Plan B, the manifest would help them determine what to do next.

He reached the door to the captain's quarters and found it locked. Darius smiled to himself; a locked door was a minor obstacle. He pulled out his picks and set to work, the tumblers clicking under his skilled touch. Within seconds, the lock gave way, and Darius slipped inside.

The quarters were richly decorated and well organized. Darius moved to the desk and located the manifest. His eyes scanned the list, noting the locations of the most valuable items: crates of rare metals, barrels of crystals, and several containers marked on the sheets with a lightning bolt emblem, indicating they contained dynamo components.

Darius folded the manifest and tucked it into his tunic. Exiting the captain's quarters, he signaled to his crew. It was time for their grand finale.

At the stern, Silas kept watch, never losing sight of the guards. His head turned toward a group of them gathering on the main dock. It wouldn't be long before they rushed Rurik and boarded the ship. If that happened, it would all be over. Silas flashed a gesture to Darius, spinning his finger around. *Speed it up.*

Darius nodded and shouted for Rurik to finish up and come on board. Shoving back a persistent guard, Rurik ran up the gangplank and toward the ship's wheel.

The remaining guards, consolidated on the main dock, shouted and started to make their way on board.

Why were they always so damn persistent? Darius grinned, grabbed a nearby barrel, and shoved it onto the gangplank. The effect was spectacular.

It toppled, rolling down the wide boards, sending two pursuers flailing into the water. Once it reached the bottom, the barrel hit a metal cleat and burst open, spilling crystals and other unidentifiable jewels all over the dock and the dark water below. A horrible waste to be sure. But now the crew no longer had to worry about any guards trying to get on board. As far as they could tell, the vessel was as good as theirs.

The men and women in the water grabbed whatever they could from the bits that fell in with them and began swimming to shore to run off with their spoils. The ones on the docks were more fortunate with their haul, running toward the spilled goods and trying to shove as much as they could into their tunics.

With a glance, Darius and Silas both arrived at the same conclusion. Time to tidy up and make it known who pulled this off. Victory would soon be theirs.

As one, they bounded across the ship's deck, snatched up a long rope, and ran down the gangplank to where the treasure-crazed guards were grappling to take advantage of the spoils. It was easy for the two thieves to encircle the greedy men-at-arms, pulling them down with the rope and binding them together. Dumbfounded, the guards didn't even know what hit them.

Darius reached down to snatch a large crystal, its clarity flawless, from the hands of a dismayed recruit caught in the rummaging. Putting two fingers to his forehead, he nodded in a mock salute and jumped back onto the ship.

"Let's go!" he shouted, and his grinning engineer Maren answered. Plugging a small copper cylinder into an exposed port at the control helm, the ship burst into life. The wind turbines mounted to the ship's three masts fed humming life to the lights and controls for the ship.

Inora whooped loudly. Together with Silas, they released all the ropes and pulled up sails to leave the harbor.

As the ship cleared the docks and glided out into the harbor, Darius allowed himself a moment of satisfaction.

They had done it. Untold treasures awaited their discovery, not to mention whatever they might fetch for such a wondrous vessel.

He looked over his team and their haul with pride, then cut through their excited shouts. "Um, guys?"

"What is it, boss?" Maren said, startled by the interruption, glancing across the ship from stem to stern to see if something was wrong.

Darius scratched his chin. "Did we ever figure out where to park this damn thing?"

The crew's laughter echoed across the water. It was a good problem to have, Darius thought. They had pulled off the most stunning heist in the history of Azoria. The rest would figure itself out.

The old warehouse on Azoria's east side was dim, with trickles of weak light filtering through the high, dirty windows. The air was filled with the scent of old wood and metal, of a place that had once been packed with activity but now stood forgotten, save for secret meetings like this. The perfect place for those who wanted to conduct business away from prying eyes.

Darius Adalan stepped through the heavy wooden doors, his footsteps echoing in the vast space. He moved with confidence, posture relaxed but alert, with an unmistakable air of triumph. The thrill of the successful heist still lingered in his mind, but here, he wore the calm, calculated mask of a man ready to bargain.

In the center of the warehouse stood a lone figure bathed in the dim light from above. Lord Cecil Thume, dressed in a tailored suit with a long paneled skirt favored among the elite of Zarakar, cut an imposing presence even in the shadows. His face was a study in control. Golden eyes narrowed as he watched Darius approach.

Thume was a man who rarely showed real emotion—it had little purpose in business—but Darius could see the subtle twitch of his lips, the flicker of something that might have been annoyance in his eyes.

"Darius Adalan," he said in a hollow tone. "I trust you enjoyed your little escapade?"

Darius smirked, eyes locking onto Thume's with a calm intensity. "It was quite the challenge, Lord Thume. But then, it's your ship. I'm sure you knew it would be."

Thume's expression didn't change. "Stealing from me was a bold move, even for you. Most wouldn't dare."

Darius shrugged as if the feat were of little consequence. "Boldness is part of the game, isn't it? Besides, you've always appreciated a good spectacle." He gave a bow and a flourish. "Consider it my way of keeping the city entertained while upholding your creative philanthropies."

There was a pause as Thume studied Darius with a piercing gaze, as if trying to see past the confident exterior to the thoughts and motivations lurking beneath. After a moment, he nodded, acknowledging the master thief.

"You pulled off something remarkable, I'll give you that," Thume admitted with grudging respect. "But, you'd be a fool to think there aren't consequences here. You've made a lot of people nervous. The harbormaster's already out of a job. And that ship—"

"Is too large for me to do anything with," Darius said, cutting him off. He leaned against a nearby crate and crossed his arms over his chest, unfazed by the man's threats. "Which brings me to why we're here. I'm willing to sell it back to you if you're interested."

Thume's lips twitched into a wry grin, a rare reaction for the stoic Zarakaran. "Hells, you've got some nerve, Adalan. But then, I suppose that makes you valuable—and predictable, in a way."

Darius tilted his head, considering Thume's words. "Predictable? Maybe. Confident, more like. No matter the stakes, I'll always come out on top."

Thume chuckled. "Perhaps. However, I wouldn't mistake my willingness to play along as leniency. The next time you cross me, there *will* be a price to pay."

"I would expect nothing less, Lord Thume. But for now, what say we focus on the matter at hand? That galleon is all yours... for a fair price, of course."

If Darius was being honest with himself, the haul on board the vessel wasn't quite as rich as he'd hoped. They found spools of copper wire, always a big win, and bags of gold and silver dynamo connectors. Then there were the crystals. They weren't the most valuable gems around, but there sure were a lot of them. Big and small, in various colors and clarities. Darius's engineer wouldn't need to buy any amplifiers or regulators for years.

Thume moved closer, his footsteps slow and deliberate. He stopped just a foot away from Darius. Liquid gold eyes locked onto the young man's with an intensity that would have intimidated anyone else. Thume studied him for another long moment before nodding. "Indeed. Very well, Adalan. You'll be paid your price."

With a swift motion, Thume reached into his coat and produced a small leather pouch, tossing it to Darius. "I trust this will serve as a deposit," he said.

Darius hefted the bag and had no doubt it would work. Thume wasn't a man to skimp on a deal—at least, not when it suited him to play fair.

"Bring the vessel back to the docks for me by sundown and we'll settle the rest."

Darius inclined his head in acknowledgment. "Pleasure doing business with you, sir."

✧

Before the first rays of light had kissed the cobblestone streets, the night's grand scheme had already begun to make its way through Azoria like wildfire.

It began at the docks, where bleary-eyed workers stumbled upon the aftermath, still shaking off the vestiges of sleep. Bruised and chagrined guards, once so sure of their control, now stood in small clusters being grilled by the city watch, their faces twisted with embarrassment. Piles of rare crystals lay in heaps, marked as evidence on the ground.

But the most glaring absence—the one detail that would light the city on fire—was the Zarakaran cargo ship, pride of a nation, now vanished without a trace.

Word traveled swiftly, first whispered in disbelief among the dockhands as they exchanged stunned glances. But disbelief soon gave way to genuine awe.

As the morning crept on, the details of the heist trickled out in bits and pieces, and the story grew legs of its own. It gained momentum, swelling like a wave crashing toward the shore, and by the time the sun climbed over the haze of the eastern sky, the tale had already become the stuff of legend.

In the busy market district, vendors paused mid-shout, their voices faltering as they caught snippets of the tale being passed from customer to customer. Eyes widened, jaws dropped, and even the hardened merchants—the ones who claimed to have seen it all, especially where theft was concerned—couldn't help but marvel at the feat.

"Did you hear? Darius Adalan and his crew stole an entire ship! A whole damn ship, right from under Lord Thume's nose!" exclaimed one vendor, his tone a mix of disbelief and excitement as he swatted the hand of a young boy trying to make off with an apple.

A stocky chili importer from Zarakar scoffed. "Impossible. No one could pull that off."

"Oh, but they did," said a wide-eyed customer. "And not just any ship—no no. A cargo galleon from your own country! They say it was loaded with enough wealth to buy a fleet, hell, maybe even a kingdom!"

By midday, the story had made its way to the taverns, where sailors, traders, and the city's more unsavory elements gathered in tight circles, leaning close to hear the latest embellishments. Tankards clinked together in mock toasts to Darius's daring while bets were scribbled on scraps of parchment. Wagers were placed on whether Lars would even attempt to top such a feat. Some said he was finished—outplayed. Others argued that if anyone could pull off something even more impossible than what Darius had done, it would be Larson Harrow.

In a rowdy tavern tucked away in the city's southwestern end, a loud group burst into laughter as a portly man with a scruffy beard acted out what he imagined Lars's reaction to the heist would be.

"Probably choked on his drink, he did! What's he going to do now, steal the moon?" The man bellowed, sending the table into another round of roaring laughter.

But while the taverns were alive with gossip and revelry, outside, the city moved on, unaware that the game was far from over. Amidst the excitement, a lean figure strode through the morning streets, slipping through the crowd with an ease that suggested familiarity with the shadows.

She was tall, with sharp features that carried the undeniable mark of nobility mixed with something wilder—something more dangerous. Her attire also set her apart: a rich, deep blue cloak, the color of midnight skies, embroidered with silver thread that caught the light with every movement.

Beneath it, her fitted bodice emphasized soft curves, though it was the grace with which she moved that drew the eye of someone skilled enough to appreciate her craft. She seemed to glide through the chaos unnoticed, a ghost in the daylight.

She approached a newsstand, plucking a fresh paper from the top of the stack. The vendor called out his thanks as she tossed a coin his way, but her attention was already consumed by the bold headline blaring from the front page: DARIUS ADALAN STEALS LORD THUME'S HAUL! THE HEIST OF THE CENTURY?

Her full lips curved into a faint smile as her sharp eyes scanned the article. The words painted a picture of chaos and daring, of a heist so bold that it had left the entire city reeling. It was almost amusing how fast the tides had turned—first in Lars's favor, then back to Darius, who always seemed to have one more ace up his sleeve.

She folded the paper and tucked it under her arm with a widening smile. "Damn, Lars. What else did I miss while I was away?"

With a final glance at the busy streets around her, the woman turned and melted back into the crowd. Things had changed while she'd been gone—that much was clear—and the stakes were raised considerably. As for Lars... well, she'd see him soon enough. There was much to discuss and even more to plan.

PART 2

SHADOWS AND INTENTIONS

5

Despite the cool night air moving through his office, a thin sheen of sweat clung to Captain Myrim's brow. He wasn't accustomed to feeling this way—outmaneuvered, outsmarted, outdone. Yet, the past week's events had left him with a bitter taste in his mouth, a gnawing sense of inadequacy that even the strongest liquor couldn't quite drown.

He stood before a map of Azoria, pins of various colors marking recent heists. Red for Darius, blue for Lars, various other colors for the less notorious thieves.

But the newest addition, a black pin with a tiny gold lightning bolt impaled through it, held his attention like a morbid fascination. The cargo ship from Zarakar. Stolen right from under his nose, with naught but dumbfounded guards and a spilled barrel of crystals left behind.

The city was still buzzing, the papers were still flying off the stands, but all Myrim felt was a rising tide of failure. This last insult from Darius Adalan wasn't some trinket lifted from a mansion; this was a direct challenge to Lord Thume himself, at the very foundation of the nation's well-constructed way of life.

A system he was sworn to uphold, and yet...

A heavy sigh escaped him as he ran a hand through his thick, black hair. He'd spent years honing his skills, rising through the ranks of the city watch, becoming the youngest captain in recent memory. He'd always prided himself on his ability to anticipate the moves of Azoria's infamous thieves, to stay one step ahead in their elaborate game of cat and mouse.

But lately, that game had changed.

The rules were the same, yet the players were bolder, their strategies more intricate, and their execution flawless. The lines were blurring, and Myrim felt himself slipping behind.

His eyes fell on a small, wrapped package on the desk, the seal unbroken. It was a gift, delivered just that afternoon, with no note or sender. Curiosity warred with caution, but in the end he couldn't resist. He broke the seal, fingers trembling as he unwrapped the package.

Inside, nestled on dark velvet, lay a single, polished crystal, catching the dim lamplight. It was smaller than the ones taken from the docks but no less dazzling. And tucked beneath it, a folded piece of parchment. Dread coiled in Myrim's gut—he'd know that arrogant script anywhere.

"*My dearest Captain Myrim,*" the note read in Darius's flamboyant hand. "*Consider this a token of my esteem. For a man of such refined tastes, I couldn't resist sharing my latest triumph. Perhaps you could use it to adorn your office? It'd liven up the place more than that lonesome plant in the corner.*"

Myrim's grip tightened on the parchment, the edges crinkling in his fist. He glanced over at the pretty plant with broad leaves and tiny orange flowers. One of his assistants had brought it in just yesterday. Fury, blazing hot, coursed through him, banishing any lingering fatigue. Darius had not only outwitted him but was now mocking that fact, rubbing salt in a wound that refused to heal.

All things considered, it was a blatant slap in the face, a calculated insult that cut deeper than any blade. In that moment, something within Myrim snapped.

His vision narrowed, the edges blurring as a red haze descended. He didn't yell, didn't curse. Instead, he shoved everything on his desk—papers, inkwells, the taunting crystal, even his half-finished glass of whiskey—onto the floor with a single, violent sweep of his arm.

The crash echoed in the sudden silence of his office. He breathed heavily, staring straight ahead at the blank wall, knuckles white as they pressed against the scarred wood of his desk. His mind, at most times a whirlwind of strategies and counter-moves, was a blank slate.

Outplayed. Outclassed. A laughingstock. Those words, laced with Darius's amusement and disdain, echoed in his ears.

For long minutes, he remained frozen, paralyzed by a fury that had nowhere to go. The air grew heavy with the mingled scents of spilled whiskey and dust, and the walls felt like they were closing in around him.

Slowly, as if emerging from a trance, Myrim straightened. He sat down, the chair creaking beneath him, and methodically adjusted the silver pin denoting his captaincy on his uniform collar. The movement was a gesture he'd performed countless times before, a small ritual of order and control in a world that by all appearances favored chaos.

But the familiar motion brought no comfort tonight.

Bending down, he sifted through the debris on the floor, brushing past shards of glass and scattered papers. He retrieved a clean, printed sheet of official city watch stationary and his best fountain pen, the nib thankfully still intact.

For a moment, he stared at the blank page, a single drop of ink welling up at the tip of the pen. Then, with a steady hand, he began to write:

To Lord Thume,

I regret to inform you that I can no longer serve as your Captain of the

The words came out stiff, formal, each a hammer blow against the anvil of his pride. He hesitated, the tip of the pen hovering over the paper as doubt gnawed at the edges of his resolve. Was this the answer? To admit defeat? To walk away from a system that had defined his life, if not his very purpose?

No. He couldn't give either Lars or Darius that satisfaction.

With a muttered curse, Myrim crumpled the paper in his fist, tossing it onto the growing pile of wreckage at his feet. He reached for a fresh sheet, a new determination hardening his jawline.

This time, he decided on a new approach:

Dear Master Braisus,

In the quiet solitude of his office, as the city around him slumbered, unaware of the storm brewing within its very own

Captain of the Watch, Myrim began to pen a different kind of letter.

The inn's common room where Lars's crew made their home was settling into its usual state of comfortable disarray.

Empty tankards and scattered playing cards still littered the worn wooden tables, remnants of the crew's celebration after the Blackwood job. They had basked in the glow of their success, but as the days passed, that excitement had dulled.

Now, the mess seemed less like a tribute to victory and more like the residue of boredom. It was their attempt to chase away the restlessness that always followed a job well done. That kind of feeling had a way of lingering, and it was made worse by the creeping sense that their success had already been overshadowed by bigger, bolder deeds elsewhere.

Sitting in his usual corner, Lars took a long drag from his pipe, a rare treat he indulged in occasionally. He exhaled a plume of smoke, gaze distant as he listened to Jax recount the city's latest exaggerated tale.

"—swear on my grandmama's forge, they found one of the guards floating on a barrel halfway out to sea." Jax shook his head in disbelief. "Said the poor sod was babbling about ghosts in the night and sea monsters."

Keer, seated across from him, chuckled into his drink. "That's not quite how I heard it, Jax."

Jax shrugged. "That's what they're saying. But no one can deny it was a hell of a heist. Darius has outdone himself this time."

Lars couldn't help but agree. Stealing an entire ship—a Zarakaran vessel, no less—from right under Lord Thume's nose was a feat worthy of legend. The papers had been beside themselves, the city buzzing with shock and awe. Keer was beyond jealous; growing up in Zarakar, it had always his dream to sail the seas aboard one of their mighty galleons.

Instead of the usual thrill of competition, a knot of worry tightened in Lars's chest. Darius was playing with a new level of brinkmanship now, one with higher stakes and what could be disastrous consequences. Lars wasn't sure he wanted to be a part of it.

"It makes no bloody sense," Liora muttered from her makeshift workbench in the corner. She was surrounded by an array of tools, wires, and crystal shards—the remnants of her ongoing investigation into the murder of Remus Switcher.

"What's that, Liora?" Keer asked.

Liora tapped a large shard of crystal with a careful finger. "This piece of crystal. It's from the murder scene."

Keer cocked an eyebrow. Liora blushed, looking at the gem with a sheepish grin. "I, heh… might have made off with it. There are inconsistencies in how it was cut, the energy signature…" She trailed off, shaking her head. "Something's not right."

If there was one thing that you could count on, it was an engineer's curiosity. Jax let out a bark of laughter. "Leave it to Liora to find a murder more interesting than a king's ransom in stolen goods!"

Keer shot Jax a warning glance. "Let her be, Jax. Something about this whole business rubs me the wrong way too." He took another sip of his drink, his eyes meeting Lars's across the room. "Wouldn't you say, Lars?"

Now all eyes turned to Lars, their gazes heavy with expectation. He knew they were looking for guidance, for reassurance. He'd always been the steady one, the voice of reason in a chaotic world.

He tamped down the tobacco in his pipe, considering his words—difficult, since he hadn't really been paying attention. "Darius is playing at a new game now," he said. "And I can't say I like where it's headed if that's what you're asking." It wasn't.

Liora snorted and rolled her eyes. "Lars! That's not even what we were talking about—"

She was interrupted as the hideout door swung open, flooding the room with the warm, golden light of the setting sun. For a moment, the figure in the doorway was nothing more than a silhouette, but then a sigh of relief rippled through the room.

"Well, look who's home," Keer said, a genuine smile spreading across his face.

Jax let out a whoop, abandoning his plans for the next story and rushing toward the newcomer. He engulfed her in a bear hug that lifted her off her feet.

"Trin! It's about damn time you got back!"

Liora, too, abandoned her workbench, a huge smile lighting up her face as she pushed her spectacles back up her nose. "Trinelle Meridia, you've been gone too long! We were starting to think you ran off to join a traveling troupe from Windale."

But Lars's gaze lingered on the woman framed in the doorway, a warmth spreading through his chest that had nothing to do with the pipe clutched between his fingers. Trin. She was home.

The woman's rich laughter filled the room. "It's good to be back," Trin said, her gaze sweeping over her companions.

Trin extricated herself from Jax's embrace, eyes twinkling. "It's so good to see you all. I come bearing gifts." She hefted a worn leather satchel that hung across her shoulder. "But first, a moment for our esteemed master of ceremonies."

She crossed the room toward Lars as he rose to greet her. A flicker of something unspoken passed between them when their hands met. For a heartbeat, their eyes locked—hers filled with warmth and a hint of challenge, and his a mixture of relief and something deeper, more vulnerable.

Lars masked the look with a wry grin. "Welcome back, Trin."

She favored Lars with a teasing smirk, stepping close and putting her hand on his arm. "Missed me, did you, Harrow?"

"Don't flatter yourself." He pulled her in for a tight embrace. "I'm just happy to have someone else to relieve the boredom around here."

From where she stood, Liora dabbed at the corner of her eye with the back of her hand, a sappy smile playing on her lips. "You two are so sweet."

Trin, ever perceptive, caught the gesture and winked at Liora. "Don't worry, dear Liora, there's plenty of me to go around." She turned to the group, a look of gravity settling on her face. "Well, talk to me. What's new?"

Lars, sensing an opportunity to regain control of the conversation, cleared his throat. "Oh, you know, the usual Azorian drama. We pulled off a brilliant heist, Liora's on the trail of a conspiracy involving a dead engineer, and Darius stole a whole hells be damned ship. But none of that matters now that you're back."

Seeing her there made the base seem whole again. Lars loved every member of his crew like family—there was no doubt about that. But since Trin had announced months back that she'd be leaving on a scouting tour around Ithris, it left a void that Lars couldn't help but feel.

"So, tell us about your trip, Trin!" he continued, nudging her shoulder playfully. "Bring anything delicious back for Jax? Poor man hasn't had but half a banquet since lunchtime."

Jax laughed and slapped his wide midsection.

Trin laughed, setting her satchel down on the nearest table with a thud. "Poor Jax is *always* a slave to his own stomach."

She unfastened the clasp and began taking out an assortment of items, placing them on the table with a flourish. Looking at the pile quizzically, she snapped her fingers and reached back in for one last item. An apple. She tossed it to the big bruiser.

"Don't worry, Jax, that's not your real gift." Trin winked at him as he took a bite with a large crunch. "Remember when I said I was looking for bigger opportunities than we'd find cooped up here in the city? Well, I had some interesting conversations. Seems word of our exploits has traveled farther than we thought."

She paused, gaze sweeping over their expectant faces. "There are those out there who are quite impressed with our work, and even some willing to invest in our future."

"Invest?" Keer echoed, his eyebrow arching skeptically. "Are we a gambling syndicate now?"

"Something like that," Trin said, a sly smile playing on her lips. "But with a bit more... discretion—and higher stakes."

Interesting. Lars had never thought of them as needing outside patrons. Their work, after all, involved the theft of valuables—and it paid. That said, the opportunity to expand with the help of an outside influence could change things for the crew in big ways. Ways, in particular, that would topple the likes of anything Darius could ever—

"Anyway! More on that later. As I said, I come bearing gifts."

"First, for Liora," Trin said, handing the engineer a small, intricate box, "the finest magnifying lenses I could find in Sarkport. Guaranteed to reveal even the most microscopic inconsistencies."

Liora's eyes widened as she took the box, tracing the delicate engravings on its surface. She opened the box, removing a sheet of tissue paper to expose round lenses, smooth and without flaws, held in delicate wire clasps. "Trin, these are incredible! Thank you!"

Trin nodded, a pleased smile playing on her lips. She turned to Keer, handing him a leather-bound journal. "And for our esteemed navigator, a collection of star charts and nautical maps from the northern end of Ithris."

Keer accepted the journal with a nod, his gaze lingering on the intricate symbols and notations within. "Intriguing," he murmured.

Next, she retrieved a heavy, ornate dagger, its hilt gleaming with inlaid silver and copper. "For Jax!" She handed the blade to him with a wink. "Something to keep those over-eager admirers at bay."

Jax took the dagger, hefting it in his hand with a grunt of approval. "Now this is what I call a gift!" He spun it, flipped it into a backhand grip, tested the balance. Giving the blade a nod of approval, the big man slid it into his belt. "Thank you, Trin."

The collection of gifts on the table had been depleted. But then Trin reached into the satchel one last time and brought out a small, silver device. It was unlike anything Lars had ever seen—smooth and rounded, with a series of intricate dials and a small, glowing crystal at its center.

"And for our fearless leader," Trin said, dropping her voice to a conspiratorial murmur, "something truly special."

She placed the device in Lars's outstretched hand. It was light but hummed with a faint energy, a subtle vibration resonating through his fingertips.

"What is it?" Lars asked, turning the device over in his hands, mesmerized by the play of light on its polished surface.

"A new toy. And it's not like anything I've ever seen."

Lars didn't even have a chance to examine the device before Liora snatched it out of his hand, eyes gleaming with an almost manic excitement. She let out a little shriek of glee and rushed over to her workbench, nimble fingers tracing the contours of the mysterious gadget.

"Oh, this is beautiful! Utterly beautiful!" Liora was oblivious to the exasperated sighs from her companions. "Where did you find this, Trin? Who made it? Where's the terminals on it? What's it made of? What in the world is it?"

Trin laughed. "Hells, she's like a tornado in the market. One question at a time. I'll tell you everything I know, but first, let the man admire *his* gift."

But Liora didn't even register Trin's words. She stood hunched over her workbench, hips subconsciously swaying and her brow furrowed in concentration as she examined the silver device under a magnifying glass, a whirlwind of muttered exclamations and technical jargon swirling around her.

"Dynamo-powered? But where's the power source? The sun? Wind? But it wouldn't keep. There's no generator here. It's not connectible to the city grid…"

Liora paced back and forth. Her shoes slapped against the wooden floor and her mind raced as she tried to unravel the device's secrets.

"It's self-contained," Lars said, joining Liora at the workbench. He couldn't help but be fascinated by the device, even if he didn't quite share Liora's manic enthusiasm. "It's got to be. There are no external power connections, but you can tell it's active. See how the crystal in the center is pulsing? It's almost like it's alive."

Liora nodded absently, staring thoughtfully at the device. "Yes, yes, thank you, Lars. We all appreciate your expert guidance. But how? What's the mechanism? It's like nothing I've ever seen before. It defies all known principles of dynamo engineering!" She shook her arms in the air as if to illustrate the importance of this groundbreaking fact.

She peered at the casing around the crystal through her magnifying glass, noting the positions of the knobs and how the dynamo vibrations resonated through it. "It's as if… as if the crystal itself is the source of the dynamo…"

Keer snorted as his eyebrows shot up in disbelief. He rose and joined them at the workbench, peering over Liora's shoulder. "What? Crystals don't generate dynamo. That's not what they do, right?"

Truth be told, he didn't know much at all about dynamo, except that—most of the time—it did what you expected it to. This sounded different.

"Could it be a new kind of capacitor? But that would have fizzled by now." Liora continued her musing, tapping a finger against her lips. "Or perhaps it utilizes some form of resonant induction, drawing power from the ambient dynamo field?"

"Or maybe it's magic?" Jax suggested with a grin, earning him a withering glare from Liora.

"Don't be ridiculous, Jax. There's no such thing as magic. Everything has a logical explanation."

She continued to pace back and forth, her mind buzzing with possibilities. "Perhaps it's a form of dynamo redirection, channeling energy from a remote source? Or... or it utilizes some form of refraction, bending the dynamo flow to create a self-sustaining loop?"

Liora paused, a look of dawning realization spreading across her face. "Nope. It has to be the crystal generating the power." Her voice rose to an almost feverish pitch. "That has to be it! It's not just any crystal either. It's different. I can feel it."

She reached out and touched the glowing crystal at the device's core. A tingling sensation shot through her fingertips, a rush of energy that surprised her.

"Careful, Liora!" Lars cautioned.

But Liora was already lost in her own world of discovery, eyes wide with wonder. She touched the crystal over and over, repeatedly zapping herself and giggling each time.

She breathed heavily, mind racing to understand. "You were right, Lars. It's alive. Somehow."

Jax, growing impatient, interrupted her reverie. "But what does it *do,* Liora? Can it blast holes in walls? Fry a man's brain from across the room? Come on, tell us already!"

Liora blinked as if startled back to reality. She looked up at Jax with a sheepish smile. "Well," she admitted, "I have no idea."

Jax tossed his hands up in mock dismay. If it didn't serve some immediate purpose, entertaining or otherwise, then it wasn't that interesting, was it?

"But," Liora added, eyes sparkling with renewed excitement, "between this little marvel and that strange crystal scrap from Switcher's workshop, I've got two mysteries to solve! Give me a few days, and I'll have it all figured out."

She glanced over at Trin, a mischievous grin spreading across her face. "Those new lenses you brought me will come in handy. Thanks again, Trin." She bounded over and gave the woman a small peck on the cheek. "It is so good to have you back. You always keep it interesting."

Two nights later, the low murmur of conversation and the clinking of glasses filled the common room of the Drowned Mermaid Inn. Sitting at a secluded table in the back, Lars took a sip of a frosty beer, gaze fixed on the figure across from him. Looking relaxed and smug, Darius leaned back in his chair, a satisfied grin playing on his lips. Trin sat beside Lars, sharp eyes scanning the room, alert as a hawk. Her presence was more like a well-honed blade at his side—ready to strike if needed, and always a comfort to have around.

"Congratulations, Darius," Lars said, raising his glass in a mock toast. "Stealing a bloody ship? That's a new level of crazy, even for you."

Darius chuckled, his eyes glinting with pride. "It was a challenge, I'll admit. But Thume needed a reminder of who runs this city."

He thinks *he* runs this city, Lars mused, taking another sip of his beer. He knew Darius enough to recognize the bravado, the calculated showmanship. But there was something else beneath the surface, a restlessness, an edge that hadn't been there before.

"So, what treasures did you unearth from Thume's little trove?" Lars asked, leaning forward casually. He needed information, but also had to play by their unspoken rules.

Darius's grin widened. "Oh, the usual spoils. Copper, crystals, and a few interesting dynamo gadgets. Nothing quite so stunning as your *little* statue, Harrow, but useful nonetheless." He gave Lars a bold wink. "Well, that and an entire cargo ship, of course."

One point to Darius. Lars felt a flush of warmth creep up his neck, and he knew it wasn't due to the ale. He glanced sideways at Trin, catching the telltale amusement in her eyes. Damn her and that knowing look.

Darius leaned closer, driving the point home. "Let's just say that Lord Thume is a man of many secrets. Some of them are perhaps even more valuable than a shipload of copper. It was time somebody pulled one over on him."

Secrets. There were plenty of those floating around these days. He thought of the device Trin had brought them, the strange crystal at its core, Liora's growing certainty that it was somehow connected to Switcher's murder. What if Darius had stumbled upon something similar? Something that had driven him to such a reckless act?

A mischievous grin spread across Lars's face. He glanced at Trin, raising an eyebrow. "Sounds like someone's been busy and is very proud of himself."

Trin's lips twitched in response. "Oh, Lars, I'm sure we have *no* idea what he's up to." Her gaze flickered toward Darius.

But Darius didn't take the bait. "I'm sorry," Darius interrupted with a smirk, "is this a private conversation between you two, or more of a trio thing? Not going to lie, I'm a little interested."

Lars couldn't help but bark out a laugh. The man knew how to banter and could push his buttons like an engineer with a dynamo switchboard. Like Lars, Darius was a true master of the craft. He knew how to read people, manipulate any situation, and turn every encounter into a performance.

"Interested enough to join our crew, Darius?" Trin asked in her silky purr that never failed to send a shiver down Lars's spine. "We're always looking for talented individuals. Especially those with a knack for grand entrances."

Darius threw back his head and laughed, the sound booming through the tavern. "Now, Trinelle, you know I prefer to run my own team." His eyes met Lars's with a challenging glint. "Besides, I wouldn't want to steal Master Harrow's thunder."

"Ha! As if you could." Lars took another sip of his beer, savoring the cool bitterness on his tongue. "But speaking of thunder, any word on how Lord Thume is taking your little display of theatrics?"

The amusement faded from Darius's face, replaced by a flicker of something darker, something Lars couldn't quite decipher. "Thume?" Darius scoffed. "He's a busy man,

Harrow. He's got bigger fish to fry than a single missing galleon. Besides, he knows better than to underestimate me."

Lars felt a prickle of unease. Darius's confidence, while at times entertaining, had just taken a sharp turn toward unnerving. If Darius was playing a deeper game here, Lars needed to learn the rules quick before it came back to bite him in the ass.

Trin, ever perceptive, must have sensed the shift in Lars's mood. She reached out and placed a hand on his arm. Her touch was a reminder that he wasn't alone in his thoughts. "Don't worry, Lars," she reassured him. "Darius is just flexing a little bit because he knows you've been without your star player."

"Star player?" Darius perked up. "Who might that be?"

Trin snorted and rolled her eyes. "Me, asshole. It's always me." She gave Lars a wink.

Her words and the warmth of her hand on his arm reminded him that he had been down one very strategic crew member in her absence, and that calmed his unease. He squeezed her hand in acknowledgement before turning back to Darius.

"Well, I'm sure you've got plenty to keep you occupied," Lars said, forcing a casual tone. "Enjoy your spoils, Darius. Trin and I have to get going. Preparing for a trip out of town and all that. But don't get too comfortable. You'll have a lot to take in when we get back."

He stood up, signaling the end of their meeting. Trin rose beside him, eyes still fixed on Darius.

"Until next time, Darius," she said in a voice as smooth as silk.

As they turned to leave, Lars glanced back at Darius. He was still seated at the table, his gaze locked on the space where Trin had been sitting, a thoughtful frown creasing his brow.

Lars turned away, wondering what the man must be thinking, a strange kind of anticipation churning in his gut.

The night air was cool against Lars's skin as they stepped out of the inn, the sounds of the city fading behind them. He drew a deep breath, savoring the familiar mix of salt air, coal smoke, and the faint metallic tang that hung over Azoria.

"Well," Trin said, her voice laced with amusement, "that was... interesting."

"Darius always enjoys putting on a show."

He glanced at Trin, noticing how the moonlight cast shadows across her face, highlighting the sharp angles of her cheekbones. "You were right," he said. "It's good to have you back."

She smiled, a flash of warmth that banished the dark. "It's good to be back," she echoed. Her fingers brushed against his arm.

They walked in comfortable silence, their steps echoing on the cobblestone streets. As they approached Lars's apartment, a sense of anticipation, a familiar pull, tightened in his chest. He hadn't realized how much he'd missed her. Not just her sharp wit and strategic mind, but her presence— how she challenged and grounded him, made him feel... alive.

At his doorway, Lars turned to face her, his attention lingering on her lips. "Come inside," he said in a tone halfway between a desire and a demand.

She met his gaze, a silent question in her eyes. Alone now with Lars, standing in front of his door, on a beautiful night... it was almost too perfect. Her look of determination and cunning, displayed before at the bar with Darius, all part of her professional persona, was replaced with a look of vulnerability and anticipation.

Lars responded by pulling her close to him. Her lean, warm body pressed against his own. Breaking the spell of coyness and questioning, he kissed her deeply and let his fingers roam up her back.

After the kiss, Trin gasped, eyes full of wonder. She followed him inside with light and graceful steps. The apartment was small but comfortable, filled with the well-worn furnishings and the faint scent of the sweet pipe tobacco that Lars enjoyed from time to time. Lars poured two glasses of wine, a rich, dark vintage that he'd been saving for a special occasion.

"To new beginnings," he said, raising his glass in a toast.

"And to old flames," Trin replied with a grin.

They sipped their wine, the silence comfortable. Lars found himself captivated by her presence, how the soft lamplight illuminated her face, the subtle curve of her smile. And the way her fingers traced the rim of her glass, a gesture both elegant and unconsciously sensual. She glanced at him through lidded eyes.

He wanted her. He'd wanted her for years, but their lives, their careers, the constant dance of danger and intrigue that consumed them, had always kept them apart beyond a few fun encounters.

And now, in the quiet intimacy of his apartment, with the buzz of the city falling away, he couldn't deny the pull any longer. The years of running, of evading the truth of their connection, seemed foolish now.

He set down his glass and reached for her hand, fingers intertwining with hers. She didn't resist, didn't speak, but her eyes met his, acknowledging the desire that flared between them. It was as if they were both suspended in time, caught in a moment where nothing else mattered but the heat that simmered between them, waiting to burst.

Lars stood, pulling her to her feet. Their bodies brushed, a spark like dynamo igniting where their skin touched. The air around them seemed to crackle, charged with the anticipation of what was to come. He leaned in and his lips found hers again. The kiss was soft at first, hesitant, testing the waters of a deep, unspoken longing. Then, as if a dam had broken, the kiss deepened. The years of tenuous restraint and professional distance melted away in the warmth of their shared breath.

She tasted of wine and something uniquely hers, a heady mix that made his head spin as though he was drinking in all the moments they'd denied themselves. Lars felt her hands on his shoulders, pulling him closer, her body pressing against his, a delicious ache that sent a wave of heat coursing through him. Trin's touch was dynamo as her fingers traced the lines of his jaw and the curve of his neck, igniting every nerve beneath her fingertips.

He led her toward the bedroom, their steps slow, deliberate. The room shrank, their world narrowing to the space they occupied together, the tension building. Lars laid her down on the bed. His body hovered over hers, and his breath caught as he searched her face for any sign of hesitation.

But her eyes held nothing but desire. A raw, unfiltered hunger that mirrored his own. The trust in Trin's gaze, the vulnerability that lay beneath, sent a thrill through him. It made him ache with the need to show her how much he wanted this—wanted her.

He kissed her again, deeper this time, his tongue exploring the sweet warmth of her mouth. His hands roamed over her curves, memorizing the contours of her body as if mapping out a sacred terrain.

Trin arched into his touch. Her skin was warm and inviting, and her breath caught in a soft gasp as his fingers traced the lines of her waist, her hips, her thighs. Lars moved slowly, savoring the feel of her beneath him, the way her body responded to his touch, each caress drawing her closer, each kiss driving them both wild.

When he entered her, it was like a rush of pure fire, their bodies fitting together with a perfect, undeniable synchronicity. Her fingers tangled in his hair, legs wrapping around him, pulling him closer, deeper. He moved with her, their rhythm a delicate balance of urgency and restraint, building and building until it was almost too much to bear.

Lars pulled back slightly, his breath ragged and eyes searching hers, their foreheads almost touching. "Trin," he said, thick with emotion, "I'm so glad you're home."

She looked at him, eyes alight with passion, a soft smile curving her lips. She pushed against him with surprising strength as she reversed their positions, moving with the confidence he loved about her.

"You're so sweet, Lars. But you're done teasing me."

Trin lowered herself onto him, hips moving against his with a tantalizing rhythm. Every movement sent ripples cascading through their bodies. Her hands braced against his chest, gaze never wavering from Lars.

The world outside faded away, the night stretching before them like a canvas waiting to be painted with their touches, their whispered confessions. The city lights flickered beyond the window, but in this moment, they were distant stars in another sky.

For now, there was only the two of them. Every touch, every caress, spoke of things that words had never been able to capture—the desire, the need, the love that had always been there, waiting for this moment to be realized.

IT'S TIME TO MOVE

6

The familiar creak of the tavern door announced their return the next morning. Lars and Trin stepped inside, greeted by the warmth of a cooking fire and the aroma of bacon and fried bread wafting from the kitchen.

In the back corner, Liora was hunched over a workbench, a tangle of wires and crystals of various types surrounding her. She was muttering to herself, brow furrowed in concentration as she peered through the multi-layered lenses Trin had brought back from her travels.

A solo game of cards occupied Jax at his usual table, though he appeared restless and bored.

From the kitchen came the clanging of pots and pans, accompanied by Keer's occasional grumbling. Surly and brash though the man might be at times, he was a damn fine cook and would always volunteer to whip up something delicious.

Liora looked up as Trin and Lars approached, a slow smile spreading across her face. Her eyes flicked between them with a mischievous glint as she cocked an eyebrow at Lars.

He responded by clasping Trin's hand and smiling.

Liora beamed at them. "Well, well, well. Look who decided to grace us with their presence."

Feeling a warmth creep up his neck, Lars squeezed Trin's hand tighter.

"Awww," Liora cooed. "You two are adorable."

Before Lars could respond, Jax slammed his hand down on the table, scattering the cards in a flurry of hearts, diamonds, and spades. "Wait a minute! Are you guys, like, *into* each other?"

Trin laughed, and her eyes sparkled with amusement. "Jax, darling, has it really taken you this long to notice?"

Lars, still feeling a bit flustered, cleared his throat. "Alright, enough with the gossip," he said, glancing at Jax, who was now gaping at them with bald-faced astonishment. "We've got business to discuss."

"Business?" Liora perked up, pushing her glasses back up her nose. "Does this business involve investigating the murder? Because if it does, I'm in!"

"Actually," Lars said, exchanging a look with Trin, "we were thinking of heading out to Stoneford. We need to meet this new patron Trin was talking about. That said, we thought you might need to come along in case any kind of tech comes up, Liora."

Jax's jaw dropped. "Stoneford? Without me? But I'm the muscle!" He lifted and flexed the stronger of his two arms as if to prove the point. "What if you run into trouble?"

"It's not that kind of trip, Jax. Besides, someone needs to stay here and supervise things. We need your eyes and ears downtown. You're the best at gathering information on the street."

Jax started to object, but Liora elbowed him in the ribs. "Ow! What was that for?" he grumbled, rubbing his side.

Liora slid closer. "Think, Jax. This is a chance for those two lovebirds to, ya know..." She trailed off, waggling her eyebrows suggestively.

Jax blinked. "Oh," he said, a slow dawning comprehension spreading across his face. "OH. Right, sure. You guys go have fun."

The red traveling up Lars's neck was now in full blush on his face. Trin giggled mischievously at his discomfort.

Just then, Keer emerged from the kitchen, wiping his hands on a stained apron. "Who's going where?" His eyes swept over the assembled crew.

"These two are going on a little... business trip," Liora explained. "To Stoneford. Just the two of them." At the table, Jax grinned and made exaggerated smooching faces.

Keer grunted with an impassive expression. "I hate Stoneford. Don't get into too much trouble." He turned back toward the kitchen. "And try not to burn down any towns this time."

Lars rolled his eyes. "It was *one* time, Keer!" The man left as the kitchen door shut behind him.

"So, Liora," Lars said, "I take it you're not coming with us?"

"Oh, I'd hate to impose, you know." Her eyes dropped to the workbench, and her fingers traced the intricate lines of the disassembled device. Lars knew the mystery would consume her until she extracted every bit of detail. "But in all seriousness, I have plenty to keep me occupied here, and it's important. I'm *this* close to discovering something big."

"Big, huh?" Lars said, taking a seat near Liora, glad to have the conversation turn away from his flames—be they Trin or that one unfortunate town. That had been a damn shame.

Adding to that, he couldn't resist looking over her shoulder to examine the captivating and enigmatic device, its delicate components spread out on the workbench like the exposed organs of some strange mechanical creature. "What have you figured out so far?"

Trin pulled up a chair next to Lars. Her expression was curious as she watched Liora work. "Yeah, Liora. What's got you so fascinated?"

Liora tapped a finger against the glowing crystal at the device's core, oblivious now to the slight zaps of dynamo it sent through her. "It's this damn crystal," she said. "It's generating its own dynamo. Or at least, that's what it seems to be doing. But like we've said, that shouldn't be possible."

Jax's eyes widened. "Wait, what? How can you know that without knowing what the damned thing does?"

Liora ignored his questions, focusing instead on the crystal. "It's unlike anything I've ever seen before. It's not amplifying or modulating dynamo like a normal crystal. It's... creating it. As if it's got some kind of internal source, a reservoir of pure energy."

"A crystal charge?" Trin suggested.

Liora nodded slowly. "That's the best explanation I can come up with so far. But it doesn't make any sense. Crystals don't hold charge. They're conduits, amplifiers, capacitors maybe. But those fizzle out. They don't hold a charge. They channel it."

She picked up a small shard of crystal from the workbench, holding it to the light. It was a jagged, uneven piece with a faint milky haze running through its center.

"This is the shard I snagged from Remus Switcher's lab," she said, voice dropping to a murmur. "It has the same energy signature as the crystal in this device, though there's no dynamo in it. But this piece at least has the same unusual cut, the same... feeling. I don't know."

She sighed, blowing a stray hair away from her face. "It just seems like they're connected somehow."

A shiver ran down Lars's spine. The murdered engineer, the strange crystal, the device Trin had brought back from her travels—it was all starting to coalesce, forming an intriguing and unsettling pattern.

"I'll tell you what I really think." Liora's eyes gleamed with fresh excitement. "I think we've stumbled onto something big here. Something that could change a lot for us."

She paused for a moment, as if considering her next words. "Anyways, the crystal is just part of the puzzle. The gadget it's powering is just as interesting. I'm calling it a dynamo lens. And I'm pretty sure it allows someone to detect the flow of dynamo energy. Imagine seeing all of the invisible currents, the connections between everything dynamo touches in the city."

"Holy shit," Jax breathed.

"Exactly," Liora said. "Mind you, I'm not sure of this yet. It's going to take some more work."

Something nagged at the back of Lars's mind. He turned and looked at Trinelle.

"Trin, you never told us where you got this device in the first place."

She cocked her head in thought. "I was just thinking the same thing. It was given to me by our would-be patron." Pausing for a moment, she threw her hands up. "Supposedly.

More accurately, a messenger of that patron. A promise, they said, of further business to come."

"A promise, huh? And what does this patron expect in return?"

Trin shrugged, a quick flash of unease crossing her face. "They didn't say. Just that they, whoever they are, were impressed with our work and had a proposition for us."

"A proposition that involves a crystal-powered device that might be connected to a murder?" Keer interjected, stepping out of the kitchen with a plate of steaming bacon, fried bread, and eggs. He set the plate down on the table with a clatter and stared at the disassembled dynamo lens. "This whole thing stinks worse than Jax's boots after a week in the sewers."

Jax, predictably, took offense. "Hey! My boots are perfectly—"

"Enough, Jax," Lars interrupted. He turned back to Trin. "Let's make sure we're careful with this, Trin. This dynamo lens and the crystal charge inside it—well, it's not just a new toy. It could be dangerous. If Thume or anyone else finds out about it..."

Lars trailed off, mulling through the questions bombarding the forefront of his mind. Did Thume even know such a crystal existed? Or a device that could apparently detect dynamo currents? Was he already aware of the power it might hold? And what would the great oligarch do if he knew they had it?

Trin nodded. "I know," she said. "I'm getting a bad feeling. But I'm too invested to back out now. We're going to Stoneford. We're going to meet this patron. And we're going to find out what they want."

Lars nodded, a surge of excitement mixed with apprehension coursing through him. He glanced at Liora, who was already back at her workbench. She sat tracing the intricate patterns and pathways of the dynamo lens, a look of fierce determination on her face. He knew she wouldn't rest until she'd unlocked every one of its secrets.

"Don't forget to sleep while we're gone, Liora," he said. "We'll need your sharp mind when we get back."

He turned toward Trin, offering her his arm. "Ready to leave Azoria behind for a while?"

Trin took his arm, fingers intertwining with his. "Let's go shake things up in Stoneford," she said with an adventurous spirit that mirrored his own.

"Guys," Keer began. "*GUYS*." They paused in their exit and turned around.

"Yes?"

Keer snorted, feigning offense. "You forgot to eat your breakfast. What the hell is with you two?"

Lars flushed and Trin laughed, then the two sat with the rest of the crew and dug in.

Days later, a carriage rattled into Stoneford, the horses' hooves echoing on the cobbled streets. Lars peered out the window, taking in the town's unique charm. Stoneford was a smaller city, nestled in a valley amidst the foothills of the mountains that formed the eastern border of Ithris.

Unlike Azoria, with its rowdy market, gleaming metallic structures, and teeming crowds, Stoneford had a more timeless feel, its architecture dominated by sturdy stone buildings that jutted organically from the surrounding landscape.

A sense of rustic industry hung in the air, a mix of coal smoke from the nearby mines, the sharp scent of pine from the surrounding forests, and the aromas of fresh baked bread and roasted meat wafting from open-air markets. In the distance, a waterfall roared down a nearby mountain, a source for both the town's water and dynamo.

"Not much has changed," Lars said, a hint of nostalgia in his voice. "Still as charming as I remember."

Trin giggled, glancing at him. "You make it sound like you spent your childhood summers here, frolicking in meadows and braiding wildflowers into your hair."

"Something like that."

The carriage pulled up in front of a modest inn, its stone facade weathered by time and the elements. Lars and Trin stepped out, stretching their limbs after the long journey. Three days on the road had been uneventful, thankfully, giving them time to rest, strategize, and... reconnect.

"Ready for your grand entrance, Master Harrow?" Trin said, a playful smirk curving her lips.

Lars chuckled, shaking his head. "I think subtlety is more our style in Stoneford, my dear." He took her arm, enjoying their closeness.

They went to their pre-arranged room, a cozy space with a fireplace and a view of the marketplace.

As they closed the door behind them, Lars glanced at Trin, a frown creasing his brow. "How the hell are we supposed to find this patron?"

Trin shrugged, crossing her arms. "Someone made contact with me before. Maybe they'll come looking for us."

"I sure hope so. Otherwise we're looking for a needle in a haystack," Lars chuckled dryly. "Literally, in this bumpkin town."

Before Trin could respond, his eyes landed on a single, sealed envelope lying on the table, addressed simply, "To the Esteemed Master Harrow."

Lars broke the seal, unfolding the crisp parchment within. It contained a single line written in elegant script:

The heart of the city holds a hidden spring.

Lars raised an eyebrow, re-folding the letter. "Cryptic. That's always fun."

"Don't worry, Lars," Trin said, looking out the window at the open market square below. "I think I know where this is going."

And so began a most unusual treasure hunt.

Their first clue led them to a weathered stone fountain in the heart of the marketplace. A young boy, face smudged with dirt and his eyes bright with mischief, approached them. He held out a single, polished stone and whispered a phrase in a dialect Lars didn't recognize. Then the boy scampered off into the crowd.

When examined closely, the stone revealed a tiny inscription: *Seek the song of fire.*

Following the inscription, they found themselves outside a blacksmith's workshop, carved into a stone embankment and reeking with the overwhelming smell of coal smoke and hot metal. A burly blacksmith, his face grimed with soot, handed them a small iron key. As Lars took it, the man pointed toward a narrow alleyway behind the workshop.

In the alley, they found a small door with the inscription, *The blacksmith sent me,* which they unlocked with the provided key. The open door revealed a steep, winding staircase that led them upwards, deeper into the heart of the city.

They emerged onto a rooftop garden at the top of the stairs, a hidden oasis of fragrant flowers and cascading vines. A young woman dressed in simple yet elegant robes offered them a cup of tea and what looked like a feather fashioned out of paper. "The eagle knows the way," she whispered.

Upon closer inspection, the paper feather bore a tiny map drawn on its surface. It depicted a winding path that they took through a maze of narrow streets and hidden courtyards, leading to a single destination: a small, elegant manor house perched on a hillside overlooking the town.

"Impressive," Lars said, admiring the ingenuity and artistry of the elaborate chain of clues as they reached their destination. "I've never experienced a meeting request quite like that."

They approached the manor house, a sense of anticipation building with each step. A servant dressed in livery greeted them at the door and led them through a series of hallways to a sun-drenched patio overlooking an expansive manicured garden.

A woman sat at a table with her back to them. She was tall and statuesque, with long silver hair pulled back in an elegant chignon. Her posture was regal and commanding, exuding an air of authority that made the room feel smaller as if everyone instinctively deferred to her presence without a word being spoken.

"You've arrived," she said in a pleasant contralto with the hint of an unfamiliar accent. "Please, join me."

She turned to face them. Lars froze at the sight of her eyes. They were the color of polished jade, a unique and provocative color. A faint smile curved her ruby red lips, a welcoming and unsettling gesture.

"Welcome to Stoneford, Master Harrow, Mistress Meridia. I am Vivienne."

Lars and Trin exchanged a look. She was not at all what they expected.

"It's a pleasure to meet you, Vivienne," Lars said, inclining his head respectfully. He sat across from her, noting the elegant simplicity of her attire—a dark blue gown that flowed around her like liquid silk, accented with a single silver pendant that shimmered with an almost unnatural brilliance. He realized he was staring and looked away sheepishly.

Trin remained standing, taking in every detail with her usual sharp observation. "You have a beautiful home, Vivienne." Her tone was smooth as silk. "And an intriguing way of inviting guests to visit it."

Vivienne smiled, an unsettling flash of amusement evident in her jade-green eyes. "I appreciate the compliment, Mistress Meridia. But I believe in making a memorable first impression." Her eyes flicked to Lars.

She gestured to the pitcher of iced tea and the plate of delicate pastries on the table. "Please, help yourselves. We have much to discuss."

As Lars poured himself a glass of tea, Vivienne leaned back in her chair, posture shifting from welcoming to something more calculating.

"I've heard a great deal about you, Master Harrow." She paused as if trying to decide on how to begin. "Your reputation precedes you. A master of your craft, they say. Bold, innovative, with an unmatched penchant for the theatrical."

A sly quirk favored her lips. "And quite attractive now that I see you for myself."

"You flatter me," Lars said, unimpressed. He was used to dealing with powerful individuals who sought his skills for their ambitions. He sensed that Vivienne was no different.

"I'm not one for flattery, Master Harrow," she said. "I deal in facts—and the fact is, I require your services." She paused again, and Lars gestured for her to continue.

"I have a proposition for you. A challenge that I believe will push your skills to the limit."

Lars snorted. "A heist then? Lady, I don't mind telling you, you didn't need such an elaborate invitation just to tip us off about a heist. Send a letter like everyone else."

Vivienne's smile widened and a hint of fire entered her tone. "Oh, Master Harrow," she said, "you underestimate me. This is no ordinary heist. This is nothing short of a masterpiece. An orchestra of daring and precision that will echo through the ages."

Lars leaned back in his chair, intrigued despite his initial skepticism, though he had heard it all before. But he sensed that Vivienne was not the kind of woman to exaggerate. Trin, still standing, remained silent. Her gaze fixed with stoic calm on Vivienne.

"Intrigued?" Vivienne asked, her voice a silken thread wrapped around Lars, drawing him in.

"I'm listening."

Lars set down his untouched glass of tea. He knew that this woman, this Vivienne, was playing a game of her own. To put it plainly, he wasn't sure if she was trying to sleep with him or rope him into a job. But he was determined to understand the rules before he made a move.

"Good," Vivienne said, smile fading as her expression turned serious. "Because what I'm about to propose is not for anyone without a strong sense of curiosity. It requires skill, daring, and, most importantly, a certain disregard for the established order."

She leaned forward, eyes piercing. "I want you to steal something for me, Master Harrow. But rest assured, it will shake the foundations of not just Azoria but all of Ithris."

Lars exchanged a quick glance with Trin. What was this woman talking about stealing? What did she know, and how did she know it? And, most importantly, would she ever get to the fucking point?

"Don't worry," Vivienne said. "All will be revealed in due time. But for now, suffice it to say that the target is significant. The security, formidable—and the reward..." she leaned forward, eyes passionate, burning, "is a reward beyond your wildest dreams."

She paused, letting her words sink in. Then she leaned back casually, the spell broken. Lars blinked and looked at Vivienne with a new, quizzical respect.

"At the least, I can guarantee it will make a legend of you, Master Harrow. More than you already are that is. And, of course, of your talented associates." Her gaze shifted toward Trin with a wry grin.

"Well," Lars asked, "what can you tell us about the target?"

Vivienne's smile returned, a slow, predatory curve of her lips that sent a shiver down Lars's spine. "A secret warehouse. North of Azoria, known to very few. The personal cache of one Lord Cecil Thume."

A heavy silence fell over the patio. Lars stared at Vivienne, mind racing.

Thume's own private warehouse, perhaps his best kept secret. It was, in a word, unthinkable. While everyone had assumed its existence—hells only knew where—no one would ever dare to make it their target. But after Darius's recent bravado…

Lars was incredulous. "You're serious." It wasn't a question, more of a statement of disbelief.

Vivienne smiled, but it remained cold. "Of course I am. Do I strike you as someone with time to waste?"

"And what makes you think," Trin said, breaking her silence, "we'd be interested in such a risky proposition?"

Vivienne raised an eyebrow, giving Trin a look that clearly questioned her intelligence. "Because you understand the game, Mistress Meridia. You know that true power lies not in accumulating wealth but in disrupting the existing order. In taking what you want, what should be yours, regardless of the consequences."

She stood up in a fluid and graceful movement, filling the patio with an almost palpable energy.

"Think about it, Master Harrow. Imagine the possibilities." She looked at Lars intently. "Think of what we could be together."

Trin snorted.

Vivienne laughed, a charming musical sound filling the air. She then gestured toward the garden, a landscape of cultivated beauty that was at odds with the clandestine nature of her words. Words that, despite the relentless nature of the one speaking them, were now ever present in the minds of Lars and Trin.

Vivienne broke their moment of contemplation. "But for now, enjoy the serenity of Stoneford. Rest, relax, indulge your… newfound passions."

Her eyes flickered toward Trin. "More information will be forthcoming. I suggest you be prepared, Master Harrow. The rules are about to change, and when they do, I want you by my side."

With that, she turned and walked back into the manor house, leaving the couple alone on the patio, the silence broken by the distant roar of the waterfall and the unsettling echo of Vivienne's temptations.

Music spilled out onto the cobblestone street, a blend of tavern tunes and the melancholic strains of a street musician's dynamo violin. Silas weaved through the crowds, scanning the faces that passed under the flickering gaslamps. He spotted Keer leaning against a lamppost, a half-empty tankard in hand, eyes fixed on the swirling dancers in the nearby plaza.

Silas approached him, a wry smile playing on his lips. "Enjoying the show, Keer?"

Keer turned, surprise crossing his weathered features. "Silas," he said calmly. "How good to see you here. I thought your crew preferred the comforts of their luxuriant hideout these days."

"A change of scenery is good for the soul." Silas took a seat on a bench beside the old Zarakaran.

Keer grunted, swigging his ale. "What brings you to this side of town, Silas? Business or pleasure?"

"I just needed some time to think, to be honest," Silas said, his eyes meeting Keer's with a prognostic glint. "You know, we go back a ways, you and I. Back to the days of the Sea's Bounty."

Though a bit suspicious of Silas's chummy behavior, a ghost of a smile couldn't help but form on Keer's lips. "Aye.

And that old grisly asshole, Captain Galdan. Those were interesting times. Long nights, rough waters, and a captain who could make any sailor tremble."

"Don't I know it. We looked out for each other in those days, remember? Always had each other's backs."

Here it comes, Keer thought to himself, deciding he'd go ahead and bite. "And how about now? This isn't a chance visit, is it, Silas? What's on your mind?"

Silas lingered a moment, staring at the plaza. He took a deep breath.

"It's Darius," he said hesitantly. "He's not himself lately. He's been reckless. Overly ambitious. Almost desperate."

This didn't have the feel of a ploy, but Keer wouldn't contribute too much of his own thoughts until he knew for sure. He took another swig of his ale, eyes fixed on Silas, waiting for him to continue.

"That ship heist," Silas said, "it was—well don't get me wrong, it was great. Stellar even. But too bold. Way too bold."

"You all got away with it, didn't you? And he's got a whole shipload of loot to show for it. Sounds like a win to me."

"It's not that simple, Keer." Silas shook his head as if organizing his thoughts. "There's something else going on. Something darker. I can feel it. It's my business to know what's happening. And right now I don't."

He sidled closer, looking around to make sure no one nearby was listening. "You heard about Remus Switcher?"

Keer stiffened, eyes narrowing as the suspicion returned. "What about him?"

"You think it was just a random robbery gone wrong?" Silas said. "An engineer like Switcher? Murdered in his own workshop? It doesn't add up."

Keer remained silent, looking straight ahead, his face impossible to read. "From what I understand, Switcher was a good man. And a halfway decent engineer. It's a shame what happened to him."

"A shame?" Silas considered the word with obvious frustration. "This is more than a shame, Keer. It's a hells damned warning. Someone's running a different hustle now, and a vicious one at that. I'm worried Darius is getting in over his head."

Keer's eyes opened wide as he turned to Silas. "You think Darius is involved in Switcher's murder?"

"I don't know…"

Silas gazed ahead, deep in thought. "No, I don't suppose I believe that," he corrected. "But something's not right. He's been acting strange ever since that score on Thume's trove. Secretive. Almost… paranoid."

He reached out and gripped Keer's arm in earnest. "Talk to Lars. Please. Something has Darius spooked, and if it has someone like him spooked, it should have the rest of us trembling. Lars needs to know if things don't feel right. Maybe he'll have some ideas."

Whatever this was about, Keer met Silas's gaze with grudging respect. He knew Silas wasn't one to exaggerate or spread rumors. If he was this concerned, it meant there was something to be concerned about.

"What makes you think Lars will listen?" Keer said. "He and Darius might have the same job but are hardly allies."

Silas paused and gave him a pleading look. "Keer, we're getting old, man. We've seen a lot. We know how this city works and how things are done around here. But something *is* changing. It's not just the stakes getting higher. There's more happening that we just aren't seeing. I don't like it. Do you?"

Keer sighed, shoulders slumping under the weight of Silas's words. He knew what Silas was saying was true. People across Azoria were feeling the pinch. It wasn't full-blown panic—yet—but more and more citizens were living on borrowed money just to get by. Prices for basic goods had soared, while jobs and stable income grew scarce. Struggling to survive, shops and businesses were cutting hours and staff, trying to stretch their resources thin. It was a slow, creeping suffocation, and the city's undercurrent of tension was growing with each passing day.

He'd felt the shift too, a growing unease, a sense that the power dynamics in Azoria were teetering on the edge of chaos—and he couldn't shake the feeling that Switcher's murder was just the beginning.

"Alright, Silas. I'll talk to Lars. But I can't promise he'll listen. He's a stubborn bastard, that one. Always has been."

Silas smiled. "Thanks, Keer. That's all I ask. I owe you."

He lingered on the dancers for another wistful moment. Keer did the same. Their carefree movements were a stark contrast to the concerns he carried.

"Take care of yourself, old friend," he said, clapping Keer on the shoulder. "And watch your back. Things are about to get interesting. I know it."

The wind howled outside, rattling the tavern windows and sending shivers down Jax's spine as he pushed open the heavy door. Rain lashed against the glass, blurring the lights of the city beyond. It had been storming since last night, casting a somber gloom over the room and Azoria at large.

More so since Keer had returned just before the storm had hit. He'd been out enjoying music in the city, but something had clearly shaken him, leaving his normally stoic face etched with worry. Despite Jax's attempts to pry, Keer wouldn't talk about it.

Jax had been trying to shake off the unease. But a knot of apprehension tightened in his chest as he stepped inside, a forced cheerfulness on his lips. He was about to call out a greeting, ready to distract his companions with the usual gossip and jokes, but the sight that met his eyes stopped him cold.

The tavern was unusually quiet. Keer was nowhere to be seen. And Liora—

She wasn't at her workbench, surrounded by her usual array of tools and gadgets. Instead, she was huddled in a dark corner, her knees pulled up to her chest and face hidden in her arms. Her shoulders shook with silent sobs, and a wave of pity washed over Jax.

He crossed the room, heavy boots thudding against the wooden floor. An urgent concern replaced his usual boisterous energy. Jax crouched beside her, the floorboards creaking under his weight. His large hand, calloused from years of brawls and heavy lifting, settled on her shoulder with a surprising gentleness.

"Liora? What's wrong?"

"It's dead, Jax." She waved her arm toward the workbench. "The crystal. It's not generating dynamo anymore. I've tried everything. Pumping dynamo into it, using different frequencies, even trying to, I don't know, jump-start it with another crystal. Nothing works. It's just dead."

She pulled away from him, scrubbing at her eyes with shaking fingers. The lenses Trin gave her, now perched precariously atop her normal spectacles, slipped down her nose. She pushed them back up with a sigh, her usual meticulousness replaced by a weariness that tugged at Jax's heart.

"It had to happen eventually," Jax said. "Right? I mean, if those crystals can hold a charge, they can lose it too. Like anything else."

Liora nodded at his observation, a glimmer of appreciation in her eyes. "Yes, you're right. It's just... this was my chance to understand them, to figure out how they work, and maybe even figure out what happened to poor Remus. Now..." she trailed off with a low, despairing moan.

Jax sat down beside her, his large frame dwarfing her slight form. He kept his hand resting on her shoulder—a solid, comforting presence—and gave her a squeeze.

"Hey. Don't give up yet, Liora. You're the smartest dynamo wrangler in Azoria. You'll figure it out."

Liora gave him a wan smile. "Easy for you to say, Jax. You're not the one staring at a scientific impossibility."

"Well," Jax said, "let's work it out together." He thought for a moment, frowning. "Those crystals, they hold dynamo, right?"

Liora nodded miserably. "That's the theory. But I can't figure out how to give it dynamo back. Or if it's even possible."

It was damn difficult seeing the spunky and energetic woman so lost and hopeless. Jax looked past Liora through the window and into the flashing storm.

He snapped his fingers, a sudden inspiration lighting up his face. "What about lightning?" he said. "I mean, lightning is pure dynamo, right? Raw power. Maybe that's what it needs, a—" he cut off but smacked a fist into an open palm. "Pow."

Liora stared at him with widening eyes. At first, she thought he was joking. But as she saw the earnestness in his look, a spark of hope flickered within her.

"Lightning..." she echoed in a hushed whisper. She considered the idea. Jax knew her mind was racing, likely picturing the jagged bolts of pure dynamo bringing her precious crystal to life. "It's not impossible. Lightning is a *very* powerful source of dynamo. But it's also very dangerous. Unpredictable. We'd need a way to harness it, to channel it into the crystal."

Jax grinned. "Leave that to me," he said confidently. "I know just the place. There's an old watch building on the north side of town, abandoned for years. It's a small building but it has a lightning rod on the roof that goes up higher than anywhere in Azoria. We can use that to catch a bolt, and you can do your dynamo magic to direct it into the crystal." He wiggled his fingers to emphasize Liora's task.

Liora sniffed and hugged him tight. "I don't say this enough, Jax. But I sure do love you."

The big man smiled wide while further considering the idea. It was risky and reckless, but it might just work. He would try anything if it made Liora happy.

The storm raged above them, a furious symphony of howling wind and blinding light. Jagged bolts of lightning tore through the sky, illuminating the rooftop in harsh flashes, painting the world in stark shades of gray. Rain lashed down, a relentless torrent that soaked them to the bone, but neither

Jax nor Liora even noticed. Their entire world had shrunk to the small circle illuminated by the dynamo lamps Liora had set up around her experiment.

Liora knelt beside the makeshift apparatus. Her brow furrowed with concentration as she connected the final wire. Her hands trembled, not from the cold or the wind, but from the raw anticipation that thrummed through her veins.

The larger crystal, the heart of the device Trin had brought back, was fastened to the lightning rod, its facets barely shimmering in the sporadic light. Beside it, the small shard she'd salvaged from Remus Switcher's lab was connected in parallel. It was a crazy idea, she had told Jax, but if she was going to risk it all, she might as well risk it all. It wasn't just a test. It was a prayer—a desperate plea to validate everything they'd been working for.

Jax, towering over her, shifted from foot to foot, a nervous energy he couldn't shake radiating from him. Lightning cracked again, splitting the sky, and a primal fear, a deep-seated instinct that told him to seek shelter, clawed at his gut.

"Liora..." He had to force the word past the tightness in his throat. "Maybe we should wait for the storm to settle down a little."

"No time, Jax," she replied firmly, though Jax saw her tremor. Her eyes, wide and bright, were fixed on the faded crystals. A web of wires that connected them to the lightning rod that reached up toward the storm-wracked heavens, daring fate to strike. "It has to be now."

Another deafening crack, closer this time. Jax flinched, instinctively reaching out to pull Liora back, but she didn't budge. "Liora, please. It's getting too dangerous."

She looked up at him, her face illuminated by the strobing lightning, a desperate determination burning in her eyes. "No. This is going to work, Jax. It has to work."

Jax nodded, but he couldn't shake this feeling of unease. He trusted Liora, but the sheer power of the storm made his anxiety worsen. Lightning cracked again, shaking them both. The tension in the air was palpable as if the very atmosphere was holding its breath, waiting for something momentous to happen.

Liora's face was alight with excitement despite the rain and danger. "We're close. I can feel it. Any minute now." It was the kind of breathless exhilaration felt only when standing on the brink of discovery. She closed her eyes, and Jax heard her whisper a silent appeal to anyone listening.

As if on cue, the heavens answered.

A blinding flash and a sound like the world splitting apart shook them both, as a massive bolt of lightning struck the rod with a force that made the rooftop tremble. The air crackled with raw energy, and a surge of dynamo, a torrent of power unlike anything Jax had ever witnessed, coursed through the wires. The metal sizzled, glowing with an intense heat. Jax shielded his eyes, the world turning white.

When his vision cleared, he turned in trepidation to Liora. His heart lurched as he saw her slumped over the device, wires tangled around her, and her body engulfed in a pulsating aura of light.

"Oh hells!" he shouted, rushing forward. But then he stopped, fear turning to awe as he saw the crystals.

It had worked.

The larger crystal pulsed with a vibrant, hypnotic glow, the milky haze that had clouded its surface vanished. The smaller shard, connected in parallel, mirrored its brilliance, casting dancing shadows across the rooftop.

With a trembling hand, Liora carefully disconnected the larger crystal. She tucked it into her pocket and held Remus Switcher's shard aloft. Her face was illuminated by its otherworldly glow.

"Thank you, Jax," she whispered.

But before Jax could respond, a sound like a thunderclap, but sharper, deadlier, ripped through the air, accompanied by a brief flash in the distance. Liora's face contorted in a silent scream, body twisting as something invisible slammed into her, flinging her backward with a force that tore the crystal from her grasp.

"Liora!" Jax screamed, his heart seizing as he watched her spin and skid along the wet rooftop. He lunged toward her, reaching out, but it was too late.

She was already at the edge.

Her scream, a raw, primal sound of terror, was swallowed by the storm as her body tipped over the edge, disappearing into the darkness below.

The world froze. Jax stood paralyzed for a heartbeat, mind reeling. Then, with a roar of desperation that cut through the storm, he tore across the slick rooftop. His heavy boots slipped on the wet tiles. Reaching the edge, he hurled himself over with reckless abandon, his massive frame crashing through the rain-soaked air. For a brief, heart-pounding moment, he was weightless. Then he plunged headlong into the violent storm, chasing Liora into the void.

THE DIE IS CAST

7

The air in Stoneford was crisp, the kind of late summer day where the sun's warmth battled with the coolness of the wind, and Lars found himself enjoying the simplicity of it all. After spending so much of his time in the madness of Azoria, the quieter pace of Stoneford was a welcome change. It was strange to think he could find some peace in a city like this, where the most exciting event of the day might be the delivery of fresh goods to the market. Perhaps it was the company that made it bearable.

Trin walked beside him with light steps, her laughter ringing as they passed a vendor selling colorful scarves. She paused to admire one, a luscious silk number with intricate embroidery, and Lars couldn't help but smile. This was good—this time with her, away from the chaos. There was plenty to worry about at home, and it was easy to forget to enjoy such moments. They came along too rarely to waste.

Lars watched as she haggled playfully, voice rising and falling in mock reaction to the overtures. The vendor, an older woman with a knowing smile, gave in to the barrage. Trin turned to Lars, the scarf draped over her arm triumphantly.

"Look what I got!" she said, holding it up for him to see.

Hells, she was adorable. He loved her excitement, even for something so simple as a new scarf. "It's beautiful. It suits you."

They continued down the narrow streets of Stoneford, passing modest homes and shops, the fragrant smell of fresh bread wafting from a nearby bakery. Lars felt a strange sense of contentment, as if the weight of his responsibilities had lifted for a moment. They had decided to stay in Stoneford a little longer than planned, sure that Liora was head-down and immersed in her work. Lars could envision the quirky engineer muttering to herself as she unraveled the secrets of the device—and its mysterious crystal.

It was a rare opportunity for him and Trin to reconnect, to deepen the growing bond between them, both physically and emotionally. He tended to be guarded, but Trin had a way of breaking through those defenses. She made him feel like there was more to life than the next problem to solve or heist to pull off.

As they rounded a corner, Lars's relaxed demeanor shifted. His eyes narrowed as he recognized a familiar figure approaching from the opposite direction. Aric Myrim, the captain of Azoria's city watch, was dressed in his usual sharp attire. His posture was rigid, shaped by the unyielding demands of his duty.

Lars felt a pang of annoyance at the sight of him. Stoneford, days away from Azoria, was supposed to be a break from the affairs of the city. So, why would Myrim be here for him?

Myrim's eyes widened in surprise when he saw Lars, but the look turned to suspicion. Lars then realized this was just a chance encounter—nothing but bad luck. Myrim changed direction, heading toward them with his gaze locked in determination.

"What a surprise to see you here, Larson. I figured Stoneford was too quiet for your tastes."

Forcing a smile, Lars could feel the tension rising. "Even a thief needs a break from the city now and then. Stoneford's a nice change of pace."

Myrim's gaze flicked to Trinelle before returning to Lars. "Is that so? Just taking in the scenery then, is that it?"

Lars shrugged, keeping it light. "Something like that. Not everything's a scheme, you know. Sometimes it's just about enjoying a good day. And," he said, "to be honest, not everything is your business."

The response didn't seem to either convince or rankle Myrim. His eyes lingered on Lars as if searching for something beneath the surface. "I've been hearing a lot about you lately. I bet you're pretty miffed about Darius showing you up the way he did."

"I'm sure you're used to this, *Captain*, but that's a bet you'd lose. Quite the opposite. The heist was impressive, to be sure. But not my style."

Myrim's jaw set, as Lars's words did nothing but deepen his suspicion and play at his nerves. "And what is your style, Harrow? Knocking over poor manor lords for their hard-earned copper?"

"Oh yes, do tell me more about these 'poor manor lords,'" Lars snorted. "Listen, we all have our parts to play. They hoard. I steal. You try to catch me..."

Though they went unspoken, the words *but never do* lingered in the air, meaning different things for both of them.

Myrim held the stare a moment longer before nodding, though he remained guarded. "Perhaps. But Stoneford's a peaceful town. People here like it that way, and I'd hate to see that peace disturbed."

"I'm not here to cause trouble. Just looking to relax." The last thing Lars needed was a lecture, but he kept his tone even.

Myrim's brow furrowed. "See that it stays that way."

With that, he turned and walked away. Lars glanced at Trin, who was watching him with a raised eyebrow.

"Well, that was fun," she said dryly.

Lars sighed, running a hand through his hair. "To be honest I'm a little surprised. He seemed angry."

"You think so?" Trin said. "I didn't get that. It felt more like wrath."

"Don't those mean the same thing?"

"Not exactly, my dear," she said. "Anger is a base emotion, something we all can feel from time to time. Wrath is deeper. It's righteous. It's anger that comes from the soul."

The veracity and vigor of her words shook Lars. "That is quite a difficult sentiment for me to parse. You have a better understanding of the psyche than I do. I'll consider it."

Trin laughed. "What you're trying to say is that I'm a bore."

Before he could protest, she continued. "No, I'm kidding. But let's be honest, we're both guessing here. Maybe he's just having a bad day."

"Maybe." Lars sounded agreeable, but he wasn't convinced. From where he stood, Myrim was changing, becoming more aggressive in his pursuits, and Lars couldn't shake the feeling that it was directed at him.

But that was a problem for another day. He was determined to enjoy the rest of their time in Stoneford and make the most of this rare opportunity to be with Trin. Without a crew or the public's expectations of their profession getting in the way.

As they continued walking, Lars forced himself to push the encounter with Myrim to the back of his mind. Stoneford might be peaceful, but his life was not. He knew that inevitably the tranquility of this small town would be shattered by the chaos that followed behind any good thief.

For now, he had Trinelle, and that was enough.

The small utilitarian house stood in the heart of Stoneford, its once-grand facade weathered by decades of wind and rain. Despite its age and plainness, the building exuded an air of quiet dignity, much like the man who called it home. Aric Myrim stood at the foot of the stone steps, hesitating for just a moment, before climbing them and rapping his knuckles against a heavy wooden door. The echo of the knock resonated through the silent halls within.

After a few moments, the door creaked open, revealing a tall, broad-shouldered man whose age had done little to diminish his imposing presence. Braisus Ekon, former Lord Captain Commander of the police force for all of Ithris, regarded Myrim with a shrewd, appraising look. Though his hair was now a grainy gray, and the lines on his face were etched deep, there was no mistaking the sharpness in his eyes—a sharpness that had seen through countless lies and confessions in its time.

"Aric," Braisus said in a low rumble tinged with the authority that had once commanded legions. "It's been too long."

"Master Ekon," Myrim replied, bowing his head with respect. "Thank you for sending for me. I wasn't sure how my letter would be received."

Braisus stepped back to allow Myrim entry. "Come inside, come inside."

The house's interior was as austere as its owner, with minimal furnishings and naught but essentials placed about in precise locations. Despite the warmth this time of the year, the fire crackled in the hearth and cast a light on the stark room.

As Myrim entered, he was hit with a wave of nostalgia. This was the room where he had spent countless hours as a young officer, listening to his master's insights and learning the ways of law and order. To him, this room was paradise, a veritable fountain of wisdom.

They walked over to a pair of chairs by the fire, and the two men sat down, appraising each other as they settled in.

"I read your letter as soon as it arrived," Braisus began while staring at the fire. "It seems you've been carrying a heavy burden."

Myrim nodded, feeling the weight of it all pressing down on him even more now that he was in the presence of his former mentor. "The world has changed, Braisus. Since the discovery of dynamo, since the Gaming Commission took over... it's not the same place you once swore to protect."

"Why do you think I retired?" Braisus turned his eyes to Myrim, expression unreadable. "The world is always changing, Aric. But that can't have warranted a trip all the way to Stoneford. What is it that's truly weighing on you?"

Myrim hesitated. His hands clenched and unclenched in his lap. "It's the thieves. The way they operate now. It isn't about giving back to the community anymore. It's become... entertainment. A joke, really. And Lord Thume, he—" Myrim cut himself off, struggling to find the right words. "He's encouraging it. No matter how obscene their scores become. I can't even be certain who's on my side anymore. I feel like I'm fighting a losing battle."

The old commander listened in silence, eyes never leaving Myrim's face. When Myrim fell silent, the older man spoke with conviction. "You've always been a man of principle, Aric. That's what made you one of the finest young officers I ever had the privilege to train.

"But it's like I said—the world is always changing, and society's principles change with it. If you don't figure out how to change too, you'll soon get left behind."

Myrim's jaw tightened. "Are you telling me to give up? To just let this madness continue?"

"Madness?" Braisus shook his head slowly. "No, madness would be getting angry at the tide, which you *cannot* control—but you may yet turn it," he said, locking eyes with Myrim. "I'm telling you to find a new way to fight, Aric. The old methods don't work anymore. You need to think like those you pursue. Understand their game, and then beat them at it."

"I don't know if I can do that, Braisus." Myrim glanced away, his thoughts racing ahead. "I've spent my entire life upholding the law, fighting for justice. But now... now it feels like justice is just another commodity, bought and sold like everything else."

Braisus reached out and placed a hand on Myrim's shoulder. "Justice isn't dead, Aric. It's just hidden beneath layers of corruption and greed. You have the strength to find it, to bring it back. But you have to be willing to change. You have to be willing to do what's necessary, even if it means bending the rules you've always held sacred."

The captain met Braisus's gaze, seeing the determination in his mentor's eyes. It was a look that showed that his old master had faced his own share of battles and had come out the other side stronger for it.

"What do I do, then?" Myrim's tone was thick with desperation. "How do I fight this?"

His mentor leaned back in his chair, steepling his fingers in deep thought.

"You start by understanding your enemy, truly understanding them. And you find their weakness. Everyone has one: Larson Harrow, Darius Adalan, and yes, even Lord Thume," he said. "When the time is right, you will strike. Not out of anger, but with precision, with purpose. And when you do, you make sure they know that the law still stands. Even in this new world."

Myrim felt a surge of resolve at his words. The fog of doubt and despair lifted for the first time in weeks, replaced by a renewed sense of purpose. He wasn't alone in this fight—with Master Ekon's guidance, he might just have a chance to reverse the thieves' momentum.

"Thank you, Braisus," Myrim said with genuine gratitude. "I needed this."

Braisus nodded, a very rare smile playing at the corners of his mouth. "Remember, Aric. You're not just fighting for the law. You're fighting for the people who believe in it. Don't let them down."

It did make sense. Yet sentiment alone wouldn't change anything. Myrim let the importance of Braisus's words sink in.

"Your advice is helping change how I see things," he said, "but even if I shift my thinking, I'm still unsure how to start. The thieves—Lars and Darius mostly—they've always been a step ahead, playing by rules I suppose I never understood. How do I catch up? What should be my next move?"

Braisus studied Myrim. "You need to do something they won't expect. They're used to being spontaneous, to always staying ahead of the law. But what if you change your methods? Turn the tables on them."

Myrim's brow furrowed. "Change my methods? How?"

"Let's think through it," Braisus continued, leaning forward. "The recent heists—Lars and the Blackwood Estate, Darius and that ship from Zarakar—what do they have in common?"

Myrim considered this. "Both were even more high-profile than usual. They were bold, unthinkable even. The kind of heists that would get people talking and that would be hard to ignore."

"Exactly. We know they thrive on attention and on outsmarting the authorities. So you could always try to take that away from them, make them irrelevant."

"You mean... undermine them?" Myrim asked, the connections forming in his mind.

"Yes, that's one way."

Braisus appeared lost in thought. He tapped his fingers against his chin as he continued mulling over the challenge. "But more importantly, strike where it hurts. Like you said, they're playing a game. But every game has rules, and every player has a breaking point. You need to find out what that is—what they can't afford to lose. It could be their reputation, their resources, or something more personal."

Myrim nodded slowly. "And once I find it, I can use it against them."

"Precisely," Braisus said. "It's not about being stronger or faster. It's about being smarter. You know these men better than they think. Use that, and learn more. Everything you can. Start chipping away at them. Set a trap that plays to their egos. Make them come to you, for example. Or…"

"Yes?"

"Employ your own network, and keep it underground. Stop being so reactive, waiting for word to get to you that they're committing a crime. By then it's too late. Learn what they're up to beforehand, employ the same methods they do, and be there to catch them in the act."

A slow smile spread across Myrim's face as the plan began to take shape in his mind. "I see it now. I'll let them think they're in control, that I'm just poking around in the dark. And then, when they think there's nothing to worry about—"

The old commander regarded Myrim with an almost paternal approval. "You strike. And this time, you make sure they know that the law is still very much alive in Ithris."

Myrim felt a renewed sense of purpose burning in his chest. He wasn't sure what the future held, but he knew one thing for certain—he wouldn't give up.

"Thank you, Braisus," Myrim said, rising to his feet. "I know what I need to do."

Braisus stood as well, placing a firm hand on Myrim's shoulder. "Go, Aric. Remember, stay one step ahead, just like they do. The law may be different now, but it still has power. So do you."

With those words echoing in his mind, Myrim left his former master's house, stepping back into the crisp air of Stoneford. The encounter with Lars earlier that day, which had driven him to anger, now felt like an opportunity—a challenge. He would find a way to restore justice to Ithris, no matter what it took. It would start in Azoria. And it would start soon.

The council chamber was a symphony of chaos, voices crashing against each other like waves in a storm, rising and falling with every heated accusation that flew across the sleek mahogany table. Like most council meetings, this was a mess of half-baked ideas, clashing egos, and short tempers, the room crackling with tension like a dynamo circuit on the verge of overload. Lord Cecil Thume, seated at the head, cast his gaze out the tall windows framing the city of Azoria. He let out a quiet, exasperated sigh.

They were stuck, bickering over adjusting the Gaming Commission's cut on smaller scores. A trivial matter. As if a few more coppers would shift the balance.

Thume had shaped this entire system—the intricate web of laws and lawlessness, of wealth flowing and being siphoned back. He and he alone grasped the delicate balancing act required to keep it all from crumbling, a vision far beyond the grasp of the narrow-minded men and women before him.

He shifted in his tall-backed chair. A wave of fatigue washed over him, a weariness that went beyond the council's endless debates and petty squabbles. It was the weight of responsibility, the burden of power, that settled upon his shoulders like a leaden cloak.

Thume closed his eyes, letting the cacophony fade into a distant drone, and his mind drifted back to a time when the world was on the cusp of a revolution...

He was thirty years old again. Young, ambitious, his heart filled with a fire that burned brighter than the molten copper flowing from his family's mines in Zarakar. The discovery of harnessing dynamo had ignited a wildfire across Ithris, a frenzy of innovation and greed that threatened to consume everything in its path.

Factories sprang up like mushrooms after a rain, belching smoke and steam into the sky. Fortunes were made and lost overnight as already wealthy inventors and entrepreneurs scrambled to exploit the new power source. But progress, as it often did, came at a cost.

The chasm between the haves and the have-nots widened into a gaping abyss. The fires of industry roared, given life by the sweat and toil of the working class, while the elite grew fat and complacent, their coffers overflowing with the profits of a technology they couldn't hope to understand. Not that they cared to anyway, as long as it kept the money flowing in and the people stayed where they belonged.

Riots erupted in the streets, fueled by desperation and resentment. The people, whose lives had been upended by the advent of dynamo—those who toiled, bled, and died in the factories and mines—saw their livelihoods vanish as machines replaced muscle. And they were hungry for change. Hungry for justice. Hungry for blood.

Thume, a man of privilege and shrewdness, watched the chaos unfold with growing interest. He saw the anger, the despair, the potential for a cataclysm that could shatter the fragile peace of Ithris. He knew something had to be done, but the traditional solutions—more laws, more police, more suppression—would do nothing but fuel the flames. And they'd be horrible for business.

They needed a different approach. A radical solution that would address the root of the problem: people being unwilling to accept the vast and growing disparity of wealth.

And so, he'd conceived of the Gaming Commission.

It was a bold, unique plan that would have been unthinkable just a few years earlier. But the times demanded bold solutions. He'd spent months traveling across Ithris, meeting with politicians, guild leaders, wealthy merchants, and even those who whispered in the shadows, those who operated outside the law. He'd presented his vision—a plan to create a system that would ease the growing unrest while also making it an asset.

"Imagine," he said, voice ringing with conviction as he addressed a gathering of influential figures in the grand hall of his estate in Zarakar. The room had fallen silent, captivated by the power in his words and the weight of his ambition. "A system where the people, those who feel disenfranchised, those who believe the scales are tipped against them, have a legitimate outlet for their frustrations. A system where they can take back what they believe to be theirs—not through violence, but through skill, cunning, and perhaps even a touch of spectacle."

A wave of murmurs rippled through the crowd. Skepticism, curiosity, even a hint of fear, reflected in their eyes.

"We're talking about sanctioned thievery, Lord Thume!" one man shouted, his arms waving. "Is that what you're proposing?"

"Controlled chaos," Thume corrected, addressing the assembled crowd and meeting their doubts head-on. "A game, if you will, with rules, regulations, and a clear set of rewards. The wealthy will have the opportunity to protect their assets, to showcase their ingenuity in crafting elaborate defenses.

"And the people," he said passionately, "will have the opportunity to challenge those defenses, test their skills, and win their share of the wealth that they feel has been hoarded for far too long."

"Madness! This will lead to more unrest, more violence!"

But Thume was steady and unwavering. "No. It will channel that unrest, that violence, into something productive. It will create a spectacle, a source of entertainment, that will captivate the masses and distract them from the true source of their misery. It will..." He paused, allowing a grin.

"It will give them hope. A chance to win. A chance to believe that equity, even in this new world, is still possible."

The debate had raged for weeks, months even, as Thume lobbied for his vision. He'd faced resistance from the old guard, those who clung to the traditional ways just as they clung to their riches, those who feared change. But he'd also found allies in unexpected places—among the reformers, the idealists, and even a few shrewd businessmen who saw the potential for profit in this new form of sanctioned chaos.

In the end, he had of course prevailed.

The Ithris Gaming Commission was born, a manifestation of Thume's vision and his unwavering determination to reshape the world in his image. He'd overseen the drafting of the regulations, the establishment of the rules, the creation of a system that would balance the scales of wealth and power in a way that had never been seen before.

In truth, he hadn't anticipated the rise of the celebrity thief, the transformation of sanctioned thievery into a form of entertainment so pervasive that it created a new wealthy class of its own, a spectacle that captivated the masses and fueled the gossip mills of Azoria. But once it began, he saw its potential. Entertainment, after all, was a powerful tool.

Thume opened his eyes, the murmur of the council chamber pulling him back to the present. A councilman was droning on about the need for strict penalties for repeat offenders as if the threat of imprisonment mattered to those who lived for the thrill of the heist and who made a living off not getting caught. Darius's theft of his ship shook them even more than it should have shaken him.

His eyes drifted toward the window, thoughts turning to a different kind of loss—a personal wound that refused to heal. His wife, Orilline. A woman of fire and passion, with a spirit as vibrant as the molten lava that flowed from the volcanoes of her homeland in Drakoria. She'd brought light and laughter into his life, a warmth that thawed the ice that had formed around his heart after years of navigating the treacherous waters of politics and power.

But their happiness had been short-lived. Orilline had died suddenly, a tragic accident, they'd said. A fall from her balcony, a cruel twist of fate. He'd mourned her deeply, his grief a dark abyss that threatened to consume him. Even now, years later, the memory of her laughter, the warmth of her touch, could bring a sharp pang of loss, a hollow ache that settled deep in his chest.

Yet, Thume had no memory of the time of her passing. And so even in his sorrow, a seed of doubt had taken root, twisting its tendrils around his heart, whispering insidious possibilities in the absence of any certainty. Had it truly been an accident? Or had he done something he couldn't remember, something he'd buried so deep that it only existed as a phantom haunting his waking hours?

The thought was repulsive, abhorrent. He, Cecil Thume, orchestrating a simple, brutal act of violence? He, the architect of Azoria's intricate system, resorting to such barbarism? It was unthinkable—and yet, the doubt lingered.

He had never been able to answer that question with any certainty. The investigation had been inconclusive. Witnesses contradicted each other. Evidence had disappeared. Or perhaps he'd arranged it all, ensuring a convenient lack of clarity, a smokescreen to hide his own guilt.

If he could only remember...

"Lord Thume?" a voice called out. It was Councilman Harkon, a thin, nervous man whose ambition often outstripped his intellect. "Councilwoman Revas has made a rather bold accusation. That you, sir, are engaging in a form of theft on a grand scale, one that dwarfs even the most daring exploits of Azoria's infamous thieves. Would you care to rebut?"

Thume turned his eyes back to the council table, expression unreadable. He met Revas's angered look, a hint of amusement playing on his lips.

"And what, Councilwoman Revas," he said, "leads you to this baseless conclusion?"

ECHOS OF THUNDER

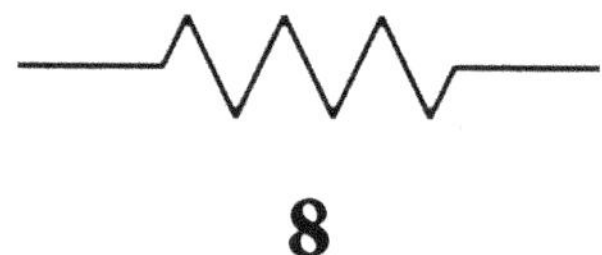

8

"I'll be back soon," Trin said with a melodic lilt as she adjusted the emerald green scarf she'd purchased earlier that day. "I just need to pick up a few essentials for the journey back. Anything you need?"

"My sanity." Lars chuckled, shaking his head at his own sarcasm. "And perhaps a map of this town that isn't drawn on a feather."

Trin giggled and kissed him on the cheek before heading off.

Lars was glad she was enjoying herself. Stoneford, despite its recent unsettling revelations, had a calming effect on him. But the encounter with Vivienne, her cryptic proposition, and the lingering mystery of her elaborate summons nagged at his mind. After Trinelle was beyond his sight, he walked in a different direction.

The heart of the city holds a hidden spring, he thought, recalling the first clue that had led them to the fountain in the marketplace.

He glanced at the swarming crowds, the vendors hawking their wares, the children chasing pigeons through the square, and a sudden urge, a compulsion he couldn't resist, took hold of him. He had to see that fountain again. He had to retrace their steps to try to understand the path that had led them to Vivienne.

He set off with long strides, soon reaching the fountain, its water sparkling in the afternoon sun. But the playful energy of their arrival had vanished. The crowds seemed indifferent, children's laughter replaced by the haggling of merchants, each trying to outsell the other behind carts bursting with fresh produce and roasted nuts.

He remembered the young boy who'd given them the polished stone, the clue that had led them to the blacksmith. He scanned the faces around him, but the boy was nowhere to be seen.

Seek the song of fire, he thought, walking toward the blacksmith's workshop.

The clang of hammer against metal rang out, a familiar rhythm that echoed through the narrow alleyway. But as he approached, Lars saw that the blacksmith from before with the soot-stained face was gone. In his place stood a much leaner, younger man. He glanced at Lars with a cheerful demeanor.

"Can I help you, sir?"

Lars looked over the workshop with a critical eye. "I was… looking for the blacksmith." He noted the subtle differences in the arrangement of tools, the lack of a certain worn leather apron hanging by the forge.

"My father's gone to visit family in the mountains," the young man said dismissively. "He won't be back for a few weeks."

Lars nodded, a strange unease settling over him. He continued down the alleyway, footsteps echoing on the cobblestones until he reached the hidden door to the rooftop garden.

The eagle knows the way.

Last time there had been a key. Lars reached for his lockpicks as he tested the handle. But this time, the door didn't resist.

He pushed it open and walked up the stairs, greeted by the fragrant scent of flowers and the gentle rustling of vines. But beyond that, the rooftop was empty. There was no sign of the young woman who had served them tea and offered the cryptic clue.

Lars felt a chill, a sense of emptiness that went beyond the physical absence of those who had guided them to Vivienne. It was as if the entire network, the intricate chain of whispers and connections, had vanished. It left behind a void, simmering with a tense and unsettling silence.

He continued, driven by a compulsion he couldn't explain until he reached the manor house overlooking the town. The sun was setting, casting long shadows across the hillside, and the once-welcoming facade now was cold and foreboding.

He knocked on the door, the sound echoing through the stillness. After a long moment, the door creaked open, revealing a middle-aged man with a bewildered look.

"Yes?"

"I'm looking for Mistress Vivienne," Lars said, glancing at the man's simple attire, the way his hands fidgeted with a set of keys.

The man shook his head, brow furrowed in confusion. "Vivienne?" he echoed. "I don't know anyone by that name.

I'm just the caretaker. The owners are away. Won't be back for several weeks."

Lars stared at the man, a cold certainty settling over him. Vivienne was gone.

And suddenly, the quiet charm of Stoneford felt less like a sanctuary and more like a trap.

Jax was beside himself with grief. He paced back and forth in the small, austere room, muttering in barely recognizable words. The storm outside may have subsided, leaving a heavy silence in its wake, but the storm in Jax's mind was heavy and terrifying. He could not come to grips with what had happened. A mechanical clock on the mantelpiece ticked off the seconds, seeming to echo the tromp of his boots.

Keer sat in a corner, watching Jax with a combination of concern and impatience.

"Jax, sit down. You're making me dizzy."

Jax stopped pacing at the sound of the gruff man's voice, and he turned to look at Keer as if he didn't even realize he was there. His gaze was unfocused, staring off into the distance. Shock, with all its cold, detached turmoil, ran roughshod in his mind. "It's my fault, Keer. I didn't even have time to grab her. I couldn't do a damn thing."

The big man ran a trembling hand through his hair. He looked with confusion at the seat next to Keer, then finally slumped down in it.

"We were on the roof. The old northern watch building, the one with the lightning rod. Liora wanted to try charging the crystal. With lightning. My idea. My stupid, stupid idea."

He shuddered, the memory of that nightmarish moment flashing before his eyes—the blinding flash of light, the deafening crack of thunder, Liora's scream as she was flung backward.

"She was so excited. So sure it would work. And then..." He choked back a sob.

Keer stood abruptly, his chair scraping across the floor, the sound sharp and jarring in the quiet room. He stood over Jax, placing a gentle hand on his shoulder. "What happened, Jax? Tell me everything."

Jax took a deep, shaky breath, the words tumbling out in a rush. "The lightning hit the rod. I saw the crystals—they were glowing—pulsing with dynamo."

"Liora was so happy, Keer. She said it worked, and she was so happy. Then there was another bolt, and another, and thunder... hells, the thunder. It was so loud I thought my ears would shatter. She screamed and spun around. And then she was gone. Just gone."

Keer listened patiently, brow furrowed in thought.

"I think that's when she was hit," Jax said, his voice almost a whisper.

"Hit? Hit by what? Did something fall on her? Was it debris from the lightning strike?"

Jax shook his head. "No, wait a minute." His face went through an almost comical transformation of emotions as the memories clicked into place.

"It wasn't the lightning. It was something else. I saw a flash from the roof across the street. That's when Liora screamed. And then she fell."

"So you're saying someone did this to her." Keer grimaced.

Jax nodded, the words confirming his own unspoken fear. "I saw it, Keer. A flash of light, a puff of smoke. Like... like from a blasting cannon, but smaller, more precise. I have no idea what the fuck it was."

He trailed off as his mind brought back the images of her falling body.

Keer cursed, his expression tightening with anger. "Who would do such a thing? Why would anyone want Liora dead?"

Now it was Keer's turn to pace. He moved back and forth across the room.

"It has to be connected to the crystals," Jax said. "That's the only thing that makes sense. Switcher's murder, the strange crystal, the device Trin brought back, and now this..."

Keer stopped his pacing, cocking his head at Jax. "You mean the crystals she was experimenting on. But why? What's so special about them, other than holding a charge, that someone would kill for it?"

Before Jax could answer, a door creaked open at the room's far end. A thin, wiry man with rolled-up sleeves and a worried mien emerged. His hands were stained with what looked suspiciously like blood.

"All set," the man said in a raspy, tired voice. "She's hurting bad. But she's recovering."

Jax choked out a relieved sob. His shoulders sagged with the release of tension. He surged toward the doctor and grabbed his arm.

"Can I see her?" His emotions were running wild. "Is she going to be alright?"

The doctor nodded grimly. "She's lucky to be alive. The thing that struck her, whatever it was, hit her satchel—full of metal scraps, thankfully." He illustrated the point by smacking a fist into his open palm. "Blunted the force of the impact. But she's got a nasty wound, a few broken ribs, and a concussion. She's stitched up and will heal, but she needs rest. Plenty of it."

He gestured toward the door. "You can see her for a few minutes. But no excitement. No questions. She likely won't be in any mood to answer them. Please, try to comfort her."

Jax and Keer exchanged a look, acknowledging the hope that was offered. They followed the doctor into the next room, hearts heavy with a mix of relief and a lingering worry.

Liora lay on a cot, taking in shallow, ragged breaths. A bandage covered her shoulder, and a dark bruise decorated her jawline. Jax winced at the sight of her.

They'd both hit an awning during their fall from the roof, rolling off and landing in a pile of trash below. Jax had grabbed Liora to cushion her fall and was banged up—bruises, a few scrapes—but he could take it. Liora hadn't been so lucky. But at least she was alive, and for that, Jax was grateful. He sat beside her, taking her hand in his. His calloused fingers, worn from years of heavy labor, were surprisingly gentle as they stroked her palm.

Keer stood at the foot of the cot, the old Zarakaran watching them with a mixture of gruff concern and something deeper, something resembling a grandfather's affection for a beloved grandchild.

Liora's eyes flickered open, a wave of confusion clouding her features. She blinked, trying to focus on the two familiar faces before her. Reaching toward her eyes to adjust her glasses, she only touched bruised skin instead.

"Jax? Keer?" she said, and her voice was so weak it was heartbreaking. "What... what happened?"

Keer took her glasses from a nearby table and slid them gently over her ears. "You fell, Liora. From the roof. Do you remember?"

She frowned, a fragment of memory returning, a shard of pain piercing through the fog in her mind. "The lightning... the crystals!" She winced. "It worked! I saw them glowing... but then..."

"I think—" she began, but cut herself off, a look of confusion taking over her. "I think something hit me. Hard."

Jax's hand tightened around hers, tears forming in his eyes. "Something did, Liora. You were attacked."

Liora stared at him, eyes wide with disbelief. "Attacked? Me? But... how? Why?"

Keer sighed, placing a hand on Liora's shoulder. "We don't know why, Liora," he said. Jax thought he suddenly looked very tired. "As for how... well, we don't know that. All we know is that you were struck from the next building over. By someone. I guess we don't know who, either."

Her eyes widened in shock as she tried to stand. "Well, time to get to the bottom of—" Her words were cut off with a wince and she fell back onto the pillow.

Keer looked down at her with obvious care. "No more detective work for you for a while, Liora. You need to rest. To heal. We'll handle this."

"But the crystals! What happened to them?"

Jax met her gaze with a reassuring warmth. "Don't worry. It's safe. The one from the device is still charged." He paused, voice catching.

"The other one, the shard from Switcher's lab, though... It's gone. Lost in the fall, I'm guessing."

Liora's face crumpled. "No," she whispered, tears welling up in her eyes. "Now we'll never know... know what happened to—"

"Hey, hey," Jax said. He squeezed her hand, his thumb stroking her knuckles. "It's alright. We can figure this out. We always do."

Keer nodded, determination etched across his face. "We'll find out who did this, Liora. To you and to Switcher. And we'll make them regret it."

PART 3

LET THE SHOW BEGIN

9

The tavern door swung open, admitting Lars and Trinelle back into the familiar warmth of their hideout. The aroma of pipe tobacco and well-worn leather mingled with the faint scent of metal and oil, a comforting blend that usually signaled a return to normalcy after a successful job. But as Lars glanced around the common room, a sense of unease settled over him.

Something was different.

Jax sat slumped at his usual table, his face etched with worry. He was fiddling with his new dagger, spinning it in his fingers, but his movements were mechanical—as if he were going through the motions without being present. The metal of the coiled hilt slapped against this palm, a dull rhythmic sound that made the silence more pervasive.

And Liora...

She wasn't at her workbench, where she always spent hours tinkering with her latest inventions. Instead, she sat by the window, a soft lavender sweater draped over her shoulders. A bandage peeked out from beneath the fabric. A tray with an untouched meal sat on a table beside her. She looked up at them, her face pale but beaming, as she tried to lift a hand in greeting. Instead she only winced, the hand falling back to her lap.

It was a far cry from the welcome they'd expected—one where Jax would jump up and give bearhugs and back slaps, Keer would complain about the latest developments, and Liora would of course chatter on about new discoveries and questions. Instead, they found silence and discomfort.

"What happened?" Lars demanded with concern. He crossed the room with a growing knot of apprehension tightening in his chest, eyes fixed on Liora. He had never seen the vibrant engineer looking so fragile.

Trin followed close behind with wide eyes. "Oh, Liora! What happened? Are you alright?"

Liora glanced up at them, smiling despite her condition. "Welcome back," she said with feigned strength. "You two look... well rested."

Jax snorted a humorless sound that grated against the tension in the room. "Rested? They were off gallivanting in Stoneford while we were here dealing with—"

"Jax!" She shot him a warning glance. "Don't—"

She faltered as she turned to Lars. "Don't worry. It's nothing. Just a little accident. Nothing to worry about. Jax is anxious for me."

Jax looked like he was about to speak up, but Liora gave him a caring smile. "But that's why we love you, Jax."

"Accident?" Lars echoed. He pulled up a chair beside her, concern deepening as he took in her pale complexion, the circles under her eyes, the way she winced as she shifted in her seat. "Liora, please tell us what happened."

Trin sat as well and looked at her friend with concern. "We should have stayed here. We would have come back sooner if we had known."

Liora shook her head, managing a weak smile. "It's not your fault. It was stupid. My fault, really."

She took a deep breath, gathering her strength. "It's the device," she said, glancing at the disassembled dynamo lens on her workbench. "The crystal lost its charge. It was devastating. Between Switcher's murder and my promise to figure out what the device did, I couldn't handle the thing fizzling out. So I was trying to recharge it."

"With lightning. Like, the kind from the sky." Jax interjected bluntly.

Liora nodded, a wry smile twisting her lips. "It seemed like a good idea at the time."

Lars's eyes widened in disbelief. Of all the ridiculous, reckless, absolutely batty things they could have gotten up to, he hadn't expected playing with lightning to be on the list. He held his cool though, not wanting to distress Liora further.

He also sensed that there had to be more to the story, something she wasn't telling them. The way she avoided their eyes, the tremor in her hands as she fiddled with the edge of the blanket, it all pointed to something more than *just* a failed experiment. "And?"

Liora was nervous. There was no trace of her usual energy. She hesitated, fingers stroking the bandage on her shoulder, looking down at the floor.

"I was experimenting with both crystals. The one that powers the dynamo lens and the one from Switcher's murder scene. But someone attacked me," she finally said. "While we were on the roof. Jax saw something on the next roof over. I was struck with a projectile, just a small metal ball. But it hit me hard, Lars. Really damn hard. And I fell."

Silence reigned, heavy like a shroud. Lars's blood ran cold, the casual warmth of their homecoming evaporating like mist under a scorching sun. His mind was struggling to grasp the enormity of what she was saying.

Someone had attacked her?

He'd faced danger countless times, navigated treacherous traps, and outwitted determined guards. But the thought of someone deliberately harming Liora, his brilliant, quirky engineer—his *friend*—filled him with a rage he had never felt before.

Trin took a deep, ragged breath. "Who did it?" she demanded sharply, her voice edged with a protectiveness that startled even Lars. "Who would attack you?"

Liora shook her head, still staring at the floor. "I don't know. I didn't see them. It all happened so fast. One minute, I was holding the crystal, watching it glow, feeling the energy... and the next, I was flying backward, the world spinning around me. All I know is that I would have been a goner if Jax hadn't jumped after me."

Jax looked at her in concern, the worry imprinted on his face. They had changed, Lars thought. Closer, more serious. Brushes with death did that to a person.

Jax grunted. "It was like a miniature version of a cannonball. *Very* small and very precise. It hit her shoulder satchel, thankfully. Blunted the force of the impact. But still..." He trailed off, unable to get the rest out.

But Lars needed more details. "And the crystal? Not that it's important compared to how you're doing."

But it was, in all honesty, and with good reason. He needed information, a starting point for the storm of anger and fear brewing inside him.

"We still have the crystal from the dynamo lens," Liora said. "And on the plus side, the lightning worked. Jax is a genius, by the way." The big man gave his first honest smile since Lars had walked in the door.

"And the other?"

"It was lost in the fall. But Lars... the lightning charged that one too. Just like the other." Liora's face grew grim.

"I don't get it," Trin said in confusion. "How could it have charged?"

Lars stood up and paced back and forth. His long strides ate up the space of the small room, and his mind was racing. "Don't you see, Trin? The shard wasn't just a minor clue to Switcher's death. It was a—what did you call it before we left?" he said, then snapped his fingers. "It was a crystal charge too. And he was killed. Now Liora's been, for lack of a better word, shot, and all while charging a crystal on the rooftop."

Trin's eyes widened as the room fell quiet.

"Which, let's remember, crystals aren't supposed to do," Liora said.

Jax shuffled his feet. "I went back and looked, Lars. Once Liora was on the mend. It was gone. I mean, it could have just been taken by a trash collector or anyone who thought they found a valuable prize—"

"I'm going to assume whoever attacked Liora took it," Lars interrupted. "Someone willing to commit murder for it wouldn't hesitate to snatch it up for themselves. The good news is that it may lead to finding them. Because if we don't find them, we won't be able to feel safe."

"You think they'll try again?" Liora said.

He wanted to lie. He wanted to tell Liora she had nothing to worry about. The energetic dynamo girl was one of the brightest spots in his life, and he hated making her worry. But, he told himself, she already knew the truth. She was too smart not to.

Lars sighed, feeling very tired. "We have to assume they will. But, Liora—and please, please listen to me here. We will protect you no matter what anyone tries."

Everyone grew silent, each of them thinking what to do next. Then, the peace was broken by the door slamming open.

The crew jumped up, their nerves shot and ready for mayhem. Jax had his dagger out in a flash, ready to attack anyone who might threaten his crew.

Keer Basar stood at the door, mouth agape. He took one look at Lars and Trin and sighed in relief. "Oh thank the hells, you're back."

Keer stepped inside, pulling the door shut behind him with a thud that reverberated through the tense silence of the room. He glanced at the assembled crew, taking in their pale faces, the lingering worry in their eyes.

"I need a drink." He pushed himself away from the door and headed straight for the bar, grabbing a bottle of amber liquor and pouring himself a generous measure.

"Keer," Lars called out. "Were you there when Liora got hurt?"

Keer paused, taking a long swallow of his drink. "No, I was out when it happened. Got back as soon as I heard though. Jax was a mess."

Trin lowered her head and murmured, "I guess I would have been too. Still, I'm glad you were able to keep it together."

Keer grunted, taking another long swig of his liquor. "Someone's gotta keep this place running while you two are off parading around. So, tell me about the trip. Any interesting treasures out there in the mountains? Stoneford still creepy as all hells?"

"It was enlightening," Lars replied conversationally. They'd get to the details soon enough.

"Stoneford's quite charming, actually," Trin said, draping her new emerald green scarf over the back of a chair. "I even managed to pick up a new scarf. Isn't it lovely?"

Liora, despite her injuries, perked up. "A scarf? Let me see!"

Jax, sitting in sullen silence, slammed his hands down on the table, making Liora flinch.

"Are you all fucking kidding me?" he roared, voice burdened with emotion, red-rimmed eyes blazing. He pushed himself away from the table and leaped up. "We're acting like this is just... an accident! Like everything's fine! But Liora's hurt, someone's out there trying to kill us, and we don't even know why!"

He stopped pacing, his gaze sweeping over the room, faltering as tears streamed down his face.

"She could be dead, damn it! Dead! And we're just sitting here, sipping drinks and talking about bloody Stoneford as if none of this matters!"

Lars started to speak to try to calm Jax's outburst, but Trin stopped him with a hand on his arm.

With a soft groan, Liora rose, each movement deliberate and measured. She crossed the room, her gaze steady on Jax.

When she reached him, her expression softened, and she rested a light, grateful hand on his arm.

"Jax. It's okay. I'm okay. You're right. We can't just ignore this. We need to figure out what's going on. But lashing out won't help."

Jax looked at her, softer now, the anger draining away.

"Sorry," he said, wiping his eyes with the back of his hand. "I... I just... I hate seeing you hurt, Liora, and I hate not knowing who did this, why..."

Liora gave him a reassuring smile and kissed his cheek. "I know, Jax. I know. We'll figure it out. Together."

She turned to Lars. "So, let's talk about Stoneford. I think it's time we all came up to speed. Did you two meet that patron?"

Lars nodded, taking a deep breath. "Yes," he said, drawing on the calmness and composure he'd cultivated over the years. "We met with her. A rather interesting woman named Vivienne. She has a proposition for us. A heist."

He hesitated then continued with a wan smile. "But it's not just any heist. She wants us to steal from Lord Thume."

Jax stopped wiping his eyes, and his expression shifted from anguish to disbelief. "Thume? Are you serious? Right after Darius stole his hells damned galleon? Not sure that's gonna work, buddy."

Keer set his glass down with a sharp clink, the liquid sloshing over the rim. "Darius," he said, the name hanging in the air. "That reminds me. Silas came to see me a while back. He has some concerns about Darius. Nothing sinister, mind you. But he's been acting more recklessly, even a bit paranoid. He thinks it has to do with Switcher, hells knows why."

"Switcher?" Liora said, eyes widening. "What about him?"

Keer shrugged. "Silas didn't have any specifics. Said it was something that had Darius spooked though."

"It all comes down to this new type of crystal. End of story," Liora said. "We got a crystal no one has ever seen before from this supposed patron. Switcher was working on something similar, and it got him killed." She glanced at Jax. "I was testing something big, and it got me shot."

"And remember Thume's little chat with Lars at the cafe?" Trin had her head cocked and brow furrowed as if trying to solve a complex riddle. "Right after Myrim showed up asking about Switcher? It's too much of a coincidence. It's *all* too much."

Lars nodded, the pieces coming together. "Thume was fishing for information. He wanted to know how we would spend the copper from the Blackwood heist. He was worried about something. And I doubt it was inflation."

"Worried enough to have Switcher killed?" Jax said. "And worried enough to try and kill Liora too?"

"It's possible," Keer said, scowling. "Thume's always been a master of control. He built this whole system, and not a damn thing happens in it that he doesn't know about."

Trin tapped her chin, eyes thoughtful. "What's your point?"

"What if he thinks he's losing control? What if he's afraid of something new, something he can't manipulate?"

"Like a crystal that can hold a charge?" Liora said. Her gaze fixed on the glowing crystal at the heart of the dynamo lens. "A technology that could disrupt everything he's built?"

The implications of their deductions hung heavy in the air, a storm cloud gathering over their usual sense of camaraderie.

"So, what are we saying?" Jax asked, the anger that had bubbled up and out of him quelled, replaced with cautious hesitance. "That Thume is behind all of this? Is that what we're saying?"

Lars met his eyes. "It's starting to look that way, Jax."

"But why?" Liora had cause to be worried. "What's he afraid of? What's going on?"

"That's what we've got to find out. And I think one person might know something we don't." Trin turned to Lars, ready for the next move and full of resolve. "We need to talk to Darius."

The Bentwire Tavern was a renowned hotspot known for its strong liquors and seafaring clientele. A low murmur of conversation underscored the energetic strains of a dynamo fiddle player in the corner. It created a vibrant backdrop for the clandestine meeting unfolding at a secluded table in the back.

Lars sipped his beer, looking at Darius, who was lounging across from him, a studied nonchalance in his posture. Beside Lars, Trin sat with her usual quiet alertness, eyes taking in every detail. The fingers of one hand tapped a rhythmic pattern against the worn wooden tabletop. Her other hand rested on Lars's thigh under the table.

Silas, seated next to Darius, mirrored Trin's observant posture. His sharp gaze flickered between Lars and his own boss.

"Thanks for meeting with us, Darius," Lars said. He was still adjusting to collaborating with his longtime rival, but the events of the past few weeks had shaken him. Attempted murder had a way of forcing a man to question everything he thought he knew about the life they led.

Darius shrugged, a careless gesture that didn't quite mask his obvious tension. "Curiosity got the better of me, Harrow. When your top lieutenant comes calling with a request for a meeting... well, it's not something a gentleman can refuse, is it?"

"Lieutenant?" Trinelle echoed, arching an eyebrow. "Is that what you call yourself these days, Silas? A bit dramatic, don't you think?"

Silas chuckled and met Trin's gaze with a spark of appreciation. "Perhaps. But every good show needs a bit of drama, wouldn't you agree, Miss Meridia?"

"Touché."

Lars cleared his throat, steering the conversation back to the matter at hand. "We're here because we need your help, Darius. We've stumbled onto something complicated. And dangerous."

Darius leaned forward, clearly interested. "Complicated? Dangerous? Now that does pique my interest, Lars. Do tell."

Lars hesitated, weighing his words carefully. He didn't want to reveal too much too soon, but he also knew they needed to establish a level of trust if they would work together.

"It started with Switcher," he said. "His murder. We believe that someone has it out for all of us."

Darius looked at the table as he tapped a finger against it. "And do you have some idea who that might be?"

Lars grimaced. He wished he knew anything right now. "We have our ideas. But we need more information. It's important we all understand what's going on."

"And you think I have those answers, Lars?" Darius asked. "Since when have we shared notes?"

The man did love to play the fool, Lars thought. But he knew behind Darius Adalan's characteristic nonchalance, there was a brilliant mind that held a web of cunning plans.

"Like I said, things are getting complicated and dangerous," Lars said. "Liora was attacked, Darius. Someone tried to kill her. With a weapon we've never seen before."

Darius sat up straighter, his act vanishing. "Attacked? Are you serious? Is she alright?"

There was genuine concern in his voice, a flicker of something akin to anger in his eyes. Despite their rivalry, a bond was forged through years of playing the same dangerous game.

"She's alive. But shaken. Someone shot her from a nearby rooftop while she was... working."

"*Shot* her? Like with a cannon?" Darius shook his head. "Wait, no, we'll get back to that. Working on what?"

Lars hesitated. He glanced at Trin, then back to Darius. "It's a long story," he said. "And it involves something unusual."

He took a deep breath, deciding to trust his instincts. "Trin brought back a device from her travels. A device powered by a crystal unlike anything Liora's ever seen. A crystal that seems to hold dynamo."

"A crystal that can hold a charge?" Darius echoed, his eyebrows furrowing. "Interesting. And you think this device is somehow connected to Switcher's murder? And the attack on Liora?"

"We're not sure. But it makes sense. Switcher also had a crystal charge. A piece of one anyway. And then there's Thume—"

"Thume?" Darius leaned back in his chair thoughtfully. "What about him?"

"He approached me at a cafe a few days ago. Out of the blue. He was asking about our recent score, about the murder, and about how we were planning to spend the copper. He seemed worried."

Darius chuckled. "I don't think that man has worried a day in his life."

Lars shook his head. He needed to get through to Darius. "Seriously. I think he's afraid of something. Something connected to these crystal charges."

"And then there's this..." Lars continued, leaning closer.

He described his journey to Stoneford, the elaborate chain of clues that led them to Vivienne's manor house, and the unsettling encounter with the woman who knew far more about their world than she should.

Lars recounted Vivienne's proposition, the promise of unimaginable wealth, the challenge of infiltrating Thume's secret warehouse, and the veiled suggestions that lingered beneath her alluring smile. As he spoke, Darius's expression shifted from amusement to intrigue, to a dawning comprehension.

Darius glanced at Silas.

Tension grew on the faces of everyone at the table as Lars finished his story. Trin's hand tightened on his thigh, eyes fixed on Darius.

Darius and Silas remained silent, their faces blank and eyes betraying nothing. It was a silence born of habit, a standoff between two masters of the same way of life, each waiting for the other to make the first move.

"For hells sake, Darius," Silas said, unable to contain himself any longer. "Just tell them."

Darius shot his lieutenant a sharp look, but the words were already hanging in the air, a challenge to the deliberate silence. "No respect for the craft," he muttered, then took a long, slow sip of his drink. He stared at the amber liquid swirling in his glass, as if weighing the consequences of honesty.

"Fine. She came to me too." He set down his glass with a decisive clink and met Lars's gaze. "Vivienne. Same proposition. Same promises."

Trin stared at Darius, eyes widening in disbelief, then narrowing with a dawning understanding. "The woman is a viper. Playing us both for fools."

"Fools?" Darius's rebuke held a hint of danger. "She's not playing me for a fool, Trinelle. That woman is sharp, resourceful, and ambitious. But so are we. Whatever game she *thinks* she's playing, I can play it just as well."

Trin gripped the table in frustration. "But why? What's so important about this warehouse of Thume's? What's she after?"

"That's what we need to figure out," Lars said, "and I think it's time we stopped marching to Vivienne's tune and started playing our own."

Darius flashed him an appraising look. "Agreed. It was intriguing when I thought it was just me she was talking to. Now it's a full-blown conspiracy. It's vital that we understand what Thume is hiding, why Switcher was killed, and what Vivienne's real agenda is."

"What we need is to find out what's so special about these crystals," Trin said. "Why someone would kill for them."

Lars nodded. "To my mind, it all comes back to power. Thume has built an empire on control. He will always manipulate the system to his advantage. It's second nature for him. Dynamo gives him that control because we all need it.

"But if we didn't rely on the city, and by extension Thume, to feed us dynamo at all times… Well, if he can't control the flow of literal power through the city, that would disrupt his entire system, right?"

"That has to be what Vivienne's after," Silas said. "Maybe she wants to use us to topple Thume and seize his power for herself. Or she wants to control the tech, become the sole supplier of these crystal charges."

Darius snorted. "Or maybe she just wants to be part of the game. To shake things up. To see if she can outsmart us all." He took a long swig, eyes meeting Lars's over the rim of the glass. "There's a certain thrill in that, wouldn't you agree, Harrow? Keeps things interesting."

Lars grinned and rolled his eyes. "Interesting, sure. But this is more than just a game, Darius. People are getting hurt—or killed. Right now the main culprit seems to be the most powerful man in Ithris, if not the world."

He leaned forward. "We need answers—and obviously, we need to make sure none of us end up as Thume's next target. No matter what Vivienne's motive is, we can't let her play us against each other. In the end, she's not the real threat. If Thume is attacking us, we attack back. As unfamiliar as it may seem, it's time we worked together. For our own survival, if nothing else."

He looked at Darius, a challenge in his eyes. "Are you with us?"

Darius favored him with a charming grin. "You're damn right I am."

Deep in thought, Silas didn't react at all. Darius slapped him on the shoulder, and he zoned back into the conversation. "Sorry, I was just thinking..."

"What? Spit it out."

"I was thinking, with Switcher's murder and them trying to get Liora too. It's because Thume wants to keep the crystal charges a secret, right?"

Lars nodded.

Silas nodded back. "Then we should make sure everyone knows about them."

"What?" Trin said. But then she leaned back and thought it through. "Oh. Oh, Silas, that's brilliant."

"Yeah. If everyone knows about them, there's no point knocking off engineers anymore. We can focus on what matters."

Lars and Darius shared a grin. "Man," Darius said. "This is going to get fun."

"Let's hope so," Lars said. "Silas, in case I've never told you this, I like your style. You're right. Let's make sure the paper gets a tip for tomorrow's run."

DANGEROUS LIAISONS

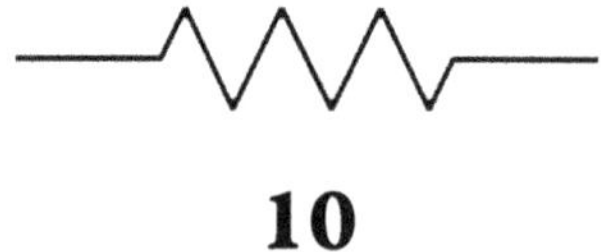

10

The carriage rolled through the cobblestone streets of Azoria, its arrival unnoticed amidst the city's usual flow of noise and motion. Vivienne, seated within its luxurious interior, watched the passing crowds with detached amusement. She was a woman of striking contrasts. Beneath her elegant attire and poised demeanor lay a carefully crafted facade, hiding a razor-sharp intellect and a ruthless determination that few dared to confront.

The carriage pulled up to a discreet alleyway, far from the prying eyes of the city watch and the curious gazes of Azoria's gossip-hungry citizens. Vivienne stepped out, silver hair gleaming under the gaslamps. She touched the silver pendant that hung at her throat and took a deep breath.

Following the alleyway to a hidden door, she rapped three times in a specific pattern. A moment later, the door creaked open, revealing Silas, face half-shadowed in the dim light.

"Vivienne, right on time. Good to see you here."

"Always a pleasure to visit the heart of the city," she said. Her green eyes sparkled like creamy jade as she passed him. "It has a certain energy I find quite intoxicating."

They passed through a maze of crates, tools, and disassembled contraptions before reaching a door marked '*Office*.' Silas knocked once, then opened the door, ushering Vivienne inside.

Her gaze swept over the austere room, landing on Darius, who sat behind a large desk. But the two figures seated across from him made her pause. Their backs were turned, but she knew in an instant it had to be—

"Master Harrow, Mistress Meridia," she said in surprise. "What a delightful coincidence."

Lars met her gaze, a knowing smile playing on his lips. "It's not a coincidence and you know it, Vivienne. Darius and I thought it was time we all had a chat."

"I'll tell you... I never expected that the two of you would share our arrangements. I believe I may have underestimated you."

Trin snorted.

Darius leaned back in his chair, steepling his fingers to his chin. "That's something you should never do."

"Look, I'm a woman who believes in options," Vivienne said. "And in hedging my bets. Don't tell me you wouldn't do the same."

"You're playing us against each other," Lars corrected.

Vivienne smiled in that predatory way that sent a shiver down his spine. "I prefer to think of it as incentivizing guaranteed success."

"By dangling the same prize in front of both of us?" Darius said, rolling his eyes. "Thume's secret warehouse, a reward beyond our wildest dreams… all very tempting, Vivienne, but a bit obvious, don't you think?"

Vivienne sat down and crossed one leg over the other, the folds of her gown parting to reveal her thigh. "Perhaps. But effective, wouldn't you say? After all, here you are at last, gentlemen, willing to put aside your differences and work together. For that, I believe I deserve a little credit."

"Credit?" Trin's voice was low and dangerous. "For manipulating us? For putting our lives at risk?"

Vivienne's gaze flicked to Trin with amusement. "My dear Mistress Meridia. Always so quick to jump to conclusions. I assure you, my intentions are every bit as pure as yours."

She turned back to Lars, holding his eyes with an intensity that made his breath catch in his throat. "I believe in progress, Master Harrow. And in challenging the established order. I believe that you, with your unique gifts, are the key to unlocking a new era of possibility."

Lars shifted in his seat, a wave of annoyance flushing through him. He took a deep breath, trying to look past Vivienne's obvious overtures. And if she'd just stop looking at him as though she wanted to take him on the table right now, it would have made things a hell of a lot easier.

"Thume is a relic of the past," Vivienne said. "A man clinging to power and afraid of change. He's holding Azoria, and more or less the world, from its true potential. I'm sure your engineer has informed you of what the device I sent you does, Master Harrow. And how it is powered."

"Yeah, about that," Darius said. "I didn't get a device."

"You didn't need to have one."

Darius snorted and opened his mouth to protest, but Vivienne had already moved on, locking her gaze on Lars. "I believe you understand that, Master Harrow. I believe you share my vision."

"Can you please stop calling him that?" Trin broke in. "And while you're at it, stop calling me Mistress Meridia."

Vivienne blinked and raised her eyebrows. "I'm sorry my dear. Trinelle. I had no idea it would bother you. Master Harr—Larson is something special, and I want to make sure he is given the respect he deserves."

This was getting out of hand. Lars tried to guide the conversation back to more reasonable topics. "We're all interested in change, Vivienne. But not danger, and not for nothing. We need more information."

Darius, clearly miffed at not being included in the conversation, jumped in. "In fact, let's lay it all out on the table. What's the story with these crystals? Do you know anything about Switcher's murder? How about the attempted murder of Lars's engineer? What is Thume so worried about? And what's in it for you?"

"What do you mean, attempted murder of Lars's engineer?" Vivienne said.

Lars sighed. "So you don't know everything. Someone attacked my engineer." He eyed her reaction critically. "With a weapon we've never seen. It was like a blast cannon, but very precise, and it fired a small metal ball at her."

"Oh my. Is she alright?" She laid a hand on Lars's arm.

"She's fine now," Lars replied, pulling his arm away. "But the unknowns are piling up and are, quite frankly, concerning as hell."

The room sat in silence for a while, which Lars was grateful for. He looked over at Trin, who was glaring at Vivienne, who was staring into her own lap. Lars put his hand on Trin's, attempting to convey assurance, but she pulled hers away and laid it on the tabletop.

Finally, Vivienne spoke. "Well, I believe I can answer at least one question based on how you described it. The weapon that was used against your engineer. It's part of the problem, something Thume has been hiding—and it's called a musket."

"A musket?" Lars echoed. "I've never heard of such a weapon."

"It's something new. A weapon of incredible power and precision. Thume has been developing it and, of course, keeping the technology secret."

"And the crystals?" Trin asked.

"I wouldn't say they're related," Vivienne said, meeting Trin's eyes with a cool intensity. "But they are both part of a larger plan. You can be sure of that."

She paused and shifted her gaze to Lars. "Those crystals, Lars, they represent something new, something extraordinary. A potential source of power unlike anything the world has ever seen. Thume is terrified of that potential falling into the wrong hands."

Darius leaned forward. "And yours are the right hands, are they?"

"You're a smart boy. You understand by now I have a different vision for the future of Azoria," Vivienne said. "A future where power is shared, not hoarded. A future where innovation is embraced, not suppressed. Just imagine a world where crystal charges are used for the betterment of all, not locked away."

Lars answered with a hint of nonchalance, his expression unreadable. "That's a noble sentiment. But it seems someone's already taken steps to make sure those secrets get out. The papers are full of it."

"Yes, it seems *someone* has. I'm sure the good Lord Thume must be fuming."

Lars shook his head. "So do you believe that's what all this is about? It's all part of Thume's plan to maintain his grip on the city?"

"Yes, and I believe he's willing to kill anyone who gets in his way," Vivienne added coldly.

"Alright, I'll buy that. We need to stop him. And we appreciate the information." Lars's tone grew cold. "But there's something you need to understand. My team, we're like family to each other. I'd imagine it's the same for Darius."

The other thief nodded.

"So trying to play us against each other, whether me against Darius or Trin against me..." Trin's eyes widened and she looked at Lars. Her hand found his and squeezed gently. "It just won't work for any of us," Lars continued, "and we won't play your game unless we know you're being honest."

Vivienne gave him a shrewd look, then she grinned. It wasn't the predatory grin that made Lars feel like she was going to smother him, but a genuine show of respect.

"Very good, Lars. And noted. Let's keep it simple then."

She slid forward in her seat, putting her palms flat on the table. "If you want to see if I'm telling the truth and understand what kind of secrets Thume is hiding, here's what I'd suggest."

"We're listening," Darius said.

"The Azoria Research Institute. There's a specialized wing that I can tell you how to find. It's where Thume runs his most significant projects. You should break in and see for yourself. Do it together."

Silas, silent for the duration of the conversation, spoke up. "I think that would raise too much suspicion."

Vivienne shook her head. "You misunderstand me. Don't steal anything. Just get in and see. Then get out. After that, you can decide if you want to trust me."

"It's not a bad idea," Lars said.

"It's a fucking horrible idea," Darius corrected. "But it sounds like our best option."

Trin stood up. As far as she was concerned, this meeting was over.

Lars looked at her and stood as well. "Thank you, Vivienne. We'll consider your suggestion."

Vivienne smiled. "That's all I ask. For now." She winked at Lars as they walked out the door.

Captain Myrim tossed a newspaper onto his desk. He'd been reading variations of the same story for days now. Rumors of a crystal that could hold a charge, a revolutionary discovery attributed to Liora Banz, the brilliant—and infamous—engineer who worked with Lars Harrow. The article even included a grainy photograph of Liora. Her multi-lensed spectacles were perched on the tip of her nose as she held up a glowing crystal, a mischievous wink directed at the camera.

Damn those thieves. A wave of frustration washed over Myrim. Years of high-stakes heists, topped off by a four-ton copper statue and a priceless galleon, and now they were making headlines with their groundbreaking discoveries. As if they needed any more reason to inflate their already overblown egos.

He stood up and paced back and forth. The news of the crystal charge had sent shockwaves through the city. Scientists were clamoring for more information, investors were scrambling to get in on the ground floor of this new technology, and the public was buzzing with excitement and speculation.

Azoria, always a city on the cutting edge of innovation, had become a whirlwind of activity. Rumors and theories about the crystal charges' potential applications were swirling through the streets, whispered in the back rooms of exclusive clubs, and debated in the halls of the Azoria Research Institute's Academy of Dynamo Sciences.

The newspapers were having a field day, churning out articles with sensational headlines: CRYSTAL CHARGES: A NEW ERA FOR AZORIA? Another predicted, SECOND DYNAMO REVOLUTION! WHO WILL CONTROL THE FUTURE? And of course, LIORA BANZ, THE CRYSTAL QUEEN!

Investors were throwing money at anything related to crystal technology, hoping to be the first in the city to discover how to mass produce them. Even the city's underworld was buzzing with excitement, with whispers of black market deals and unscrupulous figures seeking to acquire the secrets of this revolutionary discovery. But thus far, while everyone now knew of their existence, they were still a guarded secret—property of Lars Harrow and crew, and them alone.

Myrim had realized he wasn't a man to sit on the sidelines while the world changed around him. Braisus's words echoed in his mind: "*You need to think like them. Understand their game, and then beat them at it.*" He'd spent his entire career reacting to the thieves' moves, always one step behind. It was time to take the initiative, to become the predator instead of the prey.

He needed eyes and ears everywhere. A network of informants that could keep him ahead of the thieves, that could whisper secrets into his ear, and could anticipate Harrow and Adalan's next moves before they even made it.

Myrim pulled out a card, the words on it embossed in elegant script: *Need Info?*

Below the words, a single address was printed, and the ink had faded with time. He'd kept it tucked away in his desk drawer since receiving it by chance at a high-society gala years ago. Back then, he was a celebrated figure, praised for his bravery in taking on the daring thieves of Azoria—a key player in the city's grand spectacle of entertainment. Now...

He slipped the card into his pocket, grabbed his coat, and stepped out into the night.

The address on the card led him to a quiet, tree-lined street in one of Azoria's more affluent neighborhoods. The homes here were grand, their facades adorned with intricate stones and gleaming dynamo lamps, starkly contrasting the grimy streets and dark alleyways where he usually had to come calling.

He found the address, a modest townhouse with a wrought-iron gate and a heavy wooden door. On it was a sign that stated, '*Use the device to enter.*'

His eyes were drawn to a small yet complex gadget mounted on the wall beside the door.

Irritated yet intrigued, Myrim stepped closer, examining it with a critical eye. It was a marvel of gears, levers, and interlocking mechanisms, all crafted from polished brass and gleaming copper, set into a frame of stained rosewood. A small rectangular window at the bottom displayed a series of scrambled lines illuminated by a faint, internal dynamo glow.

He began by studying the visible components, noting the arrangement of gears, the position of levers, and the subtle markings etched on the surface of the wood. He tried turning a few knobs, but they met with resistance, gears clicking and whirring without any apparent change to the scrambled lines in the window. He pressed a lever, but it wouldn't budge.

He ran his fingers over the intricate carvings that adorned the rosewood frame, searching for hidden buttons or pressure points. As he did so, he noticed a subtle pattern repeating throughout the design—a stylized depiction of the constellation Ithria Ascendant, a familiar sight in the Azorian night sky.

He traced the pattern, following its path across the surface of the device, and his fingers brushed against a small, almost imperceptible button hidden beneath a cluster of gears. He pressed it, and a soft click echoed through the mechanism.

He tried the lever again, and this time it moved, releasing a series of gears that began to rotate with a mesmerizing precision. As the gears turned, the scrambled lines in the window shifted and rearranged, aligning themselves into what looked like letters.

Myrim continued to experiment, adjusting the knobs, pressing hidden buttons, his mind working to decipher the complex interplay of gears, levers, and catches. He found a hidden compartment, revealing a small crank. He turned it, and a series of internal gears whirred to life, drawing power from a concealed dynamo conduit that ran through the wall.

The lines in the window continued to shift and change, forming new letters, until finally, a single word appeared:

Welcome.

At that moment, the door unlocked with a soft click.

Myrim smiled with begrudging admiration. Whoever had designed this puzzle, this marvel of mechanical ingenuity, was a master of their craft. He straightened his uniform and stepped inside, ready to meet the mind behind this elaborate diversion.

He stepped inside, senses alert. The townhouse's interior was a study in contrasts. The entryway was bathed in a dim light, filled with the scent of beeswax and old books, hinting at a life of quiet contemplation. But as he moved further into the house, he noticed subtle touches of opulence: a thick rug with intricate patterns, a gleaming silver tea service displayed on a mahogany side table, a collection of rare gemstones arranged on a mantelpiece.

A faint hum of dynamo energy thrummed through the air, suggesting a network of hidden devices. Perhaps there were even security measures or communication systems woven into the fabric of the house.

He followed a narrow hallway until he reached a set of double doors at the end. A soft light spilled out from beneath the doors, casting a warm glow on the polished hardwood floor. He paused, taking a deep breath, then pushed the doors open. There was, after all, nowhere to go but forward.

The room beyond was a library, its walls lined with floor-to-ceiling bookshelves. A fire crackled in a marble fireplace, casting dancing shadows across the leather-bound volumes and the alluring tapestries that adorned the walls.

A woman sat at a desk by the fire, facing toward the door. She was of average height, but her presence filled the room.

Her dark hair, streaked with red, was pulled back in a loose braid that cascaded over one shoulder, a few strands escaping to frame her animated face. She wore an open, deep purple velvet jacket that hugged her curvy torso over a low-cut white blouse, the sleeves rolled up to reveal a jumble of silver bracelets that jingled as she moved.

"A city watchman solved my puzzle!" she said. "Impressive. Most men like you resort to brute force."

She leaned forward. Resting her elbows on the desk with her chin propped on her hands, the woman revealed a generous expanse of cleavage. Her eyes, a vibrant shade of blue, sparkled with challenge—and no small amount of curiosity.

"You must be Captain Myrim."

Myrim stepped further into the room, taking in her unconventional attire and the gleam of devious intelligence in her eyes. He had expected a dark mysterious figure, some kind of errant nobleman perhaps, but this woman was different. She carried herself with confidence and the slightest touch of a playful defiance.

"You have me at a disadvantage, madam. I confess I don't know your name."

"Shelina Halmuth." She offered a hand across the desk. Her grip was firm yet warm. "But you can call me Shelle. Everyone does."

"Shelle," Myrim repeated. It suited her—elegant yet with a hint of sharpness. He reached into his coat pocket and produced the worn cardstock, laying it on her desk. "I received this some time ago."

Shelle picked up the card, tracing the embossed letters with a polished fingernail. "Ah, yes. My little calling card. A conversation starter, as it were. I do love a good bit of intrigue, and I'm always happy to make new acquaintances."

She met his gaze, blue eyes twinkling. "But only if you're in a position to appreciate my gifts."

Myrim felt a warmth spread through him, a welcome surprise at her boldness. He wasn't used to being the target of this kind of attention from a woman of Shelle's obvious intelligence and standing.

He glanced around the room, noting the heavy velvet curtains drawn over the windows, the thick carpet muffling any sound, the subtle hum of dynamo energy that had to come from a network of hidden devices. "I trust this conversation will remain confidential?"

"Confidentiality is the cornerstone of my business," Shelle said. "Without it, I'd be out of a job, and I'd venture to say out of a home."

She leaned closer. "So, Captain Myrim. I don't often make a habit of dealing with the city watch, but a customer's a customer and if I'm being honest, I like a good challenge. What kind of information are you seeking? And what are you willing to offer in return?"

Myrim shifted in his seat, trying to regain his composure. "I need my own network, Shelle. A network of eyes and ears that can tell me what's happening in this city. Who's moving. Who's talking. When and where heists will happen, and how I can get there first."

Shelle cocked an eyebrow at him, and her plush lips spread into an amused smile. "How fascinating."

And with that the negotiations began. Myrim learned more about Azoria in one night than he had in years leading the city watch. Whatever would come of this odd alliance, it would certainly prove to be enlightening.

✧

The foundry hummed with a faint residual energy, the ghosts of countless inventions and forgotten dreams lingering in the air. Dust motes danced in the shafts of moonlight piercing through the grimy windows, illuminating the machinery and the scattered tools left behind on workbenches. Thanks to a picked lock, it was theirs for the moment.

People often thought of thieves as spontaneous and daring, but Lars knew that planning and understanding were key to survival. Testing the dynamo lens was the first priority—they had to know exactly what they were dealing with. If the device was as powerful as Liora suspected, it could be a game changer. But power came with risk, and Lars wasn't about to commit to anything blindly.

Lars, Darius, and Liora stood huddled around a table in the center of the vast space, the reconstructed dynamo lens resting between them. Its silver surface gleamed in the dim light, and the crystal at its core pulsed with a soft, ethereal glow.

"Alright, Liora," Lars said, gaze fixed on the device. "Show us what this thing can do."

Liora adjusted her multi-lensed spectacles, a feverish glint in her amber eyes. "Prepare to be amazed." Her excitement was as evident as her apprehension. Lars was glad beyond words that she was getting better and back to her old vibrant self.

She gestured toward a pair of dynamo lamps she'd brought, their cloth-covered wiring snaking across the dusty floor to a terminal box on the wall. "Let's start simple. These lamps are drawing a steady current from the city grid. The dynamo lens should be able to detect that flow."

She picked up the device, holding it out in front of her, and began to rotate it toward the lamps. The crystal at its core pulsed brighter, casting a focused beam of light illuminating the wiring. It traced the path of the dynamo current as it flowed from the terminal box, through the wires, and into the lamps.

Darius leaned closer to examine the illuminated circuitry. "Amazing. It's like seeing the veins of the workshop and how all the blood flows through it."

"Exactly. Now for something a bit more complex." Liora retrieved a squawk from her satchel, placed it on the table, and connected it to the terminal box. "We should be able to trace the signal from the squawk through the city's network to its destination."

She held up the dynamo lens, adjusting the dials and focusing the crystal's glow on the squawk. At first, nothing happened. Then, as if awakening from a slumber, the device sprang to life. New lines of light, shimmering threads of energy, beamed out from the Lens, tracing a path across the room. They wove through the air, disappearing into the walls and beyond.

Lars and Darius exchanged a look of astonishment. "It's... following the signal," Lars said, the revelation filling him with awe. "Through the city's grid. But how?"

"It's detecting the subtle fluctuations in the dynamo flow," Liora explained. "The way the signal modulates the current. It's like listening to a whisper in the roar of a storm, but it's doing it."

"Incredible. This little device, exposing all the city's secrets," Darius said, entranced by the shimmering lights that stretched out from the device.

"And to think," Liora added with pride, "it's all powered by a crystal charge that can be carried anywhere. Though it did take a bolt of lightning to recharge the darn thing."

Darius chuckled. "Only you could manage to harness a hells cursed storm to fuel your inventions. Maren could learn a thing or two from you."

"Oh!" Liora squeaked, "I miss Maren! Tell him I said so. Us engineers have to stick together."

Liora continued experimenting with the dynamo lens, adjusting its settings and exploring its capabilities until she noticed something unexpected. The shimmering lines were no longer tracing the path of active dynamo currents. They were fainter now, more ethereal, but still they wove through the air, tracing paths across the floor, clinging to the surfaces of objects. She gasped.

"What is it, Liora?" Lars asked, sensing her sudden shift in focus. "What are you seeing?"

"Something... different. It's residual dynamo. Traces of energy left behind, like footprints in the sand."

She pointed the lens at a nearby workbench, its surface covered in a jumble of tools. The rays converged on a soldering iron, pulsing with a faint, steady glow.

"Someone used that iron recently," she said with certainty. "And look." She directed the lens toward a cluster of dynamo terminals on the wall. "I can see traces of dynamo leading to it. Someone was working here, repairing something, maybe even modifying one of the machines."

Darius picked up the soldering iron, turning it over in his hands. "I don't understand. From the looks of this place, no one has been here for a while. How can it detect traces of energy from what could have been months ago?"

"Dynamo leaves a subtle imprint on the objects it flows through," Liora said. "Less subtle on conductive materials like copper and crystals. It's like... like an echo of the dynamo current. This device seems sensitive enough to pick up those echoes and see the remnants."

She swept the dynamo lens across the room, its crystal pulsing with a mesmerizing rhythm. The lights danced and shimmered, revealing a hidden history of the foundry: the paths of dynamo currents through the wiring, the points where repairs had been made, the machines that had once hummed with life.

"This is unbelievable," Lars said, his mind reeling with the implications. "We're looking through a window into time, seeing the flow of energy through the building's very bones."

Darius nodded, watching the intricate movements skittering across the floor. "Imagine what we could do with this. The secrets we could uncover, the mysteries we could solve—and let's not forget the scores we could pull off."

Liora nodded, thrilled beyond belief. "It changes everything. Traps, security systems, hidden compartments, they all leave a dynamo signature. We can see the flow of energy, anticipate the next move, plan our approach with a level of precision we've never had before."

She paused, gasping as she made another adjustment to the device. "Wait... there's something else."

The array of glowing beams emanating from the dynamo lens shifted, becoming more focused, more intense. They converged on Darius, forming a swirling aura of light around him.

"What... what's happening?" Darius demanded with a touch of obvious unease.

"It's reading your dynamo signature! Your personal bio-dynamo field. Dynamo flows through us too, and this can see it flowing through you!"

The glow pulsed in sync with Darius's heartbeat, a mesmerizing dance of energy reflecting his very essence. He looked down at it, growing discomfort evident on his face. "Okay, but can you make it stop? I feel violated."

Lars stared at the glowing aura surrounding Darius, a chill running down his spine. He'd always known that dynamo was the lifeblood of their world, the force that powered their inventions, their lights, the whole damned nation. But seeing it manifested so clearly, so intimately, in another human being was both awe-inspiring and unsettling.

Liora switched off the device and the crystal's glow faded to a soft murmur. Considering the implications, the three thieves stood on the foundry floor, too stunned to speak.

Autumn was fast settling over Azoria, its golden light painting the city's rooftops in shades of amber and crimson, a fleeting moment of tranquility before the long winter set in. A crispness had crept into the air, a subtle shift in the breeze that promised cooler days to come.

Keer and Silas made their way through Azoria's raucous waterfront district, the cobbled streets slick with a recent rain. The heady scents of saltwater, fish, and the ever-present pall of coal smoke from the city's countless foundries and factories filled the air. For these two grizzled veterans of the city and the sea, these smells filled the soul.

"So, the Research Institute," Silas said, pulling his worn leather jacket tighter against the evening chill. "What do we know about it? Aside from the fact that it's full of academics who couldn't tell a lockpick from a tea kettle."

Keer chuckled, a dry, rasping sound. "Don't underestimate the eggheads, Silas. They might not have your hands-on experience, but they've got brains. Sometimes, brains can be more dangerous than brawn."

He paused, sweeping his eyes over the crowded streets, taking in the usual mix of dockworkers, merchants, and sailors. "We're fairly certain that the Azoria Research Institute is one of Thume's pet projects. From what Vivienne has told us, he funds it to be the first in line when new discoveries are made. But at this point I suspect there's more to it than that."

Silas grunted. "Always is with Thume. The man's got his fingers in every pie in this city. So we've got two questions to answer. One, what is he keeping in there that's worth knocking off citizens for. And two, how do we break into this 'secret wing' Miss Charm-Your-Pants-Off told us all about.

Keer chuckled, shrugging his sturdy shoulders. "That's what we're here to find out. We need to sniff around, see what we can pick up. Talk to the right people, listen to the vibe on the streets. Aren't you a spymaster?"

Silas laughed and clapped his friend on the back. "These days I'm just an old man, Keer."

They entered a dim tavern that smelled of strong liquor, heavy labor, and stale tobacco. Add some music, and it would just be Keer's type of place. A group of dockworkers huddled around a table, arguing over a game of dice, while a lone sailor sat nursing a tankard in the back corner.

Keer headed for the bar, signaling to Silas to find a table near the dice players.

"Two whiskey sours, my friend," Keer said, placing coins on the counter. "And make 'em strong. We've got a long night ahead of us."

Silas scanned the room. He settled on a familiar face at the dice table. "Bron!" he called out with a wide grin. "Haven't seen you in ages! How's the wife? Kids all grown up by now, I imagine."

The dockworker looked up, a broad smile splitting his weathered face. "Silas! By the hells, I thought you might be retired to some island estate by now, living off your ill-gotten gains."

"Retirement's for the faint of heart. Besides, can't keep a good thief down, can we?"

"That you can't," Bron said with a laugh that boomed through the tavern. He gestured to the empty seat beside him. "Feel free to join us. We're just getting warmed up."

Silas shook his head, chuckling. "Happy to have a seat, but my dicing skills aren't a match for any of you boys. But here, are you all thirsty?" He lifted his arm. "Another round on me!"

Keer returned from the bar with two whiskey sours in hand and a knowing smile on his lips. He nodded a greeting to Bron and the other men before joining Silas at the table.

"Well, well, well," Bron said. "Look who it is, boys. Another famous old sea dog back on the prowl." He chuckled into his drink and then looked up at the pair. "You two planning to fleece us poor dockworkers or just here for the cheap beer?"

Keer grinned and signaled the bartender to hurry up with the drinks. "Good to see you too, Bron."

The barkeep waddled over, carrying armfuls of mugs for the whole table. Dice rolled, iron and gold coins clinked, and the conversation flowed, fueled by ale and good-natured banter. Silas and Keer listened intently, gleaning what they could from the dockworkers' chatter.

"Those new crystals are all anyone's talking about these days," one of the dockworkers said, shaking his head in disbelief. "Did you see the papers? That engineer who discovered them, Liora something or other—she's cute as a button. Brains and beauty, eh? Lucky bastard, that Harrow."

Keer's brow furrowed, staring at the dice rolling across the table. Liora was a good kid, smart as a whip, and she didn't need that kind of attention.

"Dynamo in your pocket," another dockworker said, shaking his head. "Who knows what those geniuses will come up with next. If I had a crystal charge though, I'd just sell the damn thing and buy myself a new ship."

A third dockworker, a younger man with eager eyes, chimed in. "I'd use it to power my own flying machine! Imagine taking her up above the city, looking down on all those rich folks in their fancy carriages. That's what I'd do."

"Flying machine? You've been spending too much time reading adventure books, lad. Those things don't exist."

"Maybe not yet," the young man said, voice filled with stubborn hope. "But with a crystal charge I bet anything's possible!"

Bron, who had been listening to the conversation with a thoughtful frown, spoke up. "If you ask me, those crystals are more trouble than they're worth. They've got everyone on edge, and the guilds are fighting over who will get them first. Who knows what Lord Moneybags Thume is going to do with it. It's enough to make a man want to pack up and set sail off somewhere quieter."

"A quieter life, eh?" Silas said, leaning back in his chair, a thoughtful look on his face. "I can understand that. Sometimes you just need a break from all the excitement."

He paused, letting the words hang in the air. "Speaking of excitement, I'm curious, Bron. You've been working these docks for years. You know everyone, hear everything about what's coming and going into the city. If a man was looking for information about where the money was flowing, who would you check with?"

Bron chuckled, taking another swig of his ale. "You asking for yourself, Silas? Thought you had all the connections anyone could need. You're Adalan's spymaster, ain't you?"

"If I went by the sources I lean on, I'd get the same kind of information I always do. I'm looking for recent info fresh off the boats. For a personal matter."

The dockworkers exchanged amused glances. "You should talk to Barto over there." He gestured toward the barkeep, a wiry man with a mop of gray hair and a face etched with a thousand stories. "Throw him a tip and he'll tell you what color his wife's underclothes are."

Silas grinned, pushing back his chair. "Thanks for the advice, lads. I'll go see what Barto's got to offer."

He winked at Keer, who was already switching to the seat beside Bron. "Don't lose all your money while I'm gone, Keer," he said, clapping his friend on the shoulder.

As Silas made his way toward the bar, Keer pulled a handful of coins from his pocket, adding them to the growing pile in the center of the table. "Deal me in, gents. Let's see if luck's on my side tonight."

The dice rolled, the conversation continued, and Keer played the role of the harmless old foreigner to perfection. He let the dockworkers win a few rounds, their boasts growing louder with each victory.

✧

Silas, meanwhile, leaned against the bar, watching the interplay with a knowing smile.

"Two more whiskeys, Barto," he said, catching the barkeep's eye. "The good stuff this time. And a word in your ear."

The barkeep's hands moved with a skilled efficiency as he poured the drinks. "What can I do for you?"

"Heard you might be able to point me in the right direction." He pushed the second drink and an extra silver coin across the counter. "I'm looking for someone who can fill me in on the latest news around crystal charges and who's spending money to make them."

The barkeep pocketed the coin. "Crystal charges, huh?" He made a show of thinking real deep, scratching his chin. "Can't say I'd know anyone."

Silas pushed a copper coin across the counter.

"I know someone," Barto said. "Been a while, might turn out to be nothing. But worth a shot from what I recall."

He reached beneath the counter, retrieving a worn piece of cardstock. "Here," he said, "take this."

Silas took the card, eyes widening as he recognized the embossed letters: *Need Info?* Below the words, an address was printed. He hadn't thought about Shelle in a spell but if she were willing to help, that would yield all the information they needed.

"Keer! Let's go."

Keer sighed and rolled the dice one last time. The dockworkers all groaned collectively as he swept the entire pot of coins into his bag. "Pleasure playing with you gents!"

He chuckled as they stepped out into the cool night air. "Those dockworkers won't be forgetting us anytime soon," he said, hefting the heavy bag of coins. "You'd think they'd learn not to gamble with a pair of thieves."

Silas glanced at him. "Speaking of that, how are things going with Harrow's crew? Still keeping you busy, I imagine?"

Keer grunted. "Never a dull moment. Lars always has something up his sleeve. Those young ones keep me on my toes. I'd imagine it's the same for you with Darius."

Silas laughed, clapping him on the shoulder. "You're not all that slow, old man. You've got a knack for playing the innocent old fool. Those boys never suspected you were a three-time dicemaster."

They fell into a comfortable silence, their footsteps echoing on the cobblestones as they made their way through the bustling waterfront district, heading toward the more affluent neighborhoods where Shelle's townhouse was located.

"You think this informant can be trusted?"

"Trust is a luxury we can't afford if we're honest with ourselves," Silas said. "But Shelle is reliable. Discreet. She's got a knack for knowing things before anyone else does. I don't know why I didn't think of her first."

As they approached Shelle's townhouse, Silas slowed his pace, studying the imposing door and puzzle lock with a critical eye. "Fun little gizmo." He turned, pulled, and pressed on the device. It unlocked in seconds.

"Still got the touch, I see," Keer said with respect as they stepped inside the townhouse.

But their progress hit an unexpected barrier—literally. A heavy portcullis, its bars thicker than a man's arm, blocked off the hallway.

"Well, that's interesting." Silas examined the formidable barrier through narrowed eyes.

On a nearby table, a note was propped against a metal box with a slit in the lid. A pile of blank papers and a pen lay beside it.

The mistress of the house is unavailable, the note read, *but if you leave a message with your name and what you need, maybe you'll get lucky.*

Silas glanced at Keer. "Do we leave a note? What should we tell her?"

Keer considered for a moment, then picked up the pen, scribbling a quick note on a sheet of paper:

Silas and Keer. Need information fast. Azoria Research Institute.

He folded the note, slipped it through the slit in the box, and turned to Silas.

"Let's grab another drink. This investigation is making me thirsty."

The Azorian marketplace buzzed with the energy of a thousand transactions, a whirlwind of sights, sounds, and smells that assaulted the senses. Vendors hawked their wares, shouting a chorus of competing claims and exaggerated promises. Shoppers haggled over prices, their faces a mixture of determination and delight as they sought the best deals.

The aroma of roasted meat, exotic spices, and fresh baked bread mingled with the oily smell of dynamo-powered machinery, creating a unique olfactory signature that was both intoxicating and overwhelming.

Trin Meridia, emerald green scarf draped over her shoulders, navigated the crowded stalls with the grace and cunning of a panther. Jax—always a magnet for curious glances and nervous whispers—trailed behind her, arms laden with coils of copper wire and sacks of components.

"When you said we were going shopping I thought we'd be looking at new clothes," Jax said, shifting the weight of his burdens. "This junk is a hell of a lot of lifting."

Trin chuckled, pausing to examine a display of custom lockpicks. "Eyes on the prize, Jax. Pulling off a heist requires more than just a flashy outfit."

"It'd be a whole lot easier my way," Jax said. "Swoop in, dazzle everyone, bump some heads, bang boom done." He emphasized this strategy with a series of arm movements, jiggling the various coils and bags of gear.

"Bang boom done," Trin said absentmindedly as she looked through various bits of gear, "is what got Liora knocked off a roof."

Her breath caught. She looked over at Jax and saw the big man's eyes widen as he frowned deeply. His shoulders drooped.

"Jax, I am so sorry. I didn't mean—"

The big man turned away. "It's fine."

"No, Jax." She laid a hand on his arm. "That was cruel and wrong of me. I'm just worried I guess."

Jax opened his mouth to reply, but she squeezed his arm. "Please, let me finish. I'm worried because this all feels wrong.

It's just not how things are done. So I said something stupid and took it out on you. And I'm sorry."

Jax looked at her, gentle face easing into a smile. Trin felt horrid for lashing out at someone who had always been there for her. For all of them.

"Trin," he said, "don't beat yourself up. It's alright. I get it. We're all feeling it I think."

He paused, a hesitant question in his eyes. "So is this all about Liora? Or is there something else bothering you?"

She hesitated as her attention drifted toward a stall displaying an array of shimmering fabrics. "I'm... concerned," she said. "About Liora, of course, and about what Thume's planning. But..."

She trailed off, hand tightening around the edge of a stall display.

"What is it, Trin? What's going on?"

She met his inquisitive look, her face clouded with a frustrated grimace.

"It's Vivienne," she said as she picked up a beautiful silk bolt, the color of a summer sky, letting it flow through her fingers. "She's so confident. Elegant. Powerful. Everything I'm not."

Her eyes softened with a vulnerability she had never displayed around Jax before. "I can't handle her smug little face. What if Lars can't see through her? What if he—"

"You cut that shit right now, Trin." Jax set down his load and reached out, taking her small hands in his. "Lars ain't falling for any snake's charms. He's smarter than that. More importantly, he cares about you. He loves you, Trin. I know it. How couldn't he? Don't you know how incredible you are?"

Trin's eyes widened, the pleasant feelings of surprise and gratitude welling up within her. She hadn't expected such straightforward reassurance from Jax, a man known for his boisterous personality and his love of a good brawl. But in that moment, she saw a different side of him, a depth of emotional understanding that touched her deeply.

"Jax… do you really think so?"

Jax squeezed her hands, the gesture firm and reassuring. "I know so. Lars might be a bit of a rogue, and he's always playing the angles, but you and I know he's got a good heart. That heart, Trin, it belongs to you. Vivienne is just trying to be a distraction. That's all she'll ever be. A shiny bauble that'll lose its luster soon enough."

He paused, as if searching for the right words. "Look, Trin, I might not be the smartest guy in the crew, but I know people. I can read 'em. And I can tell you, Lars isn't looking at Vivienne the way he looks at you. He looks at you like… like you're the only star in the sky. The only treasure he's ever wanted to steal."

Trin felt a warmth spread through her chest, a flicker of hope banishing the fear of doubt. Jax's words, so simple yet so heartfelt, felt right. She knew that Lars cared for her, but the intensity of Vivienne's presence had shaken her. No more.

"Thanks, Jax. I guess I needed to hear that."

She took a deep breath, gathering her strength. "You're right. I'm letting her get to me. I'm better than that." She straightened her shoulders, a surge of confidence settling back into her posture. "We've got a job to do, and I'm not going to let some manipulative bitch distract me."

"That's what I'm talking about!"

Trin gave him a grateful smile. "Now, come on," she said with a wink, regaining her usual spark. "Let's finish gathering these supplies. We've got a heist to plan."

Trin and Jax moved through the marketplace with renewed purpose, their earlier tension replaced by a shared determination. They gathered the remaining supplies, haggling with vendors, comparing prices, and exchanging conspiratorial, comforting glances.

They returned to their base just as the sun was setting, long shadows spreading across the surrounding buildings. Both of their arms were laden with the fruits of their trip. Jax fumbled with the heavy door, grumbling about the lack of proper lighting in the alleyway.

"First time opening a door, Jax?" Trin nudged him in the side playfully.

As they stepped inside, the expected warmth of the tavern was replaced by a chilling silence. A single envelope, sealed with crimson wax and bearing the unmistakable crest of the Ithris Gaming Commission, sat on the table.

Trin felt a sudden knot of apprehension tighten in her chest. She reached out, fingers trembling as she took the envelope and broke the seal. She unfolded the crisp parchment within.

Her eyes widened as she scanned the words, written in an elegant script:

Master Harrow, the letter began, *Urgent matters require your immediate attention. Present yourself at the Ithris Gaming Commission headquarters tomorrow at your earliest convenience. Failure to comply will be unfortunate for all parties involved.*

The letter ended with a flourish, the signoff bold and unwavering:

The Office of Lord Thume.

IMPLICATIONS

11

"Any luck with those other leads, Inora?" Darius said, feeling a weariness that went beyond a lack of sleep. The summons from Thume, arriving so soon after they met with Vivienne, had thrown them all off balance.

The old tavern felt nothing but oppressive. The dynamo lights had been dimmed low, casting a weak glow across the worn wooden tables and the mismatched chairs that had seen countless late-night strategy sessions, drunken celebrations, and moments of quiet contemplation. Maps and schematics were flung across the surfaces, a chaotic jumble of lines and annotations that mirrored the tangled thoughts and anxieties swirling through the minds of those gathered there.

Darius's infiltrator Inora, seated beside Keer at a nearby table, tossed a stack of papers onto the worn surface with a sigh. Maps, schematics, intelligence reports—the fruits of her tireless efforts to uncover the location of Thume's secret warehouse up north. So far, they'd yielded nothing but dead ends and vague rumors.

"Nothing concrete," she said gruffly, drumming a restless beat against the tabletop with her fingertips. "Thume's kept this place locked down tight. Even my best contacts are drawing blanks."

"Shelle sent over a map of the Institute if that's our next step," Keer said. He unrolled a worn sheet of parchment, its surface covered with intricate details. "Solid layout, a bit about security systems, and a recommended escape route—it's a start, I'll give her that. But nothing here about a secret research facility."

"She said she was busy with other clients," Silas added, shrugging his shoulders.

Darius frowned, his eyes slowly tracing the lines of the map with focused intensity. Each mark seemed to pull him deeper into thought. He found himself trying to strategize potential entry points, pathways, and contingencies. But it was a fruitless exercise considering their target was completely unknown.

"So we're going in blind? Relying on Vivienne's word and a map from a rushed informant? It feels reckless, even for us."

Though a fire crackled in the hearth, its warmth couldn't quite dispel the chill that had settled over them. A nervous energy hummed beneath the surface of their forced cheerfulness, a shared sense of foreboding that brought the two crews together.

Lars looked at Darius, a grim set to his jaw. "Thume summons us to see him," he said, tapping the letter with a restless finger. "What do you think he wants?"

"Oh, I'm sure he just wants to take tea, chat about the weather."

Lars didn't laugh. Darius leaned back in his chair, his gaze distant. "He wasn't happy about me stealing his ship, that's for sure. And then we made sure all of Azoria knew about crystal charges. He'll want to know whether we plan to disrupt his little empire."

"Less wondering whether we are, and more wondering how," Trin said. "He's always been fascinated by a good strategy. He's going to size us up to see if we're worth keeping on the board and try to determine our next move if so."

Darius considered Trin's feedback. They were both right.

"So, Darius, do we both go? Would that be too obvious?" Lars asked. Before Darius or anyone else could speak, he answered his own question. "Yes, it would be too obvious. We don't need him knowing we're working together. Not yet."

Inora—who had been silent until now, taking in all the shifts in the conversation—spoke up in a low rasp that cut through the tension in the room.

"Liora should go."

All eyes turned to her, a wave of surprise rippling through the room. Liora, who had been absorbed in her work, looked up with a confused expression.

"Liora?" Lars echoed, eyes shifting from Inora to Liora and back again. "Why Liora?"

Inora locked eyes with Lars, her gray gaze steady and unflinching. "Think about it. Switcher was murdered. Liora was attacked. They both had a connection to the crystal charge, and we made hers public with a big picture of her up top. It makes sense that Thume would be interested in her."

She paused, letting the import of her idea sink in.

"Let her go with you to meet Thume. See how he reacts to her. See if he recognizes her, and throw something in there about how she was shot by a mystery weapon." She shrugged.

"And gauge how he reacts," Trin added. "That's a wonderful idea."

Darius smiled, a genuine, uncalculating look that softened his sharp features. He'd met Inora a few years back in one of Azoria's less reputable gambling dens.

She had been running a rigged card game, her fingers a blur of motion as she dealt out winning hands to her accomplices. Her face was cold and calculating as she fleeced a group of unsuspecting merchants. Darius had been impressed by her skill. After the game was finished, she could disappear into a crowd as if she'd never been there.

He had offered her a place on his crew that night, and she'd accepted with a curt nod, gray eyes meeting his own with a kind of intensity that made him wonder what secrets she held. This was a woman who was economical with her words. She might be gruff, but her loyalty was unquestionable. Darius had never been able to break through the wall she'd built around herself.

But he was glad she was on his side.

Lars looked at his rambunctious engineer. "Well, Liora? What do you think?"

Facing Thume was a different kind of challenge. If Darius was honest, he didn't think the quirky engineer would be up for it. Thume was powerful, dangerous. Of course, so was lightning. And who had tamed that? Liora.

She pushed her glasses up. "You know me, Lars. Ready for anything. But let's leave the dynamo lens here."

"Of course. Just in case."

After more discussion and a round of half-worried goodbyes, Lars and Liora left the base and started heading toward the center of Azoria, where the Ithris Gaming Commission had its headquarters.

✧

As they walked, Liora couldn't help but pepper Lars with questions. "Do you think Thume will tell us about the muskets? And what do you think he'll say about the crystal charges?"

"We'll find out soon enough," Lars said, keeping his tone calm. His attention was focused on the path ahead. The closer they got to Thume's headquarters, the more Liora started to fidget and the more Lars wanted to consider their next moves in silence.

But silence wasn't Liora's strong suit. "You know... if we ever have to build a new dynamo lens, I think I'd go for a sleek, midnight blue design. With gold accents, of course. What do you think?"

Lars chuckled. "We're about to walk into a meeting with the most dangerous man in Ithris, and you're worried about the color of a gadget you don't know how to make?"

"Yet." Liora shrugged, a playful grin spreading across her face. "A girl's gotta have her priorities, Lars. Besides, a little distraction never hurts, does it?"

He couldn't help but smile. Despite the recent attack and the danger they all faced, Liora was still Liora.

"So, how about it, Lars?" Liora nudged him with her elbow. "When are you and Trin going to get hitched up? Seems like you two are finally, ya know..." She trailed off, brow furrowed, smooshing her hands together. "Hitching up," she said with a wink.

Lars felt a flush of warmth creep up his neck. "Liora, I don't—"

"Just curious. You've been dancing around each other for years. It's about time you two admitted—"

She was interrupted as they reached their destination: a grand building of polished granite and gleaming brass that towered over the surrounding structures, its facade adorned with the crest of the Ithris Gaming Commission, a stylized depiction of a golden scale held aloft by a pair of intertwined serpents.

"Here we go," Lars said, taking a deep breath, a steeliness hardening his features. He held the door open for Liora, his hand resting on her shoulder. It was a brief, silent reassurance, a reminder that he was there with her, steady and unwavering.

They stepped inside, the air cool and hushed, the comforting blend of beeswax and polished wood a stark contrast to the boisterous city streets. The lobby was a blatant show of Thume's wealth and influence, a very unsubtle display of power designed to intimidate and awe. Stunning tapestries depicting scenes of Azoria's legendary founding adorned the walls, their threads shimmering with silver and gold. A massive crystal chandelier, its facets catching the light and casting a thousand rainbows across the polished marble floor, hung from the vaulted ceiling.

On a wall hung a larger-than-life portrait of Lord Cecil Thume himself, painted in the style of the old Zarakaran masters. His golden eyes, captured with an unsettling intensity, seemed to follow their every move. Beneath the portrait, a bronze plaque proclaimed: '*Lord Cecil Thume, Founder of the Ithris Gaming Commission, Architect of Prosperity, Guardian of Balance.*'

"Bastard of Pomposity," Liora whispered. Lars gave her a sharp look.

A young woman, eyes wide with awe, sat behind a large mahogany desk. It was bare except for a simple dynamo lamp, a stack of message slips, and a small, unassuming black device. A nameplate engraved in elegant script identified the assistant as Miss Neema Vandi.

"Lars Harrow...and Liora Banz!" she squealed, "Right in front of me!" Her face became giddy and glowing. "My friends will never believe this."

Lars stood tall and adopted his most magnanimous tone. "We're here to see Lord Thume. He's expecting us."

She nodded. "Of course, of course." Her hand trembled as she pressed a button on her desk, activating a hidden communicator.

"Lord Thume, Master Harrow and Miss Banz are here to see you."

Liora nudged Lars in the side and whispered, her mouth scrunched to the side, "My squawks are better."

Neema turned back to Lars and Liora and smiled. "He should be out to get you in a moment. But... well, while we wait, can I have an autograph?"

A slight chuckle escaped from Lars. "Of course," he said. He and Liora both signed a slip of paper for her, his with the usual sharp lines and flourished curves, and Liora's with scratched letters and a sizzling lightning bolt for the final z. She handed the paper back to the girl.

"Um," the girl said hesitantly, "I hate to ask, but can you..." but she faltered. Lars grinned, knowing what she was about to ask. He reached back out for the paper—

The woman finally got the courage to finish her request. "Liora, would you add a kiss to it?"

Lars halted, eyes wide, and broke out in a huge smile. He looked at Liora, who was wearing a sheepish grin. "No problem," she said, pushing up her glasses. She took the paper and pursed her lips to add a big smooch below her signature.

"Oh wow, thank you. Thank you, I love you so much—" Neema squealed but was cut off by the sound of a heavy door opening. She grabbed the piece of paper behind the desk and stood up nervously, smoothing out her clothes.

Lord Thume strode into the room and stood with his arms crossed to look at Lars and Liora. "Well?" he prompted in his deep baritone. "Shall we go have our talk?"

Lars returned Thume's gaze as his mind raced with possibilities. Each one was a little bit more unnerving than the last.

The man's presence filled the lobby, a palpable aura of power and authority that pressed down on them. He was dressed in a tailored charcoal suit accentuating his broad shoulders and commanding stature. His burnished irises that seemed to express so much were cold now, betraying only a suppressed annoyance that made Lars's instincts scream for caution.

"Of course, Lord Thume," Lars said, walking ahead of Liora. The pair followed him down a long, bright hallway, their footsteps echoing on the polished marble floor.

They arrived at a spacious office, its walls lined with bookshelves filled with leather-bound volumes and intricate dynamo models. A large window overlooked the city, offering a wide view of the market district, river estates, and the dazzling Ithris River. This city was ostensibly run by a local government and representative council but, in reality, was overshadowed every day by this man.

Thume gestured toward a pair of chairs facing his mahogany desk. "Please, have a seat."

As Lars and Liora settled themselves into the plush chairs, Thume moved behind the desk, fixing his gaze on them with an unreadable expression. The silence stretched, thick and heavy.

"I appreciate your prompt response to my invitation, Master Harrow." He gave every indication of being calm and formal. But beneath his words, Lars could sense a dangerous edge. This was not going to be an easy meeting.

Lars nodded matter-of-factly. "We're here as requested, Lord Thume."

"Good. Then let's get down to business."

His gaze shifted to Liora with a slight hint of recognition. "And you are?"

Liora, fidgeting nervously, straightened her spectacles and smoothed her skirt. She found herself the focus of Thume's attention, and did not like it one bit. She felt a chill run down her spine, the weight of his gaze pressing down on her like a physical force.

"Liora Banz. I'm... Lars's engineer." She swallowed hard, forcing herself to meet the domineering man's gaze. "And a huge fan of the Gaming Commission. It's an honor to meet you, Lord Thume."

He responded with a faint, almost imperceptible smile, a disarming and unsettling gesture. "The honor is all mine, Miss Banz."

He leaned back in his chair, fingers steepled thoughtfully.

"So, Master Harrow, Miss Banz. Let's talk about crystal charges."

His gaze shifted, fixing on Liora with startling intensity. "I *do* remember you now. You were in the paper, the woman who developed this marvelous technology. Tell me, Miss

Banz, how do these charges work? I confess, my understanding of dynamo is somewhat limited."

Liora, clearly relieved to have the focus shift away from the more dangerous questions of intent and consequence, launched into an enthusiastic explanation. "It's remarkable. These crystals, they're unlike anything we've ever seen before. They can store a charge, like a capacitor, but on a much larger scale. And they don't fizzle out."

"A capacitor," Thume repeated, his unblinking gaze fixed on Liora. "And what are your plans for this technology?"

Liora hesitated, glancing at Lars, who was watching the exchange intently. "It's a work in progress, sir," she stammered, fidgeting with the edge of her skirt. "It's not something I can talk too much about."

"But I'm curious, Miss Banz. Do enlighten me."

"We're still exploring its potential, Lord Thume," Lars said, stepping in before Liora could reveal too much. "It's a... delicate process, and we don't want to jeopardize our research by discussing it prematurely."

"Indeed. And where did you acquire this unique crystal, Master Harrow? A trinket of such power that, somehow, no one had ever seen before."

Lars shrugged, a gesture of feigned nonchalance. "Let's just say we have our sources, Lord Thume. As do you, I imagine."

"That I do," Thume said. "And I have a particular interest in this unusual technology."

He reached beneath his desk and pulled out a large box. Unlatching the front of the box, he opened it and carefully spun it around on the polished surface of his desk.

A jagged shard of crystal, its surface clouded with a milky haze, lay gleaming under the soft light of the desk lamp.

Liora gasped, eyes widening in recognition. "Where did you get that?"

Thume raised an eyebrow, feigned surprise crossing his face. "Do you recognize it, Miss Banz?"

"Recognize it?" Liora's voice rose, trembling with unrestrained fury. "That's the crystal that—" Lars shot her a warning glance. "—that I was working on when someone tried to kill me! You son of a bitch!"

Thume recoiled as if struck. His expressive eyes, cool and calculating a moment ago, flared with a sudden, incandescent rage. "How dare you!" he thundered as he jumped to his feet, and his anger filled the room. "You will show respect in my presence, Miss Banz, or face the consequences."

Lars had had enough. He stood and stepped in front of Liora, eyes locking onto the enraged man's. "Enough, Thume. We both know this isn't a social call. You summoned us here for a reason. So let's cut the theatrics and get to the point. Because if you're trying to intimidate us, it won't work."

That was half true. He couldn't help being intimidated out of his ever-loving mind. But he would die before he let it show now.

Thume's face looked as though it might explode from rage. But after a moment he took a deep breath and got his emotions under control. He and Lars took their seats, and Thume's attention shifted to Liora. "It seems, Miss Banz, that you have a history with this particular crystal. Perhaps you'd care to enlighten me how you had it in your possession?"

Liora glared at him, lifting her chin in defiance. "I stole it," she said, pushing her glasses up. "As is my right. It was part of a score. Nothing more, nothing less."

Thume threw back his head and laughed, a harsh, humorless sound that echoed through the room. "A score?

You expect me to believe that, Miss Banz? That you just stumbled upon this crystal? A crystal that holds a power unlike anything the world has seen? That before you 'stole' it, was in the hands of a murdered citizen?"

He stood up, looming over them, burning with a fierce intensity. "I agree, Master Harrow. The time for theatrics is at an end." He regarded them both with an imperious stare. "Miss Banz. I know you didn't discover this technology. Master Harrow, I know you're working with Darius Adalan."

Lord Thume paused and leaned forward, knuckles pressing into his desk. "And I'll tell you something else I know. Someone—someone I haven't yet identified—is pulling your strings and manipulating you for their own ends. And that's something I cannot abide by."

He edged forward even closer and spoke in a low, dangerous whisper. "Be very careful what you do next. The stakes are higher than you can imagine. I may have allowed Darius to get away with his little stunt, but I will brook no more insolence toward me or my position.

"I trust you understand," he said, "and if you do not, my friends, I will not be held accountable for the outcome."

Lars wanted to respond in kind. He was moments away from telling Thume that he wouldn't be bullied. He had his own resources, and he wasn't afraid to play a dangerous game. But he did not. When the time was right, Thume would know who he was dealing with. Leaving the office with a mock bow, Lars took Liora's trembling hand and led her away.

✧

The walk down the hallway was somber. Liora's usual inquisitive and talkative attitude was muted by the angry pressure of Thume's heavy hand. As they left the building, Neema tried to get their attention once more from the front desk, but the two thieves pretended not to hear as they exited the Gaming Commission. They both breathed a heavy, shaking sigh when the familiar glow and sounds of the city washed over them.

They wandered away from the building, keeping to a track that took them out of the view from Thume's magnificent window. Though neither of them looked back at the building, they knew in their guts that Thume was standing in that window right now, watching their every move, just as he promised.

In time, they passed Tavern Row, reaching the bridges that stretched across the Ithris, leading them toward the city's south end. Though the top of the Gaming Commission building was still visible, Lars knew they were finally safe from prying eyes.

Liora leaped at him, embracing Lars in a crushing hug, all of her tension and fear lending it strength. He patted the back of her head and stayed silent. She needed to come down from the adrenaline rush. It was a feeling he had every time he pulled off a tricky heist.

Liora pulled back and turned her eyes to Lars. He saw the energy in her look, a determination he was used to seeing when she was deep in experimentation. And in fact, the air around them crackled like dynamo from tension. "Lars," she said, but faltered as the implications of her thoughts worked their way to her mouth.

But then, as he knew it would, the dam burst. Those thoughts tumbled out in a rush.

"That gold-eyed, high and mighty, hells-damned, thieving scheming lying rotten bastard! Who does he think he is, sitting up in his office like some smug, all-knowing tyrant, manipulating everyone like we're all just his little pawns in his game? He thinks he's untouchable with all his money and power, but I see through him, Lars, I see through him!"

Liora was shaking now, but not with fear. It was fury, pure and blinding, that fueled her every word. She paced back and forth, scowling with fists clenched. Her glasses slipped down her nose. Liora didn't even notice it in her rant.

"He had Switcher murdered! I know it. And the attack on me? That was him, Lars. Right? That manipulative two-bit crook's son of a rust stain has been pulling strings and thinks he can control everything—control us! Well, I've got news for him: I'm not a puppet he can play with. I'm the best damn dynamo engineer in the city and smarter than that crystal-licking sleezeball whatty-what will *ever* be. He thinks he can tell us what to do? Really? *REALLY*?"

Her chest heaved as she spun to face Lars. He had the good sense to remain silent.

"He's so full of himself, so sure that nothing can touch him. But I swear, Lars, he won't get away with it. Not after what he's done. I don't care what it takes, but we're bringing him down. You hear me? We're bringing that scumbucket *down*."

Lars watched her face and the stormclouds of righteous anger that mirrored his own feelings. Although, he had a better handle on expressing them at this moment. He'd never seen her like this. Her usual playful energy was replaced by a cold, focused rage. But beneath the anger, he saw something else: resolve. This was it for her. Liora Banz had finally had enough.

"You're right, Liora. Maybe he didn't stab Switcher—or shoot you—on his own, but he had to be pulling the strings."

"Exactly!" Liora nodded vigorously. "I'm sure of it."

Lars might not have trusted Vivienne, but she was right. They needed to see the breadth of what Thume was hiding. It seemed that the Azoria Research Institute was the best place to start.

THE INSTITUTE

12

The Azoria Research Institute sprawled across the city's southern district, a powerhouse of ambition and innovation that fueled the dynamo revolution. Its imposing facade of smooth stone and gleaming brass, surrounded by lush and meticulous gardens, stood in stark contrast to the surrounding neighborhoods. The Institute was a haven for intellectual pursuit amidst the city's commerce, not to mention its shadowy underbelly.

It was midday, and the sun shone across the manicured lawns and the wide cobbled plaza that fronted a grand entrance. Students, businesspeople, and workers from various industries hurried to and fro, their arms laden with books and blueprints. Researchers, deep in conversation, their voices buzzing with theories and equations, strode across the plaza, utilitarian tunics and robes billowing in the breeze. Carriages, emblazoned with the crests of wealthy patrons and prestigious guilds, pulled up to the curb and disgorged their well-to-do occupants.

It was a scene of frenzied, random movement and confusion—just the perfect cover for a well-orchestrated infiltration.

At the main entrance, two imposing figures stood guard clad in the crisp blue uniforms of the Institute's security force. Jax, his eyes sharp and alert, scanned the faces that passed through the arched gateway, checking credentials and waving people through. Beside him, Rurik, the short but brawny bruiser from Darius's crew, maintained a stoic silence as he stopped people to poke through their satchels and bags.

"Morning, gentlemen," a voice called out behind them. "Busy day, eh?"

Jax turned, a smile spreading across his face as he recognized the speaker from Inora's descriptions—a senior guard named Harlin.

"Always busy, Harlin. Academics don't sleep from what I can tell."

Harlin looked Jax up and down as if he wanted to say something, but the entrance was getting backed up. Giving the thief a quick salute, the senior guard turned and strode back inside. The flow of traffic continued.

Out of the corner of his eye, Jax saw Rurik nod toward the crowd. His gaze fixed on a group of people approaching the entrance. Their faces were animated with conversation, arms burdened with books and scrolls.

Amidst the group, Liora, disguised as a foundry apprentice, rushed along with the flow of students. Though a bit warm for the unseasonably mild autumn day, a canvas jumpsuit and sloop helmet provided the perfect cover for her well-known face. She adjusted the wide goggles she wore over her normal round spectacles, all the while fidgeting with the dials of a pressure gauge clipped to her belt. It was a prop she'd chosen to enhance her disguise.

Don't panic, she thought, heart pounding against her ribs. *You're just another cog in the machine.* A thief though she might be, she was used to spending her time on the outside looking in, ready to lend support with comms, gear, and dynamo pizazz. Today that was Maren's job, and Darius's engineer was behind the building with Keer, preparing the way for their escape.

She glanced at Jax, catching his eye for a fleeting moment. He gave her a subtle nod, a reassuring gesture that calmed the nervous flutter in her stomach.

She returned the nod, a mischievous spark flickering in her amber eyes. Stepping through the gateway, her boots echoing on the polished floor, Liora disappeared into the heavy crowds within the Institute's grand hall.

Across the plaza, a sleek carriage, its polished oak gleaming in the sunlight, pulled up to the curb. The driver, clad in livery of crimson and gold, hopped down and opened the door with a flourish. In the guise of a wealthy investor, Lars Harrow stepped out and adjusted his impeccable suit. His false mustache and beard lent him an air of distinguished authority.

The driver gave him a formal bow. "I hope you have a profitable visit, sir. Shall I wait for you?"

"No need," Lars said dismissively. "I have a feeling this meeting could take some time."

He handed the driver a generous tip, then turned toward the Institute's entrance. Sharp eyes swept over the throng of students, teachers, researchers, foundry workers, and patrons.

This wasn't his usual playground, this haven of knowledge and scientific pursuit. He was more comfortable in obscurity. Navigating the city's rooftops, fingers dancing across lock tumblers, his steps as silent as a whisper on the wind. But today, he was a man of wealth, a benefactor of progress. One with deep pockets and insatiable ambition.

As he approached the entrance, his confident stride drew the attention of the makeshift guards.

"Good afternoon, gentlemen," Lars said with a pompous air. "I'm here to see Professor Elmsworth. I believe he's expecting me."

Jax, never one to miss an opportunity for theatrics, straightened to his full height. His chest puffed out beneath his crisp uniform. "Professor Elmsworth, sir? And you are...?"

Lars met his gaze with an amused look of his own. "A very interested investor." He waggled his jeweled fingers. "The kind with a keen appreciation for groundbreaking discoveries. And the kind you let through the door."

"I'm sure the professor will be delighted to meet you, sir," Jax said, stepping aside with a nod. Several researchers nearby crowded close, also delighted to meet the wealthy benefactor.

Lars smiled and winked at Jax. "I do hope so."

He snapped his fingers, and a man and a woman who followed close behind hurried through the front entrance to stand at his side. Silas and Trin were dressed in professional yet modest business attire, flanking Lars as he entered the building.

Darius would be along shortly. For now, the plan was a go. Lars continued through the grand hall and toward the main hub of the academic center. From time to time he would stop to answer excited questions about the projects he was investing in, as his two associates tried to hurry him along.

Lars, flanked by his retinue, continued his steady advance toward the large double doors marked '*Offices*,' his every gesture and word crafted to maintain his persona as a wealthy, albeit impatient, investor. He fielded questions from eager researchers with a practiced ease, his responses a blend of vague promises and perceptible disinterest.

"I'm sure your work is fascinating, Professor," he said to a man with wild hair and ink-stained fingers trying to explain the intricacies of a new dynamo-powered facial hair trimmer. "But I'm more interested in projects with global implications. Excuse me." He steered his entourage toward the double doors.

Liora, meanwhile, approached the doors from a different angle. She'd planned to pose as an emergency repair worker, summoned to fix a malfunctioning dynamo conduit. Yet as she reached the doors, a uniformed guard stepped in front of her, hand resting on the handle of a small wooden club.

"Hold it right there," he huffed. "Where do you think you're going?"

A stern-faced woman in a severe gray dress, her hair pulled back in a tight bun, materialized beside the guard. "Foundry workers are not permitted in the Offices wing. The workshops are in the west wing."

"But I'm here to fix a busted dynamo conduit," Liora said, gesturing toward the doors. "The facilities manager called for an emergency repair."

"The facilities manager would have notified security if he did such a thing. And we haven't received any such notification."

He stepped closer, eyes sweeping over her. "Remove your helmet and goggles," he said. "I need to see your identification."

Liora's mind raced. She was trapped. She glanced around, searching for a distraction, but couldn't see any way out of this one. Her first time running point, she thought, and she blew it before it even began.

"What's the hold up here?" a voice shouted impatiently from behind her. Lars pushed his way through the gathering crowd, Silas and Trin flanking him. "I have a meeting with Professor Elmsworth, and I'm already running late."

"Sir," the guard said, turning to face Lars, noting his fine clothing and professional demeanor but caught in the middle of a growing crisis. "I'm dealing with a situation here. You'll have to wait your turn."

He turned back to Liora, reaching for her helmet.

"No need for that," Lars said, stepping forward, gaze fixed on the guard with intensity. "This is Miss Garockolis, my chief of labor. She's accompanying me to the meeting."

The administrator raised her eyebrows in disbelief as she stepped closer. "Wait. I thought you said you were here to fix a broken conduit."

She motioned to the guard to block entry to everyone and turned toward a large communicator set into the wall.

Just then, Darius's voice rose from the center of the grand hall, shattering the tense moment.

"Behold! The future of transportation!" he shouted. His words echoed through the vast space, drawing gasps of astonishment and murmurs of confusion. Eager passerby started milling over toward Darius.

He stood amidst the growing crowd, with wild, frazzled hair illuminated by the glow of a dozen dynamo lamps that he'd somehow managed to commandeer. Inora stood beside him with a blank, unamused look. She held a tangle of wires and gears that sparked and sputtered with alarming irregularity.

"The Aerodynamanautical Personal Leisure Flyer!" Darius shouted in a theatrical crescendo. "A marvel of engineering that will conquer the skies! Imagine, gentlemen, ladies, a world where we soar above the clouds, where distance is but a whisper, where the very heavens are within our grasp!"

He gestured toward the tangled mess of dynamo equipment, eyes gleaming with a manic intensity that was both captivating and unsettling.

"Man's a genius isn't he?" Inora yelled to a group of wide-eyed students who were getting too close. "Professor Herminorff is a true visionary. Ahead of his time, and looking for more assistants."

The younger students began to surge forward, eager to make his acquaintance. Inora stuck her foot out, tripping one of the students just as he passed another group of researchers. The chagrined student jumped up from the floor and spun, shoving another student back. Soon enough, a full-blown scuffle was taking place just outside Darius and Inora's perimeter.

The commotion drew the guard's attention. He turned to the administrator. "Stay here. I'll go see what that lunatic is up to."

He hurried toward the sound of Darius's booming pronouncements. Trin took the opportunity to lift the keyring from his belt as he passed. Her movements were as swift and precise as a striking viper.

The administrator, wide eyes flickering between the group in front of her and the commotion in the hall, reached out her arm to grab the wall communicator once more.

But she was interrupted by a huge guard who ran up, shouting, "Miss! Come quick!"

This was all too much. The administrator turned toward the running guard just in time for him to misjudge the distance and knock into her. She twisted as she fell, and before she knew it, she was flat on the ground.

Jax bent over her with worry as she lay there, shaking her and shouting, "*ARE YOU OKAY?*" His large frame, the shaking, and the increasing commotion blocked her view.

Taking the key she slipped off the guard, Trin unlocked one of the doors to the office wing and she, Liora, Lars, and Silas sped inside. Just as the door was about to close, Darius squeezed through as well, the wig of wild gray hairs removed and a giant grin on his face.

"Thought you could leave me behind, eh, Harrow?" he winked.

The group raced down the quiet but well-lit hallway until they found a turn-off. Silas peered around the corner to make sure it was clear, and the victorious gang filed into the side hall.

✧

Lars pressed his back against the cool stone wall, heart pounding a frantic rhythm against his ribs. He heard the distinct echo of approaching footsteps from around another corner, sending a jolt of adrenaline through him. He motioned to the others urgently, gesturing toward a nearby office door that stood ajar.

Silas, ever the pragmatist, was the first to react, slipping through the doorway with a practiced ease. Lars and Darius went next, and then Trin followed, eyes scanning the room for potential threats even as she urged Liora through the door.

Liora hesitated for a moment, breath catching in her throat, and then stumbled inside. She bumped loudly into Silas. Her heavy boots thudded on the wooden floor.

"Quiet, Liora," Lars hissed. He pulled her further into the room and shut the door, twisting the lock.

The footsteps outside grew louder, closer, a rhythmic thud of heavy boots on stone. The doorknob rattled, a testing twist. Lars held his breath, muscles tensed.

But the footsteps continued past, fading into the distance, leaving behind a silence almost as unsettling as the sound that had preceded it.

Lars let out a slow, steady breath, releasing the tension in his chest. He pulled out Shelle's map, tracing the intricate lines, searching for their current location.

He pointed to a spot marked '*Stairwell – Levels 1-5*.' "We're here. But this wing is a maze, and we could spend hours searching for that damned lab."

Glancing at Liora, he raised his eyebrows. She nodded, understanding his unspoken concern. It was time to call in their tenuous ally.

Liora retrieved a squawk from her satchel, copper wires trailing behind her as she crossed the room to a wall terminal.

She plugged the connector into the terminal and gave Lars a thumbs up.

"Vivienne," Lars said into the squawk. "We're in position. Now what?"

"Well done, gentlemen." Vivienne's acknowledgment came through the squawk in her smooth, seductive tone. "And ladies, of course. I'm impressed. You've gotten there quite quickly."

"Cut the compliments, Vivienne. We're on a tight schedule. Where's the lab?"

Vivienne chuckled. Through the squawk, the tinny sound was almost sinister. "Impatient, as always, Master Harrow. But I understand. Time is of the essence."

Her voice shifted, taking on a more direct tone. "Liora. Once you get into the staircase, take the dynamo lens and focus it on the blank metal wall opposite the stairs. There's a hidden sensor there which the lens should reveal. A little jolt of energy from any dynamo source will activate it."

Lars disconnected the squawk and the team ran from the office to the staircase. Despite her immense anxiety—and scientific curiosity—Liora did as she was told. She pulled out the dynamo lens, turning the little knobs until it focused a beam on the metal wall.

The lines of light emanating from the device swirled and pulsed, then converged on a single point, a faint outline shimmering on one spot in the top right corner of the metal sheet. She pressed a button on the lens. A surge of energy, drawn from the crystal charge at its heart, coursed through the device and flowed into the hidden sensor.

A low hum vibrated through the wall, and the metal of the wall slid aside, revealing a narrow doorway. A set of stairs, spiraling into darkness, beckoned from beyond.

Darius was impressed. He let out a low whistle. "Well, that's convenient."

Lars exchanged a look with Trin. This was it. It had to be.

They descended the stairs one by one, the metal steps clanging beneath their boots. As the last member of the crew stepped through the doorway, the wall panel slid shut behind them, sealing them within the hidden depths of the Institute.

The metal stairs spiraled downwards, the air growing cooler and damper with each step. A rhythmic pulsing thump filled the air, and a whirring of unknown machinery sent a prickle of unease down Liora's spine. The flickering glow of a single dynamo lamp, mounted high on the wall, cast distorted shadows that danced and twisted as they descended.

They reached the bottom of the stairs. Lars took a deep breath and pushed open a metal door. The air inside was stagnant, heavy with the scent of oil, ozone, and a faint, acrid tang that Liora recognized as the residue of high-voltage dynamo experiments.

The room was vast, its high ceilings lost in darkness. Walls were lined with workbenches, shelves, and cabinets, which were in turn overflowing with tools. Strange contraptions—hinting at the cutting edge of dynamo technology—glimmered and whirred.

Dynamo lamps cast a stark, cold light that illuminated multiple sections of the lab. Each one was separated by heavy velvet curtains hanging from brass rails on the ceiling.

"Let's see what we've got," Lars said. He stepped toward the first section of the lab, with his companions close behind.

Their breaths caught in their throats as they took in the enigmatic scene.

A sign, its letters crafted from polished brass, hung above the workbench: *Riflery*.

On the surface of the workbench, a collection of gleaming metal objects lay arranged with a meticulous precision that chilled Liora to the bone. They looked like miniature cannons one could hold in their hand, with smooth wooden grips and barrels glistening with a dark, oily sheen.

Rested beside these were larger versions, with long wooden stocks polished to a high gloss and barrels as long as Lars's arm. Piles of small, lead balls—the kind that had come close to killing Liora—glinted under the harsh light of the dynamo lamps.

"So this is Thume's new toy," Darius picked up one of the pistols and hefted it in his hand, tracing its sleek lines. He was clearly impressed by the lethal elegance of its design. "A weapon that uses neither crossbow bolts nor dynamo charges. Intriguing. And very efficient."

Liora stared at the lead balls. Her stomach churned with a wave of nausea. She could still feel the impact of that projectile, the searing pain, the dizzying terror as she'd plunged toward the unforgiving cobblestones below.

"Yeah... efficient." she whispered.

Lars placed a reassuring hand on her shoulder. "Easy, Liora. We're safe here. For now."

He turned to Darius, features hardening. "That's not a toy, Darius. This is what Thume is using to ensure his own power. He's willing to kill to get it."

"Don't dismiss those with intellect and vision, Harrow," Darius said. His eyes were fixed on the disassembled muskets with obvious admiration. "Thume's a visionary. He understands that technology is power. I'd venture to say that this is just the beginning."

He gestured toward the second section of the lab, its curtain pulled back to reveal a scene that made Liora's breath catch in her throat.

A workbench, its surface dominated by a massive dynamo generator, hummed with pent-up energy. Thick cables, their copper wires gleaming, snaked out from the generator. They connected to a series of crystal charges that pulsed with a vibrant, almost hypnotic glow.

Two of the crystals were larger than any Liora had ever seen before, their facets casting rainbows of light across the lab as they drank in the dynamo current. The internal energy they were building was remarkable, a storage of power waiting to be unleashed.

"Holy hell…" Silas said, eyes wide with awe. "Look at the size of those crystals! They're bigger than my head!"

"Crystal charges," Lars corrected, staring at the pulsing crystals. He could barely process the implications. "So Thume did know about them—and he's been hoarding them for himself after all. But why?"

"And what's he using them for?" Trin asked.

Liora stepped closer to the workbench, giddy with fascination. "Well, I can tell you one thing, at least." She pointed to a familiar-looking device that rested beside the dynamo generator, its silver casing gleaming under the harsh light of the lamps. "Looks like there's more than one of these."

Lars and Trin followed her gaze, their eyes widening in recognition. Another dynamo lens rested on the workbench, identical to the one Liora had been using. A crystal charge, pulsing with the same soft glow, sat at its core.

They moved to the third section of the lab, the air growing heavier with ozone and a tangible hum of energy that vibrated through the floor and into their bones. A small, detailed model of Azoria dominated the center of the space. Its streets, buildings, and landmarks were rendered in meticulous detail. A network of wires and cables, representing the city's vast dynamo grid, spanned the model.

Yet what intrigued the group the most—and seemed wildly out of place—was a pair of large copper prongs that jutted out from the northern edge of the model, pointing toward the wall.

"What the hell is this? I mean, I know it's Azoria, but..." Darius questioned, staring at the model quizzically.

Liora stepped closer, eyes widening as she examined the model. Her engineer's mind traced the flow of energy, the intricate connections, the subtle imbalances.

"It's a schematic," she said, almost inaudible above the hum of the dynamo conduits. "A detailed model of Azoria's grid." She got even closer, eyes level with the top of the model. "Look! There's our place, Lars. And the marketplace, my favorite copper foundry, and ooh! The building I got shot on!"

Her eyes followed the model to the northernmost end. "But the two big copper tubes up here..." She trailed off, continuing to trace the grid flows in her mind.

Lars crossed his arms, tapping his finger impatiently. They had to finish their reconnaissance soon. It wouldn't do to stick around until a gaggle of researchers came in.

Liora snapped her fingers. "That's gotta be it. They're dynamo outflows. Like a siphon. They're designed to pull dynamo from the city."

"But this is just a model, right?" Trin said.

Liora scratched her chin. "Yes..." She thought about it before responding. "So of course it's not doing any siphoning here. But—"

"But if these outflows exist in the real city," Lars said, "what would they be there for?"

Darius laughed, the sound harsh in the quiet room. All eyes opened wide in alarm and turned his way. "Sorry. But it all makes sense now."

"What does?"

"Think about it. We're here to see what Thume is up to so we'll take Vivienne up on her ultimate request, Lars. She wants us to break into Thume's secret warehouse, remember?"

"Yes, of course, but—"

"And where is Thume's secret warehouse?"

"No one knows—" Lars said, but with sudden comprehension he reconsidered. "In the north. She said it's known to very few and hidden in the north."

Liora smiled an impish grin, excited at the turn of events. "And we happen to have a tool that can trace that flow of dynamo from the city if these pipes are what I think they are."

"Let's move," Darius said. "We've seen enough for one night."

They exchanged glances, a silent agreement passing between them.

Silas stepped toward the staircase. "You coming, Liora?" he asked, glancing back at the engineer, who was still mesmerized by the model of Azoria.

"Just a bit longer." Her eyes traced the intricate network of wires and cables. "This is just too fascinating. The sheer scale of it! The precision! It's like a work of art."

Lars waved his hand impatiently, beckoning to her with urgency. "Right now, we need to get the hell out of this lab. Before someone decides to check on their pet projects."

Liora nodded and sighed, tearing her attention away from the model. She followed the others out of the lab and back up the way they came.

They climbed the metal stairs, their footsteps echoing in the silent stairwell, the oppressive weight of the secrets they'd uncovered pressing down on them. As they reached the top of the stairs, Trin checked the facade of the hidden door to ensure it was secure and then cleaned away any traces of their passage.

Back in the hallway, they raced along with as much discretion as they could, following Shelle's map toward the designated exit. The air was quiet now, the frenzied activity of midday replaced by a hushed stillness that amplified the sound of their own breaths, the thud of their hearts beating against their ribs.

Reaching a door marked '*Exit Only*' near the very back of the wing, Silas tested it and looked outside cautiously.

"This is it," he whispered, glancing at the others.

Lars nodded, looking over the deserted hallway, a flicker of unease painted on his face. He couldn't shake the feeling that something troublesome was waiting for them.

"Where to now?" Trin said.

Lars itched the back of his neck, eyes darting at the door. "Back to the tavern. It's time to regroup with the rest of the crew, compare notes, figure out our next move."

He pushed the door open, and they stepped out into the blinding sunlight of a narrow alleyway. The cool air was a welcome contrast to the stifling atmosphere of the Institute's hidden depths.

But any measure of comfort faded as Lars saw what blocked their path.

Aric Myrim stood rigidly, flanked by four uniformed guardsmen and two twitchy figures whose faces were obscured by the brims of their hats. Jax, Rurik, Keer, Maren, and Inora were bound and gagged, their wrists secured to a thick metal pole, faces pale and drawn with anger.

Myrim gave a grim smile as he met Lars's eyes. "Well, Harrow and Adalan." He laughed, and Lars couldn't help but feel like it sounded a little manic. "It seems the game is over for both of you. Nowhere left to run."

"Captain Myrim. I'm guessing Thume sent you?" Lars said, cursing inside.

Myrim's smile widened. "Thume? No. I'm afraid you continue to underestimate me, Harrow. I've learned a few new tricks and added a few new connections. It seems my timing was impeccable."

Lars felt a surge of despair. He glanced at Darius, who stood in shock, albeit with a hint of grudging admiration flickering in his eyes. Lars knew Darius well enough to recognize his appreciation for a well-executed strategy, even when it worked against them.

"Alright, Myrim. You've won this round. What's next?"

"This round?" The captain chuckled again. "You just robbed a public institution. You'll be lucky if you see sunlight again, let alone another round."

Now it was Lars's turn to laugh. "Robbed? Myrim, buddy, we didn't steal anything."

Captain Myrim rolled his eyes and snorted. "Right. Of course you didn't. We're going back to my office." His gaze swept over the captured crew, his features hard and unforgiving.

He signaled to his men, and they moved forward, flanking the thieves, hands resting on their weapons. The rest of the crew was unshackled from the pole, and they began walking with Myrim at the lead and the two unknown enforcers at the rear.

Lars's unease grew as they marched through the maze of streets and alleyways. Myrim wasn't taking them to the city watch precinct. He was leading them deeper into the city's underbelly in the eastern slums, toward an area that was as unfamiliar as it was unsettling.

They arrived at a nondescript warehouse, its brick facade grimy with soot and grime, windows boarded up. It was a desolate outpost in this forgotten corner of the city.

Lars glanced at Myrim, noticing a self-satisfied smirk playing on the captain's lips. He wondered how the captain had managed to orchestrate this ambush. How did he know where they'd be? Had someone tipped him off? The thought unsettled him—someone within their circle might have betrayed them. Could it have been Vivienne? No, that made no sense. None of this made any sense.

"Where are we?" Lars said.

Myrim smiled coldly. "You'll see soon enough. My plans required a more spacious facility. For interrogations and long-term guests. If I have my way, many more of your kind will be joining you soon."

"Interrogations?" Liora said, eyes alight with nervous energy. "But we didn't do anything wrong! We didn't steal anything! We were just... looking around."

Myrim stopped, turning to face her. "Looking around, Miss Banz?" he echoed mockingly. "In a restricted area of the Azoria Research Institute? Without authorization? Don't insult my intelligence."

"It's not like you have much to insult, is it, Myrim?" Darius said. That earned him a glare from both Lars and Myrim. The damned man couldn't resist stirring up trouble.

"Silence!" one of the unknown guards barked. His hand darted toward the weapon concealed beneath his coat.

"Easy, Kato," Myrim said with an icy calm, but his posture made it clear he would brook no insolence. He turned back to Liora. "I assure you, Miss Banz, there will be plenty of time for explanations once we're settled in."

He gestured toward the warehouse doors while glaring with disdain at the assembled crew. "This way."

As they filed into the warehouse, the heavy doors clanging shut behind them, Lars noticed Inora exchanging a worried glance with Trin. He could see the unease spreading among his crew. Something wasn't right. This wasn't just about a routine arrest. There was a ruthlessness to Myrim's actions, an almost maniacal coldness that hinted at something far more sinister.

Inora whispered to Trin behind him as they followed the others through the dim warehouse. "What do you make of this?" Inora asked.

Trin shrugged, eyes darting around the space as she took in the bare concrete walls, scattered tools, and the faint scent of oil and metal that clung to the air. "I don't know. But I don't feel good about it at all."

"I said silence!" the man Kato yelled, opening his hand as if ready to strike Trin.

Any semblance of cooperation from Lars and the two crews disappeared as the situation exploded. "Keep your goddamn hands off her!" Lars roared, lunging toward Kato. His composure shattered as a wave of fury washed over him.

The rest of the crew erupted into a chorus of shouts and threats. Jax strained against his bonds, bellowing for the guards to release them, while Rurik added his own gruff curses to the cacophony. Lars caught sight of Keer, whose sharp gaze darted around the room, likely searching for an escape route.

Myrim's face flushed crimson, his jaw tightening as he struggled to maintain control. "Kato! What the hells do you think you're doing? We don't threaten our prisoners like that, damn it! Stand down!"

Kato looked at Trin's defiant face, unwavering as she challenged him. He took a step back, eyes dropping to the floor.

Before the situation could escalate further, a new voice, cool and amused, cut through the tension.

"Now, gentlemen," Shelle said in a melodic lilt that was at odds with the raw anger that filled the warehouse. "Must we resort to violence? It's such a messy way to conduct business."

She stepped into the light. Her dark, red-streaked hair was pulled back in its usual loose braid. The short, form-fitting leather jacket she wore shimmered under the harsh glare of the dynamo lamps. Her gaze lingered on Myrim, a sly smile playing on her lips.

"Shelle?" Silas said, the betrayal etched on his face. "What the hell are you doing here?"

Darius echoed his lieutenant's astonishment. "You're working with him?"

Shelle shrugged. "Business is business, boys and girls. And besides," she said, returning her gaze to Myrim, "I rather like the captain. He's got potential."

"Potential my ass," Keer sneered.

"Sorry, I'm not taking requests."

Myrim stepped forward, his earlier amusement replaced by a cold, steely annoyance. He seemed determined not to let anything jeopardize his apparent victory.

"That's enough," he barked, cutting through the lingering echoes of anger and defiance. "It's over. You're all under arrest."

Lars took a step toward Myrim, fists clenching. "Arrest? So far all I've seen is negligence!" He was still shaking with fury.

One of the unknown guards, Kato's twin brother Luko, materialized beside him. His heavy hand rested on Lars's shoulder in warning.

"Arrested for what?" Darius said. "Trespassing? Loitering? Perhaps not turning in our books on time?"

Myrim ignored Darius's taunts. His gaze was fixed on Lars. "You were caught red-handed, Harrow." He started ticking off their supposed crimes on his fingers. "Breaking and entering. Impersonation of a public official. Conspiracy to commit theft. Possession of stolen goods."

"Stolen goods?" Lars said. "Myrim, we didn't steal a damn thing from that glorified schoolhouse—a public schoolhouse, I might add. We were just looking around. Gathering information."

"Right," Myrim said, a sardonic smile twisting his lips. "And I suppose those tools and other interesting little gadgets that my men confiscated from your associates were just for show?"

He waved at a table where the contents of their satchels and pockets lay scattered in what appeared to be a damning display of their illicit activities. A coil of copper wire sat in a disorganized jumble next to a set of lockpicks, a handful of crystals, and a leather pouch containing Maren's handcrafted dynamo tools.

They hadn't searched the rest of the crew yet, but Lars knew they would. He just hoped they could convince the captain that the dynamo lens was already theirs.

"You're grasping at straws, Myrim. We might be thieves, but we do our jobs by the rules. Those tools were for getting into and out of the Institute. For bypassing security unawares. We didn't steal anything. Not a single copper coin."

"I think he might be telling the truth, Aric," Shelle said in a calm, measured tone that belied the tension in the room. She'd watched the confrontation with a detached amusement, glancing continuously between the captured crew and Myrim.

Myrim hesitated, his gaze shifting to Shelle. He glanced at the table of confiscated items, then back at Lars and Darius.

He sighed. "Alright. You want to talk? Fine. Harrow, Adalan, let's have a private conversation."

"Trin comes with me." Lars's tone left no room for argument. "And Silas comes with Darius. No exceptions."

Myrim hesitated again, then nodded. His jaw tightened, but he seemed willing to indulge their request, perhaps believing that he had the upper hand. He gestured to a small room at the back of the space.

"Fine. Shelle will accompany me. This way."

Shelle turned to her men, Kato and Luko. "Boys, you're outside. I don't want you anywhere near the other prisoners. And, Kato? There will be hell to pay for that little outburst of yours."

The man gulped, but they both nodded and shuffled outside. Lars, Trin, Darius, and Silas followed Myrim and Shelle into the back room to make their case.

The small office was cramped, with a single dynamo lamp hanging from the ceiling. Captain Myrim sat behind a battered metal desk, eyes fixed on the four figures seated across from him. Shelle leaned against a wall, arms crossed, with an unreadable expression as she observed the exchange.

Myrim grunted. "Alright, I'm listening. But I'm not promising I'll believe a word you say."

Lars met his glare. "We're not asking you to just believe us, Myrim. We're asking you to listen. To consider the facts—and then to decide for yourself what's true.

"It all started with Remus Switcher," he said, recounting the details. "Remember? You asked me about it at the cafe the day after it happened."

Myrim felt a flicker of irritation but nodded in recognition. The unsolved murder of Switcher had been a thorn in his side, a constant reminder of his department's limitations.

"Liora managed to obtain a piece of crystal from Switcher's lab while the watch was still investigating," Lars continued.

The captain tensed. "Obtain?"

"Perfectly legal, mind you, since she wasn't caught. But listen—it was a crystal unlike anything we'd ever seen. A crystal that could hold a charge."

Myrim's skepticism battled with a growing sense of unease. A crystal that could hold a charge? If true, it could have significant implications.

"We knew this technology had a lot of potential to cause havoc," Lars said, echoing his thoughts. "And the fact that Switcher was murdered for it... well, it made us realize that the stakes were pretty damn high."

Though silent, Myrim's mind was racing. The lack of progress in Switcher's case, Thume's disinterest—it all nagged at him. He'd requested assistance, but his inquiries were brushed aside.

"Liora was experimenting with that crystal and another when she was attacked," Lars went on. "She managed to recharge it using unconventional methods. We've got a working device powered by a similar crystal—a device she calls a dynamo lens. You'll find it on her person today, but it didn't come from the Institute. It was even mentioned in the papers days back."

Myrim listened intently, maintaining a stoic exterior, but internally a flicker of doubt crept in. Could they be telling the truth?

"And you believe Thume is behind all of this?" he asked, trying to mask his apprehension.

"We know he is," Trinelle interjected. "He's hoarding these crystals. He's building weapons. He might even be siphoning dynamo from the city. We saw it all with our own eyes in his secret lab under the Institute."

"A secret lab?" Myrim's eyebrows shot up. His skepticism wavered. "What are you talking about?"

Lars exchanged a look with Darius before continuing. They described their encounter with an unnamed patron and her proposition, the clues that led them to the hidden laboratory beneath the Institute, and the unsettling discoveries they'd made there.

As they spoke, Myrim's mind churned. He'd had his suspicions about Thume—the man's true motives, his manipulative ways. The lack of interest in Switcher's murder, the dismissal of Myrim's concerns—it all pointed to something deeper. Could it be that the thieves were telling the truth while the man he served was the real criminal?

"I know it's hard to believe," Lars said, a hint of bitterness in his voice. "Trusting a thief over the man everyone thinks runs this city."

Myrim shifted in his chair, a muscle twitching in his jaw. The pieces were starting to fit together, and he didn't like the picture they formed. His loyalty to the city had always been unwavering, but now he wondered if he'd been blind.

"I'll tell you this much, Harrow," he said, leaning forward. "I'm going to search every one of your crew. Thoroughly. And I'm sending a team to the Institute to verify your story. If so much as a single copper wire is missing, you'll spend the rest of your lives rotting in the darkest cell I can find."

He paused, studying Lars's face. Despite his defiant words, a morbid curiosity gnawed at him. Shelle leaned forward as well, eyes bright with anticipation.

"But," he added, "if you're telling the truth, if nothing was stolen, and if you can show me this dynamo lens and prove that it does what you claim, then maybe, just maybe, I'll consider your theories."

"This doesn't mean I'll let you off the hook," he amended. "But perhaps we'll have more to talk about."

Lars considered his words, narrowing his eyes. "Fine by me, Captain. But we'd like to see the results of your 'thorough' search first. Then we can talk about that little field trip."

Myrim nodded curtly. "Fair enough."

They all stood and walked out of the room toward the waiting crew. Myrim followed, his thoughts a tumult of skepticism and reluctant consideration. He barked orders to the uniformed guards standing at attention near the office door. "Search them. And I mean completely. Every pocket, every seam, every hidden compartment. If they've got a spare copper washer hidden in their boots, I want to know about it."

The guards moved toward the captured thieves with practiced efficiency. Myrim watched as they frisked each member, their hands methodical, eyes missing nothing. He couldn't help but notice the camaraderie among the thieves—even in captivity, they maintained a sense of unity.

"Careful there, boys," Darius quipped as they searched his pants. "Those are delicate instruments you're handling. Wouldn't want to damage the merchandise."

Myrim ignored the remark, his gaze fixed on the growing pile of confiscated items on a nearby table. He sifted through the tools, wires, and assorted gadgets, his brow furrowing. Nothing seemed out of place. These thieves were known for grand heists, not petty thefts of trinkets.

Then Shelle pulled a small silver device from Liora's pocket, its crystal core pulsing with a faint glow.

"What's this?" Myrim asked, regarding it with renewed suspicion.

"That's the dynamo lens," Liora said, her voice a mix of pride and apprehension. "My dynamo lens. It was in the paper."

"It's what we told you about, Captain," Lars added. "The one powered by a crystal charge."

Myrim studied the device, turning it over in his hands. The intricate workings fascinated him, as did the subtle hum of dynamo energy emanating from it. He glanced at Shelle, who watched the exchange with an intensity matching his own.

"Prove it," he said, handing the device back to Liora. "Show me what it can do."

SHIFTING ALLEGIANCES

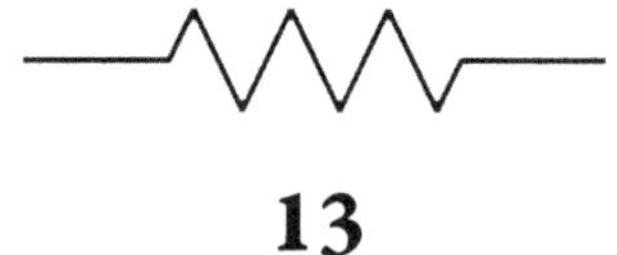

13

The northern edge of Azoria was a stark contrast to the dense city center. Here, the manicured gardens and opulent townhouses gave way to a rugged landscape of scrubland, the air scented with fragrances of cypress and salt spray. The city's border was marked with crumbled bits of granite wall, reminiscent of a time before the fires of industry were lit, when business replaced warfare, and Azoria was just another well-defended port city.

Beyond the wall, the coastline stretched northwards, a jagged expanse of cliffs and rocky beaches battered by the relentless waves of the Azure Sea. A lone lighthouse, its silhouette stark against the twilight sky, stood sentinel on a windswept promontory. Its dynamo lamp cast a lonely beam across the churning waters.

The group huddled near a break in the wall, the gateway leading to a winding gravel road that snaked its way through the scrublands. Captain Myrim stood near a break in the crumbling granite wall, scanning the desolate landscape.

"You assured me this was the right place, Harrow," he said, his posture stiff with both anticipation and unease. "Let's not waste any time."

"Patience, Captain," Lars said. "Let the experts do their work. I'm sure you can afford a few moments to ensure we can find what we claim."

Myrim grunted. His gaze returned to the bleak landscape.

Before they'd left the warehouse, he'd dispatched Kato and Luko to the Institute to verify with the administrative staff that nothing was stolen. Myrim had also warned Shelle's operatives that once they were done, they were to stay the hell away from Harrow and Adalan's crews. He regretted Kato's outburst, and the loss of control. He'd be damned if it happened again.

Beside him, Shelle stood silently, her eyes scanning the horizon. Lars, Darius, and the two engineers—Liora and Maren—were gathered around the dynamo lens. Myrim watched them closely, skepticism still gnawing at him. Part of him hoped they were lying—it would make things simpler. But another part feared they were telling the truth.

"Alright, Liora. Show the captain what this thing can do."

Liora adjusted her spectacles, standing tall and ready for scientific excellence. "Let's do it!" She held up the dynamo lens, its silver casing gleaming under the fading light of the setting sun. "This little beauty can see what your eyes can't. It can unravel the city's secrets."

"Enough with the theatrics, Banz," Myrim said. "Just get on with it."

She ignored him, turning toward the north and the remnants of the city wall. Liora rotated the dynamo lens, and its crystal charge pulsed as if searching for something, a hidden current, a whisper of energy amidst the chaos of the city's dynamo grid behind them.

Suddenly, the crystal pulsed brighter, telltale lines of light emanating from the device and converging somewhere in the distance.

"What is it, Liora?" Lars said, his eyes following the direction of the beam.

"It's a strong dynamo signature. I regulated the flow to filter out most of the city buzz. There's a massive concentration of energy. And it's coming from... that direction."

She pointed east, toward a cluster of dilapidated buildings along the city edge that huddled together like shadowy sentinels against the darkening sky.

"Let's take a closer look, shall we, Captain?" Darius said. "Unless you're afraid to find we *might* just be telling the truth."

Myrim hesitated, eyes flickering between the dynamo lens, the distant buildings, and the faces of the thieves. A war of suspicion and curiosity raged within him. He fought to maintain his composure, unwilling to show any sign of uncertainty.

"Lead the way," he said finally. "But if this is a trick—"

"It's no trick, Captain." Liora glared at Myrim with sharp intensity. "It's science. And it's the truth."

She adjusted the settings on the dynamo lens and the crystal pulsed brighter. Its beams stretched toward the east, a beacon guiding them toward their hopeful destination.

As they walked eastward, Myrim remained silent, his mind racing. The air was filled with a blend of different sounds from the city, the sea, and the wind howling over the scrublands. Ahead, the buildings loomed, shadows stretching as the sun dipped lower. He couldn't shake the feeling that he was on the brink of a revelation that could upend everything he believed about the city—and perhaps even about himself.

Maren peered over Liora's shoulder. "Fascinating. The way it amplifies the residual dynamo signature, how it filters out the background noise... it's ingenious, Liora. Brilliant even."

Liora beamed at the soft-spoken engineer. "Thanks, Maren. It took some time to master its tricks—and of course, to get the crystal charged up after it fizzled. I had a good teacher. Lightning, she's a harsh mistress." She giggled. "But she knows a thing or two about dynamo."

Maren's eyebrows damn near shot off his head. "Lightning? You're telling me you got that thing to work with lightning?"

She grinned. "I told you, buddy. Life's not worth living unless you live on the edge. Speaking of which, did you know that the energy output of a single lightning bolt is equivalent to—"

"Liora!" Lars interrupted with a growl. "Enough with the dynamo lectures. Let's focus on the task at hand."

The dynamo girl blew sharply out of her nose in a huff but moved on. The group walked eastward, keeping along the border of the city. To their right, the vibrant glow of dynamo and gas lights, smoke and steam from the markets, and the faint sounds of city nightlife assailed their senses. To their left, there was naught but the breeze blowing in from the sea. And in front of them...

The cluster of buildings that seemed dilapidated before now appeared to be anything but once the dynamo lens shone its light on the structures. As they got closer, the thin rays of light began to spread, dancing across the surface of the buildings. Then they focused on a single thick line of light at a short, squat building between the others.

Maren snorted. "Well that's a sign if ever I've seen one. Might as well have 'come look, we got dynamo' written all over it."

Liora nodded absently, brow still furrowed in thought as they kept moving forward toward the building.

They reached the building, its brick facade blackened with soot and grime and windows boarded up, a silent sentinel guarding its contents. A heavy door, reinforced with iron bars and a heavy padlock, blocked their entrance.

"Looks like someone doesn't want visitors," Myrim said skeptically, eyeballing the building's facade, searching for any weaknesses or entry points.

"Leave that to the pros," Lars said, stepping forward. He pulled out a small, customized set of lockpicks and worked with his legendary ease. As he inserted them into the padlock's intricate mechanism, a series of clicks sounded out, and the padlock fell open. Its hefty shackle clanged against the metal door.

"Always the showman, Harrow," Myrim said with grudging admiration.

They stepped inside, taking in the heady scents of dust, oil, and dynamo machinery. The interior was dim, the only illumination coming from a few flickering dynamo lamps that shone on the bare concrete floor and the rusted metal beams that supported the building's crumbling ceiling.

"Over here," Liora said, voice hushed as she pointed toward a spiral staircase that descended into darkness. "The dynamo signature is strongest down there."

Darius rolled his eyes. "Of course it is." He didn't seem excited about traipsing down into a cellar.

They all followed Liora down the stairs, its metal steps creaking beneath their weight. The air grew colder and damper with each step. At the bottom, they found themselves in a small room, the walls lined with pipes, valves, and gauges that hummed with an urgent energy. A series of large crystals, their facets gleaming in the dim light, were connected to the pipes by massive cables. Their energy pulsed rhythmically as if they were the heart of some monstrous, mechanical beast.

"What is this place?" Shelle whispered, her usual confidence shaken by the unsettling atmosphere.

"It's where Thume's doing it," Liora said with wide eyes. "Tapping into dynamo from the city."

Myrim's heart sank as he took in the scene. The realization hit him like a physical blow. He traced the path of the cables that lined the walls and ceiling, following them to a small alcove in the room's far corner. Two enormous, braided cables snaked out from the wall, disappearing into a large pipe that burrowed into the earth.

"Where do those cables lead?" Myrim demanded.

"North. Very far north, I'm willing to bet."

Liora raised the dynamo lens, aiming it at the huge cables. The scattered lights intensified, then stretched outwards, following the path of the dynamo current as it surged through the cables, disappearing into the darkness of the underground pipe.

"It's going on for miles," Liora said. "The dynamo signature is massive. I've never seen anything like it."

Myrim stared at the glowing of the dynamo lens, jaw clenched as the truth sank in. The thieves had been telling the truth.

A surge of anger and shame welled up inside him. He'd been a fool. He'd marched to Thume's tune, enforced his rules, and hated the city's thieves with a growing passion and intensity. But behind the scenes, Thume was stealing from the city with a blinding ferocity—financially and in dynamo.

All the while, it seemed, with Myrim as his willing pawn.

He glanced at Shelle, noting a similar look of unease on her face. Had she known? Was she also a pawn in this game? The thought made his stomach churn.

Turning back to Lars and Darius, he felt a newfound understanding—and a heavy burden. His duty was to the city, and he'd failed it by blindly following Thume. Despite his disciplined, sometimes cold-hearted efficiency, Myrim knew when it was time to shift his thoughts in a new direction. There was no longer any denying that the time had come.

"I'm going to need to meet this patron of yours," he said.

The old warehouse echoed with a disappointing silence. Myrim paced back and forth, heavy boots rapping against the concrete floor. The captain's mind was a whirlwind of conflicting thoughts. He'd secured this warehouse as a new headquarters, where he could operate outside the constraints of the city watch precinct. A blank slate where he could build his own vision of justice.

He'd imagined rows of cells filled with Azoria's most notorious criminals, interrogation rooms where secrets would be revealed, evidence rooms overflowing with confiscated loot. As for himself, he'd be a new breed of lawman, an arbiter of justice who would restore order to a city teetering on the edge of chaos.

Instead, Myrim found himself standing amidst a group of thieves. His own men were guarding the perimeter, and his plans crumbled around him. The revelations about Thume—the dynamo siphon, the crystal charges, these muskets that could kill with terrifying precision—it was all too much, too overwhelming. And it was impossible to ignore.

He glanced at the assembled crew, their faces alight with defiant apprehension. Lars, Darius, Trin, Silas, Liora, Jax, Keer, Maren, Inora, Rurik—a formidable collection of talent, cunning, and criminal activity. He'd spent his career trying to bring them down, and now they were his only hope to make sense of the world he once knew.

"So who is she?" he asked, eyes fixed on Lars. "This patron of yours. She sent you to the Institute?"

Lars met Myrim's inquisitive gaze, his expression unreadable. Myrim wondered what was going through the thief's mind. Did Lars trust him? Probably not. Trust between a thief and a lawman was a precarious thing. Still, Myrim realized they needed his resources—and perhaps, even if the thieves didn't realize it, they needed his insights as well. At the very least, they all shared a common enemy.

"She's a business associate. Someone who is interested in seeing Thume brought to justice."

Myrim snorted. "Justice? I don't think you know the meaning of the word. She sounds more like someone who wants to take his place."

"Maybe," Lars said. "But her motives aren't our concern. She's given us information. Valuable information—and she's offered us a chance to level the playing field."

Trin burst out in anger. "By using us as unwitting pawns? By putting our lives at risk? By manipulating us repeatedly? Yeah, she's great."

Myrim nodded, understanding in his eyes. He'd seen that kind of manipulation before, witnessed firsthand the seductive allure of power, the way it could twist even the most honorable intentions.

"She's good, I'll give her that," Darius said. "Charming, devious, and she knows how to push our buttons." Myrim noticed Trin's glare aimed at Darius, so intense it seemed it could burn a hole through him. "But she also delivered. She gave Liora the dynamo lens and led us to Thume's secret lab."

Myrim shot an accusing glance at Liora. "*She* gave you the lens. And what about the crystal charge? Did she give you that as well?"

"She did," Liora said. "At least the one I have. The crystal charge powers the dynamo lens, so it can be used without plugging it into the city grid."

Curious, Myrim thought. Anything independent of the grid meant it wasn't dependent on Thume's influence. That would rankle the man.

"To what end? What did she ask for in exchange?"

Darius rolled his eyes and grinned. "Oh, you know, cleaning services, cook a meal for her here and there." Myrim's eyes narrowed at him, but Darius laughed. "What do you think, Captain? She wants us to steal things."

"Us?" Lars raised an eyebrow.

"She came to me too, Lars," Darius said. "Remember that. You're not the only hotshot in town."

It seemed like Lars was going to respond to the taunt. Trin put a warning hand on his arm to silence him, but Inora cut through the mix instead with a raspy laugh. "Get to the point, you asses."

A sultry giggle rang out at Myrim's side. He glanced at Shelle, noting the amusement dancing in her eyes. She seemed to be thoroughly enjoying the exchange, her lips curved in a sly smile.

"Both of you?" Myrim said, glancing from one thief to the other. "She wanted both of you to steal from Thume?"

Darius snorted. "What can I say, Captain? We're the best in the business, and Thume's got something she wants. Badly enough to pay a hefty price."

"What did she offer? What's so valuable in this secret warehouse of his?"

"We don't know."

Myrim's eyebrows shot up. "You don't know? Did you not ask?"

Lars hesitated and glanced at Trin. A silent conversation passed between them.

"She wasn't forthcoming with the all the details," Lars said. "The usual promise of wealth and fame of course." He waved his hand dismissively. "But the real goal is apparently something that will shift the balance of influence in this city."

"And you believe her? You're willing to risk everything on the word of a woman you don't even know?"

"No. At least, we weren't," Trin said, brow furrowed, "until Liora got shot, and we saw Thume's plans at the Institute."

Darius cut in. "We're not risking anything. We've been gathering information. Assessing the situation and deciding whether her proposition is worth the complications."

"Complications?" Myrim shook his head. "You make it sound like a game, Adalan. A game with rules. But there are no rules here, not anymore."

"Perhaps you should be telling that to Thume, Captain, not us," Lars said with a bitterness that Myrim couldn't quite decipher.

The air in the room crackled with a tension like a sputtering dynamo connector. Myrim's eyes locked on Lars. For a moment, the years of rivalry, the countless chases and near-captures, the unspoken rules of their way of life hung between them.

But just then, a soft knock sounded at the warehouse door, a rhythmic pattern that sent a wave of anticipation through the room.

Myrim looked sharply at Lars, eyes narrowed. "Expecting company, Harrow?"

"You're the one that asked for her," Lars said. "Our patron is here."

A wave of apprehension, cold and unsettling, washed over Myrim. He'd faced down hardened criminals, stared into the eyes of murderers, and navigated the treacherous undercurrents of Azoria's underworld. But this... it felt different.

He was about to meet the person who had orchestrated the alliance between Azoria's two most notorious thieves, who set in motion a chain of events that threatened to unravel the very fabric of the city he'd sworn to protect.

What kind of person could wield such power?

The door swung open, and the figure that stepped into the room shattered Myrim's carefully constructed image.

Vivienne stood before them, a vision of elegance and power. She was tall and noble, silver hair shimmering under the dim light of the warehouse lamps, eyes sparkling with a confident amusement. Her crimson gown, its fabric a luxurious blend of silk and velvet, flowed around her like liquid fire.

"My, my," she said with a low, melodious introduction that caressed the air, "the party just keeps growing, doesn't it? First, our esteemed thieves decide to collaborate. Then they invite the captain of the guard to join their impromptu team. The wonders never cease."

She moved toward them with graceful steps, filling the cramped office with an intoxicating blend of perfume and a subtle hint of danger. Lars watched her closely, aware of the effect she had on those around her.

"Gentlemen, ladies," she continued. Vivienne swept her eyes over the assembled group, a knowing smile playing on her ruby lips. "Captain. Shall we dispense with the pleasantries and get down to business?"

She crossed the room and settled into a chair, gown cascading around her like a pool of spilled wine. Lars noticed Myrim's gaze briefly follow her movements before the captain averted his eyes, a flush of discomfort visible on his face. He could relate.

"Let me start, Captain," Vivienne persisted. "You've seen the truth, haven't you? The man you've sworn to serve, the architect of this city's entire system. You've seen that he's the greatest thief of them all."

She paused, expertly allowing the weight of her words sink in. "He hoards wealth, manipulates the law, controls the flow of power, and now—from what Lars tells me—he's tapping into the very lifeblood of Azoria.

"He's not content with playing the game, Captain. He wants to own the whole board. He wants to control it and you."

"And what about the muskets we found?" Liora's tone was sharp with indignation. "Those weren't toys, Myrim. They were weapons. Deadly weapons." She faltered, her expression tightening as if reliving the attack.

"To silence those who get in his way," Vivienne finished for her coldly. "Switcher. Liora. Perhaps even you one day, Captain. Anyone who dares to question his authority. The question is, what are you going to do about it?"

Lars observed Myrim as the captain's jaw tightened, his gaze fixed on the table. It was clear that he was grappling with the implications. Lars wondered what was going through his mind. Had the steadfast captain begun to doubt the very system he upheld?

"What do you propose we do then?" Myrim finally asked. "Even if what you say is true, what can we do to stop him? He's too powerful and far too well-connected."

Vivienne smiled. "That, Captain, is where this whole escapade comes in. We need to expose him. The way forward is to show the city the truth about their beloved Lord Thume."

She paused, gaze lingering on Lars in a subtle challenge. "And I believe my talented Master Harrow knows how to do that."

Trin's eyes narrowed dangerously.

Lars met Vivienne's look with an amused detachment. He knew she was playing to Myrim, using her charm and insistent narrative to draw the captain further into her web. For that matter, she was trying to once again play him against Trin. But he also knew that she wasn't wrong. Thume was a threat, a danger to them all, and they needed to act.

"We've been discussing that, Vivienne," Lars replied. "But even if we accept your assessment of what needs to be done, we're still facing a considerable challenge. He's not going to give up his power easily. He has more resources and influence than we can imagine."

"And let's not forget the muskets," Keer said. "Those weapons are a game-changer. They could escalate the situation beyond our control."

Darius, who had been watching the exchange with uncharacteristic intensity, leaned forward. His eyes gleamed with a dangerous light. "I'm not afraid of a little escalation, Keer. In fact, I rather enjoy a bit of chaos. It's good for business."

"Chaos isn't a solution," Trin said to Darius, but her attention was fixed on Vivienne. "It's a distraction. A way for Thume to tighten his grip on the city. I am sure we can be smarter than that. We need a plan."

"No, Mistress Meridia," Vivienne said wryly, "you only need me."

Trin rolled her eyes and snorted. Vivienne ignored her, eyes on Lars. "The work you've done thus far is admirable, and I feel you've earned my trust at this point.

"Captain Myrim," she said, pausing in her uncomfortable inspection of Lars. "I do not know you. Yet. But you're here, and I'm going to assume that if I'm working with him," she said, nodding at Lars, "then I'm working with you?"

Myrim nodded. "It would seem so."

"Excellent," she said, smiling at Lars. "Well, Lars, my sweet, will you accompany me outside to fetch what I've brought?"

The room fell silent with disbelief and discomfort at Vivienne's boldness. Trin shot an apprehensive look at Lars, and he tried to reassure her with a knowing wink. Her fists clenched, but she nodded back to Lars. Apparently she had decided not to give Vivienne the satisfaction of a reaction.

Vivienne stood and her gown swirled around her. She offered Lars her arm with a seductive smile. "Shall we, Master Harrow?"

Lars looked once again toward Trin. He saw the hurt and suspicion on her face, the unspoken plea for him to stay. But he knew this was a part he had to play, a risk he had to take.

And yet... deep inside, did he also feel some measure of curiosity about the woman herself, the power she wielded, and the allure that drew him in despite his better judgment?

He offered Trin a reassuring smile, a silent promise to explain everything later, and then turned to Vivienne. He did not accept her arm but gestured toward the door with his best showman's flourish. "Lead the way."

As they stepped outside, Vivienne stopped and turned to face Lars, blocking the narrow alleyway with her presence.

"Please, walk with me." She pressed herself against him in a way that felt like dynamo coursing through his veins. She looked at him with wide, pleading eyes, and he felt himself being drawn in, whether he wanted it or not.

She led him down the alleyway, nestled close and conspiratorial. "Tomorrow, I want you to meet me at my estate to discuss the next phase of our plan."

Lars froze but she persisted, fingers brushing against his arm. It was a touch that promised something more than just business. "Alone, Lars. No Trinelle. No Darius. Just you and me."

"Vivienne, you and I both know that's not happening."

"It's not a request, Master Harrow. It's a necessity." She squeezed his arm. "For the mission and our success. You must learn to trust me, Lars."

Her features softened, and she leaned closer. Her lips almost brushed his ear. "I'll be expecting you."

Trust her! How could he, when what she said in one moment defied what she said in the next? Did she think he couldn't pick up on her overt, seductive cues? Or was she that damn confident that he'd follow her blindly...

But he had to, didn't he?

With an enigmatic smile, Vivienne turned and walked toward a waiting wagon. Its cargo was shrouded in heavy canvas tarps. And Lars followed.

Coming to the wagon, Vivienne lifted the edge of the canvas to reveal a cloth bundle and two small crates. "Help me with these, will you, darling? They're a bit heavy."

Lars swallowed hard, forcing himself to regain his composure. He lifted the two crates, their weight substantial, and followed Vivienne back toward the warehouse.

"Remember," Vivienne whispered just as they were entering the door. "Tomorrow."

Lars entered the warehouse first, setting the crates down on a table near the center of the room. Vivienne followed, laying the cloth bundle beside them. Her eyes swept over the assembled group as she flashed a triumphant smile.

The warehouse fell silent, all eyes fixed on the bounty they'd brought inside—except for Trin's, whose eyes were locked on Lars. Myrim leaned forward, brow furrowed, with a sharp and assessing gaze. Darius shifted his weight from one foot to the other, his usual swagger momentarily subdued.

Liora and Maren looked like they were about to explode with excitement. Both wore wide grins, shoulders shimmying back and forth in eager anticipation of what Vivienne would soon reveal.

Trin reached out her hand to Lars, fingers intertwining with his. Lars squeezed her hand in return, settling close. It seemed to reassure her. For that matter, it reassured him as well.

"Well?" Darius said. "Don't keep us in suspense, Vivienne. What have you brought us?"

Vivienne's smile widened, amusement evident in her jade eyes. "A few essentials for our mutual endeavor."

She reached down, untying the rope that secured the bundle. She unwrapped the cloth, revealing two gleaming muskets, their wooden stocks polished to a high gloss and metal barrels gleaming under the harsh light of the warehouse lamps.

"Oh hells," Jax said, eyes widening as he recognized the weapons. "She's got muskets!"

Myrim's jaw tightened. His eyes fixed on the muskets, a mix of fascination and fear evident on his face. Lars hadn't seen the captain react this way before. Myrim glanced at Shelle, a silent question passing between them.

Lars, his stomach churning with a mix of anger and apprehension, picked up one of the heavy muskets. "Where did you get these, Vivienne?"

"I have other resources, my dear, just as I have you. I get what I want when I want it."

She turned toward the crates and unlatched the clasps. "But these," she said, lifting the lids, "are for my dear engineers. Consider it a token of my appreciation for your unique talents."

The crates contained a dazzling array of crystal charges, their facets shimmering under the warehouse lamps. Two of the charges were massive, their pulsing energy casting shifting patterns of light across the room. Nestled beside them were two more dynamo lenses, their silver casings gleaming and crystal cores humming with power.

"Unbelievable," Maren said with wide-eyed awe. "Look at the size of those charges! And the clarity, the purity... it's extraordinary."

Liora, itching to examine the crystals, couldn't contain her excitement. "Where did you find them, Vivienne? These must have come from the deepest mines in Zarakar."

"Perhaps," Vivienne said slyly. "Or perhaps from somewhere closer to home."

She glanced at Myrim, lingering for a moment. "You see, Captain? There are forces in this city that even Lord Thume can't control. Forces that are eager for change."

"Rest assured, my friends," she said to the whole crew. Her eyes flashed with a fierce determination. "I have the resources, the connections, and the will to bring Thume down. With your help and your unique talents, we will succeed. Azoria will be free."

The early morning Azorian air was crisp, the sky a canvas of pale grays and blues, the kind that was sure to herald in a clear autumn day. But within the walls of the old tavern that Lars and crew called their base, a different kind of storm was brewing, a tension that crackled with anticipation.

Lars, Darius, and their crews stood huddled around a map spread out on a table, their faces illuminated by the glow of a dynamo lamp. The map was a meticulous creation from Shelle, depicting the northern reaches of Azoria. It was a vast expanse of scrubland and jagged coastline that stretched toward distant mountains and wildernesses that held unknown dangers.

"You're sure about this, Lars?" Keer said, studying the map intensely. His weathered face was etched with concern. "Heading north? Could be risky... we have no idea what Thume has going on up there."

"It's a necessity, Keer. We need to know what Thume is doing. If possible, what he's planning." He waved a hand at the map. "Hells, we don't even know where the damn warehouse is."

Darius shrugged. "Yet Vivienne says it's the key to taking him down. And who are we to question the wisdom of our benefactor?"

Trin snorted. "I don't trust her either, Darius. She's playing a game of her own, and how she's doing it is quite frankly disgusting."

Lars rubbed his temples, feeling the exhaustion settling on him like a shroud. "We don't have much choice, Trin. We're already too deep in it. At this point, I think we can all agree there's no choice but to see this endeavor through."

They had argued last night after Vivienne left, and the memory of it still lingered in Lars's mind. It was like a dull ache that mirrored the guilt twisting his gut. Accusations flew as freely as the tears did, and the hurt in Trin's eyes was almost too much to bear. He'd tried to explain, to reassure her. He reminded her that their bond, the years they'd spent together, the risks they'd taken, and the trust they'd forged meant more to him than any woman's seduction.

He'd held her close that night, whispering apologies, promises, and reassurances, until the anger had faded, replaced by a fragile understanding, a shared determination to face the coming storm together. He knew it wasn't over yet and that their relationship would be tested further. But for now, he needed her by his side.

He turned to Keer, Rurik, and Maren. The men stood by the window, outfitted for travel. They had what they needed; it was just a matter of dealing with whatever they found out there.

"You're our eyes and ears, gents," Lars said. "Follow the dynamo trail. Find that warehouse and report back. But be careful. Thume is a dangerous man, and he won't hesitate to protect his secrets." He glanced at the muskets on a nearby bench with a collection of ammunition. "As we know."

Liora bustled forward, eyes shining with a feverish excitement. Her arms were laden with a sizable crate of equipment.

"I've packed you a few essentials," she said, setting the crate down with a thud that rattled the table. "Just in case you run into trouble."

Rurik grunted, eyeing the heavy crate skeptically. Keer nodded, though Lars could sense his reluctance. None of them wanted to send their friends into danger, but it was a necessary risk.

Liora stepped closer to Keer. "Sorry to weigh you down with all this gear. But it's important. Trust me on this one. Come on, Maren." She beckoned to Darius's engineer. "Let's go over the instructions."

Keer started to walk away, but she grabbed his arm and pulled him back. "Not so fast. You'll need to check behind him, Keer. Make sure he lays it properly along the way."

With a resigned sigh, Keer followed Liora and Maren out of the room.

A few minutes later, the rumble of a departing carriage echoed through the quiet streets surrounding the tavern. Keer settled into the worn leather seat at the front, taking the reins firmly in his calloused hands. Rurik and Maren climbed into the carriage behind him. The vehicle—a sturdy but unassuming model drawn by a pair of stocky piebald horses—was one of Darius's less conspicuous acquisitions. It was perfect for blending into the flow of traffic and avoiding unwanted attention.

As they left the city center behind and the familiar landmarks of Azoria faded into the distance, Keer felt a chill settle over him that went beyond the crisp autumn breeze. They were venturing into unknown territory, and he knew they would need to be both quick and cautious if things went sideways.

Eyes fixed on the road ahead, Keer felt a familiar knot of nervousness tightening in his stomach. He'd sailed treacherous seas, faced down storms, and navigated the darkest corners of Azoria's underworld. But this journey—a mission into the heart of Thume's territory—felt different.

Beside him, Rurik sat in stoic silence, his stocky frame snug within the confines of the carriage. He scanned the passing landscape, cracking his knuckles—a sound like dry twigs snapping underfoot. Keer glanced at him, appreciating the silent companionship.

Maren perched on the edge of his seat, eyes bright with feverish energy as he adjusted the dials of the dynamo lens. The focus beams were fixed on the massive dynamo flow beneath them, surging from the city. Keer was fairly certain that Maren had never been outside Azoria before; the young engineer's wide-eyed gazes at the passing scenery made that evident.

"Ready for an adventure?" Maren said, a ridiculous grin spreading across his face.

Keer grunted, keeping his eyes on the road as the shadows of the cypress trees lengthened with the sun's slow descent toward the horizon.

"Let's just get there and back in one piece, Maren. That's all the adventure I need."

PART 4

POWER DYNAMICS

14

The city watch archives were a labyrinth of dusty shelves, forgotten records, and the lingering scent of a thousand unsolved cases. Myrim, brow furrowed in concentration, sifted through stacks of reports. His fingers traced the faded ink as he searched for patterns, connections, anything that could shed light on Thume's clandestine activities.

He'd spent the past few days immersing himself in the city's underbelly, utilizing his authority and Shelle's ever-expanding network to gather information. He'd interviewed informants, questioned guild leaders, and even pulled a few strings to gain access to confidential records. The more he learned, the more unsettled he became.

Thume's influence was everywhere, his tendrils reaching into every corner of the city. It seemed as though his control over Azoria and its dynamo infrastructure was absolute.

Myrim had discovered permits for a series of underground construction projects, all authored by Thume himself and all signed by Thume himself. He had found records of unusual shipments arriving at the docks, crates filled with components that even Liora, with her vast knowledge of dynamo technology, couldn't identify.

And he'd uncovered whispers, rumors of government operatives working at all levels within the city. A group loyal only to Thume, their activities hidden beneath layers of bureaucracy and plausible deniability.

He sat at a desk. The surface was worn and scattered with the ink stains of countless investigations. His head throbbed as he spread out the latest reports Shelle had provided. Her network was proving to be invaluable. Various agents in her employ moved through the city's dance, their eyes and ears attuned to the slightest shift in power.

Whereas information on Thume's activities was hard to get to, any intelligence on Vivienne was vague and conflicting. Rumors painted her as a wealthy merchant from Drakoria, a shrewd businesswoman with a talent for negotiation and a knack for getting what she wanted. Others whispered of a darker past, a connection to the criminal underworld, a ruthlessness that belied her elegant facade.

Myrim rubbed his temples. He couldn't shake the feeling that he was caught in a web of intrigue—just another fly struggling to break free before the spider closed in.

He needed to talk to Shelle. He needed her insights, her connections, her... something.

He plugged in a squawk, courtesy of Liora. That girl might be twitchy and excitable but she made some damn fine dynamo gadgets. This new squawk had easy buttons to reach out to Lars, Darius, or Shelle with a simple tap. Who would have thought he'd be reaching out to thieves on a regular enough basis to need such a thing?

He pressed the button that would connect him to his informant. "Shelle, I could use your insight. I'm at the archives if you're free."

"Make it a drink to go with the insight and I'm all yours," Shelle's playful lilt crackled through the squawk.

Less than an hour later, she swept into the archives—a splash of color and energy amidst the dusty silence. She carried a bottle of ruby-red wine and two crystal glasses, their facets catching the light of the overhead lamps.

"I thought we could use a little refreshment," she said, blue eyes twinkling as she set the bottle and glasses on the desk. Her voice and the jangle of her silver bracelets were a delightful change. Myrim had heard nothing for hours but the rustle of papers and the creaking of ancient shelves.

She poured two generous measures of wine, handing one to Myrim, her fingers brushing against his. A warmth spread through him, a pleasant tingle where her skin touched his. He withdrew his hand, trying to maintain a professional demeanor though he couldn't quite suppress his smile.

She took a seat beside him, eyeing the scattered reports. "So, tell me, Captain. What secrets have you unearthed for all your trouble?"

Myrim took a long swallow of wine, savoring the rich, fruity flavor as it warmed his throat, loosening the tension in his chest. "Thume's been busy. Busier than I ever imagined."

He gestured toward the spread of reports and summarized his findings: the construction permits, the unusual shipments, the whispers of a lobbying organization loyal to Thume.

"It's like he's building an empire within an empire," he said with a mixture of disbelief and grudging admiration. "He's got his fingers in everything. And he's covering his tracks with a precision that's... well, it's impressive, to say the least."

"This, coming from mister meticulous." Shelle giggled, and the sound brightened Myrim's mood. "He's always been a master of control, Aric." She swirled the wine in her glass thoughtfully. "But this is different isn't it? It's like he's preparing for something."

"The crystal charges are a part of it. That much is clear," Myrim said, tapping a finger on a report that detailed the rumors swirling through the city. "But what's he planning to do with them? Power a new weapon? He's already got the muskets. Control the city's energy flow? He already does that, doesn't he?

"And then of course there's Vivienne," he added. "What have you learned about her?"

Shelle took a sip of her wine. "Ah, Vivienne. A fascinating woman, isn't she? Beautiful, intelligent, ambitious... and dangerous. Very dangerous."

She leaned closer to Myrim, her perfume a heady blend of spices and exotic flowers, speaking in a low, confidential murmur. "She's not just a wealthy merchant, Aric. She's got connections that reach far beyond Drakoria or Ithris. Political influence. Financial resources and a network of associates who are as loyal as they are ruthless."

Myrim snorted. "I get it. She's a major player. But what's her endgame? What does she want?"

"The same thing all people in power want, Aric. More power. If she's trying to take down Thume, then she wants power over the Gaming Commission. Which gives her power over Azoria and, from there, over Ithris. She's obviously willing to use anyone—thieves, lawmen, even you—to achieve her goals."

She held her hands up, looking Myrim in the eyes. "On this side, we have Vivienne the viper, and she's got her fangs sunk deep into Azoria. Over here, we have Thume, the grand architect of our fair city and patron saint of intrigue." She clapped her hands together. "And in the middle of all this, gangs of thieves and the man who chases them."

Myrim chuckled humorlessly, taking another sip of wine. "So, it seems I've traded one master manipulator for another. Wonderful. And what about me, Shelle? Where do I fit into this game?"

Shelle leaned forward. The cloying perfume she wore filled his nostrils and delighted his senses. "That, my dear Captain," she said, fingers tracing a light path along his arm, sending a shiver down his spine, "is for *you* to decide."

Her words hung in the air, a warning and a temptation. For a moment, Myrim was lost in the intoxicating possibility of choosing a different path, a path that led away from the rigid confines of duty and into a world of shadows and secrets. A world where the rules were fluid, the stakes were high, and the rewards exhilarating.

He pulled back, clearing his throat, forcing himself to regain his composure. "Thume's been playing me for a fool. Using me to maintain his control and enforce his rules while he's been breaking those rules and manipulating the system for his own gain."

He smacked his hand on the table, making the wine glasses clink. "I won't be his pawn any longer," he said.

"Then choose your side, Aric," Shelle urged, eyes fixed on him. "Choose wisely, and you might just find yourself winning."

The soft chiming of her silver bracelets broke Myrim from his dark musings as he met her gaze with a determined look of his own. "I'll choose my own side."

Shelle's smile widened as she leaned toward him once again, speaking in a sultry whisper. "And is that all you choose?"

Myrim felt a slow heat spreading through his chest, a pull he no longer wanted to resist. He didn't answer immediately; instead, he let the silence linger, taking in the soft lines of her face as if for the first time. His eyes wandered over her, savoring every detail—the way her hair fell over her shoulders, the rise and fall of her chest, the way her fingers toyed with the edge of the table.

He stood slowly, pushing his chair back with a deliberate motion. She watched him, expression shifting from sultriness to a burning curiosity. He stepped around the table, closing the distance between them with measured steps as if counting each moment, each heartbeat that brought them closer.

When he reached Shelle, he paused, fingertips pressing against her jaw, tracing the line of her cheek. His touch was firm as he looked deeper into her wide, blue eyes. Shelle didn't move. Her breath caught in her throat, waiting, watching him intently.

Myrim leaned in closer. His lips hovering near hers, their breaths mingling in the small space between them. "No," he answered, "that is not all."

And then he kissed her, his lips moving over hers with the hungry ferocity of suppressed desire. Shelle melted against him, her hands sliding up his chest to his neck, fingers splayed against the warmth of his skin.

He deepened the kiss, hands slipping down her back and clenching the fabric of her soft purple skirt, pulling it up as she leaned back onto the table. The scattered papers of their work crinkled beneath her. But that work, the wine, and their plans were forgotten.

Shelle's hands gripped his shoulders. Her breath came in soft, shallow gasps, as Myrim moved against her, slow and steady, with every touch deliberate and every motion a slow, simmering burn. Their bodies moved together harmoniously, a rhythm that grew with each passing moment. She closed her eyes and tilted her head back. A soft moan escaped her lips as the tension built, a slow, delicious climb toward the peak.

Myrim's hands moved over her with a knowing touch, as if he could read every desire she hadn't yet voiced. He felt a shiver run through her body, an urgency in the way she arched her back as he gripped her backside. He matched her movements with his own, the slow, deliberate strokes becoming faster, more powerful, bringing them ever closer to the edge.

And when the release came, it was like the breaking of a storm, a rush of heat and light that flooded through them, overwhelming and all-consuming. They held onto each other, their breaths mingling. Their bodies trembled with the force of it, savoring every lingering moment of the aftermath.

They stayed like that, clinging to each other, feeling the echoes of their shared passion settling into a quiet calm. Myrim's lips brushed against her forehead, a gentle, lingering kiss as he whispered against her skin, his breath warm and soothing. "Our side."

The Salty Sark, a tavern nestled amongst the warehouses and workshops of Azoria's waterfront district, was a haven for weary dockworkers, thirsty sailors, and those seeking solace in the bottom of a mug. Scents of ale, salt fish, and pipe tobacco settled over Jax like a comforting blanket and set his mouth to water. He pushed open the heavy wooden door, Inora following close behind, thin-lipped with her wide hat pulled low.

The tavern buzzed with a restless energy, a tension that crackled beneath the surface of the usual boisterous laughter and drunken boasts. Jax, sharp eyes scanning the room, sensed a shift in the atmosphere. Where there was once a camaraderie, a shared sense of pride in the city's thriving industry and its unique brand of sanctioned chaos, there was now a current of unease. It was a simmering discontent that ran roughshod through the crowd.

A group of dockworkers huddled around a table, faces grim as they argued over a game of cards, their voices rising with a bitterness that had nothing to do with their losses. At another table, a cluster of foundry workers, their faces grimed with soot and sweat, slumped over their mugs of ale, their conversation a low murmur of complaints and grievances. Even the barmaid—always a source of cheerful banter—was silent as she moved through the tavern with a heavy step. Her tray was laden with half-empty mugs and meager plates of food.

"Something's not right," Inora said in a low rasp as she surveyed the scene.

Jax nodded. "People are worried. They're feeling the pinch."

He gestured toward a table near the back, where a group of men in soot-stained overalls were engaged in a heated debate. "Let's see what those foundry workers are grumbling about."

They made their way through the crowded tavern, the floorboards creaking beneath their boots. As they approached the table, they caught snippets of the conversation, a litany of complaints and anxieties that echoed the growing unrest throughout the city.

Taxes were too high, wages were stagnant, and the prices of necessities, from bread to metal, were rising faster than a belch of steam. The recent influx of copper from the thieves' tributes, once a source of civic pride and a symbol of Azoria's unique system, no longer seemed to be returning to the pockets of the working class.

"Where did all that copper from the Blackwood heist go?" one of the foundry workers said. "A thousand pounds of pure copper, they said. Enough to build a new schoolhouse, to fix those damn leaky conduits in the east end, and maybe even lower our taxes for a year or two. But what did we get? Nothing. Not a single iron chit."

One of his colleagues also chimed in. "Didn't see any from the ship heist either. That Zarakaran bastard's keeping it all for himself." His face was dark with resentment. "Tell me I'm wrong. He's lining his pockets while we're struggling to make ends meet. He's the biggest thief in the city."

Jax and Inora exchanged a look, both of them noting the simmering anger and growing sense of betrayal that permeated the tavern.

Sensing an opportunity, Jax leaned against the edge of the table, his imposing frame drawing the attention of the disgruntled foundry workers. "Rough day, ladies and gents?"

One of the workers, a stocky man with a thick mustache and a scowl etched deep into his face, grunted in response. "Every day's a rough day." He drained his mug of ale with a bitter sigh. "Working our asses off, barely making ends meet, while those fat cats in their fancy carriages get richer by the minute."

"You're telling me," Jax said, shaking his head in sympathy. "Seems like the only ones getting ahead in this city are the thieves and the guilds. The rest of us are just scrambling for scraps."

Inora glanced at Jax and jumped in. They needed to steer the conversation toward their target. "Don't forget the politicians. They're lining their pockets too, all while making speeches about how they can't do anything for us."

"Speaking of politicians," Jax said casually, "what's the word on the street about Lord Thume? Is he doing all he can to help us poor sods? Or is he just causing more problems?"

One of the foundry workers spat on the ground, but another worker cut in.

"Thume's a complicated man," he said hesitantly. "He's done a lot for this city. I mean, he brought order to the streets and made Azoria a beacon of progress, right? But—" He trailed off, eyeing the bar nervously.

"But what?" Jax pressed. "What are people saying?"

The foundry worker hesitated again but answered in a hushed tone. "People say—not me, mind, but other people—they say he's not the man he used to be. They say he's become obsessed with power. And that he don't care about anything else."

Inora peered at the man. "And?"

He was about to respond but must have thought better of it. "And nothing. Ask them folks what said it. I told you it wasn't me."

Silence fell over the table. Jax wanted to push him, but Inora elbowed him in the ribs. He winced and rubbed his side, but got up and tromped out of the tavern.

They walked through the door, and the cool night air was a welcome relief from the stifling heat of the crowded tavern. Inora turned to Jax with a thoughtful glance.

"He stopped talking because he's afraid. Afraid of us."

Jax frowned. "Afraid of us? Why the hells would he be afraid of us?"

"Because he figured us for Thume's enforcers," Inora said. "He thinks we'll report him for speaking ill of the boss."

Jax let out a humorless chuckle. "Thume's enforcers? That's rich. We're the ones he's trying to crush."

He shook his head, a wave of anger washing over him. "That bastard's got the whole city living in fear. Whispering in the dark, afraid to speak their minds. It's not right."

"It's what he wants, Jax. Control through fear. Silence through intimidation. Makes sense to me."

They walked in silence for a moment, footsteps echoing on the cobblestones. The sounds of the city—the rumble of carriages, the distant clang of a foundry bell, the laughter spilling from a nearby tavern—starkly contrasted the quiet unease that had settled between them.

"It's getting worse, isn't it?" Jax said in a low murmur. "This whole situation. It's not just about fortunes and games anymore. It's different. More dangerous."

Inora nodded, her gaze fixed on the shadows that danced beneath flickering gaslamps. "Thume's been shifting the ground beneath us. And we're all caught in the landslide."

She lapsed into deep thought with a frown. Jax thought it best to let her think in silence.

"I'm worried about my crew," she admitted with a raspy whisper.

Jax looked at her, a flicker of understanding in his own eyes. He knew what it meant to be loyal, to protect those you cared about—to face any danger or threat—to keep them safe.

"Me too," he replied with emotion. He thought of Liora with her infectious enthusiasm and brilliant mind. But also with a vulnerability that belied her outer cockiness. He still couldn't shake the memory of that night on the rooftop, the terror in her eyes as she'd plunged toward the unforgiving street, the cold grip of fear that had clutched at his heart.

Inora spoke hesitantly. "Me and my crew, we're not as close as you all seem to be. But that doesn't make me worry about them any less."

"I get what you mean."

"I thought you might," she responded with a wry grin. "Just a big softy under all that muscle, aren't you?" She punched the big man in the shoulder.

Damn, that woman packed a decent punch. It's true, Jax realized. They all had their gifts, and cared in their own way, but he was the protector for all of them. The one who would do anything to ensure they didn't suffer.

Hell, even going to jail. It felt like years since he was in the clink, but that was just months ago. He had marched to the magistrate and turned himself in to cover for Keer. Not because the man asked him to—but because Jax needed to.

"I guess it's the same for Rurik, huh?" he asked.

Inora looked at him and snorted. "Rurik? Why, because he's a big bruiser like you? Naw. He's just in it for the fight. Man of few words and even less emotions."

She let out a sigh. "No, that title falls to me. You'd never know it to look at me, but if any of them—Silas, Maren, Rurik, and... and Darius—were hurting, I'd be the first to fall to despair about it. Or to violence." She looked at Jax sadly, eyes conveying an emotional depth that startled him. "I can't imagine what you went through when your dynamo girl got shot. I felt for you then and I still do now."

"We can't let Thume win," Jax said with bitter determination as he wiped his eyes. "We have to stop him. For our crews and the city, sure. But also for us protectors."

Inora nodded, and a new resolved settled over both of them. They might be from different crews, their loyalties divided and methods often clashing. But at this moment, united by a shared enemy, they were more than just thieves. They were guardians, and the heart and soul of their crews.

Lord Cecil Thume strode through the halls of the Gaming Commission headquarters, footsteps echoing on the polished marble floors. His presence was a wave of authority that parted the sea of clerks and assistants who scurried to and fro. He was a man accustomed to deference, to the subtle bows and hushed whispers that accompanied his every move.

He'd just finished a frustrating meeting with the Council, a contentious debate about allocating resources for the upcoming Dynamo Festival. Those fools, with their petty concerns and their short-sighted ambitions, had no understanding of the larger game. It was a delicate equilibrium of control that he'd spent his life crafting. They bickered over copper coins while the very foundations of their city and their nation were shifting beneath their feet.

He reached his office with its heavy oak door and pushed it open, expecting to find the usual scene: his desk organized, the latest reports stacked in neat piles, a crystal decanter of chilled Zarakaran buuka awaiting his arrival.

Instead, a woman sat in one of the chairs facing his desk, her back to him. Silver hair shimmered under the soft glow of the dynamo lamps, and her posture was both relaxed and commanding. She wore a deep emerald dress that shimmered with a subtle iridescence, its fabric clinging to the curves of her body like a second skin.

"Who are you?" Thume demanded in a low boom that echoed through the spacious room. "And what are you doing in my office?"

The woman turned in a smooth movement, eyes meeting his. A faint smile curved her lips, a gesture that seemed welcoming on the surface but felt unsettling nonetheless.

"So this must be the great Lord Cecil Thume." Her voice was melodic and carried the hint of an accent Thume knew all too well.

"I am," Thume said shortly. "And you are?"

"Vivienne," the woman said, rising from her chair, extending a hand toward him. "A pleasure to meet you, Lord Thume. I've traveled a great distance to be here."

He studied the woman for a moment, lingering on her outstretched hand, weighing her demeanor and boldness. There was something about her that he couldn't quite place. He took her hand in a firm grip that remained cool and impersonal.

She was not welcome here. Not without his invitation or his blessing. And despite her attempts at blatant flattery, Thume felt no hint of desire for her. He had forsaken such feelings years ago.

"And what brings you to Azoria, Mistress... Vivienne? Business or pleasure?"

"It's always both, my lord, as I'm sure it is for you. I'm a merchant, Lord Thume. From Drakoria. I've come to Azoria to explore some magnificent opportunities. I've learned a great deal about your city, its thriving industries and innovative spirit—and of course its unique approach to maintaining order. All, I'm told, by your design."

"I'm flattered," Thume said. He gestured toward the chair she'd vacated. "Please, sit down. Tell me more about these opportunities."

He observed Vivienne as she settled back into the chair, her gaze sweeping over his office. He followed her eyes as they moved from the intricate dynamo models to the maps adorning the walls, and then to the carefully arranged artifacts. Each piece was a reflection of his life—a life meticulously crafted at the intersection of power, wealth, and a cultivated taste for the finer things.

"I'm a woman who appreciates vision, Lord Thume. And I see a great deal of promise in this city. In its people. In its leadership."

Vivienne's eyes met his. "I'd like to learn more about your vision, Lord Thume. About your plans for the future of Azoria. And perhaps," she said slyly, "I might even be able to offer a few insights of my own."

Thume leaned back in his chair, fingers steepled thoughtfully, studying Vivienne with his intense eyes. He let the silence stretch to the point of discomfort, ensuring that he would regain and remain in control of this unexpected conversation.

"Insights?" he echoed. "You intrigue me, Mistress Vivienne. But before we speak about anything, perhaps you could enlighten me on the specific nature of your interest in Azoria. What brings a wealthy merchant from Drakoria to our humble city?"

Vivienne met his gaze, smile unwavering. She leaned forward, resting her elbows on the armrests of the chair, the movement causing the fabric of her emerald gown to shift, offering a view of well-defined collarbones atop the smooth curves of her cleavage.

"Drakoria is a land of fire and passion, Lord Thume. But it's also a land of limitations. Our resources are vast, our people are skilled, but we lack the infrastructure to harness our own potential. We've heard quite a lot about Azoria's progress of late. Specifically regarding your more recent innovations in dynamo technology."

She paused, a calculated warmth lighting up her eyes. "I'm eager to learn, to collaborate, to invest in a future where our two nations can prosper together. I represent a consortium of Drakorian investors. We have significant resources at our disposal—copper, crystals, the finest engineers and craftsmen Drakoria has to offer. We're seeking a chance to be part of Azoria's ascendance.

"We're willing to invest heavily, Lord Thume," she concluded, "and as you are at the center of that ascendance, I have come to you. And only you."

"That was a fine pitch," he said in a bored tone. "One I hear almost every day—and ultimately, nothing more than a pathetic attempt to buy a seat at my table."

Vivienne straightened, sudden annoyance plain on her face, which she quickly masked with a composed smile. "You misunderstand me, Lord Thume. I'm not begging for a place at your table. I'm offering you a partnership. A collaboration of equals, a chance to expand your influence and power far beyond the borders of Azoria."

"A partnership?" Thume sneered at her. What a waste of his time.

"Tell me, what kind of partnership exists between a man who has built an empire and a woman who peddles trinkets from her quaint firepit of a country? You offer me copper, crystals, a few skilled laborers?" He stood up, looming over her. "I have access to the riches of Zarakar, Mistress Vivienne. My influence already stretches across continents. What, pray tell, do I need you for?"

Vivienne rose from her chair, eyes never wavering from his. "You underestimate me, Lord Thume. And you underestimate Drakoria. We are a force of significance with a power waiting to be unleashed. If you're not willing to be part of my vision... well, I'll find others in this city hungry for change. Others who are willing to take what they deserve."

"Change, Mistress Vivienne?" He barked a mirthless, dangerous laugh. "This city is built on change that I allow. On a game that I designed. And you, with your veiled threats and your provincial ambitions, you are no different than any other pawn in my game. A pawn I can sacrifice whenever I want."

He leaned closer. "Let me make one thing clear, Mistress Vivienne. Without my blessing, you will not succeed in this city. You will not secure a single contract, a single partnership, or a single iron shilling. Your influence ends at my doorstep. This meeting is over."

Vivienne met his glare, but her amusement was replaced by a cold, calculating scowl. "I understand, Lord Thume. Perhaps, in time, you'll come to appreciate the value of working with me. But until then..." She made a mock curtsey, lips curled in a sneer. "I wish you continued success in your endeavors."

She turned and walked toward the door, gown swirling around her.

✧

Once she was beyond the sight of Thume's office, Vivienne's smile vanished, replaced by a look of cold satisfaction. She reached into a hidden pocket beneath the folds of her gown and retrieved a small silver device, no larger than a small carafe. It was a marvel of Liora's ingenuity, powered by a tiny crystal charge. Similar to a squawk, but capable of recording sound and storing it within another integrated crystal.

She pressed a button on the device, and Thume's menacing voice filled the air.

"*You are no different than any pawn in my game. A pawn I can sacrifice whenever I want. Let me make one thing clear, Mistress Vivienne,*" Thume's voice went mercilessly on, the device carrying his threatening tone perfectly, "*Without my blessing you will not succeed in this city. You will not secure a single contract, a single partnership, or a single iron shilling. Your influence ends at my doorstep.*"

Vivienne chuckled, a musical sound that echoed in the empty hallway.

"Foolish man," she whispered, tucking the recording device back into her gown.

WICKED GAMES

15

The late afternoon sun shone upon the manicured lawns of Vivienne's estate, painting the vibrant flowers and cascading fountains in beautiful hues of gold and crimson. The air smelled of jasmine and honeysuckle, a cloying sweetness that contrasted with the tension that thrummed beneath Lars's constructed calm.

He stood on the patio, taking a deep breath and looking over the estate's sprawling grounds. The manor house, a masterpiece of Ithrisian architecture, its white marble facade gleaming in the sunlight, rose from the surrounding gardens.

What the hell am I doing here? A wave of doubt washed over him, cold as the autumn sea. He should be back at the tavern with Trin, with his crew, planning their next move, strategizing how to counter Thume's growing threat. But here he was, alone, a guest in the lioness's den. Drawn by a woman whose methods were as dangerous as a wildfire, with motives as elusive as smoke.

He heard the click of heels on the marble floor behind him, and a shiver ran down his spine as Vivienne stepped onto the patio. It was the way she carried herself, Lars decided. Her noble bearing was as intoxicating as Drakorian wine.

She wore black leather pants that hugged her slender curves, accentuating her long legs and the sway of her hips. A deep purple silk blouse, its neckline plunging daringly low, revealed a tantalizing glimpse of her cleavage, a delicate silver and crystal necklace glimmering against her pale skin. Her silver hair was pulled back in a fashionable bun, a few strands escaping to frame her face, jade eyes gleaming with a predatory hunger that made his pulse quicken.

"You came." Vivienne's smile was thrilling, lips painted a deep, luscious red. Her confident and triumphant attitude made Lars shift uncomfortably.

"I always keep my promises, Vivienne." He turned to face her, subconsciously taking in the curves of her body despite his better judgment. He knew she was trying to unsettle him, to draw him into her game, and he couldn't deny a swift rush of heat at the sight of her. He needed to cool down. And to remain impassive.

"Such a gentleman. And so punctual. One might almost think you were excited to come here." She gestured toward a pair of wicker chairs arranged near a low table. "Come, sit with me, Lars. We have much to discuss."

Lars hesitated, then crossed the patio, settling into one of the chairs, careful to maintain a distance between them. He watched as Vivienne poured two glasses of wine, a deep, rich vintage that shimmered like liquid rubies in the fading light.

"Drakorian wine," she said, handing Lars a glass, fingers brushing against his. "A taste of home. I thought you might appreciate it."

He took the glass, swirling the wine, inhaling its intoxicating aroma, but he didn't drink. His mind was sharp and alert, senses attuned to her every move subtle shift in expression.

She raised her glass in a toast. Her dazzling eyes met his over the rim. "To new beginnings."

"To new beginnings," he echoed, taking a sip of the wine and letting the rich flavor linger on his tongue. It was a delicious, full-bodied and complex wine with tantalizing hints of spice that lingered on the palate.

"Tell me, Lars," Vivienne said, leaning back casually, "what are your aspirations? What do you desire beyond the thrill of the heist and whatever you manage to score from it?"

Her soft and seductive voice told him she didn't care about what he wanted at all. He could feel the heat of her attention, the intensity of her presence, and he knew she was offering him more than just an alliance. She clearly wanted to ensnare him, like a fly caught in a spider's web.

But why him? What could he offer her, with all her wealth and power?

Vivienne leaned forward, speaking to him in a sultry whisper. "I'll tell you what I desire, Lars." Her fingers traced a delicate path along the rim of her glass. "I want power. Real power. The kind that shapes destinies, that controls empires, and not just in Drakoria. In Ithris. In Zarakar, and even beyond."

She paused, giving him a moment to consider her words. "It all starts here. Thume has held this city in his grip for too long. He hoards wealth, he manipulates the law, he crushes anyone who dares to challenge his authority. Azoria deserves better. It deserves a leader who understands its potential, embraces innovation, and will guide us into a new era of prosperity."

She met his look, eyes burning with an ambition that both intrigued and unsettled him. "I can give Azoria that future, Lars. But I can't do it alone. I need someone capable. Someone with a unique understanding of the city's inner workings, who will challenge the status quo, work the people and government both, and help me usher in that vision."

She reached across the table and brushed her hand against his, a touch that sent a jolt of heat through him. He didn't pull back.

"Imagine what we could accomplish together, Lars. You and I—a partnership forged in ambition... and desire. We could reshape this city. We could rewrite the rules. I see it in you. We could build an empire of our own."

Lars could feel his head swimming, whether from the wine or her, or more than likely a mix of both. This woman was compelling, obvious in her intentions, and in all too much to handle. He set his glass down and stood up from his seat.

A flash of disappointment—and was that anger?—washed over Vivienne's face. But it was gone in a moment. "Leaving so soon?"

"No. No, I just need to stretch and think about what you're saying."

"Of course, darling," Vivienne said, rising from her chair to stand beside him. "You're a man of action, always on the move. I understand."

She stepped closer. Her body brushed against his, the warmth of her touch a stark contrast to the cool evening air. "Walk with me, Lars. Let's enjoy the sunset and the possibilities."

She led him along a winding path that snaked through the gardens, the fragrances of jasmine and honeysuckle heavy in the air. They reached a small gazebo, its white marble pillars gleaming under the fading light, and Vivienne paused, turning to face him.

"Thume is a fool. He thinks he can control everything and everyone. But he's blinded by his own ambition, and his ridiculous arrogance. He doesn't see the cracks in the foundation. There are whispers of discontent, Lars. It's a rising tide of men and women tired of his flagrant abuses of power."

She stepped closer, eyes searching his. "Azoria is ready for a new era. An era of prosperity, innovation, and freedom. And you, my dear, you can be a part of that future. A vital part.

"You have a choice to make, Lars. You can cling to your crew and the life you've always known." She reached, boldly tracing the line of his jaw. His body responded to her touch in ways he very much wished it wouldn't. "Or you can step into the light, claim your rightful place beside me, and build a legacy that will echo through the ages."

Vivienne leaned closer. Her lips brushed against his neck, her breath warm on his skin. "Do choose wisely."

Lars felt his head spinning. It wasn't just the wine. Vivienne's words—and her touch—were a potent cocktail that clouded his judgment, fueled a desire he hadn't dared to acknowledge. He felt a hunger for something more than the fleeting thrill of the heist, the hollow victories of a game rigged against him. And a hunger for this woman who wielded power and sexuality in ways he could barely understand.

"What do you want from me, Vivienne?"

"I'm suggesting a partnership, Lars. A *true* partnership. One built on shared ambition and our mutual desire. I have the resources, the connections, the influence to make our dreams a reality. All I need is you."

She cupped his face in her hand. Her touch sent a wave of heat through him. "What do you say? Will you join me? Will you help me build a new Azoria?"

Lars stepped back, breaking the spell of her touch and the heat of her passionate intensity. He could feel his heart pounding, his mind a whirlwind of conflicting emotions. The allure of power, the promise of a new life, the intoxicating scent of her perfume, the warmth of her body against his...

"What about my crew?" he stammered, the question forcing its way past the desire clouding his judgment. "What role do they play in this new Azoria? Do you have plans for them as well?"

Vivienne's smile softened and her hand lingered on his cheek. "You're such a good man. They'll be rewarded, Lars. Their talents will be recognized, and their contributions appreciated. They'll be protected. By you. By me. By our partnership."

He could see the truth in her words but also the veiled threat that lurked beneath her seductive promises. Those who were loyal would be rewarded. Those who weren't...

"And Thume? How do you plan to deal with him? What's your strategy?"

Something cold and ruthless crossed her features. "Thume is a problem that will resolve itself in time. You must trust me, Lars."

He looked away. He didn't even trust himself.

Vivienne reached toward his chest, wrapping her fingers around the folds of his shirt. "Come inside," she said in a pleading, husky voice. She pulled him toward her home.

"No! I..." He paused, calmed his thoughts, and backed away. Reaching his hand up, he uncurled her hand from his shirt and released it. "This is a lot to process. I need time to think."

"Of course, darling," she said with a brilliant smile. "Take some time if that's what you need. But don't wait too long, Lars. Opportunities like this... they don't last forever."

He walked back along the winding path, the scent of jasmine and honeysuckle now rotten in his nose, the beauty of the gardens now a gilded cage. He needed to get back to Trin, his crew, and the familiar chaos of their world.

As he reached the edge of the patio, Vivienne's voice, an almost sibilant hiss, stopped him.

"Lars. Don't forget, I only want you."

He paused, then turned to face her, a forced smile on his face. "I... I'll think about it."

Then, without another word, he walked away. His footsteps echoed on the marble, the sound a hollow counterpoint to the silence of the gardens.

The summons arrived just before noon, delivered by one of Thume's couriers, a grim-faced man whose silence spoke volumes. Myrim set the envelope down on his desk, its crimson wax seal bearing the snakes and scales of the Ithris Gaming Commission. He regarded it with a mix of annoyance and curiosity.

He hadn't expected this. He'd been meticulous, careful, operating outside the confines of the city watch. He utilized Shelle's network to gather information, meeting with the thieves in secret. He'd been certain to ensure that Thume remained oblivious to his shifting allegiances.

Breaking the seal without ceremony, he unfolded the crisp parchment. The words, penned in an elegant script, were brief, formal, and devoid of warmth.

Lord Thume requests your presence in his office this afternoon.

Myrim reread the brief summons, brow furrowing as he considered the possibilities. What could Thume want? Did he know about his alliance with the thieves? Had he discovered their investigation into the secret warehouse?

He set the parchment down on his desk. Standing abruptly, he walked over to a cabinet and poured himself a double shot of whiskey. Taking a long swallow, the amber liquid burned a fiery trail down his throat as he contemplated his next move.

Just then, the office door swung open and Shelle entered with her usual air of playful confidence. She crossed the room, bracelets jingling softly, and her fingers ran up his arm as she kissed his cheek. Leaning down, she read the summons over his shoulder.

"Sounds ominous. What do you think he wants, darling?"

Myrim turned to face her, a silent question on his lips. He'd never been one for sharing his doubts and vulnerabilities. But with Shelle, it was different.

"I don't know. But I guarantee it can't be anything good."

Shelle straightened up, eyes sweeping over the scattered reports and maps littering Myrim's desk. They were all the product of tireless efforts to unravel Thume's secrets. "Well, we shouldn't borrow trouble. It could be a promotion, you know. Perhaps Thume is impressed with you."

Myrim snorted. "Impressed? I'm sure he's furious. Let's not mince words, I've been stepping on his toes and poking around in his business. He doesn't like that. Not one bit."

"He wouldn't dare touch you, Aric. Not with the influence you have. You're the captain of the damn guard." She leaned closer and put her hand on his. "You're too valuable to him, darling. He needs you. At least for now."

"Maybe. But I'm not going in blind. I need to be prepared. I need to know what he wants before he tells me."

He turned back to his desk. His mind was racing as he sorted through the reports. "I need leverage," he said, more to himself than to Shelle, "if such a thing is possible with him."

"I'll get my people on it. I'll have everything you need by the time you go see him."

Myrim nodded, a surge of gratitude and something deeper that felt suspiciously like hope warming him from within. He wasn't alone in this fight. He had Shelle and all her cunning, which he never would have imagined he'd need to lean on. But here he was, and it was good.

He crumpled the paper in his fist in anger. It was the same feeling he used to get when a theft occurred in the city and he was powerless to do anything about it. But then took a deep breath, forcing himself to calm down, to think strategically. He couldn't afford to act rashly, not now. Not with so much at stake. Certainly not with Thume involved.

"It's alright, Shelle," he said, unclenching his fist and smoothing out the crumpled paper. "Hold off on the network for now. No need to risk exposing your people. Thume's playing his games, but we've got our own."

Shelle's brow furrowed in concern. "Are you sure, darling? You're walking into the lion's den after all. He could—"

"He could try," Myrim interrupted grimly. "But he won't. Not yet. He needs me. As you said, at least for now."

"You do sound more confident about it. So what do you think he wants?"

Myrim stood up, pacing restlessly. He was desperately trying to anticipate Thume's next move. What indeed?

Shelle joined him, bumping into him playfully. Her arm brushed against his as they paced side by side, their steps in rhythm. They both stopped and chuckled, the moment of levity breaking the serious mien that had tried to take hold of their conversation.

She paused. "I think he's fishing. He's trying to figure out where you stand. Thume has to know you're questioning his authority and that you're investigating him. With this summons, we'd be stupid to assume otherwise." She tapped her chin thoughtfully. "He needs to know if you're a threat. Or if he can still control you."

Myrim nodded slowly, the pieces falling into place in his mind. "He's going to try to figure out what I know, obviously. And if he feels like I know too much, he'll try to remove me." Shelle's eyes narrowed. "No no, I don't think it will be anything sinister. But it could be a promotion, a transfer, something like that."

"And would you accept?"

Myrim smiled, a rare, genuine smile that transformed his stern features. "Hell no," he said. "I'm done playing by his rules. I'm committed to exposing him, Shelle."

He turned to her, speaking in earnest. "It won't happen with your network, not yet." He reached out, entwining his fingers with hers. "But with your other talents. Your ingenuity. Your knowledge of dynamo. I need you to connect with Liora. Work with her. See what you can come up with together."

Shelle's eyes widened. "Dynamo? Now that sounds like fun."

They left the warehouse together, stepping out into the fading light of the afternoon, the cool autumn air a welcome contrast to the stifling tension of the office.

"It's a shame we didn't have more time to play some games of our own today, darling," Shelle said in a husky murmur, smacking his backside as they walked.

Myrim blushed and opened his mouth to respond, but she cut him off with a laugh.

"Go get 'em, Captain. I'll do what I can on my end."

She turned and headed toward Lars's base with light, swift steps, her purple jacket disappearing into the crowd.

Myrim watched her go, his heart pounding a strange rhythm, the result of anticipation and a newfound excitement. Then, with a resolute nod, he turned and set off for the Gaming Commission headquarters in quick strides.

The heavy oak doors of Thume's office swung open, admitting Myrim into his world of polished mahogany, gleaming brass, and the subtle hints of power and wealth. Myrim's boots echoed on the polished marble floor as he crossed into the room, warily inspecting the imposing figure seated behind the massive desk.

Lord Cecil Thume, dressed in a bespoke suit of midnight blue, his bald head gleaming under the soft light of the dynamo lamps, looked up as Myrim approached. His golden eyes were piercing and unreadable.

"Captain Myrim," Thume said in his booming baritone. "Come in, my friend, come in. Have a seat."

Myrim obeyed, posture stiff at Thume's pleasant tone. He settled into the chair facing the desk. A silence stretched, a heavy, expectant silence that amplified the faint hum of the dynamo conduits that snaked through the walls.

"You requested my presence, Lord Thume?" Myrim was guarded, a knot of apprehension tightening in his chest. He'd spent the past few hours reviewing Shelle's reports, memorizing the details of Thume's clandestine activities. The evidence of his betrayals was astounding, all hints of darkness that lurked beneath the man's charismatic facade.

Thume leaned back in his chair, staring at Myrim with an intensity that made him shift uncomfortably. "Indeed, Aric. I hope I may call you that? There are matters we need to discuss. Matters of mutual benefit."

"Benefit?" So it's the carrot then, Myrim thought with an internal grin.

The imposing Zarakaran arched an eyebrow. "Of course. Do you have any reason why it wouldn't be so?"

Myrim's jaw tightened. "No, Lord Thume." His pulse quickened, a wave of adrenaline sharpening his senses. "But I've learned that assumptions can be dangerous. Especially in city affairs."

"Wise words. Wise words indeed. Which is why I wanted to have this conversation. To clear the air, as it were. To ensure that we're both on the same page."

He paused, tapping his fingers on the desk, eyes never leaving Myrim's. "You've been a valuable asset to the Gaming Commission, Aric," he said, a touching paternal concern in his tone. "A loyal servant of the city. You've dedicated your life to upholding the law, maintaining order, and protecting the delicate balance that has made Azoria prosperous."

He leaned forward intently. "But I sense a weariness in you, Aric. A disillusionment. I'm wondering if your heart is still in the business of bringing criminals to justice."

He paused again, letting the silence stretch, allowing his words to sink in, then continued in his grandiose declaration. "It's time for a change. A change of pace if you will. A new challenge."

"What kind of a challenge?" Myrim said, brow furrowing. He knew what was coming. The offer. The promotion. The gilded cage.

Thume leaned back in his chair, fingers steepled under his chin. "I have a proposition for you, Captain Myrim. A chance to serve Azoria in a new capacity. A role that requires a different kind of skill set and utilize your unique talents."

"What are you suggesting, Lord Thume?" Myrim very much wished the man would get to the point. He had no patience—or time—for intrigue.

"I'm suggesting that it's time for you to leave the city watch and all its chaos behind." Thume smiled with a warmth that didn't reach his calculating golden eyes. "Think about it, Aric. A position of influence. One that utilizes your strategic mind, your understanding of the city's people. A place on the council, perhaps. Or a more advisory role. My trusted confidant, someone who can help me guide Azoria toward a brighter future."

Myrim's jaw tightened. He wasn't surprised by the offer. It was exactly what he'd expected. A way for Thume to neutralize and silence him, to remove him from the board without resorting to anything messy. But upon hearing the words, seeing the calculated gleam in Thume's eyes, a wave of anger, hot and immediate, surged through him.

"A desk job," he said flatly, the words tasting like ash in his mouth.

"A position of power," Thume corrected as his smile faded. "You'd have access to resources, information, and influence that would far exceed your current limited scope."

"And what about justice, Lord Thume?" Myrim said, unable to keep the bitterness out of his voice. "What about the law? What about protecting the city from those who abuse their power?"

"Justice." Thume's eyes narrowed as he snorted, a flicker of something dangerous flashing in their depths. "Justice is a fluid concept. It's a tool to be wielded, a weapon to be deployed, not an abstract concept to blindly follow. I control the flow of justice in this city, Captain. I suggest you remember that."

Myrim met Thume's gaze, and a defiant spark ignited upon him. He'd spent years upholding Thume's vision of justice, enforcing the laws of the land, turning a blind eye to the subtle manipulations, the whispers of corruption, the imbalances that festered beneath the surface of Azoria's glittering facade. But no more. Something within him had shifted. The line had been crossed.

"And what if I refuse your generous offer, Lord Thume?"

Thume's smile vanished, replaced by a cold, calculating mask. He leaned back in his chair, fingers drumming a rhythmic beat against the polished mahogany. Relentless eyes bored into Myrim—assessing, weighing, judging.

"Refuse?" he echoed, the word hanging in the air, a challenge, a threat. "I can't even fathom why you might do that. To be blunt, it would be most unwise. You've served this city well, Captain. You've earned your place. But even the most loyal of servants can outlive their usefulness."

The warmth of their earlier exchange was now a distant memory. "Are you threatening me, Lord Thume?"

Thume's chuckle was a low, humorless sound that echoed through the room. "No, my friend, I don't make threats. I offer advice. Friendly advice. From one who understands the ways of the world to anyone who may be blind to them."

He leaned forward. "You're playing a dangerous game, Myrim. And it's a game you don't understand. Align yourself with the wrong players, ask the wrong questions, and you might find yourself removed from the board."

He paused, letting the obvious but unspoken consequence hang in the air, making sure Myrim understood that nothing he had been doing had gone unnoticed.

Regaining a touch of its previous warmth, a mask slipping back into place, Thume continued. "But there's still my offer. You can reconsider your allegiances. Serve Azoria, and therefore me, as you once did."

He extended a hand across the desk in an offer of reconciliation and forgiveness.

Myrim stared at Thume's outstretched hand. The man offering it now seemed like a symbol of everything he loathed and had been blind to for far too long. Thume's manicured fingers, adorned with rings of gold and gleaming gemstones, represented a world of privilege, of power built on manipulation and control. It was a world that Myrim had served for years.

And suddenly, the dam within him burst, a torrent of words, a flood of emotions he'd suppressed for far too long, surging forth.

"The city watch," Myrim said, trembling with a passion he hadn't felt in years. "It's more than just a job, Thume. It's a responsibility. A sacred trust."

He stood up and stared Thume down in challenge. "Those men and women who wear the uniform put their lives on the line every day to protect this city. To uphold the law. To serve the people. They don't answer to you. They answer to a higher calling. A calling rooted in justice, fairness, and the belief that everyone, regardless of their wealth or status, deserves protection and a chance to live a decent life."

His words echoed in the silence of the room, a challenge to Thume's carefully constructed world, a crack in the foundations of his power.

He doesn't control everything, Myrim realized, a surge of clarity washing over him. He might own the factories and control the flow of dynamo, but he doesn't control the law. The council, and therefore the people, hold the power to appoint and dismiss the city's servants. And they, not Thume, would decide his fate. Thume did not know what justice was.

He straightened his shoulders, his gaze hard and unshakable. Resolve flowed through him. He would not back down.

"No, Lord Thume. I won't be your pawn. I won't be silenced. And I damn well won't be controlled." Myrim's jaw hardened as he stood tall and proud.

Thume's eyes widened. The audacity of the man before him clearly shook him to his core. "Aric Myrim, you are a fool."

"Lord Thume," Myrim growled, low and dangerous, "you can go fuck yourself."

✧

Liora's workshop was a scattered mess of instruments of chaos just like her brilliant but often messy mind. Wires snaked across the floor, tools were scattered across workbenches, and the air was filled with the faint scent of soldering flux and ozone, a familiar aroma that brought a sense of comfort and focus under normal circumstances. But today, a nervous energy sparkled inside her, a blend of anticipation and a touch of apprehension as she waited for Shelle's arrival.

Shelle had called earlier. Her usual energetic tone sparkled through the squawk as she proposed to come by and combine their talents to make ready for the upcoming warehouse infiltration.

Liora was secretly thrilled. Shelle, with her sharp wit, effortless confidence, and playful danger, was unlike anyone she'd ever met. Those eyes, that piercing blue gaze that seemed to see right through her and understand her mind's whirring gears and tangled wires just made her go gooey inside. And, she had to admit, she did love being called darling.

The workshop door creaked open, and Shelle swept into the room, a whirlwind of confidence. She wore a sunshine-yellow dress that hugged her voluptuous figure, its fabric stretching taut over her ample curves. A short, cropped teal jacket, its sleeves ending just above her elbows accentuated her look and added a splash of eye-popping color contrasting her pale skin. Matching black boots, belt, and lace gloves completed the ensemble.

"Darling, what a delightful mess you've created!" Her eyes twinkled with amusement as she surveyed the workshop. She gave Liora a tiny peck on the cheek that brought a flush to the engineer's face.

"I've been working on something ambitious," Liora said with excitement and nervousness. "I call it biodynamics. It's all about using dynamo to detect and analyze places and even living beings."

She gestured toward a bundle of wires and sensors connected to a small dynamo generator. "I think it's possible to use subtle fluctuations in a person's bio-dynamo field to identify them, to track their movements, even to... well, to eavesdrop on their conversations."

Shelle's eyebrows rose. A flicker of admiration and a hint of concern crossed her face. "That's quite a discovery. A bit dangerous, perhaps. But undeniably fascinating."

She shifted in her chair. "So tell me... can any of this biodynamic wizardry of yours help us with our little secret warehouse problem?"

Liora blushed, fidgeting with a small, silver device she'd been tinkering on. "Well, not exactly. But I did have an idea."

She held up the device, its surface gleaming with a subtle dynamo glow. "This little beauty is a sound recorder. It's a bit like a squawk, except it captures sounds and converts them into dynamo pulses, storing them inside a crystal."

Grinning with near-manic excitement, she thrust the device into Shelle's face. "Would you mind saying something? As fun and cute as you'd like."

Shelle laughed and placed her hand over Liora's, pulling the device close to her lips. "For you, darling?" she simpered in an exaggerated seductive voice. "I'd be delighted to."

Liora giggled, fingers fumbling as she pushed a button to stop recording. A moment later, she played back Shelle's words. The voice was only slightly distorted but every bit as musical as the real thing.

Shelle clapped her hands in delight, eyes bright with admiration. "That's brilliant, Liora! You're a genius!"

Liora beamed as her cheeks flushed pink with pride. She tucked the recording device away in her pocket.

"Wait a moment," Shelle said, brow furrowing as if a sudden realization had struck her. She paced back and forth, boots scuffing against the floor, mind racing. "I know I'm a simple dynamo dabbler, but... could this device be modified? To trigger a circuit instead of just storing a sound?"

Liora, caught up in Shelle's energy, nodded eagerly. "Of course! It's just a matter of redirecting the output signal. Instead of sending it to a crystal storage unit, we could route it to a relay switch, a detonator, anything that a dynamo pulse can activate."

Shelle's eyes gleamed with excitement. "And could that trigger be, somehow, from far away? Could it be activated without any wires connected to the button?"

Liora hesitated. "Theoretically, yes. We could use a focused beam of dynamo energy, a specific frequency that would activate the receiver. But it's never been done before. Not on a practical scale."

"What about using sound? Forget storing it in crystals. What if we used sound waves to activate the circuit? A specific frequency, or a coded sequence... it could trigger a switch on the other side!" Her words came quick and excited now. "So you'd push a button, which would play a sound or squeal or something, and it would get picked up by the other device which would play, I don't know, a recording of someone saying 'Come quick!'"

Liora's eyes widened, a spark of understanding igniting in her mind. "We could make distractions and place them all over to play when we want to confuse the guards!"

"Exactly!" Shelle exclaimed, clapping her hands together. "And if it works, we could embed a receiver in any device, any mechanism, like lights or squawks or fans... and then activate it remotely using a coded sound sequence. Imagine the possibilities!"

"But we'd need a way to transmit that sound over a distance," Liora said, brow furrowed. "A frequency high enough to be inaudible to the human ear, but still detectable by the receiver."

"We can figure that out." Like Liora, Shelle wouldn't be deterred by trivialities. "This is what happens when you get the dynamo girls together!"

The dynamo girls! Liora had never heard something so amazing in her life. Best team name ever.

"Yep, we can do it," she said, eyes gleaming with a newfound determination. "I'm sure of it."

She grabbed a handful of wires, already itching to start experimenting, to translate their ideas into reality.

Just then, the kitchen door creaked open, and Jax stepped inside, his imposing frame filling the doorway. The bruiser's face was a mix of curiosity and concern.

"What are you two up to? Sounds like you're plotting world domination in here."

Liora focused on the wires in her hands and waved a dismissive hand. "Shhh, Jax! You're disrupting the dynamo flow." She glanced up at him, eyebrows drawn together. "Can't you feel it? The air's buzzing with ideas!"

Jax blinked. "Dynamo flow?" he echoed, looking around the workshop, eyes settling on a half-eaten sandwich resting precariously on a stack of blueprints. "All I feel is hungry."

Shelle chuckled, eyes twinkling with amusement. "Leave her to her tinkering, Jax. She's on the verge of a breakthrough."

"Oh, yeah?" Jax perked up with interest. "Does that mean we can finally blast a hole in Thume's fancy warehouse and get this over with?"

"Not exactly," Liora said with enthusiasm. "But close. See, what we're doing is, we're taking sound waves, and we're converting them into coded dynamo pulses that can be transmitted over a high frequency, inaudible to the human ear, and—"

She launched into a detailed explanation of their concept, complete with diagrams, equations, and passionate discourse on the principles of sound wave propagation, dynamo resonance, and the potential for remote activation of dynamo devices. Jax listened patiently, head nodding slowly, eyes clouded, wearing a mask of polite interest.

At last, Liora concluded her explanation with a triumphant flourish. "And that's how we're going to revolutionize the art of the heist! Remote activation, Jax! We'll be able to control everything from a distance. Lights, alarms, even locks. We'll be unstoppable! Dynamo girls!"

Jax blinked. "That's... great, Liora," he said hesitantly. "Really impressive. I think I'll leave you two to your dynamo flow." He walked away mumbling to himself. "Crazy engineers..."

He slipped out of the workshop, leaving Liora and Shelle to their brainstorming session.

Shelle and Liora turned to the workbench, their minds abuzz with possibilities. Tools clattered, wires sparked, and myriad clicks and whirs filled the workshop as they began to experiment with their new ideas in mind. Liora, fingers working overtime, soldered wires, adjusted dials, and tested circuits.

Meanwhile, Shelle passed her tools, offered suggestions, and marveled at Liora's ingenuity. "I never realized dynamo could be so versatile," she said, watching as Liora connected a series of crystals to a modified squawk, a collection of wires snaking across the workbench. "It's like magic."

Liora snorted. "There's no such thing as magic, Shelle. It's all about understanding the principles, the laws of physics, the flow of energy. Once you grasp the fundamentals, the possibilities are endless."

"Who knows, you might even be able to use this sound transference to talk from squawk to squawk without wires," Shelle said. "Just imagine instant communication across the city or all of Ithris."

Liora stopped what she was doing and stared at Shelle. Her eyes widened behind her spectacles. A jolt of excitement that felt like pure dynamo shot through her.

"You know," she said, pushing her glasses up her nose, breathless with a sudden realization, "I bet I could."

The hours melted away, the sun sinking toward the horizon, painting the workshop windows in hues of fiery orange and deep violet. Sparks flew, wires twisted, and tools clattered as Liora and Shelle worked side-by-side, the dynamo girls in action making magic—no, wait, science—happen. Shelle's infectious laughter mingled with Liora's excited gasps and the occasional triumphant squeal.

✧

The carriage rattled its way down the narrow alley, its wheels bumping over cobblestones, its arrival a hodgepodge of creaks and groans that echoed through the quiet streets surrounding the crew's base. Exhausted from days on the road and nights spent under the open sky, Keer climbed out of the carriage and surveyed the familiar surroundings.

The journey north had been... enlightening, to say the least. Following the huge flow of energy with the dynamo lens, they'd found the warehouse. It was a sprawling complex hidden amidst a desolate stretch of coastline, its defenses formidable, its secrets buried deep.

They'd gathered what information they could, utilizing the lens to map the flow of energy and peer into the heart of Thume's operation. And they'd carried out Liora's instructions, deploying the mysterious equipment she'd packed with such meticulous care. They left behind a trail of wires and crystals that would hopefully—well, he wasn't quite sure what she was planning, but he trusted her genius.

He'd left Rurik and Maren at their base, where Silas, Inora, and Darius greeted them with open arms. He was sure they'd jabber through the day with their own tales of adventure. Keer made his way home, eager to see his crew, tell them what he'd learned, and hear what had transpired while he was gone. And, truth be told, he could use some of that good whiskey he kept hidden on the corner shelf of the bar.

He reached the tavern door, its heavy wood scarred with the marks of countless late nights and close calls, and grasped the handle, expecting it to open with a flood of light, scents, and voices. Though the handle turned, the door wouldn't open.

That's odd, he thought. He tried the handle again, jiggling it, but the door remained locked.

He called out. "Liora? You in there?"

Silence met his words. Something wrong with the lock, he thought. Keer fumbled in his pocket for his key and brought it out.

Suddenly, a tinny voice crackled to life, startling him.

"State your name and purpose."

Keer jumped back, reaching for the dagger concealed beneath his coat. His eyes darted around the alleyway, searching for the source of the voice, but he saw no one.

"Liora, is that you?" he said, looking around for her. "Where are you?"

"Name and purpose please, Keer," the voice said.

"You damn well know my name. You just said it." He snorted and shook his head.

A giggle, light and mischievous, echoed from the hidden speaker. He heard a faint click and tested the handle again. This time the door swung open easily, as light and four grinning faces flooded his vision.

Keer stepped inside, looking around at the familiar surroundings—the worn wooden tables, the glowing dynamo lamps, and—most important right now—the shelves lined with bottles that promised warmth and solace. It was a good welcome home.

Lars, Trin, and Liora were gathered around a table, studying a map spread out before them, their faces illuminated by the the overhead lights. Jax sat nearby, cleaning his prized dagger with meticulous care that belied his usual boisterous nature.

"Keer! You're back!" The dynamo girl jumped up from her chair and rushed toward him. "How was the trip? Did you find the warehouse? Did you lay out the cable?"

Keer chuckled. "Before we get into that... what the hell was that voice? You trying to give me a heart attack, Liora? And what's with the new lock?"

Liora giggled and blushed. "It's a new dynamo tech I'm working on. Just a prototype. Thought I'd test it out, you know, make sure it's effective."

"Effective? It scared the wits out of me."

A collective chuckle filled the room.

Trin sat with a hand on Lars's thigh and smiled at Keer warmly. "So, how did it go?"

"Everything went smoothly." Keer settled into a chair and accepted a mug of ale from Jax with a grateful nod. He took a long swallow, savoring the cool, bitter flavor.

"We managed to get a good look at the exterior. I mapped out the security systems and identified potential entry points. And..." He paused, eyes meeting Liora's with a wink. "We completed your little side project. Just as you instructed."

"Yay! That'll help us get out of there when we're done."

"Well," Lars said, "we have to get in first, don't we."

It was the curse of the well-established thief. Always seeking every possible angle, always looking for the perfect heist. When you got too successful, thinking that getting in and finding what you came for was a foregone conclusion, you just needed to worry about getting out.

Keer coughed. "Yeah, about that. Thume's warehouse. It's... well, it's something else. Bigger than I imagined. More heavily guarded—and there's a hell of a lot of dynamo flowing into that place, that's for sure."

He took another swig of his ale. "Add to that, there's a whole contingent of Zarakaran guards. Elite mercenaries by the looks of them. We couldn't get close enough to know for sure. And searchlights patrolling the perimeter. They light up the scrubland for miles around. Eyes everywhere.

"Lastly, there's a network of tunnels," he added, "loads of them from what we could tell. We tried—"

Lars, who had been listening with evident disappointment, perked up. "Tunnels? Well that's promising."

"You didn't let me finish. They flood. At high tide, when it rains, or when rain comes down off the northern hills." Keer shook his head. "No, there's no way we can count on those. Too risky."

"Damn," Lars muttered, brow furrowing.

"And there's something else," Keer said, recalling Maren's confusion at the phenomenon. "Something strange. Whenever we got close to the warehouse, we felt this... buzzing sensation. Like a static charge in the air. The closer we got, the more intense it became. The dynamo lens was going haywire. The readings were erratic."

Liora leaned forward, eyes widening. "Erratic? What do you mean?"

"It's hard to explain." Keer shook his head. "It was like invisible walls of energy. Pulsing, shifting, almost alive. We didn't dare get any closer."

"That's... troubling," Liora said. She glanced at the dynamo lens on the table.

Lars and Trin looked at each other, and Keer watched as he gave her hand a reassuring squeeze. He was glad they truly had each other now. They'd faced difficult odds before, countless times. It came with the job. But this sounded like it would be their most difficult score yet.

Lars sat, lost in thought for a moment. "You didn't mention muskets. Did you see any of those?"

Keer grunted. "Not a single one."

"That is surprising."

They had all assumed that Thume would have deployed his new weapons to protect his most valuable assets, assuming that's what he kept in his secret warehouse. But perhaps the muskets were still under development, or Thume was saving them for a more strategic purpose.

"Anything else?" Trin said sharply.

"What more do you need, Trin?" Keer rubbed his eyes with an exasperation born of tiredness. "The place is crawling with guards, rigged with traps, and buzzing with enough dynamo to fry a man's brains. It sounds like a suicide mission to me."

"I'm not planning on backing down, Keer," Lars said, his jaw set with a determination that brooked no argument. "The man tried to kill Liora, and that's the end of it for me. That warehouse is where we'll find what we need to expose him."

He turned to the others. "I'm not going to lie to you. This is going to be dangerous. Maybe even impossible. But we've faced impossible odds before. And we've always found a way."

He paused, giving his crew time to think it over.

"I'm not asking you to follow me blindly. I understand if you think this is too much or you're unwilling to take the risk. Say you want to sit this one out and there will be no hard feelings. But if you're ready to get to work, let's do it. This game's not over, not by a long shot."

"Personally I feel like that stuck-up bitch Vivienne can storm the damn keep herself if she wants it that badly," Trin said with a determination that matched Lars's own. "But I'm not backing down from a challenge. Not when it comes to protecting what's ours."

A murmur of agreement rippled through the room. Jax thunked his sharpened dagger into the table and nodded to Lars. They had reputations and each other to protect.

"Let's do this," Liora said with a determined squeak. "Let's show Thume what happens when you mess with the best damn crew in Azoria."

SETBACKS

16

A strange stillness had settled over Azoria, a windless day that held a weight of anticipation as if the city was holding its breath, bracing for a storm. Inside the old tavern, Lars and his crew oversaw a whirlwind of activity—maps spread across tables, tools scattered across workbenches, crystal charges humming and various bits of metal and wire strewn about.

For a week, they had immersed themselves in preparations for the heist of Thume's warehouse, their usual rivalries with Darius and the city watch set aside, and all of their resolves firmed in their course of action. But while they plotted and strategized, a new round of the game was beginning on a windless day in their city.

The morning sun, a pale disc obscured by a veil of smog and smoke from Azoria's countless factories and foundries, cast a sickly glow upon the city's streets. The usual energy, the vibrant hum of commerce and innovation that pulsed through Azoria's veins, felt subdued, replaced by a nervous tension that crackled in the air like an unregulated dynamo current.

Newspapers, their headlines screaming accusations and pronouncements, flew off the stands, snatched up by eager hands. Unlike those following a good heist, these headlines were far more foreboding. Their contents were devoured, dissected, and debated in hushed whispers and angry shouts.

MYRIM OUT! THUME CITES CAPTAIN'S INCOMPETENCE, APPOINTS NEW GUARD LEADER, one said.

Or as another alleged, *CRYSTAL CHARGE CONTROVERSY: THUME ACCUSED OF HOARDING REVOLUTIONARY TECH*

And of course there was the Azoria Star, paper of the people, which noted: *CITY ON THE BRINK? PETTY THEFT, VIOLENCE ON THE RISE AS AZORIANS FEEL THE PINCH*

Groups gathered on street corners, their faces grim, their voices a chorus of discontent as they argued over the latest news, their anxieties amplified by uncertainty of the future and the shifting tides of power. A growing sense that the laws of the land they'd trusted in for so long were being rewritten. It was as if forces beyond their control were manipulating their destinies.

A wary silence had settled in the market district, where vendors once hawked their wares with boisterous enthusiasm. Shoppers clutched their purses and haggled over prices with a fierce intensity, their eyes darting nervously, their trust in their fellow citizens eroded by fear gnawing at the edges of their once-carefree and prosperous lives.

The whispers started in the taverns, spreading through the back alleys and disreputable corners of the city, carried on the breath of rumors and a potent brew of fear and resentment.

"Thume's gone mad with power," some said in hushed tones, their gazes darting around as if afraid of being overheard. "He's hoarding those crystals, building weapons, spying on us... he's turned this city into his own private battlefield."

Others blamed Myrim, the disgraced captain of the watch, whispering tales of corruption and incompetence, their anger fueled by the rising tide of petty theft and violence that had plagued the city of late.

Pickpocketing, once a rare occurrence in a city that prided itself on *honest* thieves, was becoming commonplace. Copper cables vanished from workshops, purses were snatched in broad daylight, and brawls, fueled by cheap gin and simmering resentment, erupted in the taverns, leaving a trail of broken bones and bruised egos in their wake. The city watch, under the command of Thume's freshly appointed captain—a stern-faced woman with a reputation for ruthlessness and blind loyalty to her patron—seemed powerless to stop the escalating chaos, her presence more a symbol of Thume's authority than a force for order.

"Where are Harrow and Adalan?" the people asked with heavy suspicion and a desperate longing for the familiar order, the comforting chaos of the old game. "Why aren't they stopping this? They're the ones who are supposed to keep those gangs in check, to balance the scales. Have they turned on us too?"

The rumblings of discontent, the whispers of fear and suspicion, grew louder with each passing day. The very air of Azoria crackled with a volatile energy as unpredictable as a lightning storm. The city, once a beacon of prosperity and innovation, was now a tinderbox. And it was ready to ignite at the slightest spark.

Rumors of Thume's secret projects, of muskets, crystal charges, and dynamo manipulation, spread like wildfire through the streets, fueled by both the insidious effects of fear and a need for answers. Investors, their fortunes built on the city's thriving dynamo industry, poured money into clandestine research projects. Their engineers toiled night and day, desperate to unlock the secrets of crystal charge technology and to replicate the lethal precision of the muskets.

Yet, even as they gambled on innovation, the fear of the unknown drove many of Azoria's elite to seek refuge outside the city walls. Once reserved for weekend retreats and hedonistic summer parties, lavish country estates were now fortified with armed guards and the latest security measures. Their dynamo generators hummed with a constant, reassuring power. Rumors spread of secret bunkers being constructed around the city, hidden sanctuaries where the wealthy could weather the coming storm, their status and privilege shielded from the chaos now unleashed.

The city held its breath, waiting for the spark, the catalyst that would ignite the powder keg.

And then the spark came, not a flash of light or a crash of thunder, but a single, horrifying act of violence that shattered the city's fragile peace, sending shockwaves of grief and outrage through its heart. A young girl named Yina, no more than eight years old, was murdered in broad daylight, caught in the fray of a petty theft gone wrong.

A thief, desperate for a few copper coins, had snatched her father's wallet in the crowded marketplace, and the girl, in a moment of innocent bravery, had tried to intervene. Panicked and trapped, the thief had lashed out. His blade silenced her cries, and her blood stained the cobblestones crimson.

The city erupted in a fury of grief and rage. Crowds gathered, their voices a thunderous roar as they demanded justice, their anger directed at the thieves, the city watch, and Thume himself. The newspapers, their headlines screaming for vengeance, fanned the flames of discontent. Their pages were filled with lurid details of the girl's death, the growing sense of lawlessness, the fear that had gripped the city.

Thume, sensing the power shift, made a rare public appearance. His commanding presence blazed with a powerful anger, and he spoke with a reassuring boom that echoed through the streets.

"This madness has gone too far. The time for games is over. The root of this disease must be excised. Justice will be served."

As Azoria stood on the precipice of a new day, the air was frantic with the kind of tension that only accompanied righteous indignation.

An unspoken anxiety settled over the entire crew, the echoes of laughter and boisterous banter replaced by an almost manic intent.

Lars and the crew spent the morning scurrying around their base, poring over maps and schematics. Their fingers had jabbed out at random to trace the intricate lines. Every mind grappled with the implications of Yina's death and

Thume's proclamations. What would Thume do? Would it interfere with their plans?

And of course, there was the new and uncertain challenge of working not just with another crew but with a disgraced captain of the city watch and his devious—if vibrant—partner.

When Myrim had told the crew about his exchange with Thume, including the final bit telling Thume what he could do with himself, the combined crews had laughed uproariously. It had gone a long way in cementing their trust.

But the good captain had been removed from his post and was taking the girl's death very hard. Harder still, since he couldn't do anything about it now. Truthfully, the city's descent into incivility and violence weighed on them all. They were thieves, masters of deception and manipulation. But they were also citizens of Azoria, their lives intertwined with the fate of the city they both exploited and, in their own way, protected.

As the day went on, the mood livened a bit. They had a job to do, and they were all damn good at doing it.

Liora, surrounded by a growing mountain of tools, wires, and crystal charges, hummed Dynamo Daydream to herself. Her fingers moved with practiced skill as she assembled a new device. Sparks flew, gears whirred, and the air bubbled with the faint scent of ozone. She'd been working nonstop since she and Shelle had put their heads together and came up with a few new tricks.

The workshop had transformed into an innovation playground. Lars had commented to Trin that it seemed Shelle had lit a fire under his engineer's bottom, what with how hard she was working. Trin had laughed and told him he had no idea.

"What are you making this time, Liora?" Jax said, peering over her shoulder with nervous curiosity. "And none of that technical mumbo jumbo. Are we finally going to blow something up?"

Liora giggled. "Something even better." She held up a small, silver device as she pushed her glasses up. "This little beauty is a... well, you'll just have to wait and see."

Trinelle, seated beside Lars at a nearby table, chuckled. Their fingers intertwined, their bodies leaned close together, and a silent language of shared affection passed between them. The events of the past few weeks—the attacks, the revelations about Thume, the unsettling alliance with Vivienne—only strengthened their bond. Though in truth, it helped that Vivienne had been absent for weeks.

Lars glanced at Trin, a warmth spreading through him that had nothing to do with the crackling fire in the hearth. She smiled in return, clearly feeling the same.

The aroma of roasting pork, spiced apples, and fresh baked bread wafted through the air. It was a comforting blend of scents that had Jax looking repeatedly toward the kitchen with yearning.

A sharp rap on the front door shattered the mood, echoing through the tavern like a musket shot. Lars and Trinelle's hands moved toward the weapons concealed beneath their clothes. Jax rose from his chair with narrowed eyes.

Liora glanced nervously at the door, her eyes wide. Her fingers tightened around a small wrench she'd been using to adjust a dynamo circuit.

Lars growled in alarm. "Who is it?"

"City watch!" a gruff voice barked from the other side of the door. "Open up!"

Lars exchanged a look with Trin. "Myrim?" The anxious fear that the captain's dismissal was just a ruse and that he would betray the crew bubbled to the forefront of his mind.

"It's not Myrim, Lars," Trin said sharply, eyes fixed on the door. "He wouldn't bother knocking."

Before Lars could respond, the door swung open. A contingent of city watch guards filed into the tavern, grim-faced with hands resting on the hilts of their swords. At their lead stood a tall, lean woman with a face as sharp as a honed blade. Her black hair was pulled back in a tight bun, her gray uniform starched and pressed, and the silver badge on it gleamed with a cold, impersonal light. But it was her eyes, a dispassionate gray that pierced through any pretense or facade, that made Lars's blood run cold.

"Secure the premises," Captain Harrick commanded. "And find any other members of Harrow's crew. Bring them to me. Now."

The guards fanned out, their movements swift and efficient, their heavy boots thudding across the wooden floor. A moment later, Keer was dragged from the kitchen, face flushed with anger and his dark brown skin smeared with flour. They shoved him into a chair beside Lars, the aroma of roasting pork and spiced apples still clinging to his clothes.

"What the hell is the meaning of this?" Lars said, rising to his feet. "This is a private establishment, and I won't have you—"

The captain cut him off with a slashing gesture. "Silence, Harrow." She stepped closer. Her presence was a palpable force that seemed to shrink the room and suffocate everyone in it. "I'm not here to play your games."

Thume had handpicked Captain Dalini Harrick for this position. A career officer, she'd risen through the ranks of the city watch with a ruthless efficiency. Her loyalty was unquestionable.

Harrick's ambition was limited to the pursuit of order, and her only pleasures were a well-executed arrest and the clink of silver coins in her pocket. She had no patience for the theatrics of Azoria's celebrity thieves, no tolerance for their particular form of chaos, no understanding of the intricate dance they choreographed within the city's heart.

She was here to enforce the law, as dictated by Lord Thume, and she would carry out her duty with a cold, unflinching precision.

"Liora Banz," she said haughtily, "you are under arrest for the murder of Remus Switcher. By order of Lord Cecil Thume."

Liora's eyes widened into a mask of terror and shock.

Lars snarled. "Murder? That's insane! She had nothing to do with Switcher's death! She was trying to help find the bastard who did it!"

Trinelle kept her eyes fixed on Captain Harrick. Her tone was deceptively calm as she tried to reason with the implacable officer. "This is absurd, Captain. You can't just barge in here and arrest someone based on hearsay. Where's your warrant? Where's your evidence? Where's your authority?"

"My authority comes from Lord Thume himself, Mistress Meridia," Harrick said coldly. "And I suggest you remember that."

Jax, face flushed crimson, surged to his feet. His massive frame towered over the guards. "You're not taking her anywhere! You lay one finger on her, and I swear to—"

Before Jax could finish his threat, two guards lunged at him, their combined weight tackling him to the floor. He struggled, muscles bunching, fists pounding against the floorboards. But their grip was relentless.

Harrick let loose a sharp shout, cutting through the chaos. "I said silence!" She turned back to Liora with a cold, unwavering calm.

"You're coming with us, Miss Banz. The rest of you are under house arrest pending the outcome of the investigation. No leaving this tavern. No communication with anyone outside these walls. No contact with Darius Adalan or his crew. Lord Thume is determined to unravel this conspiracy and will not tolerate any further insubordination."

"Lars!" Liora squeaked, "What—"

Captain Harrick whirled on her, and Liora's mouth clicked shut. The captain paused, gaze sweeping over the stunned and disbelieving faces of the crew.

"Good day," she said with a final, curt dismissal. Then, gesturing to her men, she turned and strode out of the tavern. Liora, struggling with her wrists bound in cuffs, tried to pull away but it only resulted in her glasses being flung from her face. They clattered to the ground as the guards pulled her chains and led the frightened engineer away from her crew to an uncertain fate.

✦

The fire crackled in the hearth, casting dancing shadows upon the luxurious furnishings of Vivienne's private study.

Jasmine and sandalwood lingered in the air, a cloying sweetness that masked the icy chill that emanated from the woman who sat alone by the fire, a glass of wine untouched in her hand.

Vivienne's face, usually a canvas of elegant composure and seductive charm, was now a mask of cold, calculating ambition. Her eyes, devoid of their usual playful sparkle, reflected the flames, a dangerous ruthlessness burning in their depths.

She swirled the wine in her glass, watching the ruby liquid catch the firelight. Her thoughts were a vivid tapestry of intricate plans. Everything was unfolding according to her design. Switcher's death, the attack on Liora's life. Myrim's disillusionment, the raid on the Institute, Lord Thume's fury—every move, every countermove, an orchestrated step in a symphony that only she understood.

"Poor Remus. Such a brilliant mind, wasted on petty ambitions."

Switcher had been an obstacle, a loose thread that threatened to unravel her plans. His curiosity and relentless pursuit of knowledge had led him too close to discovering crystal charges on his own. She'd eliminated him swiftly, decisively, a calculated sacrifice that had served its purpose.

As for Liora... well, she had never meant for anyone on Lars's team to get hurt. But that damn engineer's tenacity, both a blessing and a curse, made it necessary. The attack on the rooftop had been a risky move that could have backfired. But the outcome—Liora's fear, anger, and her renewed determination to find answers—had played into Vivienne's hands.

A cruel smile, devoid of warmth, stretched across Vivienne's lips. The muskets weren't Thume's creation at all—they were hers. Years ago, she'd tasked her most trusted engineers in Drakoria with developing this new technology, a weapon of unprecedented power and precision. She'd seen the potential for disruption, for shattering the established order, and had seized it with ruthless ambition. And once the prototypes were ready, she'd moved the project to Azoria. Vivienne had established a secret lab beneath the very institute Thume believed he controlled. It was poetic, really.

The crystal charges, too, were her doing—a revolutionary discovery she'd kept hidden from the world, waiting for the perfect moment to unleash their potential. They were the perfect bait, a lure to draw in Larson Harrow and his crew. And to manipulate them into playing her game.

Thume's unwavering belief in his own power and an arrogant conviction that Azoria danced to his tune was a delicious irony to Vivienne. He was a king on a borrowed throne, ruling a city he only thought he controlled.

But what about Lars Harrow? Even with her ruthless focus on destroying Thume, she had to admit that her pursuit of the attractive and daring thief was a bit uncharacteristic.

Initially she had thought to sway Lars against his woman—that hateful little trollop Trinelle Meridia—and his crew. Give people something else to focus on, to distrust, to hate, and they'll be less likely to probe the depths of your plans. But over time, her attraction to Lars grew, and now... well, now she had decided he would be hers. And Vivienne always got what she wanted.

She pictured him with his easy confidence, mischievous grin, and eyes that held a spark of danger and vulnerability. He was a challenge, a worthy prize, a man who could match her wit and her ambition. He could be her king, the ruler at her side. He would help her reshape Azoria, to build an empire that would stretch far beyond the confines of this city and the nation of Ithris.

She'd already laid the groundwork, planting seeds of doubt, offering glimpses of power, whispering promises of a future where they could rule together. She had seen the flicker of desire in his eyes, the way his gaze lingered on her curves, the way his pulse quickened beneath her touch. He was tempted. She could feel it.

And soon, she would break him. She would bend him to her will.

But first, he had a job to do. They all did.

Of course, Thume had tried to throw a pathetic wrench into her plans. The old fool had disgraced Captain Myrim, but the new enemy he created with that action would do nicely to correct the balance of her scheme. A pawn removed from the board, only to be resurrected as a more powerful piece. Yes, Myrim's anger and thirst for revenge would serve her purposes quite well.

She had already contacted the stodgy former captain, offering him solace, a listening ear, a chance to reclaim what he'd lost. She'd played him expertly, appealing to his sense of justice and his wounded pride. He was falling into her web, just as she'd planned.

"Lars. Darius. Myrim. Shelle. My loyal and effective flies," she murmured.

With Darius and his crew under house arrest, there wasn't much he could do to remedy the situation with Liora, Lars, and the rest. She'd have to handle that too. But for now…

Vivienne rose from her chair, crimson gown swirling around her, and crossed the room to a writing desk with an arrangement of quills, inkwells, and parchment. She dipped a quill into a silver inkwell, its surface adorned with a swirling pattern of illustrated circuitry, and began to write. Her movements were swift and precise, the words flowing from her pen.

The door creaked open. A pale and wide-eyed young man entered the room.

"You summoned me, Mistress?" He bowed his head respectfully.

"You're here, Aminn, excellent." She folded the parchment, sealed it with crimson wax, and handed it to him. "Take this to Captain Myrim. It's of the utmost importance."

"*Captain* Myrim?" Aminn echoed, his brow furrowing. "But... he's no longer at the city watch headquarters. Where should I—"

Vivienne raised her hand and his mouth clicked shut. "He's at a warehouse. On the east side of the city, near the old foundry district. I'll give you the location."

She watched as Aminn hurried out of the room, the parchment clutched in his hand. His footsteps faded into the silence of Vivienne's sprawling estate.

The pieces were falling into place, a web of chaos woven with a precision that even Thume—with his vast network of spies and meticulous control over the city—couldn't fathom. Liora's arrest would be the catalyst, the spark that would ignite Lars's rage, Myrim's devotion to justice, and Trinelle's willingness to accept what must be done. The others in his crew, and Darius with his, would also fall into line.

Thume, in his arrogance and blind pursuit of power, had made a fatal mistake. He'd underestimated her. He'd underestimated them all.

She was the weaver, the one who spun the threads of fate, manipulated the players, and orchestrated the dance of chaos and order. Soon, very soon, she would bring his empire crashing down. She'd replace his vision with her own. A new order, a new Azoria, a city and nation forged in her image.

She finished her wine, the crystal goblet cool against her lips, savoring it along with the sweetness of her victory and the intoxicating anticipation of claiming her prize. And Lars Harrow... he would be her plaything king. The jewel in her crown.

NO TIME TO WASTE

17

Lars's base was shrouded in a heavy silence. Rain pattered against the windows, the wind howling like a banshee as Azoria was bathed in cool autumn rains.

Lars paced back and forth in frustrated steps thudding against the worn wooden floor. His mind was a whirlwind of anger, fear, and a desperate need for action. Liora, their brilliant, quirky engineer. The brains and spirit of their crew were locked away in Thume's prison, accused of murder, a pawn in a game that was spiraling out of control.

"We have to get her out," Jax said, clenching his fists as he glared at the storm raging beyond the windows. A fierce protectiveness replaced his usual jovial demeanor. "We have to storm that damn prison and get her back. I've been in there, Lars. Liora won't last a minute in the clink."

"Calm down, Jax," Trin said sharply. She sat at a table, staring at one of Shelle's maps. "Brute force isn't going to get Liora out of jail. We need to be smart about it. Strategic."

Keer snorted and rolled his eyes. "Smart? We're thieves, Trin. Not diplomats. And right now, our friend is locked up, accused of a crime she didn't commit." His face was clouded with bitter anger. "Jax is right. We need to get her out."

Lars stopped his pacing and looked at the gruff old sailor. "She's right, Keer. We need a plan. But we also need to be careful. This isn't just about Liora anymore. Thume knows what we're up to. It could be that our entire plan is cooked. Yes, we must get Liora out, yes, Thume needs to pay, but yes, we could be well and truly fucked."

Trin cleared her throat.

He turned to Trin. "Yes? Do you have an idea?"

"First, let's figure out what Thume's got on Liora. What evidence he's using to hold her. Then, we need to make sure he can't arrest her again. I've done a bit of research." She gestured at stacks of papers and books on a table nearby. "And I believe that we can plan a heist to break Liora out and get away with it as theft, making it legal in the eyes of the law."

Just then, a muffled click echoed from behind the bar. The crew jumped up as one and ran over to the bar, peering at the panels of wood on the floor behind it. A hidden door swung open, and Myrim stepped into the room. His face was pale, eyes shadowed with weariness. Hadn't been sleeping much, that one.

"How the hells did you get in here?" Jax blurted.

Myrim gave a wry smile. "I was the captain of the watch for years, Jax. And a pretty successful one despite what Thume says. I know a thing or two about secret passages.

"Besides," he added sheepishly, "Shelle provided me the intel. It's her job to know the ins and outs of every hideout and rat's nest in the city."

"That woman is a marvel," Lars said, shaking his head. "A true human dynamo."

"Oh, you have no idea."

Lars peered again at the former watch captain, feeling... well, concerned for him, to Lars's vast surprise. "What are your plans, Myrim? What's been going on?"

"Well, you know Liora's in prison by now," Myrim said, a muscle in his jaw twitching. "They have her in the violent offenders' wing."

Jax groaned and Trin cried out in dismay, the painful sounds wrenching Lars's heart.

"Vivienne sent me. She's... worried about Liora. About all of you. She said this is it, that you'd know what to do, and that it's time to act. Now."

Lars threw his hands up. "Well, she's right about one thing. This is it. As for me knowing what to do, I have no fucking clue."

"Captain Myrim?" Trin put a hand on his arm. "We're stuck here. Thume's got us trapped, and the bastards made off with our primary squawk so we've had no way to connect with Darius and his team."

That had been a punch to the gut. Watching Liora get dragged away was devastating, and realizing that the guards had cut off their contact with anyone who could help was worse still. They were under constant surveillance.

"So, if you have any ideas on what we can do to get us out of this mess, get Liora back, and not all end up joining her... well, we're all ears."

Myrim gave Trin a sharp look. "Pretty demanding for a virtual prisoner who's out of options, aren't you?"

Trin glared at him, but then paused and looked at the rest of the crew. "I'm sorry," she said. "Truly. It's just—"

"I know, Miss Meridia." Myrim gave her hand a reassuring pat. "We're all on edge."

He sighed, and it sounded like the weight of everyone's troubles was rushing out of him. "Shelle's working on it. She and I have mutual contacts. She's working on communication. And I'll be getting Liora out personally."

"You?" Lars said. That was unexpected, despite the captain's dismissal from the guard.

Myrim cast a sharp look at Lars, but his response was warm. "Yes, me. Believe it or not, I've come to respect what your team does and how you look out for each other. Not the thieving. I still despise that. But we both know Liora didn't murder Switcher. We both know who did, and we both know she deserves to be set free."

"And what about us?" Keer said. "We're stuck here, Myrim. Trapped. What good is breaking Liora out if we're all just going to end up back in Thume's pokey?"

"You got yourselves into the Institute, didn't you?" Myrim nodded toward the hidden door behind the bar. "I'm sure you can find a way out of your own base."

He paused, eyes sweeping over their faces. They held a blend of determination and a newfound confidence that replaced the uncertainty that had plagued them since Liora's arrest.

"But we have to do more than just escape," Myrim said. "We need to take the fight to Thume."

He pulled out the silver device, activating it with a gleaming button. "Shelle, we're ready. Send the package to Darius. Tell him to meet us north of the city. Near the buildings with the dynamo siphon chamber."

Shelle's voice, a playful tinkling that belied the urgency of the situation, crackled through the device. "Already on it, darling. And Aric? When you see her, give Liora a big kiss for me and tell her that her little invention works like a charm."

Myrim pressed the button again, ending the communication, a smile tugging at the corner of his lips, and tossed the device to Lars. "Darius will have one of those soon, as will Vivienne. Consider it a lifeline. Stay in contact, share information, and trust no one but yourselves."

He stood up and clapped Lars on the shoulder. "Get out of the city. Head north. Vivienne's arranged for transportation. With any luck, Liora will be waiting for you there."

The cell was cramped and cold, and it smelled of sweat, fear, and a lingering hint of something Liora couldn't quite place— it reminded her of a badly wired dynamo generator. A flickering gaslamp spread a weak glow upon the rough stone walls and the six women huddled around a rickety table. They were brimming with curiosity, yet their faces betrayed a wary respect for the newest member of their makeshift gang.

Liora sat at the head of the table, deftly twisting and braiding wires, brow furrowed in concentration as she assembled a small, intricate device. It would have been a lot easier with her glasses, she thought with a pang of loss.

She'd been in this cell for three days now, accused of murder, a pawn in a game she didn't understand. The first day had been rough, the guards rougher, but she determined that fear was for the weak. Now, it was the guards who were apprehensive as she moved through the cell block, her chin lifted and her eyes sharp, her voice a quiet command that even the most hardened criminals rushed to obey.

A woman with a mass of tangled black hair stood near Liora, tears running unchecked down her face. "So do you think he really loved me? Even though he ran off with that bitch from the bakery?"

"He didn't love you, Zara," Liora said. She glanced up from her work. Her gaze met the woman's with warm sympathy and understanding. "And that's okay. Men are simple creatures. They crave sweets. And you..." She gave the woman's shoulder a comforting squeeze. "You are a feast fit for a king."

Zara sniffled, wiping her tears. "You think so, Liora?"

"I know so," Liora said. "You're strong, Zara. Smart. And those eyes could melt a glacier." She flashed a wry grin. "He'll be back. You'll see. Crawling on his knees, begging for another chance. And when he does, you'd better tell him exactly where he can shove his honey cakes."

A gruff voice echoed from the hallway, interrupting their conversation. "Banz! On your feet! You've got a visitor."

The women in the cell, a rough mix of seasoned criminals and first-timers entangled in the nets of Azoria's escalating chaos, bristled at the guard's intrusion. In only a few days, they'd come to see Liora as their figurehead—the one who could fix a broken device, rig a card game, and dispense advice on matters of the heart with equal skill.

"What do you want with her?" One of the women blocked the guard's path.

Another woman joined her, glaring at the guard. "Leave her be. Can't you see she's busy?"

Liora held up a hand, silencing their protests with a gesture. She was curious. Who would come to see her?

"It's alright, ladies," Liora said, meeting each of their worried faces in turn. "I'll be back in a bit. Don't fret. No one's going to mess with you... not while I'm around."

She stood up. Her movements were a bit stiff from the old pain in her shoulder and poor sleeping conditions. But she followed the guard out of the cell, walking like she owned the prison. She had no idea who this visitor could be, but she wasn't afraid. Not anymore.

They walked down a dim corridor, the air reeking of sweat, disinfectant, and despair.

"In here," the guard said, gesturing toward a small, windowless room. "Don't try anything stupid."

Liora suppressed a giggle as she entered the interrogation room, the door clanging shut behind her. What could she try in this cramped little room with a locked metal door? The room was almost bare, with a single metal table and two chairs bolted to the floor. A flickering gaslamp sputtered on the ceiling, its weak illumination doing little to dispel the oppressive gloom.

She expected to see Thume, golden eyes gleaming with a cold triumph, or perhaps the new captain, with her bitter little face basking in satisfaction. But as her eyes adjusted to the dim light, she gasped.

Aric Myrim leaned against the back wall of the room, decked out in full prison guard regalia, brass buttons and shoes polished to a high gleam and cap pulled low.

"Myrim?" Liora squeaked with excitement. "What are you doing here?"

He looked up and flashed her a quizzical look. "What does it look like? I'm here to break you out of prison." He handed her a pair of familiar round spectacles.

"Oh my!" Liora said, taking the glasses from him and putting them on. Her vision cleared, and she peered at her rescuer, a giddy excitement mixing with surprise. "Thank you!"

Myrim grimaced at her. "You doing alright?"

Liora grinned back. "Better now that I've seen a friendly face."

"Good," Myrim said, eyeing her solemnly. "We need to get outside. Now."

"But how?" Liora said in confusion. "There are guards everywhere. And I'm, ya know, a pretty famous prisoner."

"Leave that to me."

He pulled a hefty ring of keys from his pocket, and their jingling echo was the sweetest sound Liora had heard in days. "I still have a few friends in the guard," Myrim explained as he unlocked the chains that bound her wrists.

"Alright. Stay here and keep quiet. In fact, sit at the table with your hands in your lap. If anyone shows up, just look scared and don't answer their questions."

He disappeared through the door, leaving Liora alone in the interrogation room, rubbing her wrists. She sat at the table as Myrim demanded, but giggled at the thought of looking scared. That wasn't her anymore.

A few minutes later, the door creaked open again, and Myrim reappeared, pushing a wheeled stretcher. "Get on. And pull this blanket over you. No talking. No questions."

Liora, trusting Myrim's judgment, obeyed without hesitation. She settled onto the stretcher, pulling the scratchy wool blanket up and over her head. Her heart pounded as Myrim began to wheel her out of the room with quick, purposeful steps. The wheels of the stretcher squeaked and clattered against the stone floor.

They passed through a maze of corridors, the air growing colder, the stench of disinfectant stronger, the echoes of their passage amplified by the silence. Myrim's voice, a low murmur in her ear, broke the tension.

"We're heading for the medical wing. It's near the side entrance. Less security there. Shelle's waiting for us a ways out with a carriage. Just keep your face covered and stay quiet. No matter what you hear, no matter what happens, don't make a sound."

She gave a little thumbs up under the blanket. Myrim rolled her through the corridors for what felt like an eternity, the stretcher clattering along the stone floors and shaking her around like a loose bolt in a generator.

"Almost there," Myrim said, just as he hit a large bump in the floor. The stretcher shuddered, bouncing up into Liora's tailbone and pulling the blanket down.

"Ouch!" she shrieked, then covered her mouth.

"Liora?"

It was Zara. Oh no.

The wide-eyed woman looked from Liora to Myrim and then to the stretcher. "What's wrong with Liora?" she shrieked. "What did you do to her?"

Myrim tried to make a shushing gesture, and Liora sat up to show her everything was fine, but it was no good. Zara's worry carried through the hall, bringing a senior guard running around the corner between them and the exit.

"What is going on here?" he shouted, seeing Zara on her knees grasping Myrim's coat and Liora sitting up waving her arms at the woman. "Liora Banz? What is the meaning of—"

Myrim didn't wait for him to finish the question. Steeling himself, he shoved the stretcher forward causing Liora to flop back onto it. Myrim raced down the hallway like dynamo through a copper wire, careening into the shocked guard and knocking him to the wall.

He barreled around the corner. Thank the hells, the metal bars leading to the door were unlocked and wide open, an abandoned stool and table tucked into the corner of the small secured area.

Picking up speed, ignoring Liora's frightful shrieks and grunts, he burst through the door, the stretcher bumping on the threshold, shocking two guards who were standing outside smoking pipes. Without sparing even a second to look at them, he kept running, crossing the busy street as shocked onlookers jumped out of the way. On the other side of the road he turned down an alley and brought the stretcher to an abrupt and jarring stop.

Liora jumped off and winced, rubbing her backside. "Well, that was—"

"Hsst!" Myrim cut her off as they both peered around the corner.

The two smoking guards were still just standing there, mouths agape. Two more guards ran through the door, looking up and down the street.

Turning to Liora, Myrim put his hands on her shoulders. "Do you know where the Avardis Art Museum is from here?"

"Yep," she said, nodding westward, "right around that corner."

"Go," he said, turning to run back out into the street. "Shelle will be waiting there with a carriage."

"What are you going to do?" Liora said, eyes wide.

"Distract them," Myrim replied and ran off without another word.

✧

The dilapidated buildings huddled together at the city's northern edge, their facades blackened with soot and grime. The last time they'd been here, Lars and company had led Myrim down into a hidden cellar, found courtesy of the dynamo lens. At the same time, it had given them the key to their next big move.

Lars, Trin, Jax, and Keer approached the designated rendezvous, their breaths forming clouds of vapor in the cool night air, footsteps crunching on the gravel. The tension of the escape, the adrenaline rush of evading the city watch, was giving way to both weariness and a gnawing worry about their missing comrade.

"I hope Myrim's plan worked," Trin said, staring at the darkened windows of the squat building.

"He'll get her out, Trin." Lars was reassuring despite a knot of apprehension that tightened in his chest. He couldn't shake the image of Liora's terrified face, glasses falling to the ground as the guards dragged her away.

Keer grunted, putting a hand on Trin's back. "She's a tough one. I'll bet she gave those guards a run for their money."

As they approached the building, a figure emerged from the shadows, a familiar silhouette that brought a wave of relief washing over Lars.

"Darius!" he called out, genuinely pleased to see the rival thief.

Darius grinned, stepping forward. Silas, Inora, Rurik, and Maren stood behind him. They all beamed at Lars's crew with relief.

"Harrow," Darius said, nodding in greeting. "You made it. I was starting to think you couldn't slip past a little pack of guards."

Lars laughed, but it came out tired. "Darius, I don't even have the energy to banter back right now."

"How'd you make it out?" Trin said as she swept her gaze over the assembled crew.

"Shelle's people created a distraction at the back of our place," Silas said. "A little fireworks display, courtesy of Maren's ingenuity. Drew the guards away long enough for us to slip out."

Inora grunted, looking at the bone-weary expression on Lars's face. "And you? I'm guessing your escape was a bit more dramatic."

"We weren't so lucky," Keer said. "Those bastards were watching our every move. We had to create our own diversion."

Lars glanced at Jax with a weary grin. "Let's just say that Jax has a... unique talent for persuasion."

Jax chuckled, flexing his massive bicep. "Those guards won't be forgetting it anytime soon."

The night was quiet in this part of the city. No crowds milled about, and even the ever-present hum of dynamo seemed far away. Lars looked past Darius's crew, searching for his star engineer, but she was nowhere to be seen.

What if something had happened to her? They couldn't pull this off without her, but that wasn't what mattered to Lars. He wouldn't be able to forgive himself if something had happened to the bright and inquisitive dynamo girl.

"Have you seen Liora?" Trin asked Darius and his crew.

"Nope," Rurik said, walking over to Jax to compare bicep girth. "Ain't she in prison?"

Lars grimaced. "Well, we'd hoped—"

"Quiet!" Darius said, slipping back into the dark spaces between buildings. Lars, Trin, Jax, and Keer joined him, breaths puffing in the chill. Someone was coming.

The sound of hoofbeats and clattering wheels grew louder, heading toward their direction. Jax and Rurik pushed forward, peering around the corner, ready to stomp anyone who tried to sniff them out. The sound stopped.

Jax whooped a great cry and leaped out of their hiding place, rushing forward. Lars thought he must have lost his damned mind until he heard a familiar voice.

They exited the building crevice to find Jax picking up the wiry little engineer and spinning her around in a crushing hug.

"Ow ow ow, Jax!" Liora shrieked, though there was absolute joy painted all over her face. "I'm still hurting from Myrim's so-called escape plan."

Thank goodness she was okay. Lars owed Myrim a huge debt for getting her out of that hellhole. "Liora! Is the captain with you?"

The carriage door opened and the driver stepped out, tight leather pants around curvy hips and a tighter black corset over a blue flowing shirt. "I may not be as pretty as Myrim, but I've got a faster carriage." Shelle beamed at Lars as she put an arm around Liora's slim shoulders. "The good—well, he's not a captain anymore, but he's been delayed. Don't worry about him."

Liora nestled close to Shelle and looked up at her sparkling eyes. "Dynamo girls."

"Dynamo girls," Shelle agreed with a grin.

"Alright alright," Darius cut in gruffly. "I'm sure we're all excited and we all love the touching reunion. Really, my eyes are moist. But I believe we have an escape to make and a warehouse to rob."

Trin rolled her eyes at Darius. "Is there even a heart under all that bluster, Darius?"

"Probably not. I'll steal one when we get back from this trip."

Inora chuckled heartily.

Lars grinned despite his weariness. Darius did have a point. "Well, we can't all fit into one carriage. Any ideas on how we're going to get there? Keer said it was a long ways away."

"Don't worry about that, Lars," Shelle said. "Vivienne has two fast carriages ready and waiting for you." She nodded her head up the street along the old city wall. "My people made sure to gather all your gear from your respective bases and load it up."

She smiled at Liora. "By the way, darling... Vivienne told me to tell you the carriages were crafted to your specifications."

"Oh," Liora breathed. "This is going to be fun."

The crews walked along the wall together, ribbing at each other with genuine camaraderie. This was what their whole world was about. The daring plan, the race for the prize, and the flight from capture. They were, each of them, in their element.

Some more than others, Lars thought, watching Jax and Rurik compare their muscles and give each other workout tips. Though Rurik was far shorter than his big friend, he was just as stocky. Lars was glad Jax had a bruiser buddy to relate with.

Circling a small building, they came upon the carriages. They were sleek and sturdy, made of polished black wood that converged on a metal-reinforced base. Each was tethered to two gorgeous horses, their breaths creating great huffs of vapor in the night air as their hooves clattered on the cobblestones in impatience. Lars had no doubt they would make their way north with impressive speed.

"Alright, load up," he said to the crews. Each headed toward a different carriage. He eyed the single horse-drawn carriage Shelle rode.

"Shelle, I assume you're staying here in the city?"

The mischievous spy let her lip puff out. "I see," she pouted, her voice coming out as a sultry sigh, "I'm not welcome here."

"No! That's not what I—"

Trin giggled from behind him, wrapping an arm around his waist. "Lars, you are so gullible, my love."

Shelle joined her in laughing at Lars's discomfort. "They usually are," she agreed. "Yes, Lars, I'm staying here. I'm on my way to pick up Myrim and take him back to our hideout. We'll be waiting for you when you return."

"Shelle?" Liora said. "I don't know if I've told you this, but I love your optimism."

The crews finished loading up and said their goodbyes. Shelle hopped back into her carriage, and with a flick of the reigns through a small front opening, her horse pulled her back toward the heart of the city.

Silas and Keer were set to commandeer the two carriages on their trek through the scrublands. Checking one last time to make sure everyone was packed up and ready to go, they began their long ride north toward Thume's warehouse and to a hopeful victory.

✧

A scraggly line of twisted trees marked the edge of the scrublands, their bare branches creaking in the wind like bones rattling in the cold night air. The air smelled of damp earth and wet leaves, a far cry from the streets of Azoria where the scents of smoke and spice always lingered. Lars crouched low behind the ragged treeline, surveying the warehouse in the distance. His eyes scanned for any sign of movement among the guards patrolling the perimeter, though he could hear the rustle of leaves and shifting bodies as his crew huddled nearby, waiting for his signal.

It had been a long, arduous journey north, each day bleeding into the next as the landscape grew more barren and hostile. They had ridden hard—harder than usual, even for Lars—pushing their horses through endless fields and rocky plains until the city had become a distant memory. By the time they had made camp each night, exhaustion had set in, and they took what little rest they could get.

Meals had been light, just enough to stave off the hunger but never enough to fill them. Jax had complained, his stomach growling louder than the campfire they'd huddled around, but he'd fallen silent when Keer started taking potshots at empty cans with a musket, each shot echoing across the empty plains like a thunderclap. It was just to pass the time, Keer had claimed, but Lars knew it was more than that. It was preparation. Gearing up for one hell of a storm.

The nights were restless, with only the flickering firelight and the occasional howl of some unseen creature to keep them company. Inora had spent her nights maintaining her musket, every piece of the device as precise as her movements. When she wasn't sharpening her blades or adjusting her gear, she watched the others with a hawk-like gaze. Her mind never stopped calculating the next move, even when there was no move to be made.

After days of riding, they'd arrived at the edge of the compound, the bare trees giving way to the looming silhouette of the warehouse. The tall, imposing structure stood like a sentinel in the darkness, surrounded by tall metal fences and the occasional gleam of torchlight from the guards making their rounds.

"This is it," Lars said, standing against the backdrop of the night. He glanced over his shoulder at his crew, each poised and ready, tension rippling through the air like a coiled spring. They were ready to move, to act. Mostly, they were ready to see what secrets Thume had buried in the depths of that warehouse.

The time for preparation was over.

Lars crouched low, gesturing with quick, decisive motions as his crew huddled closer. The warehouse loomed in the distance, its walls illuminated by the roving searchlights.

He looked at both crews, eyes shifting between each of them. "Alright, listen up. Two crews, one objective. We get in, find out what Thume's up to, and get out. No complications."

Standing at Lars's side, arms crossed, Darius flashed a wry smile. "No complications, Lars? Since when have we ever had a job that didn't have complications?"

Lars shot him a sideways look but allowed himself the smallest smirk. "Touché. But we stick to the plan, and we minimize the chaos."

"And maximize the profit," Darius reminded him. "Remember, this is Thume's own private warehouse. Hells only know what kind of riches he has holed up inside."

Lars saw fit to ignore him. Of course they were going to make off with everything they could.

He pointed toward the northwest side of the compound, where the fence dipped into a natural gully, and the guards' presence looked thinner. "That's our entry point. It's the least guarded section of the compound. We make our approach from there, split into two teams once we're inside. Maren, Inora—you're on rooftop duty. Disrupt the dynamo systems, create as much confusion as you can. If anything goes south, make sure the guards can't get their systems back online. Keep them blind."

Inora nodded, a determined look painted on her face. Maren gave a quick, playful salute, fingers twitching as he fiddled with one of his gadgets.

Darius interjected, shifting his weight as he spoke. "While they're causing mayhem, I'll distribute Liora's sound devices. Those should keep the guards running in circles while you all make your move."

Lars nodded. "Exactly. You keep them distracted, Darius. Make sure they're too busy chasing their own tails to notice us."

Turning to the rest of the group, Lars continued, taking on a more urgent tone. "The rest of us—Jax, Rurik, Trin, Liora, and me—we'll move to the main warehouse level. That's where the dynamo signature is strongest and where we'll find our answers. Keer, Silas, you're with us too.

"Jax and Rurik, you'll handle the guards at the door. Knock them out, strip them of their uniforms, and get them tied up. Silas and Keer will wear the uniforms and return to the carriages to bring them to the depot bay. That'll be our escape route."

Keer leaned forward, sharp eyes narrowing as he considered the plan. "And if we get caught?"

Lars shot him a grin, though it didn't quite reach his eyes. "Don't."

Keer raised an unconvinced eyebrow but said nothing. Silas, beside him, gave a quiet nod.

"We move in pairs," Lars said, looking at each crew member. "Wait for the searchlights to pass, then run for cover. We regroup at the base of the warehouse walls and take it from there. No one gets left behind, got it?"

A grin split Jax's face. "Got it. This is going to get good."

There was a murmur of agreement as the group shifted, the nervous energy palpable. The quiet hum of distant dynamo systems drifted through the trees, a reminder of the power that lay just beyond their reach.

"Alright, enough talk," Lars said. "Everyone knows their role. We do this clean, we do this fast. There's no way we'll do this unnoticed. Try not to get yourselves killed. Or caught, which might be worse this time around."

With a final glance at the looming warehouse, Lars signaled for them to begin. There was no more time for second thoughts or doubts. The ante was already collected on the table, and the crew of master thieves were about to play their hand.

Lars waited. His heart pounded in his chest as the searchlights swept over the compound. The beams of light sliced through the night like knives, but Lars remained calm, crouched low alongside Trin. Two by two, the crews began to move. They darted forward, running across the open space toward the perimeter fence.

Keer and Silas were the first to dash across the gravel and dirt. They found cover behind a stack of old crates. Pulling a set of metal shears from his pack, Keer quickly made an entrance in the wire mesh surrounding the warehouse.

Lars nodded to Jax and Rurik, who slipped forward next, their large frames somehow moving with the grace of men a third their size. As soon as the searchlight passed again, Inora and Maren made their way across, Inora helping shoulder the load of all Maren's gear.

Lars motioned to Trin and Liora. "You two, now."

Trin gave him a quick smile, and with a deep breath, she and Liora darted out of cover, their forms low to the ground as they sprinted toward the safety of the wall. Lars waited, watching as they slid behind a rusted metal barrel just as another searchlight passed by.

The tension was palpable, each heartbeat a countdown to the moment the guards might catch them. The seconds stretched into an eternity.

"You ready for this?" Lars asked Darius.

Darius flashed him a wry grin. "You already know the answer to that. Don't slow me down, Harrow."

The searchlights passed, Lars signaled, and they made their move. They darted forward, joining the others at the wall just as a guard began his patrol.

The guard was a Zarakaran elite, his ebony skin gleaming under the harsh lights, and Darius let out a low whistle as they ducked behind cover. "Thume pulled out all the stops, huh?" he whispered.

Keer peered out cautiously. "Grand Legion of Zarakar. Mercenaries." He spat on the ground to show just how he felt about that squad. "I'd know their emblem anywhere. We need to move quickly."

The guard passed by, oblivious to their presence, and Lars signaled for the next phase of the plan. Darius, Inora, and

Maren moved toward a ladder leading up to the warehouse rooftop, climbing the rungs to the top of the first platform. Darius gave his crewmates a quick nod before splitting off, heading along the building to plant Liora's sound devices. His footsteps were silent as he ran along the low rooftop toward the main gate area, slipping in and out of view like a ghost. Inora and Maren continued up the ladder, disappearing into the darkness above.

Meanwhile, Lars led the remaining group toward a small metal door on the side of the warehouse. The door was guarded by two men, armed with sabers, their eyes scanning for any sign of intruders.

Lars motioned to Jax, who cracked his knuckles with a grin before nodding to Rurik. The pair rushed forward in perfect sync, moving like wraiths as they closed in on the guards. In a blur of movement, Jax grabbed the first guard from behind, wrapping a massive arm around the man's neck, cutting off his breath in an instant. The guard struggled for a moment before going limp, and Jax lowered him to the ground.

Rurik dealt with the second guard just as fast, slamming a heavy fist into the man's temple. The guard crumpled without a sound, and Rurik began stripping him of his uniform.

Lars stepped forward, eyes scanning the area. "Damn fast work, you two," he said. "Get them bound and gagged."

In a matter of moments, the guards were tied up and hidden behind a stack of barrels. Silas and Keer grabbed the uniforms and pulled them on, the oversized clothes hanging like tents on their frames.

Keer buttoned up the high collar of his stolen uniform. "There. How do I look?"

"Like you're playing dress-up," Liora said with a grin. "Just keep your head down."

They turned their attention back to the metal door, but Lars frowned as he tried the handle. "It's locked. And no keyhole."

Lars pulled out his squawk and pressed a button on its side. "Maren," he called, "can you unlock this door?"

The squawk only crackled, but then Maren's voice came through. "Sorry. We're only just getting into place. It will take a while before I'm set up. I think you need to find another way."

For a moment, uncertainty hung in the air as the crew exchanged glances. Rurik pointed to a small duct high up on the wall, just above the door. "There. That's our way in."

They all turned to look, and Lars nodded in agreement. "Sharp eyes, Rurik. That'll work. But it's tight." He glanced at Trin. "Think you can make it through?"

Trin raised an eyebrow and grinned. "You know it."

Jax and Rurik moved to Trin's side, giving her a boost to shimmy into the narrow duct. Trin crawled through the tight space with nimble ease, heart racing with excitement. She could hear the muffled sounds of the crew outside as she made her way through the duct, and after a few tense moments, she reached the other side.

With a soft thump, Trin dropped down into a small corridor. She listened intently, senses heightened, and after hearing no one nearby, she crept forward. She spotted a pressure plate on the floor and rolled her eyes. Even a child could avoid that trap. She continued forward toward a guard who stood by the door, his back turned.

Moving fast, Trin grabbed a nearby metal rod and knocked the guard out cold with a swift, precise strike. He collapsed in a heap, and Trin bound his hands and gagged him. A moment later, there was a quiet click, and the door unlocked from the inside.

The metal door swung open, revealing Trin standing in triumph over the unconscious guard. "Piece of cake," she said with a grin.

Lars chuckled as he, Jax, and Rurik raced inside, their eyes scanning the area for any other threats. But just as they were about to move deeper into the warehouse, Jax cursed as a panel thunked beneath his foot.

A click sounded, and a low hum emanated from the walls. The heavy open door started to close with a loud, menacing groan.

"Shit!" Lars hissed as the door began to shut, trapping Keer, Silas, and Liora outside.

Keer acted without hesitation. He slammed his body against the door, trying to keep it from closing. But the door, charged with dynamo from the trap, sent a jolt through his body. He collapsed to the ground in a heap. The door stopped moving, but Keer did as well.

"Keer!" Liora cried out, rushing to his side. She knelt with trembling hands and checked his pulse. "He's still breathing." Trin gasped in relief.

But they had no time to waste. Jax glanced down the hall with narrowed eyes. "We've got company," he warned as the sounds of guards approaching grew louder.

Silas crouched beside Keer. "I'll take him back to the carriages. We need to reposition them anyway. I'll make sure he's safe."

Lars nodded. "Take care of him, Silas. We'll meet you back there."

As Silas hoisted Keer's limp form onto his shoulder and retreated toward the sparse treeline, Jax and Rurik moved forward to meet the oncoming guards, their fists already clenched and ready for action.

Lars raised the squawk to his mouth and pressed a button on the side. The crystal charge in its center lit up, indicating it was ready. Lars spoke into it calmly despite the chaos. "Darius, Keer's down, but we're still moving forward. What's your status?"

Darius's voice crackled back through the squawk's pinholes. "Planting the last of the devices. I'll meet you at the north end of the warehouse in five. Keep moving."

Trin watched as Liora stood up, fists clenched and face set in determination. She saw her friend sling Keer's musket over her shoulder, the weight of it pressing down visibly. Trin knew how much Liora hated that weapon—it had once injured her, leaving wounds deeper than just the physical scar. Yet here Liora was, ready to carry it for the sake of their survival. A mix of admiration and concern welled up inside her.

"Inora," Lars said into the squawk. "Security systems?"

Inora's voice came through, a hint of dismay in her gruff tone. "Disabled, now. Don't worry. Silas and Keer made it back safely. Now get moving before more guards show up."

With a nod, Lars led the way deeper into the warehouse. Liora and Trin stayed close behind, ready for whatever came next.

The air inside the warehouse smelled of oil and metal, the quiet hum of dynamo systems thrumming behind the walls. The crew sped down dimly lit corridors, seeking cover in shadows wherever possible. Despite the tension that radiated from them, the guards this deep into the warehouse were unaware of their presence. Their defenses were fixed on the patrol routes and the areas around the gates, leaving the inner sections of the warehouse more vulnerable than they should have been.

Lars crouched behind a stack of crates, sharp eyes scanning the area ahead. A group of armed guards stood vigilant in the main doorway leading to the section of the warehouse they needed to reach. The door loomed large behind the guards, the one remaining barrier between them and Thume's inner hold.

He raised the squawk to his lips, filled with urgency. "Maren, now."

From his position on the rooftop, Maren heard the call. Lars waited as he shut down the dynamo system to the entire area. The lights flickered once, twice, and then went out completely, plunging the warehouse into darkness.

Shouts of confusion erupted from the guards. One of them barked a command in Zarakaran, the loud boom cutting through the blackness. The sound of boots shuffling on the floor echoed off the walls as the guards scrambled to regroup.

Suddenly, a tinny voice echoed from a far wall, startling them further. "Over here! Help!" it cried out, the words shrill and desperate.

Red backup lights flickered to life, bathing the area in an eerie crimson glow. Confused by the unexpected sound, two of the guards rushed toward it with their weapons drawn. "This way!" one of them shouted, trying to direct the others.

"No, you idiots! Here!" another voice rang out, further away, causing more confusion.

Liora, hiding in the darkness with Lars, stifled a giggle. She could hardly contain her delight as they watched the guards fall victim to her sound devices. Each one was placed to perfection, emitting recorded voices that led the guards on a wild goose chase.

But even with the distraction, several guards remained in front of the door they needed to get through.

"We'll take care of this," Rurik growled as he prepared to charge forward.

Lars raised a hand to stop him. "There's too many of them. We need a bigger distraction."

Darius, waiting in the rafters above, dropped down gracefully beside them, landing in a crouch. His lips curled into a rictus grin. "Looks like we don't have much of a choice."

Rurik, grinning as well, snatched the musket from Liora's shoulder. "Time to make some noise."

Without waiting for a go-ahead, Rurik aimed at the far wall of the warehouse and pulled the trigger. The crack of the musket reverberated through the entire building, the sound deafening in the enclosed space. The guards jumped, startled by the sudden, terrifying noise. Then all at once, they rushed in every direction, trying to locate the source of the new threat.

The team heading for the door used the chaos to their advantage. Staying low and keeping to the shadows, they edged forward, inching closer to the main door while the guards scrambled around them.

Jax and Rurik, on the other hand, didn't bother with subtlety. The two men charged headlong into the fray, their fists flying as they knocked out guards left and right, sowing further confusion among Thume's elite forces.

At last, Lars reached the door with Liora, Trin, and Darius close behind him. Glancing over his shoulder to make sure they weren't being followed, Lars pushed open the door, and the three of them slipped through. It closed behind them with a quiet click.

Testing the handle, Lars frowned. "Locked."

Trin looked concerned, but Lars shook his head. "We'll solve that problem later. Let's move."

The thieves made their way through the silent room beyond the door, the air growing heavier with each step. Unlike the rest of the warehouse, this room was eerily quiet, save for the constant hum of dynamo that pulsed around them. Lars felt a chill creep up his spine.

"This is where the dynamo signature is strongest," Liora said in awe. "This is what we've been looking for."

They could feel it as they ventured deeper into the room—an unseen force humming all around them. Dynamo flowed everywhere.

They were close. Very close.

Lars, Liora, Darius, and Trin moved further into the room, the hum of dynamo growing louder, almost as if the very air was vibrating with energy. The dim, red emergency lights cast eerie shadows on the walls, making the space feel even more ominous.

"Stay close." Lars glanced around cautiously. Whatever they were about to find was more than just another one of

Thume's schemes—it was something far bigger and more dangerous.

They rounded a corner and entered a vast, open chamber. Liora gasped, eyes wide as she took in the sight before them. In the center of the room stood a massive bank of dynamo equipment, cables and wires stretching in every direction, feeding into large crystals stacked near the walls. The entire system buzzed with power and glowed faintly, like beating hearts pulsating with life.

As they stepped forward, dynamo lights flared to life, bathing the room in a sterile glow.

And then they heard a new sound coming from the dynamo devices in front of them. It was a low, constant murmur of voices layered on top of one another, as if a thousand conversations were happening all at once.

Darius stopped dead in his tracks, his brow furrowing. "What the hells is that?"

Liora moved forward cautiously, trailing her fingers along one of the wrapped wires leading into the crystal bank. She pressed her ear closer to the hum, trying to isolate the noise.

"It's... people," she gasped. "Voices. Conversations. Hundreds of them."

Trin's eyes widened. "Is this... Is this coming from Azoria?"

"I think so," Liora said. "Listen over here. You can hear music playing. I bet that's Tavern Row!"

Lars listened, tried to tune in on one or two conversations. He heard merchants, customers, thieves, lovers. Dozens of conversations, all flowing through this room on the wings of copper wire.

"He's listening. Thume. He's using Azoria's dynamo grid to monitor everything and everyone in the hells damned city."

Lars's mind raced as the implications hit him. Thume wasn't just tapping into the city's power—he was tapping into its secrets. Every conversation, every whisper, every plan—Thume had access to it all. This wasn't just surveillance. It was abuse of power on a scale Lars had never imagined.

Liora pointed to the thick wires leading to the crystals on the walls. "These are for storing sounds. They're like the ones we've been experimenting with. Thume's been collecting all of these conversations—who knows how long he's been doing this?"

Lars felt a surge of anger and revulsion. This wasn't the wealth or weapons they had expected to find—it was far more insidious. Thume had been playing a different game altogether, one that went beyond copper and crystals. He had been building a web of control, a way to monitor and manipulate the entire city.

"This is worse than we thought," Lars said, clenching his jaw tight. He reached into his satchel and pulled out a bag. "We're taking as many of these as we can as evidence. We'll show the city what Thume's been up to."

Liora sped to the crystal bank and disconnected several of the storage crystals as quickly as possible. Each one hummed as she placed it into the bag, the glow from within fading as the connection was severed.

"Got it," she whispered. "This should be more than enough, I hope."

But even as the haul was secured, a heavy disappointment settled over the group. There were no weapons, no crystal charges. No treasure trove of wealth that could make up for the risks they had taken. All they had found was a dark revelation that left a bitter taste in their mouths.

Darius shook his head in frustration, the anger visibly bubbling up inside him. "I was promised a score. Vivienne said this would be the haul of a lifetime. But instead, we find this? More intrigue, more lies?"

A grimace crossed Lars's face, yet his words were calm. "We already knew Vivienne was using us to get to Thume."

Darius clenched his fists. "I don't care about her games. I care about getting what's owed to us. This... this isn't it."

Lars knew Darius was right, but there was nothing more they could do here. They had what they needed to expose Thume's surveillance operation. But beyond that, their hands were tied. The best reward they could hope for now was to get home safely and take Thume down before he could have them all in chains.

Lars hit a button on the squawk. "Maren, open the door. We're done here."

There was a brief pause before the door clicked open. As they stepped back into the dim warehouse, they could hear the chaos Rurik and Jax had created—shouts, scuffles, and the occasional musket shot echoing through the space.

Lars glanced over at Darius. "We'll figure this out. But first, and I can't stress this enough, we have to fucking *move*."

Darius nodded. "Let's just hope we still have a way out."

The group fled through the warehouse, keeping low as they navigated through the maze of corridors and crates. They could see Rurik and Jax leading the guards on a merry chase, the two men ducking in and out of cover, using the confusion to keep the guards off balance. Here and there, a device would call out, "Over here! No, over there!" It was madness.

Rurik paused long enough to fire another musket round into the air, sending the guards scrambling again. He grinned as he saw Lars and the others approach.

"Took you long enough," Jax said with amusement. "Ready to make a run for it?"

Lars nodded, raising the squawk to his lips once more. "Everyone, let's go!" he barked, the urgency unmistakable.

With a final burst of energy, the crew sprinted toward the far door leading to the loading docks, the shouts of the guards echoing behind them.

As Lars, Trin, Liora, and Darius raced to escape, the clash of musket shots and angry shouts behind them echoed through the air. The chaos grew louder with each step. But the far door to the loading docks was in sight now. And beyond that was the relative safety of their waiting carriages.

Lars pushed forward, urgency driving every step. Jax and Rurik had kept the guards occupied in the distance, but they knew their window was closing quickly. Lars could feel the promise of freedom so close he could taste it.

They burst through the door, spilling out into the cool night air. The carriages were there, horses stamping nervously, ready for a fast getaway. Lars felt a brief flicker of relief. But then, just as they emerged from the exit, a shadow moved.

Without warning, a guard lunged from behind a stack of crates. He shot an arm out like a snake and grabbed Trin. She cried out in surprise, stumbling as the guard yanked her back with a violent pull. His arm locked around her waist, grip unrelenting as he hauled her backward. She could feel his breath on her neck, hot and determined, as he tightened his hold.

Lars skidded to a stop, spinning around just in time to see the terror flash in Trin's eyes. The guard, sword drawn, held her as a human shield.

"Don't move!" the guard said in passable Ithrian, his face alight with malice as his blade gleamed in the moonlight. He was ready to strike if anyone dared approach.

Everything slowed. Lars's heart hammered in his chest, instincts screaming at him to act, but the wrong move could cost Trin her life. His hand twitched toward his blade, but there was no time—

A sharp crack split the night. The guard stiffened and his grip on Trin loosened as a single musket shot slammed home. His body swayed for a moment, the life draining from his eyes before he crumpled to the ground.

Trin stumbled free, gasping as she staggered back and regained her balance. She looked up, breath catching in her throat as she saw Inora perched on a nearby rooftop.

The musket still smoked in Inora's hands. She gave a curt nod as her sharp eyes scanned for more threats.

Lars didn't waste a second. He grabbed Trin by the arm, pulling her toward the carriages. "We need to go!" he shouted, cutting through the din. There was no time to thank Inora now—their escape was still on the line.

The crew sprinted across the platform, with the sounds of pursuing guards echoing closer by the second. As they neared the carriages, Lars glanced over his shoulder and spotted Rurik and Jax breaking from the fight, racing toward them.

Their faces were flushed with exertion, but they were grinning, adrenaline coursing through them. They had done their job, keeping the guards at bay long enough for everyone to make their escape.

Inora and Maren were already scrambling down from the rooftop, their boots hitting the ground just as Darius leaped into the lead carriage, where Silas sat waiting with the reins taut in his hands.

Rurik barreled toward the carriage, throwing himself onto the seats with a quick nod to Darius. "Go, go, go!" Rurik yelled as Inora and Maren climbed aboard.

"Unhitch the horses!" Lars shouted as Liora circled the carriage.

Darius smirked at Lars. "Thanks, Harrow, but I'm done with this mess. Silas, ride!"

Lars lunged forward, trying to stop him. "Wait!" he called out, but Darius was already pulling away, urging his spymaster on.

With a shout, Silas cracked the reins. The carriage bolted into the night, speeding away from the warehouse at full gallop.

Lars clenched his fists in frustration but had no time to dwell on Darius's departure. He and the rest of his crew had to make their own escape, and fast. He turned to Jax, who was already untying the horses from the second carriage.

Jax slapped the lead horse's rump, and they both galloped away from the depot, leaving the carriage untethered and ready for the crew to pile in. He flashed his engineer a nervous look. "Let's hope this works, Liora!"

Lars, Trin, and Jax scrambled into the carriage, the tension in the air crackling with dynamo-like energy. Trin turned her attention to Keer, who was still slumped against the side of the carriage, unconscious but alive. She smoothed his hair back with obvious and overwhelming concern. Lars urged Liora to hurry—the guards had regrouped and were closing in fast, nearly at the door. In seconds they would be overrun.

Liora's hands trembled with anticipation as she found what she was looking for. A long cable interspersed every few feet with amplifier crystals that stretched underneath the carriage and beyond, leading south.

Keer and Maren had laid this cable on their scouting trip weeks back, stretching just shy of fifty miles from Thume's siphoning chamber in Azoria all the way to the warehouse in preparation for this moment. Liora grasped the end of the cable and dashed to the depot's dynamo terminal. Once it was plugged in, she leaped onto the carriage and into Jax's arms.

Just as the pursuing guards closed in, Liora blew them a kiss and hit a button on a small device.

Suddenly, the warehouse exploded with sound. A drumbeat began, blaring from the carriage and all the tiny devices Darius had scattered throughout the warehouse. The guards stumbled in confusion, just as a wild dynamo fiddle riff sizzled through the air.

The bottom of the carriage lit up with glowing blue energy, crackling with power as it attuned to the long, snaking cable—just as the opening lines to Dynamo Daydream blared through the speakers:

I'm a dynamo dreamer, charging in the night
Got my wires crossed, but baby it feels right
Dynamo currents flowing, through copper veins
We'll light the sky up bright, and burn away the chains

The carriage jolted forward, rocketing down the thin cable like a high-speed tram, racing out of the depot at breakneck speed. The sheer force of the acceleration shoved the crew back into their seats, their hearts pounding as they hurtled across the land faster than they or anyone else in the world had ever traveled.

As they raced away from the warehouse, the landscape blurred around them, and in the distance, they could see Darius's carriage moving at a far slower pace. They shot past him, the air filled with wild music and the thrill of their explosive escape.

In the back of Darius's speeding carriage, Maren leaned over to Darius. "Told you we should've waited," he said with a wry grin.

Darius could only shake his head, a chagrined smile on his lips as he watched Lars and his crew disappear into the night, back toward Azoria and their uncertain fate.

ASCENT

18

The night sky blurred overhead as the carriage shot across the landscape, riding the dynamo wire with a speed that defied belief. Lars sat near the front, mind racing almost as fast as the carriage, replaying the events of the past few hours.

After what felt like only moments, the familiar silhouette of Azoria came into view. The towering headquarters of the Gaming Commission and sprawling streets loomed before them, lit by the soft glow of street lamps and the ever-present hum of dynamo energy. They had covered what should have taken days in just a couple of hours, and as they approached the outskirts of the city, Lars could feel his heart rate slowing along with the carriage. Their wild journey was almost at an end.

The carriage shuddered to a stop at the northern edge of Azoria.

"That," Liora said, "was fucking awesome."

Lars hopped off first and turned back to the crew. Trin was already jumping down, grabbing her pack and slinging it over her shoulder. Jax followed, landing on the cobblestones with a soft thud. Eyes wide with manic energy, Liora scrambled out last, clutching her equipment and the pilfered crystals to her chest.

But Lars's eyes shifted to the back of the carriage, where Keer lay slumped against the wooden planks, still unconscious from the jolt of dynamo that had taken him down at Thume's depot. His face was pale as he took ragged breaths. Lars felt a pang of worry twist in his gut.

"We need to get him to Myrim's base. Shelle will know where we can take him."

Jax grunted as he hoisted Keer's limp body over his shoulder, carrying the man's weight with ease but not without a grim look on his face. "Alright, let's go. He needs help bad."

Lars nodded, raising the squawk as they moved. "Shelle, do you copy?"

No response.

Lars tried again, a touch more urgency in his tone. "Shelle, it's Lars. We're back. Keer's down—we need help."

Still nothing but static. Lars lowered the squawk, muttering a curse.

"Shelle's not answering. We'll have to make it to the base on our own."

"Something's not right," Trin said, eyes scanning the narrow streets that stretched before them. "It's never this quiet."

Lars nodded toward the nearest alleyway. "Stay sharp. Let's keep off the main roads. We'll cut through the back streets and head for Myrim's base. The first priority is getting Keer help."

They crept into cover one by one, their footsteps light but quick as they made their way through the alley. The air was colder here, biting at their exposed skin.

The once-frantic city now felt like a graveyard. Shops were shut tight, stalls abandoned, and the few lanterns that flickered in the dark cast eerie shadows against the walls. The crew moved in silence, the tension palpable. Lars watched his team closely, every sense heightened as they crept through the quiet streets. What the hell had happened here?

They moved as fast as they could, darting between buildings and sticking close to the walls, keeping as low and quiet as possible. The familiar hum of dynamo energy felt louder in the absence of city noise, and every creak of their gear felt magnified in the silence. Lars kept his eyes moving, searching for signs of life—or worse, signs of danger.

The crew followed silently, the weight of the past few days heavy on their shoulders. Their escape from Thume's depot had been nothing short of miraculous, but they weren't out of the woods yet. The safety of familiarity loomed just ahead, but it felt like a distant dream.

Finally, Lars signaled for them to slow as they approached a narrow street toward Myrim's makeshift hideout. He could see the glow of dynamo lanterns in the distance, but something about it made his stomach churn. The city wasn't just quiet—it was shut down.

"I'm not liking this," Jax said, adjusting Keer's weight on his shoulder. Lars grunted in agreement.

They rounded the corner, and the street narrowed further, pressing in around them. Myrim's base was just ahead—just past the final stretch of a broad cobblestone street.

"Wait a moment," Lars said, scanning the rooftops. That's when he saw it—just a flicker of movement, the flash of metal catching the moonlight. Lars froze, squinting up at the darkened rooftop. There, perched like a vulture, was a lone city watchman.

His face turned toward them.

"We've been made," Lars murmured, trying to keep his voice steady.

Trin followed his gaze, and her eyes narrowed when she saw what Lars was looking at. "The city watch," she whispered, despair lacing her words. "Damn it."

Lars bit back a curse. "We're too exposed to backtrack now," he said through clenched teeth. The streets were far too open for any sort of retreat, and with Thume's lackey watching from above, any sudden moves could tip them into a full-blown ambush.

Liora shifted beside him, clutching the stolen crystals tighter. Her eyes darted around nervously. "What do we do?"

Weighing their options, Lars decided there was only one. "We keep moving. Stay cool. Act like nothing's wrong." He glanced at the others calmly, even though every instinct told him this was bad. "Whatever happens, we stick together."

Jax grunted in agreement, rolling his shoulders in preparation for whatever came next. Trin gave a small, tight nod and clenched her jaw. Liora, still jittery, swallowed hard but fell in step without hesitation. Keer bounced against Jax's back as they moved forward, their hearts pounding in unison. Lars led the way, every sense heightened, strolling across the street as if he didn't have a care in the world.

Suddenly, harsh dynamo lights flared, bathing the cobblestone street in a dazzling white light.

✧

In the dark, standing triumphantly at the warehouse entrance, was Lord Cecil Thume.

A dozen of his elite guards flanked him, each combat-ready and standing at rigid attention. The dynamo lamps cast confusing shadows across their faces, but the smirk on Thume's lips was unmistakable. Lars felt his stomach drop. Though the street was wide, the guards spread out in a rigid formation, trapping the thieves with nowhere to go.

Thume stepped forward—relaxed, regal, and beaming with confidence. He gestured with a lazy hand, and two figures were dragged into view from behind the line of guards.

Myrim and Shelle were both shackled in heavy chains, looking battered but alive. Shelle's usual boisterous mien was gone. Myrim's jaw was clenched as his eyes locked with Lars. He shook his head as if to say, *There's no way out*.

"I'm so glad you made it, Master Harrow," Thume mocked. "I was wondering when you'd show up. I must say, your timing is impeccable." His attention flicked over each member of the crew, lingering a moment on Jax, who still carried Keer. "Though it seems you've had a rougher night than expected."

The crew froze, tension rippling through them like a dynamo current. Lars clenched his fists, feeling the totality of their situation settling in. They were outnumbered, outmaneuvered, and their usual routes for escape had already been cut off.

Thume's smirk widened. "You're all under arrest," he said. "And this time, there will be no breakouts, no clever tricks. You've had your fun, but the game is over." He gestured toward his guards, who began tightening their circle around the crew, weapons raised and ready.

Lars's mind raced, searching for an opening, a strategy—anything. But even he knew the truth: they were cornered.

Thume stepped closer, his boots clicking against the cobblestones as he surveyed the group. "Look around you, Larson. You're done. You've lost."

Thume's smirk grew into a full grin as he paced back and forth in front of the crew, the gold in his irises gleaming in the harsh dynamo light. He was in complete control now, and he knew it.

"You know, Master Harrow, I do admire your nerve. Breaking into my warehouse, hoping to steal what belongs to me—quite the move. I'm sure you gave a wondrous performance. But, as they say, every show must come to an end."

He stopped pacing, fixing his gleaming gaze on Lars with a predatory gleam. "You think you're clever, don't you? But you're not the first to try and challenge me, and I doubt you'll be the last. Yet here you are, just like all the others—trapped, beaten, and ultimately, defeated."

Thume gestured toward the city around them, the dark streets and empty buildings. "Azoria belongs to me. This city moves because I allow it to. Its people breathe because I permit it. You see, I don't just control the Gaming Commission, Harrow. I control the very lifeblood of this city, don't I? I know every move that's made, every word that's spoken. I am everywhere, watching, listening. You can't so much as whisper without me hearing it. I own this place."

His smile widened, a cruel, almost triumphant grimace. "And you, with all your little tricks, thought you could stop me? You thought you could outsmart me? You're just a *thief*, Larson. You only exist because I allow it. And you've been nothing more than a distraction, a brief annoyance that I've tolerated for far too long."

He stepped closer, growing more menacing. "But now, you are finished. And the consequences? Well, let's just say they're not as light-hearted as you might have hoped." He glanced at Myrim and Shelle. "The city will see you for what you are—failures, pests that have tried to remain relevant that must be eradicated."

A satisfied smirk played on his lips as he folded his arms across his chest. "Any last words before I take what's left of your little crew into custody? Any witty banter you'd like to play out before the bars slam home?"

Lars clenched his jaw, mind racing.

But before he could respond, a calm, measured voice cut through the tension, echoing out of the darkness. "You see? This is the man you have entrusted your city to, Councilwoman Revas."

The sound of footsteps followed, steady and deliberate, coming closer. Thume's smug expression faltered. His eyes narrowed as he turned toward the source of the voice.

Out of the shadows stepped a figure draped in a long, flowing cloak, the glint of her silver hair catching the light as they approached. Behind her, emerging like wraiths from the darkened alleyways, came several more figures, their faces obscured but their presence unmistakable.

Vivienne.

Thume's eyes widened, the realization hitting him like a cold wind. His eyes flashed with a mixture of anger and surprise as the figure came to a halt beside the crew.

And just behind her, Councilwoman Revas, flanked by the other city council members, emerged into the glow of the beaming lights.

✧

Vivienne stepped forward. Her cloak brushed the cobblestones as her eyes flicked from Thume to the crew. Her face was calm but resolute, and her tone carried a weight that silenced the entire street.

"Guards," she commanded, gesturing toward Jax, who was still holding the unconscious Keer. "Get this man medical attention immediately. We are not monsters. Let us remember our humanity."

The guards hesitated, glancing with uncertainty between Thume and the council members. But a command from Councilwoman Revas tipped the balance. "You heard her. Help him."

Two guards broke rank, stepping forward obediently.

Thume's smirk had disappeared. "What is the meaning of this? You think you can undermine me with this farce, Mistress Vivienne?"

Vivienne's eyes hardened, and her features turned to steel as she addressed Thume directly. "This is no farce, Thume. This is the reckoning you've long delayed. Your time of terrorizing this city is over."

Thume sneered, his eyes boring holes into her. "Terrorizing? In what way? You have no proof. No evidence. This is nothing more than a poorly orchestrated coup—"

But Vivienne was already reaching into her cloak, pulling out the device she'd used in his office when they met. She held it up for the council to see, its faint glow casting an eerie light across the faces of the gathered officials.

"I've already played this for the council," Vivienne said with cold precision. "Shall I play it again?" She clicked a button on the side of the device.

"You are no different than any pawn in my game. A pawn I can sacrifice whenever I want. Let me make one thing clear, Mistress Vivienne. Without my blessing you will not succeed in this city. You will not secure a single contract, a single partnership, or a single iron shilling. Your influence ends at my doorstep."

"That was enough to get the council's attention, Lord Thume." She spat his name.

The Zarakaran's eyebrows climbed his forehead. "A boast. You all know this. Just the way politics are played and nothing more. This is hardly evidence of—"

Liora, shifting the bag on her shoulder, called out. "We found your secret spy chamber!"

Thume's face froze as he turned to look at the defiant engineer. Liora pushed her glasses up with her free hand and glared back. Then she stuck her tongue out at him.

Lars stepped forward. "We found crystals that contain the voices of the people of Azoria—conversations, secrets, everything. All of it recorded without their knowledge and without their consent. Thume has been using the city's dynamo grid to spy on every one of its citizens, manipulating and controlling them behind the scenes."

A shocked murmur rippled through the gathered council members, their eyes wide. Councilwoman Revas stepped forward, her expression darkening with realization. "You're saying he's been listening to all of us? Watching us?"

Lars nodded gravely. "Everything. Every private moment, every word spoken in confidence. He has been feeding on the very lifeblood of this city—its people—and using it to consolidate his power. These are just some of the ones we were able to bring back." He signaled to Liora who opened her pack so they could see the collection of storage crystals inside.

Vivienne met Thume's gaze again, eyes gleaming with the satisfaction of this new revelation.

Thume paled but quickly recovered. "Lies. All of it. You have no authority here, Vivienne. And these criminals are hardly credible witnesses."

But Vivienne was undeterred. She turned to the council, and her voice rang with conviction. "These 'criminals,' as this man calls them, are why we know the truth. He would still be operating unseen without them, tightening his stranglehold on Azoria and keeping this esteemed council in the dark."

Councilwoman Revas nodded slowly, shifting her attention from Thume to Vivienne, then to the thieves. "This is damning evidence. If what you're saying is true—"

"It is. And I have no doubt that if you examine the crystals, you will find undeniable proof of Thume's treachery. The people of Azoria deserve to know the truth. They deserve to be free from his surveillance and control."

The council members exchanged glances, their thoughts growing darker with each passing second. Thume, sensing the shift in the air, straightened and raised his voice, desperation creeping into his tone. "You're being manipulated! Vivienne is no different—she is an interloper using you to seize power for herself!"

But the damage had already been done. One by one, they began to nod in agreement, their decision clear.

Councilwoman Revas turned to the guards. "Take him into custody. Immediately."

For a moment, Thume stood frozen in shock and disbelief. The guards hesitated, glancing at one another. Thume's smirk returned briefly. "I control this city. Azoria belongs to me. Don't you dare forget that."

But Councilwoman Revas stepped closer, staring at him in disgust. "Not anymore, Thume."

At her command, the guards moved swiftly, surrounding Thume and locking heavy manacles around his wrists. Thume struggled and tried to fight them off in a frenzy, but there was no escape. The tables had turned, and his power had slipped through his fingers.

As Thume was pulled to his feet, his golden eyes locked with Lars's one last time, filled with a mix of hatred and disbelief. Lars met his gaze without flinching and gave a mock salute as the man was dragged away.

With Thume dragged away in chains, the tension in the air dissipated for a moment. Some members of the council exchanged shocked comments. Others were shaken beyond words at the violation of their trust and possibly at what secrets of their own might soon be open to the public. They all left, fading back into the backdrop of the city.

But Lars knew this was far from over.

His mind raced as he watched Vivienne, and he saw her sharp eyes gleaming with satisfaction as she surveyed the aftermath.

Vivienne stepped close. Her voice came out low and intimate as her breath brushed against Lars's ear. Her lips curved into a sly smile, eyes gleaming with both triumph and desire. "This is just the beginning, Lars."

Her eyes flicked to Trin, who was watching them with a palpable dismay and anger before settling back on Lars. "The real work is about to begin, and I want you by my side. Just as we talked about."

Vivienne emphasized the last part with a slow, deliberate look at Trin. She went on, relentless. "You remember, don't you? When you joined me at my estate. The plans we made... the power we could wield together.

"This is the moment, Lars. If you want to join me, you have to choose now. There won't be another chance."

She stepped closer still, hand gripping his arm. "Think about it. Everything we've dreamed of is within our grasp. But only if you come with me now."

She smiled, exuding confidence that radiated off her in waves, sure of herself and her ability to get what she wanted. Vivienne knew how to pull a man's strings, playing to his ambitions and instincts. There was no room for hesitation in her offer, only a demand wrapped in an enticing promise. She wanted Lars with her, and she wouldn't let him forget it.

Lars felt the urgent push of Vivienne's words pressing down on him, each syllable heavy with calculated intent. Her presence was magnetic, the lure of power almost a tangible thing.

But this wasn't just about ambition. Lars knew that. He had known it from the moment she first proposed their secret alliance. He cast a quick glance at his crew, lingering on Trin, who stood rigid with unbridled anger.

Vivienne watched him closely with unwavering confidence, eyes sharp and unblinking as if she could will him to move with her thoughts alone. Lars knew what she was doing. She wasn't just extending an offer—she was staking her claim.

The choice was clear and ruthless: join her, and the world was his for the taking. But it meant leaving everything, everyone in his life, behind.

Lars took a halting step toward Vivienne.

At that moment, he felt Trin's gaze sear into his back, an intensity that was impossible to ignore. He didn't need to turn around to know what he'd see—the shock, the disbelief, the betrayal etched across her features. Yet he turned around anyway, giving her one final look.

Trin was trying so hard to hold it together, to stay strong. But Lars could see the cracks forming in her armor, the way her lips trembled despite her best efforts to stay composed. Her eyes, once filled with fire and determination, were now glassy with unshed tears, shimmering in the light of the street. She took an unsteady step toward him, speaking in a low whisper.

"Lars..." Her voice cracked, raw with emotion. She swallowed hard, but the tremor in her tone betrayed her, no matter how much she tried to suppress it. "Don't do this. Don't... don't just walk away."

Her words hung in the air like a plea, laced with all the history they shared. Every moment of trust, every whispered secret, every night spent in sensual embrace.

There was nothing she could do to stop the tears now. Several drops rolled down her cheek, catching the light before she swiftly wiped them away as if denying the evidence of her hurt would somehow erase the reality of what was happening.

Jax, tensed with shock, stepped forward. "Lars, what the hell?" The question barraged Lars with unconcealed anger. "This isn't you, man. You're just gonna bail on us? On Trin?"

Lars felt the pit of his stomach twist as his crew—his family—looked at him, pleading for him to stay. Every instinct told him to walk away from Vivienne right now. To stand with the people who had been by his side for years, through every heist, every close call. Still, his expression stayed cool and indifferent.

"I have to," Lars said simply, even though his heart hammered in his chest. He stepped closer to Vivienne, hand brushing hers for just a moment as if solidifying the choice. "This is bigger than us."

Trin's face fell, the sadness radiating off her in waves. "No," she breathed, shaking her head. "Don't you dare do this to us. Don't you dare do this to *me*."

Jax clenched his jaw, shaking his head in disbelief. "This is wrong, Lars. You know it is."

But Lars held firm. "It's what has to happen." He forced himself not to look back at Trin again. He couldn't afford to falter.

It was Liora's voice that broke through the tension, soft but piercing. "Lars... you can't leave us." She clutched the crystals they had fought so hard to obtain, trembling as if her hands could barely hold on. The excited energy that once fueled her was replaced by a fragile uncertainty. Her wide eyes, filled with desperate hope, searched his face for any sign that he might change his mind. "We need you. We love you."

Vivienne smiled—a cold, satisfied smile. She reached for his hand, tugging him closer to her side. "You've made the right choice, Lars. Now let's go. We have so much to accomplish."

She turned, pulling him along as she moved toward a waiting carriage, her heels sharp against the cobblestones echoing in the tense silence. The crew watched in stunned disbelief, their faces a mixture of shock and betrayal.

Lars kept his face forward, forcing himself to stay focused on the path ahead.

When they reached the carriage, Vivienne climbed in first, her movements graceful and composed. She settled into her seat, eyes never leaving Lars as she waited for him to follow.

Lars hesitated at the door. His hand hovered just above the handle as he felt the weight of everything he was leaving behind pressing down on him. Despite his better judgment, he glanced back at the crew. At Trin's tear-filled eyes, Jax's clenched fists, and Liora's desperate hope. But he forced himself to push those feelings aside.

He couldn't afford to falter, not now. Not when Vivienne's eyes were fixed on him, expectant and hungry for his decision.

Without another word, Lars took a deep breath and stepped into the carriage, the plush interior swallowing him up as he settled into the seat beside her. The door slammed shut behind them with a heavy finality, the sound cutting through the air like a blade.

THE RECKONING

19

The carriage rolled to a stop outside Vivienne's sprawling estate, tucked behind the looming structure of the Azoria Research Institute. It wasn't a grand structure like the mansions along the coast, but a collection of smaller buildings connected by beautiful and intricate gardens.

Lars stepped down from the carriage first, boots crunching against the gravel as he took in the estate's surroundings. It was quiet—eerily so. The wind rustled through the trees, and the distant hum of the city faded away. Behind the imposing sprawl of the Institute, it was as though they had crossed into another world, a quiet paradise of wealth and power in the heart of an otherwise chaotic city.

Vivienne stepped out beside him, movements smooth and deliberate as her cloak trailed behind her. She gave him a sidelong glance, her lips curving into a pleased smile, though there was no warmth to it. The early rising sun caught the silver strands in her hair, making her seem almost ethereal against the backdrop of the darkened estate. A triumphant glow dominated her features, the kind that came from someone who had just won a game no one else knew they were playing.

"Welcome back," she said, with an air of intimacy that made the space between them feel smaller. "To my home—and now yours." She led the way inside, walking across the stone floor with a sense of purpose, hips swaying with each step.

The interior of the estate exuded a quiet elegance, its design understated but deliberate. Dark wooden beams crisscrossed the ceiling above, their rich, polished surfaces gleaming in the dim light cast by strategically placed lanterns. The floors beneath Lars's feet were smooth and flawless, polished to a high sheen that reflected the warm glow of the room.

There was no clutter, no signs of wear or imperfection—everything looked as though it had been arranged just so, as though nothing had been left to chance.

The faint, delicate scent of jasmine lingered in the air, subtle yet intoxicating, a unique fragrance that added to the sense of refined tranquility. It was a scent that invited calm, yet something was disconcerting about it, like a veil drawn over something darker. The walls were adorned with a blend of artwork—abstract pieces that didn't demand attention but added to the room's atmosphere of cultured restraint.

Even the furniture appeared more like art than utility, with its clean lines and soft, muted colors. Cushioned chairs and low tables were arranged in perfect symmetry, as though each item had been placed after careful consideration of balance and form.

Every detail had been curated to project an image of control and sophistication. It was a room that mirrored

Vivienne herself: beautiful, poised, and controlled, with an undercurrent of calculation running beneath the surface.

Lars followed her inside. His mind buzzed with the consequences of everything that had just transpired. Thume, imprisoned. Vivienne, triumphant. And him... here, in the heart of her domain. The crew he had called family was miles away, reeling. He forced the thoughts back, trying to steady himself.

Vivienne's voice broke the silence as she turned to face him. "I told you we'd do it, Lars. And I promise you, my dear, this is only the beginning."

She stepped closer to him, reaching out to brush against his arm. It was a soft touch, but there was intent behind it. "And now, we'll be unstoppable. Together."

Lars tensed as her hand lingered on his arm. He knew what she was doing—pulling him in, tying him to her in more ways than one. She had never hesitated in her advances toward him, and he had always been able to maintain restraint despite his body's urging. But now, here in her estate, it felt more dangerous than ever.

Vivienne came closer, breath warm against his neck as her hand slid up to his chest. "You've made your choice, Lars," she said, lips caressing the edge of his ear. "Let me show you what victory feels like."

Lars swallowed hard, forcing himself to step back. "Not now." He gently removed her hand from his chest and took a step back. "Everything's still... too raw."

Vivienne's expression faltered for the briefest moment, a pall of frustration passing over her face before she masked it with a cool smile. "I understand," she said, though her eyes told a different story. "But don't keep me waiting too long. Power demands commitment."

She let her hand fall from his chest and stepped back. Her posture regained its usual poise. "If you aren't ready to claim what you've won, then I'll have to claim my victories elsewhere. The council will want to discuss the future of Ithris and Azoria, and I intend to make sure they know exactly where I stand."

She paused, eyes lingering on him as if appraising his reluctance. "But you must be exhausted. Executing a heist of this magnitude, escaping back to the city in record time, and then facing down Thume in a battle of wits. All of it must be weighing on you."

Her fingers drifted over his shoulder before she turned away, gesturing toward the grand staircase that led to the upper floors of the estate. "Settle in, Lars. Get some rest," she urged. Her tone was somewhere between a command and an invitation. "You've earned it, after all. If you are to stand by my side, I'll need you sharp and ready."

She tilted her head, eyes narrowing with a hint of warning, the smile on her lips fading into something more serious. "Then, perhaps, we can discuss what it truly means to have a place in this new life we will create together."

Without waiting for his response, Vivienne turned with effortless grace, sweeping out of the room as though the air parted for her. Her cloak billowed behind her like a queen's train, the sharp noise of her heels striking the polished floors with purpose. Each step echoed through the empty halls.

Lars stood there, momentarily stunned by the sudden shift in her demeanor. The sound of her footsteps faded into the distance, leaving him alone in the quiet stillness of her domain. He drew a deep breath, his gaze fixed on the doorway through which she had disappeared. Something about her pulled at him, as it always had. A magnetic allure that filled his head with captivation and caution.

✧

Two days had passed since Lars had arrived at Vivienne's estate. Two days of endless persistence from her—subtle touches, whispered promises, and increasingly pointed remonstrations. She had been relentless. Her eyes were always watching him, expecting him to give in, to commit to her fully. But Lars had held firm, assuring her time and again that he just needed a little longer.

Still, the pressure weighed on him. Vivienne was not the type to wait patiently, and he could feel her frustration growing.

He was standing in the main sitting room of the estate, staring out at the intricate gardens that sprawled outside. It was a place of order and beauty, meticulously curated just like everything she touched. The morning sun filtered in through the tall windows, casting a golden hue over the dark wooden beams and polished floors. The faint scent of jasmine lingered in the air as always, an ever-present reminder of Vivienne's control over this place—and over him.

Just as she was now pushing for control of the city.

Vivienne was out again, attending yet another council meeting, her influence growing with each passing day. Each morning, she left with an air of calm command, her head held high as if the city's future belonged to her. She would return late, flushed with success, and press him again, reminding him of what they could achieve together if he would just commit fully.

Her absence should have been a relief, a break from the constant pressure she applied, but instead, it heightened the sense of unease that gnawed at Lars. Even when she wasn't physically present, Vivienne's shadow lingered, suffocating in its quiet persistence.

Every corner of the estate reminded him of her—of the power she wielded and the control she sought over Azoria and him. Despite his best efforts, he couldn't shake the feeling that he was being ensnared beyond any measure of redemption.

Then there was a knock at the door. It was sharp and insistent, breaking through the quiet of the estate like a jagged crack in the polished surface of his thoughts. Lars frowned—he wasn't expecting anyone. No one ever came here for him. They came for her.

Lars looked through the window, brow furrowed, but he couldn't see anyone there. Shrugging, he walked over to the door and pulled it open to see who stood outside.

Darius.

He stood in the doorway, arms crossed over his chest, raw anger painted on his face. Lars felt a jolt of shock run through him—Darius was the last person he expected to see here. And the look in his eyes... Lars knew this wasn't going to be a happy visit.

Darius stepped inside, boots thudding against the polished floor as he approached Lars. There was no greeting or friendly banter this time. His face was drawn in bitter anger as he jabbed a finger at Lars's chest.

"What the hell are you doing, Lars?"

Lars straightened, forcing himself to stay calm despite his heart pounding in his chest. "I'm where I need to be."

Darius snorted and stared at Lars through narrowed eyes. "Where you need to be?" he echoed, shaking his head in disbelief. "With her? After everything we've been through, after everything your crew has done for you... you're just going to throw it all away?"

Lars met his gaze with indifference, even though every part of him screamed to open up to the man. The tumult of emotions he was trying to keep in control were crushing him. "This is bigger than us, Darius. Bigger than the crew. You don't understand."

"Don't give me that bullshit."

He stepped closer, anger radiating off him in waves. "You're chasing power, Lars. You're letting her get in your head and throwing away everything you built—for what? Some promise of power and glory? Sex?"

Lars felt the sting of his words, the sharp cut of truth hidden within them, but he forced himself to remain cold, distant. He couldn't afford to let his emotions get the better of him—not now. "It's not that simple," Lars insisted, the words ringing hollow even to his own ears.

Darius let out a bitter, humorless laugh, shaking his head in disbelief. "You're wrong, Lars. It is that simple." His voice dropped, but the intensity grew. "You're choosing her—some two-faced, narcissist *bitch*—over them. Over Trin. Liora. Jax. Keer."

He took another step closer, relentless in his accusation. "Do you even give a damn that Keer's getting better? That he could've died because of this mess you've dragged us into? Or are you too busy getting cozy in Vivienne's arms to care?"

The mention of Keer sent a jolt through Lars, the memory of his friend's battered body flashing in his mind—the sound of his labored breathing as they carried him from the depot.

He'd heard that Keer was recovering well, regaining his strength thanks to the care Vivienne's medical team had provided—a gift, she'd told him coyly. But Lars had kept his distance, allowing the relief to come from afar rather than rushing to his side.

"Keer's in good hands," he said bluntly. "I knew he'd be fine."

"That's it?" Darius spat, disbelief and disgust coloring his words. "You knew he'd be fine?"

"This is my choice, Darius. You don't have to understand it. You just have to accept it."

Darius stared at him, his eyes blazing with rage and something else—something like grief. "Accept it?" he echoed incredulously. "You've lost yourself, man. When you wake up and realize it, when you realize what you've thrown away, it'll be too late. There won't be anything left for you to come back to."

Darius stared at him for a long moment. His eyes searched Lars's face for any sign of the man he thought he knew. Finally, Darius shook his head, a look of raw disgust crossing his face. "You're a fool, Lars. A goddamn fool."

He turned on his heel and stormed out of the room, leaving Lars standing there in the silence of Vivienne's estate.

The air in the prison block was oppressive and damp, the faint stench of mildew clinging to the stone walls. Gaslamps flickered against the cold, gray surfaces, and the sound of dripping water echoed in the distance, the only noise in the otherwise ominous silence.

Vivienne strode with a purpose down the stone hall as she descended deeper into the bowels of the prison. Her rich purple and gold cloak swept behind her like a shadow. The guards who flanked her stood rigid, keeping a respectful distance, their faces devoid of emotion. None dared to speak, though they exchanged uneasy glances as they led her down the winding passageway toward the cell where Thume was held.

At last, they arrived at a heavy iron door, sturdy and imposing, with a single barred window near the top. The guard unlocked it with a sharp turn of the key and pulled it open with a creak of rusted hinges. Vivienne stepped inside with her chin held high, eyes gleaming with icy resolve.

Thume sat in the corner of the small, austere cell with his back against a stone wall. The proud, golden-eyed man she had once feared was gone. Now he was nothing more than a shade of himself—disheveled, shackled, and stained with dirt and sweat.

Vivienne took a step closer, lips curving into a cold smile. "The mighty Lord Thume. What a disgrace you are," she sneered. "You always thought yourself untouchable, didn't you? But look at you now—rotting away in this miserable cell."

Thume's jaw clenched, but he said nothing. He glared at her with a venomous intensity, his eyes reflecting a mixture of anger and disbelief.

She watched him intently, savoring the silence between them, captive and victor. Thume's attention remained steady, unflinching, but Vivienne could see the cracks forming beneath the surface—the uncertainty that flickered behind his usually confident eyes.

She let the moment stretch on as she took a deep breath. Her heart beat steadily in her chest as she willed her fury to simmer just beneath her cool exterior.

Then, she took another step closer, eyes narrowing and a twisted snarl forming on her lips. "I hate you."

Thume's eyes flickered with surprise—just a momentary flash, raw and unguarded. His composure wavered for the briefest of instants. But his expression soon returned to its familiar mask of indifference.

"I hate you," she repeated with more strength, each syllable laced with years of buried anger. She could feel her heart pounding harder now, the anger that had simmered for so long threatening to boil over.

Thume leaned back and grinned ruefully. "Hate? Why would you waste such a fragile emotion on me?"

His tone grew smoother, more confident, as he shook his head, chuckling under his breath. "You should know that hate—anger, even—is for the weak," he said. "It clouds your judgment, makes you vulnerable. Look at you now—gripped by it, letting it fuel you. You think I am a disgrace. Look at yourself, Vivienne."

Lifting his brow, Thume's expression shifted to one of false concern. "Let me give you a bit of advice. There's no room for hate in this world, no place for soft emotions like that. They'll drag you down in the end."

Vivienne gave him a tight, mirthless smile. She could see what he was doing—trying to reduce her to some misguided fool caught up in her own emotions. But she would not be dismissed so easily. Not by him. Not now, not ever.

"Oh, Thume. You have no idea, do you? No idea what I've carried all these years, what you've made me into. You think

I'm weak because I hate you? You think that makes me less capable?"

She took another step, standing so near to him now that she could feel the unease behind his facade. "You've spent your whole life controlling people through fear and manipulation, but you've never known what it's like to have something taken from you—to have someone rip your life apart and leave you with nothing."

Her eyes narrowed as she continued with rage. "I hate you because you're why I had to become this person. You're the reason I had to fight and claw my way to the top, to build an empire from the ashes of the life you left behind."

She paused, trembling. Not with weakness but with the raw anger of a wound left to fester for years. "I hate you because of what you did to my mother."

Thume's mask of indifference cracked, and at that moment he broke.

"My mother," Vivienne repeated. Her words were sharp and biting as she stepped closer. "Orilline. The woman you claimed to love. The woman you cherished, and yet... the woman you left to die and forgot."

Thume flinched, the accusation seemingly cutting deep. A shadow of pain flickered across his face.

"Do you have nothing to say?" Vivienne hissed, continuing with a fury that matched his own guilt. "You left her behind, Thume. Maybe you didn't kill her with your own hands. Maybe you did. But either way, you let her die. You turned your back on her and walked away, thinking you could bury the memory and move on."

Vivienne to notice the torment behind his eyes. It was as delicious as she always hoped it would be.

"Nevee? Is that really you?" Thume moaned. "Yes... yes, I see now. But you know she was everything to me. I never wanted to leave her. I didn't want to—"

Vivienne's eyes flashed with anger. "You didn't want to? What a lovely sentiment. And yet you left me to fend for myself, your stepdaughter, technically, the one you never even bothered to acknowledge. And I don't go by that name. Not anymore."

Thume opened his mouth to respond, to regain some semblance of authority, but the words came out weak. "I did what I could, Nev—Vivienne. I sent regular tributes to her estate. It wasn't as if I left you entirely—that copper should have ensured—"

Vivienne cut him off with a sharp laugh, eyes flashing with anger. "Oh yes. Thank you so much for those kind tributes, stepfather."

She continued as her features hardened with cold satisfaction, "I'm here to repay the favor. I've spent years building my power—first in Drakoria, then here in Azoria. All the wealth I've gained, all the influence I've built—it's all thanks to you. Your 'regular tributes' helped fund my rise to power since I was a newly orphaned toddler." She let out a bitter laugh.

His eyes widened ever so slightly, a flicker of realization crossing his features as he stared at her. But Vivienne pressed on. "You will rot in this prison," she said coldly, and her words came out like a death sentence. "And I will make sure that you never have the chance to destroy anyone or anything else."

She stepped back with a bitter smile as she watched the weight of her words sink in. Thume stood there, silent and defeated, the once-powerful man now shackled by his own guilt and the vengeance of a woman he had helped create.

Thume found his voice, but it was hoarse and filled with disbelief. "Vivienne..."

But she cut him off, straightening to her full height and regarding him with icy disdain. "You are nothing to me. You never were. But now... now you are an obstacle who will soon be erased."

Without waiting for a response, Vivienne spun and swept out of the cell. The iron door slammed shut with a final, resounding thud, sealing Thume in his cell—and sealing his fate.

She walked back down the corridor with chilling determination. The guards fell into step beside her, but they said nothing. She had no need for their words nor for Thume's. She had what she wanted.

AFTERMATH

20

The heavy iron gate creaked as it swung open, and Vivienne stepped through to the polished stone path that led to her estate. The soft glow of the fading afternoon light bathed the gardens, and for a moment, she allowed herself a smile of triumph. The satisfaction of bringing Thume to his knees still pulsed through her veins, each step reminding her of the sweet, intoxicating revenge she had waited so long to fulfill. His downfall had been inevitable, but witnessing it had filled her with a deep, unrelenting sense of victory. Thume, once untouchable, was now rotting in a cell beneath the city, and it was all her doing.

But that wasn't the only victory. The next would be Lars. She had felt his resistance wavering, his reluctance wearing down under the pressure of their shared ambition. He had held back, citing the need for more time, more space. But Vivienne knew the truth—he was just waiting for the right moment to give in completely.

He couldn't resist her forever, not after everything they'd accomplished. Today would be different. Vivienne was sure of it.

She quickened her pace as she approached the entrance, a sense of eager anticipation building in her mind. Her thoughts spun with thoughts of what was to come, the fire, the passion, the thrill of the conquest that she would share with Lars. The estate was her fortress of power, and he was waiting inside. He would be lounging in the sitting room, or perhaps he'd already poured them a glass of wine to toast to their mutual success.

She pushed open the door, the familiar scent of jasmine hitting her immediately. Stepping inside, she called out to him, breaking the eerie silence of her home. The estate was immaculate as always, every surface polished to perfection, every piece of furniture arranged exactly where it should be. But there was no sign of Lars.

Vivienne's breath hitched, the cold tendrils of uncertainty creeping into her otherwise ironclad confidence. She clenched her jaw, willing herself to remain composed. This wasn't like Lars. He would never just vanish—he was too entwined with her now. They had been through too much together, shared too many ambitions, whispered too many plans in the dead of night for him to walk away without a word. She pushed the thought aside, refusing to entertain it. Lars was still here. He had to be.

She strode through the many rooms, eyes darting around the corners of the estate. The air felt heavier, the scent of jasmine oppressive, clinging to her like a shroud. She stormed through the sitting room again, eyes lingering on an untouched wine bottle. Vivienne couldn't shake the gnawing sense that this silence wasn't just coincidence. Something was *wrong*. It wasn't peace. It was absence.

Her hand brushed the polished wood of the grand staircase as she took a steadying breath. The entire estate was too still and perfect, as if Lars had never been there. But she knew better—his presence had been real, tangible, undeniable. She had felt it. Every time he promised he would come around, that he would be hers... he had meant it. She had made sure of it.

Still, the silence persisted, and a knot of unease twisted in her stomach. Her eyes scanned the corridor that led to the upper floors, but no matter how hard she looked, there was nothing—no movement, no sound.

Vivienne's calm exterior crumbled, the fear she had worked so hard to suppress now bubbling to the surface. Her heart pounded in her chest as her thoughts spiraled into panic. Her breath quickened, and with a sharp intake of air, she turned on her heel, her movements frantic and uncharacteristically clumsy as she made a beeline for the basement.

She descended the stairs with feverish speed. Her feet slipped on the polished wood as she raced downwards. Thoughts tumbled over themselves as she tried to piece together what could have happened. Calculations and suspicions danced through her head like wildfire.

Every fiber of her being screamed that something was wrong, horribly wrong. She could still feel the phantom presence of Lars, hear the echoes of their whispered plans. But now... now everything was unraveling.

As she reached the bottom of the staircase she paused. Her eyes darted around the room, scanning every corner, every object. Everything was where it should be—the sparse furniture, the shelves lined with books and artifacts, all in their proper places.

Yet, the stillness itself felt out of place. It was too quiet and orderly, as if mocking her. Her breath came in short, shallow gasps as she moved deeper into the basement, and her steps grew more urgent with each passing second.

Her mind reeled with possibilities. Could Lars have…? No, she shook her head, forcing the thought away. He wouldn't betray her, not like this. Not after everything he had left behind for her. Not knowing what they were going to build. What he promised her he'd build with her, at her side, where he belonged. Her hands brushed against the sleek surfaces of her devices as she passed them, barely registering the cold metal beneath her fingertips.

Gaze locking onto the back wall at the far end of the basement, she sped forward. Her heart lurched, the knot of dread tightening in her chest.

The sleek metal door, disguised within the wall, was wide open, swinging on its hidden hinges. The sound of metal creaking against metal filled the silence like a death knell, and Vivienne's blood ran cold. She let out a strangled cry, half a scream, half a curse, as she bolted toward it, shaking as she reached for the door.

Panic gripped her, twisting in her gut as she threw herself through the doorway.

The tunnel stretched out before her, lit by the harsh glow of industrial dynamo lights along the smooth, sterile walls. Her feet pounded against the hard floor as she ran, breath coming in ragged bursts. She could feel the panic closing in around her, squeezing her chest like a vise.

The tunnel appeared endless, the closeness of the walls smothering as she raced through it. Vivienne's mind screamed at her to move faster. The cold, clinical air of the hidden passage burned her lungs as she sprinted toward the end. The thoughts running through her mind were a chaotic mess of fear and fury.

After what felt like an eternity, she reached the other side of the tunnel. She burst through the final doorway, trembling with a dangerous blend of terror and adrenaline, and found herself standing in the secret lab of the Azoria Research Institute. *Her* secret lab.

She stopped dead in her tracks, eyes widening as she took in the scene before her.

The room that had once been filled with rows of muskets gleaming under the stark lights, racks of crystal charges pulsing with latent energy, and shelves stacked with experimental gear and prototypes were all stripped bare. Not a single weapon, not a single crystal remained.

Once cluttered with her tools and devices, the polished metal tables now lay empty, their surfaces gleaming under the harsh, sterile light. Cabinets that had once housed precious materials and delicate gems now stood ajar, their contents ripped from their places.

Vivienne's pulse quickened and her heart hammered against her ribs. Her mind raced, calculating how this could have happened, though she knew the answer.

The panic twisted into anger, the familiar fire of rage building in her chest as she stepped further into the room, hands brushing against the cold, barren tables. Her eyes swept every corner for some clue or trace of Lars's presence.

Her eyes landed on the center of the room, where a detailed model of Azoria once stood, a three-dimensional blueprint she had used to plan her future domination of the city.

Now, the model had been disassembled, reduced to mere fragments. Her hands curled into fists at her sides, trembling with fury.

Amidst the wreckage of her carefully constructed empire, there was a single note, placed as if mocking her.

It was never yours to begin with.

Respectfully,
Trinelle Meridia

Vivienne's fingers tightened around the note, crumpling the parchment as anger and fear surged through her in equal measure. The woman she had underestimated, the inconsequential bitch she had mocked, had taken everything from her.

Vivienne stood in the middle of the empty lab, the note still crumpled in her fist, the mocking words of Trin burning like acid in her mind. The fear was still there, but now it was mingled with something darker. She would not be rejected like this. She would not be abandoned.

They may have struck the first blow, but this wasn't over.

Vivienne emerged from the tunnel. Her heart still pounded from the rush of anger and fear that had flooded through her in the lab. Her footsteps echoed in the quiet basement as she made her way back to the entrance.

When she reached the top of the stairs, she paused, closing her eyes and taking a deep breath. The hollow echo of the empty basement still lingered in her ears, mocking her, but she couldn't let that control her now. Not here. Not in her home. She straightened her shoulders and lifted her chin as she moved with deliberate grace toward the sitting room.

Once there, she moved to the side table where a crystal decanter of wine stood waiting. Her hand trembled as she reached for it, the glass clinking as she poured a generous amount of deep red wine into the waiting goblet. She held the glass for a moment, watching the wine swirl as the rich scent filled her senses.

Vivienne sank into a chair by the fire, the flames casting a pleasant glow against the dark wooden beams and polished floors. The warmth brushed her skin, but it couldn't thaw the icy grip of fear and anger tightening in her chest. She took a slow sip of the wine, focusing on its bitter undertones. The familiar taste grounded her and pulled her back from the edge of panic.

She exhaled slowly, forcing herself to focus, to regain control. She could feel her pulse beginning to steady as her thoughts sharpened once more. The firelight danced across her skin, and the spark of resolve slowly returned in her eyes.

No matter what had happened in that lab or what Lars, his little summer fling, and the band of thieves had done, this wasn't the end. They had blindsided her, humiliated her, but they hadn't broken her. Not yet.

She took another drink, the wine burning a little hotter as it slid down her throat. She let her eyes drift shut, savoring the quiet as she gathered her strength, rebuilding the walls around her.

But then, an unexpected sound cut through the silence—the sharp, deliberate knock of someone at the door. The sound echoed in the quiet estate, shattering the calm Vivienne had spent so much effort constructing.

Her heart leaped into her throat, a flash of hope sparking to life inside of her before she could stop it. For just a fraction of a second, she dared to think it could be Lars, that he had come back, that this had all been some twisted test of her resolve.

But even as the thought crossed her mind, she cursed herself for being so foolish. No, it wouldn't be Lars. It couldn't be. The rational part of her knew that. And yet, she hated how much she wanted it to be him. The betrayal of her own emotions sickened her, and she scowled, setting the glass down with a little too much force, the sound jarring in the silence.

She stood, smoothing her dress, straightening her posture as she moved toward the door. Her mind raced with possibilities. Whoever was at the door could be a threat, or worse—someone here to deliver another blow to her pride. She couldn't allow herself to be caught off guard again. She reached the door, hand hovering over the handle for just a moment before she steeled herself and pulled it open.

Her breath caught in her throat as she was met not with Lars but Aric Myrim.

The man lingered in the doorway, dark eyes scanning Vivienne's face with a curious intensity. At first he didn't say anything, meeting her gaze with that same calm, unreadable expression.

"Captain Myrim," she said, more controlled now, a polite mask of warmth slipping back into place. "What brings you here this evening?"

Myrim's lips twitched into a faint smile, but it didn't reach his eyes. "I'm not a captain any longer. But I have something I'd like to discuss with you. If you'll allow me inside."

Vivienne studied him a moment longer. Her sharp eyes caught the subtle tension in his posture, the way he shifted on his feet. Whatever this was, it wasn't just a casual visit. She nodded, stepping aside with a graceful gesture toward the sitting room.

"Come in." She was all business. There was no trace of the usual seduction she often wielded as a weapon. Instead, there was a quiet resolve in her eyes, a firmness in the way she moved as she led him into the room.

Myrim followed her inside. The crackling fire filled the space with warmth, and the scent of jasmine lingered in the air.

Vivienne moved toward the side table where she had left her glass of wine, the decanter still sitting half-full. Without missing a beat, she poured a second glass for Myrim and handed it to him with a cool, steady hand.

"Wine?" she offered cordially but with an underlying firmness. She wasn't interested in playing games tonight.

Myrim accepted the glass with a nod, taking a small sip before lowering it to his side. However, his eyes never left Vivienne's.

Vivienne settled into her chair by the fire, posture poised yet relaxed, an air of quiet command about her. She watched Myrim, waiting for him to speak.

"Thank you," Myrim said after a moment. "I'll get right to the point. Azoria is changing."

Vivienne's eyebrow arched though she remained silent, waiting for him to continue.

"With Thume gone, the city is in a state of flux. The power vacuum left behind has already started to stir unrest. You can feel it in the air—the tension, the uncertainty. Thieves, gangs, and opportunists will be looking to carve out their piece of the city. I know it as well as you do... we've both had dealings with them after all. The question is: what's next?"

Vivienne tilted her head and traced the rim of her wine glass with a polished fingernail. She of course knew what was next, but her curiosity was piqued. "Go on."

Myrim shifted his weight as if considering how to proceed. "We've all played our part in your game, haven't we? You've risen to power with a level of finesse and control that few can match. But this chaos, it creates new opportunities—and I've been thinking.

"What if we used the chaos to our advantage? What if we elevated the thieving industry in this city to a new level?"

Vivienne's eyes narrowed. "And what exactly do you have in mind?"

Setting his glass down, Myrim leaned forward. "Vigilante justice," he said, the words slipping out like a challenge. "I've watched this city decay from the inside. Thume's reign was one of control and fear, but now that it's crumbling, the city needs something else. What if we created a new force within Azoria—enforcers of a different kind of justice, operating in the shadows, taking down both the thieves and the worst of the criminals that would seek to rise in Thume's place."

"A vigilante force," she repeated in a thoughtful tone. Vivienne's eyes widened as she considered his proposition. "And you propose to lead it?"

Myrim nodded. "Yes. I've spent years as a captain of the watch, enforcing the laws of this city. But I've seen how corrupt those laws can be—how easily they're twisted to serve the powerful. What I'm suggesting is something different. A new kind of order, one that operates outside the traditional boundaries. One that answers to no one. Part of the same system that gives thieves their power."

She steepled her fingers thoughtfully, interest piqued. "And what would be my role in this new order?"

Myrim smiled faintly. "You would continue to grow your influence, as you've been doing. But with this new force as your ally, you would have eyes and ears in every corner of the city. Not like Thume," he amended, "but I'll commit that you would know what's happening before anyone else. You could control not just the politics of Azoria—but the streets as well." He slapped a fist into the palm of his other hand.

Vivienne's lips curved into a slow smile as the potential of his idea settled in. She could see it now—the potential in what Myrim was proposing. It wasn't just about maintaining power, it was about expanding it and deepening her control over the city in ways that even Thume hadn't achieved.

For the first time since discovering the lab empty, Vivienne felt a new rush of excitement. She took another sip of her wine, and her eyes gleamed with renewed ambition.

"Tell me more, Captain. I'm intrigued."

The moon hung low in the sky, casting a soft, silvery light over the secluded hideaway where Lars and his crew had gathered. The distant hum of the city was nothing more than a faint echo, drowned out by laughter and clinking glasses. A fire crackled in the center of the gathering, casting flickering lights on their faces as they huddled near each other, reveling in the warmth of both the fire and their victory.

Lars sat back against a rough-hewn log, a rare smile tugging at the corners of his mouth as he watched his crew—the family he'd built—celebrate the success of their greatest victory yet. His eyes lingered on Trin, who was laughing at something Liora had just said. For just a blessed moment, he allowed himself to savor the feeling, the sense of completeness that came from a job well done. And from being surrounded by the people who mattered most.

"It still doesn't feel real," Trin said, leaning against Lars. Her shoulder pressed comfortably against his as she gazed up at the stars. Her eyes reflected the silvery light and a contented smile played at her lips. "We did it."

Lars chuckled, his laughter mingling with the crackle of the fire. He shook his head in disbelief, marveling at the magnitude of what they had accomplished. "I know. We pulled off the greatest series of heists in history and lived to tell the tale. Not just one score, but all of them—one after another, like clockwork. And now, here we are."

Trin smiled up at him, the warmth between them undeniable as she nestled closer. Her fingers brushed against his as she let out a soft, contented sigh. "It's crazy. All that planning, close calls, and a masterful betrayal... now we're legends."

Across the fire, Jax leaned forward with a wide grin, his booming voice cutting through the night air with infectious energy. "And let's not forget," he said, chest puffed out with pride and his rich cloak swirling behind him, "the biggest legend of them all!"

He paused for dramatic effect, grin widening as the others turned their attention to him. "That's right," he continued, pointing a thumb at his broad chest. "If it weren't for my expert timing—and my sheer intimidation, of course—we'd all be dead meat in Thume's warehouse."

Trin raised an eyebrow with a teasing smirk. "Oh? And what *exactly* was your 'expert timing,' Jax? I seem to remember you almost running into a locked door."

Jax waved a dismissive hand, laughing heartily. "Details, details! The important thing is, we got in and out, didn't we? And once we were in, it was all about muscle and charm, baby!" He flexed his biceps for emphasis, earning a round of good-natured laughter from the crew.

Sitting beside the fire with a half-empty mug of beer, Liora giggled and wiped a tear of laughter from her eye. "Charm, huh? I think the rest of us were doing the heavy lifting while you were busy playing hide-and-seek with the guards."

Jax huffed playfully, shaking his head. "Hey, someone had to distract them while you tinkered with your little knobs and gears and whatnot! And besides, that last punch I threw—right before we bolted? Thing of beauty." He mimed the motion, swinging his hand through the air with an exaggerated flourish. "The guy never knew what hit him."

Lars laughed and shook his head, beaming at Jax. "I'll give it to you, Jax," he said, "you did keep them off our backs long enough for us to get in and out. We wouldn't have made it without you."

Jax's grin widened as he leaned back, crossing his arms and giving a satisfied nod. "Damn right."

Liora giggled, nudging him playfully. "Oh please, Jax, we all know you just enjoy the attention. But you're right. It was pretty impressive. Almost as impressive as my brilliant planning." She winked with infectious enthusiasm as she bounced in her seat, unable to contain the excitement. "No one's ever going to forget the night we turned Azoria upside down!"

Still recovering but sitting proudly with a glass in hand, Keer raised it in a toast. "To us—the greatest thieves to ever roam these streets. And to a swift recovery, because I want to be the one out there laughing at Darius next time." His voice was strong despite the slight strain in his tone, and everyone cheered in agreement, raising their drinks high.

Lars laughed as the memory came rushing back—their modified carriage tearing across the landscape, hurtling past Darius and his crew like a tornado. "You should have seen his face," Lars said, shaking his head with amusement. "It was a blur, but I'm sure he was fuming."

Trin grinned, resting her head on Lars's shoulder. "The best part," she said, her words filled with warmth. "Was that moment when we knew we were free and that absolutely nothing could stop us."

Lars turned to look at her. For a long moment, they just sat there, the fire crackling between them and the rest of the world falling away. Trin reached up to brush a stray lock of hair from his face, fingers lingering on his cheek. "I'm proud of you. Of all of us. But especially you."

Lars swallowed hard, his throat tight with emotion. He wrapped an arm around her, pulling her closer as he softly kissed her forehead. "I couldn't have done any of this without you, Trin," he said quietly, with a rare vulnerability. "You kept me going when I wasn't sure we'd make it."

She smiled up at him with shining eyes. "That's because I never doubted you. Not for a second."

As they sat there, wrapped in each other's warmth, the sound of the others' laughter and conversation washed over them like a soothing balm. This was what they had fought for—this moment of peace, of unity, of triumph.

"I guess we're going to need a new base now," Liora said suddenly as she looked around at the group. "Something bigger, more fitting for our new status. A manor, maybe?"

Jax let out a booming laugh. "A manor? That's right! We've got enough copper to buy half the city. Why not go big?"

Keer grinned, shaking his head. "You know, I never thought I'd live to see the day when we're sitting around discussing what kind of estate to buy. But here we are."

Lars chuckled, feeling a lightness in his chest that he hadn't felt in years. "I suppose we've earned it."

The group erupted into laughter, the firelight dancing across their faces as they shared stories, relived the highlights of their heists, and reveled in the joy of their success. For tonight, they didn't need to worry about the future.

But as the night wore on and the laughter faded into a comfortable silence, Lars couldn't shake the thought lingering at the back of his mind. Azoria was changing. Vivienne wouldn't let this go easily. The first shot had been fired, and there would be consequences. But for now, surrounded by his crew—his family—he let those worries slip away.

Tonight, they were legends. And tomorrow... tomorrow would take care of itself.

APPENDIX

The Ithris Sanctioned Heists Act (ISHA)
Treatise on Dynamo Engineering and Its Applications

The Ithris Sanctioned Heists Act (ISHA)

Authored by Lord Cecil Thume, Chairperson of the Economic Betterment Committee

Preamble

In the interest of promoting economic opportunity, fostering innovation in skillful acquisition, and supporting the broader welfare of the Ithrian people, the following legal provisions are hereby established to regulate the act of burglary and related activities, henceforth referred to as "heists." These regulations are intended to maintain order while capitalizing on the public's enthusiasm for gamesmanship, risk, and strategic ingenuity.

Section 1. Definition of Heists

A heist is any coordinated operation designed to acquire, relocate, or exfiltrate valuable assets—whether physical (e.g., currency, materials, artifacts) or intellectual (e.g., proprietary information, designs)—from a designated target location. For the purposes of this law, all such actions fall under the term heist, regardless of size, complexity, or method.

1.1 Heist Classifications

Heists are categorized into four distinct types based on scope, target, and operational risk:

- **Class I Heist ("Petty Heist")**: Small-scale theft involving assets valued under 500 Ithrian coppers (approximate equivalent). Targets may include private homes, small businesses, or personal vehicles. Typically carried out by a small crew of 2-3 thieves.

- **Class II Heist ("Commercial Heist")**: Mid-range theft involving valuable assets from commercial or corporate entities. Targets may include warehouses, trading companies, or merchant vessels. Often conducted by crews of 4-6 thieves, and may involve moderate risk from traps or private security.

- **Class III Heist ("Elite Heist")**: Large-scale operations targeting high-value assets, such as major corporations, nobles, or government officials. These heists are high-risk, often involving advanced security systems and requiring intricate planning. Crews generally consist of 6-12 members.

- **Class IV Heist ("Grand Heist")**: The most complex and high-stakes operations, often involving public institutions, heavily fortified locations, or irreplaceable artifacts. These heists typically have citywide implications or large-scale public attention. Only crews with established reputations and additional permissions from the Ithris Gaming Commission may attempt such heists.

1.2 Heist Tools and Techniques

All methods of entry, theft, and escape fall under this law, provided they adhere to the sanctioned guidelines for permissible tools and techniques. This includes the use of:

- **Traditional Tools**: Lockpicks, grappling hooks, and lightweight carrying equipment.

- **Dynamo-Powered Tools**: Tools powered by the city's dynamo grid for more complex heists, including communication devices, magnetic lockpicks, and cutting tools.

- **Tactical Entry**: Utilizing creative methods to breach fortifications, such as climbing, tunneling, or diversionary tactics.

Section 2. Allocation of Proceeds

A minimum of one-quarter (1/4) of the net proceeds from any successful heist must be remitted to the Ithris Gaming Commission. These funds are allocated toward maintaining the infrastructure required to support the gaming and economic system.

2.1 Welfare Contributions

An additional one-eighth (1/8) of the net proceeds shall be allocated to the General Ithrian Fund, which supports:

- Public infrastructure projects such as roads, bridges, and schools.

- Funding for the healthcare system, with special attention to compensating victims of heists who suffer undue financial harm or injury.

- Social programs designed to assist lower-income citizens, offering basic services, education, and workforce development to reduce economic disparities.

2.2 Alternative Payment Structures

For Class III and Class IV Heists, where the value of the assets exceeds 100,000 Ithrian coppers, the Ithris Gaming Commission may offer an alternative payment plan, allowing crews to remit proceeds in staggered installments over a 12-month period to minimize economic disruption.

2.3 Incentives for Innovation

Crews that demonstrate unique or innovative methods during a heist (e.g., the use of novel technology or exceptionally creative execution) may receive a reduced Gaming Commission fee as a reward for advancing the art of thievery. A petition for reduced fees must be filed within 30 days of the heist's completion, along with supporting documentation of the innovative methods used.

2.4 Late or Non-Payment Penalties

Crews failing to remit the required fees within 30 days of a heist's completion will face escalating penalties, including:

- An immediate doubling of the fee owed to the Gaming Commission.
- Bounties placed on the heads of non-compliant thieves, to be pursued by bounty hunters or the Azoria city watch under the Gaming Commission's authority.

2.5 Transparency of Proceeds

The Ithris Gaming Commission is required to issue an annual public report detailing the total proceeds received from heists and how these funds have been allocated. This transparency ensures public trust in the legal heist system and allows citizens to see the tangible benefits of sanctioned activities.

Section 3. Scope of Legal Heists

This law applies exclusively to heists that target established entities, such as homes, businesses, warehouses, vehicles, or governmental institutions. Heists conducted outside these boundaries will not be protected under the Ithris Heist Sanctioning Act and will be treated as unlawful theft.

3.1 Exclusions from Sanctioned Heists

- **Peer-to-Peer Theft**: Theft involving individuals in direct interaction, commonly known as pickpocketing, mugging, or swindling, does not fall under the protection of this law and is punishable under standard criminal law. Theft must involve an intermediary structure (domicile, vehicle, etc.) to qualify as a heist.

- **Common Dwellings and Small Businesses**: Theft from low-income homes, ordinary citizens, or small businesses is expressly forbidden. Any heist conducted against such targets will be deemed illegal, and all proceeds must be returned. Additionally, offenders will face fines, imprisonment, or loss of legal status.

3.2 Wealth-Based Target Restrictions

To further discourage theft against citizens of modest means, the Ithris Gaming Commission uses a wealth threshold system to determine permissible heist targets. This threshold is based on:

- The net worth of the target, calculated annually.
- The market value of property and assets in possession of the target.
- The social or economic impact of a heist on the target's broader community.

Targets that fall below this threshold will be exempt from legal heists, and attempts to breach these rules will result in penalties ranging from fines to disqualification of the heist's legality.

3.3 Duration and Legal Boundaries

The act defines the temporal and spatial boundaries within which a heist must occur to remain legal:

- **Timeframe**: A heist must begin and end within a set timeframe as established by the Ithris Gaming Commission. Heists exceeding this duration, even if successful, will be considered illegal.

- **Geographic Boundaries**: Once the crew crosses the legally defined boundary for the heist's completion, as established in the annual heist guidelines, the stolen goods are considered the legal property of the crew. Pursuing the crew beyond this boundary will violate the "Done is Done" provision (see **Section 7**).

Section 4. Wealth-Based Fee Adjustment

To dissuade acts against common citizens and small business owners, a Reverse Proportional Fee Scale shall be applied. Heists targeting high-wealth individuals or organizations shall pay the minimum outlined fees, while heists targeting lesser-wealthy individuals will see an increased fee proportional to the target's lack of wealth. This measure is designed to ensure that only those capable of bearing the loss are subject to sanctioned heists.

4.1 Base Fee Calculation

All heists are subject to a base fee of one-quarter (1/4) of the net proceeds, as outlined in Section 2. This base fee is applied to heists targeting high-wealth individuals or entities (those exceeding the wealth threshold set by the Ithris Gaming Commission). The fee is calculated before any adjustments based on the target's wealth.

4.2 Reverse Proportional Fee Scale

To discourage theft from low-wealth individuals, a reverse proportional fee scale will be applied to heists based on the net worth of the target. The fee increases as the target's wealth decreases below the Commission's minimum wealth threshold.

4.3 Upper Cap on Fee

To ensure fairness, the maximum fee that can be applied to any heist, regardless of target wealth, is capped at 50% of the net proceeds. This prevents punitive fees from completely erasing the profitability of a heist, even if the target is of lower wealth.

4.4 Failure to Comply

If a crew fails to remit the adjusted fee, or attempts to falsify the target's wealth to reduce the fee, they will face immediate asset seizure, as well as bounties placed on individual crew members.

Section 5. Punitive Measures for Non-Compliance

Any heist crew or individual thief that fails to remit the required fees to the Ithris Gaming Commission within 30 days of completing a heist will be subject to immediate penalties. These penalties are structured to ensure timely compliance and the integrity of the legal heist system.

5.1 Primary Penalties

- **Doubling of Fees**: The owed fee will immediately double, increasing both the base and adjusted fees. Failure to pay within an additional 30 days will result in further escalation, as outlined below.

- **Suspension**: The legal protections of the offending crew or individual will be suspended, prohibiting further legal heists until the outstanding fees are settled. All planned or active heists will be canceled, and any new operations will be considered illegal under Ithrian law.

5.2 Secondary Penalties

- **Asset Seizure**: The Ithris Gaming Commission will have the authority to seize any assets derived from the unpaid heist. This includes stolen goods, monetary proceeds, or any related equipment. Seized items will be either auctioned or returned to the original target, depending on the circumstances of the heist.

- **Public Bounty**: A bounty will be placed on the offending crew or individual members, offering monetary rewards to bounty hunters, rival crews, or city watch who capture them. Bounties will be proportional to the value of the unpaid fees and will be publicized citywide.

- **Property Confiscation**: The registered base of the offending crew may be confiscated by the Commission. If the crew operates from a designated safehouse, workshop, or headquarters, this property may be forfeited, either to the Commission or auctioned to new crews.

5.3 Exemptions and Appeals Process

In rare cases, a crew may appeal their penalties to the Ithris Gaming Commission if they can provide evidence that their failure to pay was due to unforeseen circumstances, such as:

- **Unlawful Interference**: If another crew unlawfully interfered with the heist or stole proceeds from the original thieves, a formal investigation may be initiated, and penalties could be reduced or deferred.

- **Heist Malfunction**: If technological or dynamo-based equipment malfunctioned, preventing timely fee payment, the crew may apply for a grace period to resolve the issue.

- **Natural Disaster**: In cases where natural events (e.g., flooding, earthquakes) directly impacted the completion or profit from a heist, the Commission may issue a temporary fee reduction or deferral.

All appeals must be filed within 15 days of the penalty being issued. The Commission will conduct a review, and a verdict will be delivered within 10 days. During this review period, no additional penalties (such as fee doubling or bounty issuance) will be applied.

5.4 Commission Audit Rights

The Ithris Gaming Commission reserves the right to conduct audits of crew finances to ensure the correct allocation of fees. Random audits may occur on a quarterly basis, or if suspicious financial activity is reported. Crews found guilty of falsifying heist records to reduce fees will face penalties equivalent to non-compliance.

Section 6. Damage Limitations

During the execution of any heist, certain levels of property damage and physical harm to non-combatants or security personnel are permissible, provided these damages remain within the annual limit set by the Ithris Gaming Commission. This limit is reviewed each year to balance public safety with the expected risks and thrills of sanctioned heist activities.

6.1 Damage Threshold

The Commission establishes a monetary value for permissible damage that may be inflicted during a heist, including:

- **Property Damage**: This includes damage to physical infrastructure such as windows, doors, safes, security systems, and interior furnishings.

- **Physical Harm**: Limited non-lethal physical harm to security personnel or individuals guarding the target property, provided injuries fall under "reasonable force" guidelines. Lethal force is strictly prohibited unless the target initiates lethal action.

6.2 Annual Damage Limit Review

The permissible damage limit is set annually by the Commission and published in the official **Heist Code of Conduct**. The limit is adjusted based on:

- **Historical Data**: Averages of damage from previous heists, including frequency, scale, and cost of damages.

- **Public Safety Concerns**: Ensuring that public sentiment and safety are considered, particularly in densely populated areas of Azoria.

- **Insurance Claims**: Coordination with private insurance firms to ensure compensation mechanisms remain intact for targeted businesses and entities.

6.3 Reasonable Force Guidelines

Heist crews may incapacitate guards or personnel to complete a heist, but excessive or disproportionate force is strictly prohibited. Guidelines for force include:

- **Non-lethal methods**: The use of non-lethal incapacitation tools (e.g., taseshots, stun darts, gas canisters) is allowed.
- **Lethal force**: Lethal force is forbidden unless the crew faces immediate lethal danger from the target or its defenders. This must be documented in post-heist reports.

Violations of the reasonable force guidelines will result in additional fines and penalties, including potential bans on future heists and imprisonment.

6.4 Exemptions for Dynamic Environments

Certain high-risk environments, such as military installations, government treasuries, or high-security vaults, may have higher damage limits due to the advanced security systems and defenses in place. In these scenarios, damage limits may be increased by special permit, allowing for the use of more aggressive techniques (e.g., explosives, advanced dynamo-based devices).

Section 7. The "Done is Done" Provision

Thieves who are captured within the temporal and spatial boundaries of a heist, as designated annually by the Ithris

Gaming Commission, are subject to legal judgement. This includes fines, imprisonment, or other forms of punishment.

7.1 Heist Boundary and Completion

Under the "Done is Done" Provision, a heist is considered complete once the crew successfully exits the predefined heist zone with the stolen goods. The boundaries of the heist zone are determined annually by the Ithris Gaming Commission and vary depending on the target's location, type, and security level.

The heist zone is a geographical perimeter established around the target property or location. Once the crew crosses this boundary with the stolen goods, the heist is considered legally completed, and the stolen goods become the property of the crew, free from further legal pursuit or claims by the target.

7.2 Heist Zone Parameters

The parameters of the heist zone are set by the Ithris Gaming Commission based on the complexity of the heist, the value of the target, and the surrounding environment. These parameters include:

- **Urban Zones**: In cities like Azoria, the heist zone may be confined to a specific number of blocks surrounding the target building or facility. For high-security targets, the zone may be smaller to increase the challenge.

- **Rural Zones**: For heists in rural areas, the zone may cover several miles, especially if the target is located on a vast estate or secluded region.

- **Special Zones**: High-risk targets, such as military installations or government facilities, may have tighter and more complex zones, including checkpoints or layered perimeters that must be breached before a heist is complete.

7.3 Legal Protection Upon Boundary Exit

Once the crew has exited the heist zone with the stolen goods, all pursuit or reclamation efforts by the target or law enforcement are prohibited. The crew and their loot are granted legal protection under this provision, meaning:

- **No Further Legal Action**: The target of the heist, regardless of the losses incurred, cannot seek legal recourse to recover stolen goods once the heist is complete.

- **No Retrieval**: Any attempt by the target or their agents to recover the stolen goods after the crew has exited the heist zone will be considered an illegal act, and the crew has the right to defend themselves without fear of legal repercussions.

- **Ownership of Goods**: The stolen items are now the legal property of the crew, and any attempt to claim or repossess the items will be treated as theft against the crew.

Section 8. Back at Base Provision

If the thieves' established base of operations is within the boundaries of the heist, and the goods are returned to this base without capture, the heist is considered completed under legal parameters. The address of each crew's base must be registered with the Ithris Gaming Commission to qualify for this protection.

8.1 Definition of Base

- A "base" refers to the primary operational headquarters of a heist crew, where stolen goods, plans, and crew members retreat after a heist. This base must be an officially registered location with the Ithris Gaming Commission to qualify for protection under the Back at Base Provision.

- Bases can include private homes, safehouses, underground hideouts, or mobile vehicles, provided they meet the necessary criteria for registration (see **Section 8.2**).

8.2 Base Registration

Crews must register their base with the Ithris Gaming Commission at least 30 days before conducting any heist. Registration includes:

- **Exact location**: The base's geographic coordinates must be submitted. If the base is mobile (e.g., a ship or caravan), the Commission must be informed of its operating range.

- **Security Capabilities**: Basic security features of the base (e.g., alarms, traps, guards) must be detailed to ensure it is a secure location.

- **Ownership or Lease Agreement**: Proof that the base is under the legal control of the crew, whether owned, leased, or rented.

Crews may only register one primary base at a time, though they may apply for special permits to maintain secondary hideouts if they operate across multiple regions.

8.3 Safe Return with Goods

The Back at Base Provision grants full legal protection to a crew if they can successfully return to their registered base with the stolen goods before being captured. Once the crew reaches the base:

- **Completion of the Heist**: The heist is legally considered complete. All stolen goods, regardless of their value or origin, become the lawful property of the crew.

- **Immunity from Pursuit**: Law enforcement, rival crews, or the original target of the heist may not pursue the crew once they have entered their base. Any attempt to breach the base will be considered a violation of Ithris law, with severe penalties.

8.4 Seal of Completion

Once the crew reaches the base, they must report their success to the Ithris Gaming Commission within 24 hours to receive an official Seal of Completion for the heist. This seal legally affirms their ownership of the stolen goods and protects them from future legal claims by the target.

8.5 Multiple Crew Bases

In rare cases, crews may collaborate and use multiple registered bases for particularly large-scale heists. If more than one base is used, the following rules apply:

- Each base must be individually registered and meet the proximity requirements to the heist target.

- Goods may be split among the bases, but at least 50% of the total stolen value must reach one base to trigger the Back at Base protection.

8.6 Joint Accountability

All collaborating crews must report the heist jointly to the Commission, and any penalties for non-compliance will be shared among all parties.

Enactment & Oversight

This law shall take effect upon ratification by the Azorian City Council, with oversight granted to the Ithris Gaming Commission, which shall also handle yearly assessments, revisions, and sanctions related to ongoing heist operations.

Lord Cecil Thume
Chairperson, Economic Betterment Committee
Azorian City Council

Treatise on Dynamo Engineering and its Applications

*Submitted to the Azoria Research Institute's
Advanced Dynamo Lab by Liora Banz*

Azoria thrives not because of the iron and stone that frame its body, but because of the dynamo energy coursing through its veins. The city's energy network, or dynamo grid, is a marvel of ingenuity—a complex system that harvests the raw kinetic forces of nature and transforms them into the very lifeblood of our daily existence. In its simplest form, dynamo energy is generated by harnessing motion. Azoria has mastered this process by tapping into every available force—wind, water, and the sea itself.

Our windmills, scattered along the ridges outside the city, catch the coastal winds that sweep in from the Azure Sea and the southern plains. These winds, while gentle to the casual observer, turn the massive blades of the windmills, converting their motion into mechanical energy. This force, captured and directed, is sent into the copper-wound turbines in various storehouses and basements below the city, where it becomes part of the grid.

Various watermills dot the Ithris River, which divides the city into north and south. These add to this energy flow, taking advantage of the city's powerful natural waterway. Each rush of water spins these wheels, powering turbines with a constant, reliable source of mechanical force.

The true brilliance of our engineering lies beneath the waves in the form of underwater sea sails. Hidden beneath the surface of the Azure Sea, these massive sails harness the natural ebb and flow of the tides. As the tides shift, the sails rotate in response, driving submerged turbines that generate dynamo energy. With each movement of the water, the system efficiently converts the ocean's kinetic force into a reliable source of power for the city.

It is not just Azoria that benefits from these methods. Other cities across the world have adapted their own ingenious systems. Stoneford, another city in Ithris, has harnessed its massive natural waterfall, embedding turbines into the rock to capture the immense power of water crashing down from the heights above.

All of these forces—wind, water, and tidal motion—are funneled into the dynamo generators, where magnetic fields rotate within copper coils to produce dynamo. This is then distributed throughout the city, feeding into everything from household gadgets to the squawks that keep thieves connected on the go.

The Role of Metals in Dynamo Engineering

The dynamo system owes its existence to the conductive and structural properties of specific metals, but the availability and practicality of each metal varies widely. Chief among these is copper, the most essential and sought-after resource in dynamo engineering.

Copper's high conductivity and relative lightness make it the ideal material for drawing into wires, coils, and components that power the grid. However, it is also the most difficult to mine and the most in demand. Copper veins tend to run deep and are often buried beneath difficult-to-reach terrain, making extraction a costly and labor-intensive process. Its scarcity is reflected in its value, making it the cornerstone of the world's economy.

Silver, while possessing the highest conductivity, is too heavy to be practical in large-scale applications. Its weight makes it inefficient for use in long-distance transmission or high-volume energy systems. Additionally, silver is often found in small deposits, and its malleability is limited, making it difficult to form into the fine wires and components required for precision engineering.

Gold, though more resistant to corrosion and highly prized for its stability, is similarly limited by its availability. Gold is commonly found in small, scattered deposits, and while it is more abundant than copper in some regions, its softness and difficulty in forming it into intricate parts mean that it is reserved for specialized applications where its anti-corrosive properties are most needed.

Iron, on the other hand, is abundant and versatile, though its poor conductivity limits its use in the grid. Instead, iron serves a critical role in structural components of dynamo systems, especially in the cores of the turbines where its magnetic properties are harnessed to enhance the interaction between the rotating magnetic fields and the copper coils. It also serves as shielding to protect delicate components from magnetic interference.

Most of these precious metals and crystals are mined in Zarakar, which has become the wealthiest and most powerful nation since the advent of dynamo engineering. Zarakar's vast mineral reserves and access to precious crystals make it the hub of dynamo technology, driving its economy and global influence. Drakoria has also seen success in mining, though its treacherous waterways make the transport of materials hazardous and trade routes difficult to maintain.

Ithris itself maintains only a few provincial mines, supplying just enough copper and other metals to supplement its needs, while Aelyndor remains without any significant mining operations or widespread dynamo use.

This dynamic has shaped both the geopolitical landscape and the economies of the nations, with copper serving as the foundation for power, both literally and figuratively, in the world of dynamo engineering.

The Science of Crystals in Dynamo Technology

While metals like copper and iron form the foundation of dynamo engineering, it is crystals that unlock the true potential of energy regulation, storage, and transmission. The unique properties of various crystals make them indispensable in controlling the flow and distribution of dynamo energy, transforming raw kinetic power into something manageable, scalable, and precise.

Crystals serve as the regulators in the dynamo system, acting as resistors, transistors, capacitors, and amplifiers within devices, circuits, and the dynamo grid itself. Each type of crystal has its own intrinsic properties, determined by its structure, conductivity, and capacity to interact with dynamo energy. These qualities are what allow them to play such a critical role in Azoria's power infrastructure.

Resistor Crystals

Crystals like feldspar act as natural resistors, absorbing excess dynamo energy and dispersing it safely through the grid. These crystals are embedded within circuits and energy lines to prevent overloads and ensure that power surges don't damage the system. By regulating the energy flow, resistor crystals protect sensitive equipment, especially in areas with fluctuating energy inputs, such as windmill farms and tidal generators.

Capacitor Crystals

The ability of quartz crystals to store dynamo energy has revolutionized energy management in Azoria. These crystals work as capacitors, holding a charge until it is needed and then releasing it in controlled bursts. In everyday applications, quartz is used to smooth out energy flows, providing backup power during temporary grid shortages or equipment failure. This ability to store energy makes quartz essential in both industrial and household contexts, as well as in personal devices like squawks.

Transistor Crystals

Tourmaline crystals play a critical role as transistors, modulating energy flow and amplifying signals. These crystals are found in many advanced technologies, including long-distance communication devices, where they can boost the strength of dynamo energy to relay messages across vast distances. Tourmaline's ability to act as a switch or amplifier makes it indispensable in the most complex systems that demand precision in energy transfer, such as the defensive systems of Azoria or in high-end crystal arrays used by elite engineers.

Amplifier Crystals

Sapphire and certain rare diamonds are highly prized for their ability to amplify dynamo energy, making them crucial in energy-intensive applications. Amplifier crystals are used in devices where power needs to be concentrated, such as in the city's protective barriers or large industrial equipment.

These rare crystals are difficult to mine and are usually reserved for elite thieving crews and high-level governmental use due to their scarcity and cost.

Crystals as the Core of Dynamo Engineering

The interplay between metals and crystals in dynamo technology is what makes Azoria's grid so sophisticated. Copper and iron lay the groundwork, but it is the crystals that enable precise control over energy. Without the natural resistance, capacitance, and amplification that crystals provide, the dynamo grid would be prone to destructive surges and inefficiency.

Each crystal acts as a filter, shaping the raw energy into a usable form. For instance, as dynamo energy travels through the city's grid, resistor crystals ensure that excess energy is safely dissipated, while transistor crystals direct the energy precisely where it's needed, such as powering vital communication lines or factories. Capacitor crystals store any leftover energy to be used later, when demand peaks or when a temporary outage occurs.

Even personal devices like the squawks rely on a fine balance of tourmaline and quartz crystals, which regulate and amplify the energy that powers long-distance communication over the city's grid. The squawk's capacitor stores small amounts of dynamo energy, ensuring the device functions without interruption even if the city's grid momentarily falters, which could result in loss of life or imprisonment during a heist.

The geopolitical power dynamics of the world are heavily influenced by the availability of these crystals. The vast majority of high-quality crystals are found in Zarakar, which has solidified its status as the wealthiest and most powerful nation. Zarakar's mines produce a wide range of crystals, from feldspar and quartz to rarer varieties like tourmaline and sapphire, which are shipped across the continents to fuel the dynamo requirements of cities like Azoria. The rarity of these crystals, especially those with superior energy-regulating properties, makes them as valuable as metals like copper.

Drakoria, known for its treacherous terrain and waterways, has also emerged as a supplier of high-quality crystals, though its difficult geography complicates trade routes. Drakoria's volcanic regions yield unique crystal formations that are unmatched in their ability to withstand extreme temperatures and pressures, making them ideal for use in amplifiers and heists.

Example: Construction of a Squawk Device

The squawk is one of the most exemplary applications of dynamo energy—a portable, handheld communication device that allows for real-time, long-distance messaging across the city of Azoria and beyond. This device taps directly into the dynamo grid, using a combination of metal conductors, crystal arrays, and intricate components to transmit and receive signals with remarkable clarity.

Copper Coil Array – Energy Conductor and Receiver

The copper coil is the backbone of the squawk, acting as both the primary conductor and receiver of dynamo energy. Copper, being the most efficient conductor, is used to draw dynamo energy from the city's grid and channel it into the device. The coil is tightly wound within the housing, creating a field that responds to the dynamo grid's energy pulses.

- **Function**: When connected to the grid (via public energy ports in Azoria), the copper coil gathers and channels dynamo energy, which is then regulated by the crystal array. The coil's ability to conduct energy is critical for maintaining a consistent power supply to the squawk without causing overheating or surges.
- **Design**: The coil's winding is done with extreme precision to maximize conductvity while minimizing space. Thin copper strands are used to increase surface area, further enhancing energy flow and efficiency.

Gold Contacts – Stability and Durability

While copper serves as the main conductor, gold is used in the contacts and connection points within the device due to its resistance to corrosion and long-term durability. Gold is especially important in the squawk's power ports, where it ensures that the squawk remains connected to the grid in environments where exposure to the elements might otherwise degrade the components.

- **Function**: Gold is used at key contact points to prevent corrosion and ensure a consistent, stable connection with the dynamo grid. This is particularly important in the volatile environments of Azoria's markets and docks, where salt air and moisture could damage less stable metals.
- **Design**: Thin gold plating on contacts ensures durability without excessive weight or cost. These contacts are precision-fitted into the squawk's power intake ports to create a seamless connection with the city's grid.

Tourmaline Crystal Array – Signal Modulation and Amplification

The tourmaline crystal array is the heart of the squawk's communication function. Tourmaline's ability to modulate and amplify dynamo energy is what allows the squawk to send and receive clear, long-distance signals. This array consists of several small tourmaline crystals, arranged in a complex circuit that balances signal strength with energy efficiency.

- **Function**: The crystals act as transistors, modulating the dynamo energy that powers the device's communication features. They amplify weak signals received from distant squawks and boost outgoing signals, ensuring clear communication even across long distances.

- **Design**: The tourmaline crystals are set in a delicate arrangement, each placed at key points in the circuit to ensure the strongest possible signal without overloading the device's small energy reserves. Their placement also allows for energy conservation, minimizing the power needed to transmit long-distance messages.

Capacitor Quartz – Energy Buffer and Regulation

A small quartz crystal capacitor is embedded within the squawk to act as an energy buffer. Quartz's natural ability to store and release dynamo energy in controlled bursts ensures that the device operates smoothly, even when disconnected from the grid or during periods of fluctuating power.

- **Function**: The capacitor stores excess dynamo energy, which can be released when needed—such as when the device temporarily loses connection to the grid or when extra power is required to boost a signal. This prevents the device from losing power unexpectedly during crucial moments of communication.

- **Design**: The quartz capacitor is placed near the power intake, where it intercepts and stores surplus energy. Its compact design allows it to fit within the tight confines of the squawk's casing while providing enough buffer power to sustain the device for short periods.

Crystal Lattice Interface – Combining Metal and Crystal Components

A critical but often overlooked component of the squawk is the crystal lattice interface, which integrates the different crystal types into a single, harmonized system. This interface is responsible for balancing the energy drawn from the copper coils with the needs of the tourmaline crystals and quartz capacitor.

- **Function**: The interface ensures that the various crystals (tourmaline for signal modulation, quartz for energy storage) work together efficiently. It regulates the flow of dynamo energy through the system, ensuring each crystal receives the exact amount of energy it needs.

- **Design**: The interface is a delicate crystalline matrix, carefully grown to fit the specific energy flow patterns of the squawk. It is this interface that allows the squawk to remain both efficient and powerful, harmonizing the flow of energy between the metals and crystals without overloading any single component.

Assembly and Usage

The assembly of a squawk requires not only technical skill but an intimate understanding of how metals and crystals interact with dynamo energy. The metals (copper, silver, gold, and steel) provide the conductive pathways and structural framework, while the crystals (tourmaline and quartz) manage the energy flow, amplify signals, and store power for future use.

When activated, the squawk draws power from the city's grid, regulated through the capacitor and crystal array. As the user sends a message, the tourmaline crystals amplify the signal, sending it through the grid to the receiver's device. If the device loses grid connection, the quartz capacitor steps in, ensuring the device continues to function for short periods without interruption.

In an environment like Azoria, where communication and power are critical, the squawk's balance of efficiency, durability, and innovation makes it an indispensable tool for everyone from thieves to the merchants they steal from.

Conclusion and Future Crystal Charge Research

In conclusion, the intricate interplay between metals and crystals forms the backbone of dynamo engineering, driving the technological advancements that power cities like Azoria. The efficient harnessing and regulation of dynamo energy have not only shaped the infrastructure of modern society but have also influenced geopolitical dynamics, economies, and daily life. Devices like the squawk exemplify the remarkable potential of combining conductive metals with specialized crystals to create tools that are both powerful and essential.

However, as our reliance on dynamo technology grows, so does the need for continued research and innovation in crystal charge applications. Future studies aim to explore new crystal formations with enhanced properties, such as higher energy storage capacity, improved signal modulation, and greater durability under extreme conditions. Researchers are particularly interested in synthetic crystals, which could offer customizable properties and reduce dependence on scarce natural resources.

Advancements in nanocrystalline structures and composite materials may lead to more efficient energy regulation and miniaturization of devices without compromising performance. Additionally, investigating the integration of alternative metals and alloys could open new avenues for reducing costs and increasing the accessibility of dynamo-powered technology across different regions.

The future of dynamo engineering lies in our ability to push the boundaries of current technology, striving for greater efficiency, sustainability, and innovation. By deepening our understanding of crystal charge mechanisms and exploring novel materials, we can unlock new potentials in energy management, communication, and beyond— paving the way for a brighter, more connected world.

THANK YOU

Words cannot express how much I appreciate you reading (and hopefully enjoying!) this book. If you'd like more updates, you can find me on:

My Page: sgkaram.com

Instagram: @yaystevek

TikTok: @sgkaram